PRAISE F

SUGAR CAGE

"Mixing magic with touches of political realism, Connie May Fowler has written a strangely beautiful novel about love and human frailties."

—*San Francisco Chronicle*

"A beautiful, taboo love story."

—*Chicago Tribune*

"A first novel suffused with the lushness and heat of a Florida night. Fowler introduces her unusual characters one by one, letting several of them narrate this muscular, mystic, and alternately hilarious, charming, and melodramatic saga. . . . A seductive and impressive debut."

—*ALA Booklist*

"*SUGAR CAGE* is one of the most accomplished, haunting fictional debuts since Amy Tan's *The Joy Luck Club*."

—*Atlanta Journal-Constitution*

"To read Connie May Fowler's *SUGAR CAGE* is to be a child, sitting on the bottom porch steps on a hot summer evening, listening to the grown-ups talking. . . . Hold quiet, save it all to sort through later, but don't miss a single word."

—*Kansas City Star*

A Literary Guild Featured Alternate
A Doubleday Book Club Featured Alternate

"Fowler has a trusting and attuned ear. Her characters are right on the money, and their simple, lush, infuriating voices roll along on the pride, fear, sadness, alienation, struggle, and uncertainty that ended Southern innocence and isolation at the beginning of the civil rights movement and the start of the Vietnam war."

—*Miami Herald*

"There's a lot to admire in *SUGAR CAGE*. . . . a tale of family struggles and the universal search for love."

—*New York Newsday*

"In *SUGAR CAGE*, Ms. Fowler has inventively worked the notion of 'sweet poison' into the lives of her characters . . ."

—*The New York Times Book Review*

"Fowler nicely balances the mythic with the realistic, the comic with the tragic. *SUGAR CAGE* has both the sweetness and grit of real sugar."

—*Orlando Sentinel*

SUGAR CAGE

CONNIE MAY FOWLER

WASHINGTON SQUARE PRESS
PUBLISHED BY POCKET BOOKS

New York   London   Toronto   Sydney   Tokyo   Singapore

A Washington Square Press Publication of
POCKET BOOKS, a division of Simon & Schuster Inc.
1230 Avenue of the Americas, New York, NY 10020

Copyright © 1992 by Connie May Fowler

Published by arrangement with G. P. Putnam's Sons

ISBN: 0-671-74809-2

First Washington Square Press trade paperback printing March 1993

10 9 8 7 6

WASHINGTON SQUARE PRESS and colophon are registered trademarks of Simon & Schuster Inc.

Cover design by Brigid Pearson
Front cover photo by William Johnson/Stock Boston/PNI

Printed in the U.S.A.

The author acknowledges permission to reprint lyrics from "I Wished on the Moon" by Dorothy Parker and Ralph Rainer, copyright © 1934 and 1935 by Famous Music Corporation, copyright renewed 1961 and 1962 by Famous Music Corporation.

I wish to offer my thanks and gratitude to the following people: John Fogarty, for sharing his memories about Vietnam; Ellie and Bob Gilder, for telling me to go to Kansas but to come straight home; the University of Kansas and University of Tampa English departments; my agent, Joy Harris, whose enthusiasm and nurturing spirit are unyielding; my editor, Faith Sale, whose sensitivities and perceptions sweeten every page; my dear friend and teacher Carolyn Doty, because without her belief in a few pages attempted long ago this novel would have never been written; and mostly I thank my husband, Mika, who never stops listening and believing and caring.

For my parents, Henry and Lee,
whose love was as inexplicable and as lovely as air

And for Deidre

Inez Temple

I don't know if it was luck or providence that put me in Rose Looney's motel room the day after her wedding. But sure enough, I was there—a young woman scared to death because I'd just left my hometown of Eatonville, and I no longer had any family to speak of because both Mama and Grandmama had died within three months of each other, and after their awful passing and after the weight of my loneliness got to be too much I had said to myself, You've got to go on and make a life for yourself, missy.

So I left Eatonville, which sits almost dead-center in the middle of Florida, and took a Greyhound bus to the coastline. Thought the ocean might do me good. But being a Negro woman in 1945—despite my high school diploma—meant the only job I could find in this beautiful place, where the sky shined so blue and the water glittered like lapis and the sea breeze cooled your skin, making you forget all about those windless, stinging days down home, was as a maid.

Now I knew had my mama and grandmama been living they would have said to me, Miss Inez, there's nothing in the world wrong with being a maid as long as in your soul you know that you fly just as bright and pure as anybody else. See, my family, from way back, they were good, old-fashioned witches. Mama and Grandmama never had a dime to their names, but because of the healing teas and protecting rituals they worked up for our neighbors, we were never lacking for a thing. Always had food and shelter and our dignity. Always had a bright smile and good things to say to folks. But as I stood in that motel room looking at the tangled sheets and the empty Jack Daniel's bottles and trying to breathe the air that was choked with the scent of half-smoked cigarettes, I thought,

11

Not only do I not have any family left, I don't have any good feelings about myself either.

It was right then, with me thinking those dark, down-in-the-mouth thoughts, that the door swung open and a startled Rose Looney stumbled in. "Well, hello there," she said. "How are you doing?"

And I'm afraid I have to say that I lied. I said, "Just fine." And then I said, "I can come back and clean later if you'd like."

But she waved me away. "Oh no, honey, that's all right. I'm just coming in to get out of the sun for a few minutes. Don't stop on my account."

Now I already knew some things about Rose Looney that she didn't know I knew. That's because I was standing in the Coquina Motel office getting some fresh towels when she and her husband got in the previous afternoon. Her husband was a big blond man. He was wearing a blaringly white Coast Guard uniform. His hat was tipped back on his head in a very unmilitary fashion. Rose had on a yellow cotton dress with flowers embroidered around the collar. In her pretty little fist was a bouquet of black-eyed Susans. Her husband hit the door and said, "Hello, sir." He was addressing Mr. Tucker, the owner. "Me and the new Mrs. Rose Looney just tied the knot. We need us the biggest, grandest honeymoon suite you've got."

Now that Mr. Tucker, he didn't seem amused. The Coquina Motel was not one of those huge, mansionlike hotels the rich northern folks stay at when in St. Augustine. The Coquina was plain as water—clean, efficient, and not very fancy. Its one nod at luxury was its thatched-roof tiki-tiki bar facing the ocean. And its rates were dirt low compared to those in town, so I knew that the new Mrs. Rose Looney had not married a man of means.

I studied the newlyweds. Mr. Looney sure was exuberant. All his gestures were oversized and his gaze seemed to skim over everything, snapping here, snapping there with judgments. He spied the newspaper laying on the counter. Its headline screamed AMERICA DROPS BOMB ON JAPAN! He threw his head back and laughed. "Well," he boomed, "the goddamn Japs are finished now. The little slant-eyed bastards must be begging us to let them surrender."

Mr. Tucker said, "Sir, I believe you are right."

"Rosie"—Mr. Looney put his arm around his wife—"looks like I'll be trading in this Coast Guard uniform for my old policeman blues sooner than later."

And Mrs. Looney was just beaming and looking all around the office. She noticed the tourist brochures and she admired Mr. Tucker's shell collection that he displayed in a fishnet on the wall. She looked out the window and said, "The water sure is beautiful." Everything about her seemed wide-eyed and a little gullible.

The next morning as I pushed my cleaning cart down the walk I noticed the newlyweds were at the bar. Rose Looney was wearing a big wide-brimmed white hat with a polka-dotted bandana. And her little bathing suit matched the bandana—all black and white and polka dots with a big black bow at the waist and a little skirt to boot. She was really done up. There was a skinny white woman with them, and the three of them were standing—drinks in hand—watching somebody in the Atlantic. The skinny woman was hopping up and down and waving. Completely excited. She yelled out, "Hey, Junior, baby, I love you."

So my curiosity got the best of me. I left my cart in front of unit number 3 and ventured out to the seawall so I could get a good look at this Junior. I figured he'd be some beach bull, for that lady to be so worked up. But no ma'am. A little thin white man was all he was. And he was a wonder. Out there all alone in that surf, giggling and flapping his arms, jumping the waves with all the joy of a child. I suspected he was a gentler soul than Rose Looney's new husband.

But I couldn't dawdle all day. I had to get to work. So I went back to my cart and got my glass cleaner and a rag and unlocked Rose Looney's honeymoon door. And like I was saying, I was standing there feeling down in the mouth when she walked in. I offered to leave, but she said she was coming in for just a few minutes. Then she shut the door and kicked off her beach slippers and sunk down in the green swivel chair next to the bed. She murmured, "Boy, I don't feel so hot."

I decided it would be best if I just minded my own business. I went over to the sink and started my straightening. I heard a match strike, so I knew she was lighting up a cigarette. And then she said to me, "My name's Rose."

"How do you do?" I returned softly, but at that very moment I was wishing I was back in my tiny, comfortable, dirt-floored shack in Eatonville.

And then she said, "You know, on second thought, why not just leave us some fresh towels. I can straighten this room. There's no need for you to be doing it."

I sprayed a healthy dose of cleaner on the bathroom mirror. As my rag squeaked against the glass I took account of myself. My skin is very black—almost purple like an eggplant. And my hair is always under some kind of cloth. My family never let anybody in the whole world see our hair, and we never cut it either—it's the Temple family's secret, my mama always said. The white scarf I wore that day looked like a billowing cloud, a wild crown. But it didn't go at all with the gray, faded cotton uniform Mr. Tucker made me wear. I said, "No ma'am, that's all right. I get paid to clean your room."

But Rose said, "My husband always says what people don't know won't hurt them."

I paused from my cleaning for a second. "Well, ma'am, my mama always said what people don't know may very well come up and bite them on the butt."

From my vantage point at the mirror I saw Rose giggle. Then she puffed on that cigarette for all she was worth, and I decided that a sweet hope and sorrow masked her.

She said, "I'm a newlywed. My husband and I just got married yesterday. At the courthouse in St. Augustine. And we met another newlywed couple here. They got married yesterday too, by the same judge. And now they are staying at the same motel as us. They seem real nice. Don't you think that's weird?"

"Yes ma'am, I'd say that was a little odd." I began to tidy their toiletry knickknacks. Pushed her husband's shaving kit and aftershave up against the mirror. I noticed that Rose had broken out in a sweat—even though the window fan was cranked full blast. She seemed a little pale.

"Those people we met, the other newlyweds, their names are

Eudora and Junior Jewel. Jewel—don't you think that's a nice last name? My new last name is awful—Looney."

I smiled. "No ma'am, it just sounds like a nice, strong Irish name to me." I wiped down the countertop.

Then she tapped out her cigarette but straightaway lit another one. She reminded me of a smokestack, just puffing away. "My husband is a police officer in St. Augustine. Well, actually, right now he's in the Coast Guard, but that's just something temporary due to the war and all."

"I see." I went over to the bed and started changing the sheets.

"Junior Jewel—the fellow we just met—he said he wanted to join the Army but they wouldn't let him. Something to do with his spine. But the war's all over. That's what everybody is saying, anyway."

Mrs. Rose Looney sure wasn't having trouble finding something to blabber about. I started untangling the sheets from the blanket as she chattered on: "You don't suppose, do you, that it is some kind of bad luck that I got married on the same day we dropped that A-bomb, do you? I mean, since I was a little girl I imagined that my wedding day would be perfect. Birds singing and cloudless skies. That I'd be wearing a beautiful long white gown and it would be a church wedding—maybe a cathedral—and I'd have a little flower girl and five bridesmaids and a whole crowd of people there to wish us well." And then little Rose Looney, right before my very eyes, burst into tears.

I was at a loss. What to do now? I stopped fiddling with the sheets. I went to the sink and rinsed out a glass that reeked with whiskey odor, and filled it with some cold tap water. I walked over and sat on the bed real close to her chair. "Here, sweetie, you need to drink this."

I put my hand over hers, but what I felt was more than flesh and bones. I was feeling something inside her, something I couldn't name. Mama and Grandmama always told me I had the same ability to see as they did. I never believed them. But Mama's face would just glow as she said, "Miss Inez, you're a Temple. All us Temples can see."

And I thought as I held Rose Looney's hand that maybe Mama

was right. Maybe I was seeing. I was for sure feeling something. I decided the woman needed some strength, something more than just water. So I said, "Wait a minute." I fished a sugar packet out of my pocket—I had taken an extra one that morning from the coffee shop. I tore it open and poured the sugar in the glass. "Here, drink this," I said.

My voice was so sure and forceful it caused Rose Looney not to question me. She took the glass and drank that mixture down. And as I watched her, what I had felt when I touched her but couldn't name began to take shape. Just a shadow at first, swimming inside her. And then a sweet, watery face, and almost deerlike eyes, and pretty, newborn skin. Just as sure as I knew the ocean was singing outside that door, I knew Rose Looney was pregnant.

She handed me the glass. I noticed that she hadn't drunk down all the sugar—it was clouded on the bottom. I said to myself, Inez, you should have stirred that sugar up. You should have made it dissolve. Because the last thing on this earth that I wanted was to look in that glass and see a sign. I was past all that, too smart for it. I wasn't in Eatonville anymore, playing with hoodoo. So without looking at it, I set the glass down on the nightstand next to the Gideon Bible. Then I took hold of both of her hands and said, "Ma'am, you need to lay down and rest. There's no bad luck going on around here." I got up from the bed.

Rose Looney shook her head. "No, no, that's all right. I'm okay." But her pale face told me otherwise. And then she said, "Well, maybe you're right. Maybe I'll lay down for just a minute or two."

And I didn't want to, but I couldn't stop myself from speaking. The words seemed to blurt out on their own, even though my brain was saying to me to mind my own business. I said, "You need to settle down for a while. Maybe quit the liquor and the late nights and just take care of yourself, missy." Because I felt this need for that child of hers to be all right.

Then I told her, "I'll just leave you some fresh towels, like you said. I'll come in and clean tomorrow. You don't need me in here rattling around." And then, "You need something else, some more water, or a cold towel for your head, or anything?"

Rose returned, in a very sweet voice, "No, dear, that's all right. I'm okay. Thank you. You're a very nice lady."

And my daily self said to me, Inez, don't do it. Just leave that water glass alone. But the old part of me—the part brought up on spells and potions—said, You've got to. You've got to see what's in it. As if I had no choice in the matter, I gave in. I picked up that water glass and walked it over to the sink. And by the time I got there I knew what was glistening at the bottom of that glass. A sign of Mrs. Rose Looney's future. A sign that would tell me she was going to let love eat her up. With my heart beating like crazy, I brought the glass right up close to my face and I stared down into it. And sure enough, this is what I saw: bars glittering like white sand under the sun.

Now when I met Rose Looney again it was two years later. But I had gained a lot of weight, and my confidence in my ability to earn a living had grown, and I was no longer working at the Coquina Motel. So she had no idea that I was the same woman who had held her hand in her honeymoon room that morning. I thought that was just fine—no need for her to have that little tidbit of information.

But despite me holding that back from her, I came to know Rose and her husband better. I even came to know Eudora and Junior. Yes, I'm saying the four of them were best friends and best enemies. And I cared about them simply because I'm a decent woman, and I came to care for the children they would give birth to also.

Some days, it's true, I was haunted by a twinge of guilt. Because maybe if I had not been so helpful that morning, maybe if I hadn't poured sugar into that water, there would have been no cage. Now I know what Mama and Grandmama would have said. They would have said, The cage was always there, Inez—you just happened to see its deceiving bars.

But for a long time, for the life of me I wondered if there wasn't a way to dissolve that sugary curse. At least, I thought, the children those women would bring into this world ought not to suffer too.

Sweet Poison

Emory Looney

This here, in the early summer of 1960, is how it ended. I mean, there was lots of other fights after this one. Other reasons why I decided I couldn't take no more of my daddy. But what happened on the field that day underneath a hot sun with the whole town watching—that was the event that ended my childhood. The other fights were just gas in the wind.

I think that on the first day of summer vacation a lot of other kids sleep in. They dream about all those ball games they'll play until way after dark or about swimming so long their fingers wrinkle up like crocodile skin or about playing pool at the colored pool hall without their mamas ever knowing about it. But me, I didn't have time for any of that. I woke up as soon as the sun started shining through the navy-blue curtains Mama had sewed a couple of weeks before. They were blue with white jets, and they were neat because if you squinted your eyes as the wind blew them you'd think that the jets were real, that they were zooming in amazing flight patterns before your very eyes.

But on this first day of freedom from school I couldn't be bothered with imaginary jets because, see, it was also Game Day. Tiama's yearly Free Men and Prisoners Baseball Game. In just three hours, criminals and businessmen would walk together, play together.

I got out of bed and pulled open my curtains. Our house is across the street from the fed and my bedroom is situated so as I can see it perfectly clear. I looked past the oleander in our yard and spied on the guard in his tower. I wondered if he was itching as bad as I was to get to the game. I wondered if the prisoners were already in their baseball getups. Maybe they were practicing pitching and batting in the prison yard. Last year my class took a field trip over there, and it was real different seeing those convicts under those circumstances. I'd seen them only at the game before that. But

21

being behind those huge granite walls, hearing not just one but two monster gates clang shut behind me, and seeing the prisoners in their rec room leering at us with cigarette smoke shading their eyes— well, I knew there was another side to those guys, one that didn't show at the game. But that was okay. It didn't really scare me. In fact, it made me want to play in that game more than ever. Just imagine pitching to some guy who was so mean he'd just as soon knife you as look at you. I'd spent hours supposing what I'd do if after they played the scratchy National Anthem record over the PA and as the two teams went to shake hands a murderer or a car thief or a bank robber squeezed my hand till it hurt, and growled, "If you tag any of us you're a dead man." And in my mind I always laughed straight in his face. And then I'd be the first baseman and like a major leaguer I'd do it: I'd tag the dog-faced convict a clear two feet from the base, and the crowd would roar as the ump screamed, "Out!"

And see, I had more than just a faint notion that all this might come true. I had kind of a guarantee from my daddy. After the last game, after Tiama got whipped for the eighth straight year, my daddy, he said to me, "Shit, son, next year we're going to put you out on that field."

And I was going to hold him to it. Yes, sir. A dream come true. He'd be so proud of me.

But I couldn't do it straightforward. He could be real disagreeable. I would have to coddle him into a good mood and then remind him.

That's why I couldn't lay there dreaming about long days of freedom with nothing to do but fool around town. I had to devise a plan.

As I stood at my window watching that guard pace, I decided the one thing I'd seen Daddy do that he seemed to really enjoy was eat. So it was easy. I'd get into his good graces by fixing breakfast. I thought, Do something with eggs and toast and ketchup and tomatoes. Keep his cup filled with hot coffee and rub Mama's shoulders. Don't make any faces, even behind their backs, and don't pop the question until after he has lit up his first cigarette.

It was a good plan. So I put on some shorts and my Mickey

Mantle number 7 New York Yankees T-shirt. I went into the bathroom and shut the door behind me real quietly. Mama had recently bought a bunch of yellow ceramic fish and hung them on the bathroom's green walls. The fish had long black eyelashes and red puckered lips—not like any fish I'd ever seen. They looked real stupid swimming above the commode. But Mama thought they were gorgeous and said she was going to go downtown to the Woolworth's and buy those fuzzy commode covers in a shade of yellow that would match the fish. "That'll look damn good," she'd told my daddy.

I turned on the faucet and ran some water over my face. I looked up into the medicine cabinet mirror and stared closely, checking for the possibility of whiskers. I had just turned fourteen. Seemed like what Mama called peach fuzz should show up any day. But no, all I had was a couple more pimples. I suspected that the pimples was getting in the way of whisker growth. Last week Mama bought me a tube of that stuff Clearasil. She hadn't said a thing. One day I come home from school and there it is, sitting on the table by my bed, next to my goldfish bowl that was empty because Oscar the Fourth had recently kicked the bucket. Oscar One, Two, and Three I had buried in the backyard, kind of like a funeral. But by the time Oscar the Fourth died I'd had it with goldfish. Him I just flushed down the toilet. As I watched his shiny orange body swirl down and away, I screamed at Mama, "Don't you get me any more fish." And even though Mama was nice enough to buy me something like Clearasil even after I'd yelled at her about the fish, I don't think the stuff worked. I still had pimples and I still didn't have any whiskers. I looked over at Mama's ceramic kisser fish. I thought about how I had convinced myself that Oscar the Fourth would live a long, healthy life just because I had wanted him to. Then I thought, Well, maybe my plan won't work. Maybe nothing I'd do would make any difference. But then I said to myself, No, Emory. You may have a baby's butt face, but you're good. Good enough, old enough, to play ball.

I opened the medicine cabinet, and there between the shaving cream and a tube of lipstick and some iodine was Daddy's Aqua Velva. I took it out and splashed some on my face. I patted it on hard the way Daddy always did. Mama likes to say that I'm the spit and image of Daddy. I don't recognize it so well. Except maybe the head hair. We was both thick with it. I stared at my aging face and deepened my voice. "Well, Daddy, what order do you think we'll be batting in?"

And I heard his voice trickle in my mind: "I'm not sure, son, but let's get going. We don't want to keep the team waiting."

I put up the Aqua Velva and knew I'd make Mama and him proud. I'd play almost as good as Daddy. Might hit a home run, maybe off Ezekiel Williams, he's the state pen's star player. Hell, Jack Higgensmith, owner of the white pool hall, he'd probably give me a few games on the house. Maybe even slip me a beer or two.

See, in Tiama, this ball game was the biggest jag in town. Prisons, that's all we had. The state pen, the fed, the women's prison, the juvenile detention center, plus the city jail. My teacher, Mrs. Hoffman, she said she suspected that was some sort of American record, all these prisons.

St. Augustine, that's north of here, they're known as the oldest city in the United States. They get lots of money that way. Dumb Yankees come down here and spend hard, cold cash to see Ponce de León's Fountain of Youth, when we all know it isn't anything more than a spring fed by some stupid river. So one year the Tiama City Council got disgusted with St. Augustine's oldest this and oldest that. They decided to lure some of those tourists down here and they started a town motto, "Prison Capital of the World."

And they made another decision. They said that from then on, the prison team would be sort of a criminal all-star team. No more would just prisoners from the state pen play. But the feds and the locals too. That way everybody but the women and the juvenile delinquents would be represented. And I'd be there. And I'd help us win.

I was pretty confident as I walked into the kitchen and threw open the icebox door. I got the egg carton out and found Mama's big red mixing bowl beneath the sink. I cracked open the first egg, then another. I cracked four eggs in all, as I'd heard Daddy speak fondly of four-egg omelets. But since I didn't know an omelet from a hole in the ground, I planned to scramble these.

24

I stared down into the bottom of the bowl and realized I'd landed four perfect yolks. Each was unbroken and glistening. Good sign. Maybe means four homers. A splash of milk, a pinch of salt, two dashes of Tabasco. A few whirls with my fork was a tour around the bases. I'd watched Mama do this a million times.

I buttered two pieces of bread and put them on a cookie sheet. Broiled toast. I buttered a third piece for me. I sliced a tomato and set it on a plate, just like Mama always did. I figured it was all going perfect, until I realized I had no idea how to make the damn coffee. Potential strike.

I ran my finger along the butter and then stuck it in the sugar bowl. I sucked the sugar butter off my finger. Through my head I tried to piece together what I'd seen Mama do. I couldn't figure out if she put the coffee in the water and it boiled through the basket, or if the coffee sat in the basket, totally separated from the water. It was a mystery, but I knew if I screwed it up Daddy would never let me forget it.

The game isn't over yet, I coached myself.

I heard the toilet flush. I froze. Please, God, I prayed, don't let it be Daddy, not without my plan, my cooking, fully executed. Someone was standing behind me. I held my breath. I turned around. Thank you, God, it was Mama.

On Mother's Day I'd given her a rose-colored quilted bathrobe, because Rose was her name, and she wore it now, even though it barely stretched across her big belly, because she was pregnant. Both she and Aunt Eudora was pregnant, and it made for some awful times, believe me.

"Well, look at you, sweetheart. What's all this, dressed and combed and cooking?" Then she sniffed real deep. "Oh my God, you're wearing your daddy's Aqua Velva." She smiled like she knew all my secrets, and then messed up my hair. I pulled away and wished with all my heart I hadn't put that stuff on.

"I just thought I'd help out," I grumbled.

But she ignored me. She just sat down at the table and groaned. The table was one of those aluminum jobs with a yellow surface that sort of looked like ice cubes. And the chairs were the same yellow, but plastic with about five years' worth of cigarette burns.

Sitting in the middle of the table was a little plastic pot blooming with faded yellow plastic daisies. She sure was fond of yellow. She yawned and then rested both hands on her belly. "Sweetheart, reach up and get me that peanut butter."

Lately, her pregnancy had put a strain on me. Maybe it was her and Eudora being pregnant together. I became their hands, their feet. They would have made me eat for them if they could have swung it.

For instance, if Eudora was home by herself and needed her and Junior's laundry hung to dry, what do you think happened? That's right, no matter what I was doing—listening to the radio, geography homework, getting ready to play ball—Mama would say, "Emory, you go on over to Aunt Eudora's house and help her hang those clothes right now."

And at home all I heard was, "Emory, get me a cold drink." "Emory, help me put that roast in the oven." "Emory, honey, don't you think you could get Daddy's beer for him."

And sometimes when Daddy would come home late from singing or drinking in the bars, I would hear Mama yell at him, "Listen, you son of a bitch, you're the one that got me in this condition. You'd better straighten up until I get out of it."

But when the order came for the peanut butter, I didn't roll my eyes. I went over to the wooden cupboard that was painted white, with yellow daisy decals stuck on the doors—kitchens needed a theme, Mama liked to say—and found the jar beside a big box of Epsom salt, and I got it down and then fished a spoon out of the dish drainer and handed it to her as nice as could be and very politely asked, "You want bread or a saltine with that?"

"No, honey, this is fine."

"Mama?" I hid my finger, which wasn't entirely clean of sugar butter, in the tail of my T-shirt.

"Yes, honey?"

"How do I make coffee?"

"Are you kidding me? Are you really fixing us breakfast?" she asked as she hooked a lump of peanut butter near the bottom of the jar.

"Yes, ma'am," I said. But I offered no reason.

"On second thought, go ahead and get me those saltines," she said.

I walked back over to the cupboard. They were way up there, on the top shelf. Since she got pregnant she'd been buying the giant-size saltines—those in the big tin can. I jumped up and batted it off the shelf like it was a basketball. I started to toss it to her, but something inside me said, "No."

Instead I set the can on the counter, popped off the lid, tore open the wax wrap, and arranged a few crackers in a circle on a plate—I wanted everything to look nice.

I set them in front of her.

"Thanks, sweetheart," she said. Then she bit into one. I looked at her close. Her eyes was puffy and red, like she'd stayed up crying. She always looked like that the morning after Daddy came home late and they'd had a fight. Some of the fights were loud, with pushing and shoving. During those I turned up my radio or buried my head in my pillows.

"You been crying again, Mama?" I asked her, but she didn't hear me.

She was just looking sad. She stared out the kitchen window and out the side yard, as if me or the ticking wall clock or the icebox motor that had just clanked on didn't exist. Then, with a sudden loud voice, she blurted, "Coffee. Sure. I'll show you how to do that. Just fill up the pot, up to where the water line is, where the inside of the pot isn't dull."

Okay, I could do that, and I did.

"Got it?" she asked.

"Got it."

"Now put six scoops of coffee in the basket and set the basket in the pot so that it stands straight up."

So I did that, but I wondered if she was playing a joke on me. "How's that going to make coffee?" I asked.

"Because you heat the water until it boils up through the basket."

I should have known it was something simple like that. My mind tends to go for the complicated. I turned the burner on high. I liked the way the blue flame stretched flat when I set the pot on it.

"No, no, honey, not on high."

27

"Why not?" I figured Daddy would be up any minute; I wanted the coffee done.

"Because if you put too much heat to it, you won't get a gentle boil, you'll get a rumble. Nothing left but mess."

I guess I have to admit that Mama talked me through that breakfast. At least got me to first base. I never knew scrambling eggs could be so tricky. I thought all I had to do was shake the pan. I didn't know about scraping them off the bottom with a spatula. "Emory, eggs stick. They burn to the bottom of the pan." And then she said, like it was a matter of life or death, "Everything sticks in that good-for-nothing pan."

But I had no time to figure out why that was important. I had to keep on with my plan. So I finished those eggs, and Mama had me put a lid on the pan to keep them warm.

When that was done I looked around the kitchen, impatient, anxious for Daddy to wake up, but I didn't dare make any out-of-the-way noise, for fear of riling him. I stared down at the linoleum floor. It was supposed to look like little blocks of white and yellow tile, but it didn't fool anybody. Mama was a good housekeeper, but this floor was dirty. She was forever saying, "With you two traipsing dirt in and out of here and spilling whatever you drink or eat, it's a wonder I can clean this floor at all."

But standing there, I realized there was also bacon grease on the floor. I'd say that was her mess, but I knew I'd better never point that out.

I watched Mama finish off the peanut butter, and as she screwed the lid back on the jar she said, "This child is going to be strong. All it wants is peanut butter, spinach, liver."

"What about me, what did I want?" I asked.

"You were a sugar baby. I gained fifty pounds carrying you. God, I was fat. But I just couldn't get enough sugar. Candy bars, honey buns, ice cream. And your daddy just kept feeding it to me. He'd say, 'If that baby inside you wants another honey bun, by God, he's going to get one.' Your daddy always knew you were going to be a boy." She stretched her arms over her head and yawned real big.

Her words surprised me, talking about Daddy knowing things

about me before I was born. I wanted to ask Mama if they fought a lot when she was pregnant with me or if there was a time things was just quiet in the house, but I couldn't bring myself to ask.

Mama looked at the wall clock. Actually it was a plastic red rooster with a clock for a stomach. The clock ticked real loud, so that early in the morning or around midnight, when everybody was asleep, it shouted at you.

"Mama, when I was born, Daddy was a policeman, wasn't he?"

She reached for her cigarettes, and I thought I saw her face soften. She lit one up. "Yes, sir, he was. He was on the motorcycle patrol up in St. Augustine. The handsomest man on the force."

"Why isn't he a cop now? Why's he selling cars?" I asked.

She looked at the cigarette like she was studying it. "He had an accident. A bad one. Snapped his leg in two and called it quits." Then in a louder voice she said, "And speaking of your father, if he doesn't get his lazy ass out of bed, he's going to miss the game."

"Whose lazy ass are you talking about?" said my daddy. He was standing in the doorway, rubbing his hand across his blond and white chest hairs. He looked hung over; his eyes were red and half shut, like he was in pain.

I immediately felt angry. I thought the possibility of a foul ball was rolling around on my tongue.

"There's scrambled eggs in the pan and toast in the basket. Here's your plate." Mama tapped the table, and I handed him the dish with its sliced tomatoes. "Emory fixed breakfast this morning. Even the coffee. Awfully nice of you, Emory," Mama said.

Daddy grunted. "What's the boy cooking for? Next damn thing I know, you'll have him sewing ruffles on those apron strings of yours."

"Emory, get me a Coca-Cola out of the icebox, please," Mama said. "At least I'm here when he needs me. That's more than some people in this room can say."

Daddy sat down at the table and didn't look at nobody. He just mixed all his food into one big heap and then reached for the saltshaker that was shaped like a cactus. You always knew which was the salt and which was the pepper because the pepper was one

29

of those Mexican sombreros. "Jesus Christ, Rose, get off my back. I just woke up. Emory, don't we have any ketchup? I need some ketchup."

I handed Mama the Coke and she patted my hand. "Get Daddy some ketchup, Emory."

I beelined back to the icebox and stuck my tongue out at the OJ carton just to take off some pressure. I got a Coca-Cola for myself and the ketchup for Daddy.

I set the ketchup on the table and then, like it was no big deal, sat back down.

Mama leaned back in her chair and yawned again. Daddy leaned over his plate and said, "Jesus, what's that smell?" Mama just grinned and winked at me. And I wished with all my heart that I'd never put that Aqua Velva stuff on.

Then Mama said, "Well, I guess I'd better get dressed soon, if Eudora and I are going to make the game. What are you wearing, Charlie, your band shirt? You want me to iron it?"

Daddy nodded. Then he tried the coffee. "Good coffee, son." He set down his cup. He lit a Camel. He inhaled, and then, with his eyes almost slits, he blew a long stream of smoke out of his nose. Dragon head, I thought.

"Emory, what are you doing drinking a Coca-Cola this early in the morning? You're too young to be drinking cold drinks so early in the day," Mama complained.

"Oh, Jesus Christ, Rose, leave the boy alone. Hell, in a couple of years he'll be old enough to perform the old in-and-out, if he isn't already." Daddy slapped my arm and laughed.

I squirmed. I stared at the cold yellow patterns of the kitchen table. And then I thought, Well, he does seem in a pretty good mood. There's your opening. I rolled the Coke bottle between my palms. I decided it would do me no good to put it off. I might as well hit it straight. "Daddy, I was thinking." I made real sure my voice wasn't shaking. "You know how last year Mr. Lewis and his son both played on the Free Men's team? And this year, the prisoners, they're going to be tough, coming from all the different prisons. And so, what about it? This year, you and me? They could probably use us both." My heart was pounding. I worked at keeping

30

Sweet Poison

my face steady. In my mind my bat cracked hard and loud against a well-thrown ball.

Daddy didn't say a word. He stared at his half-finished breakfast. I figured the ball was sailing through the air, somewhere over mid-field. Still silent, he soaked up some tomato guts with his toast. He chewed. The only sounds were him eating, the rooster ticking on the wall, the icebox clanking on, and a mockingbird outside warbling a catcall.

I looked at Mama, who was completely ignoring me and the entire situation. As if it was a normal day, she just poured herself some more Coke. I noticed one cuff of her housecoat was torn. And Daddy kept on with his breakfast. I was about to think they'd both gone deaf on me, when Daddy finally said, "Look here, Emory, your mother insists on going to the game. I don't want her and Eudora up in those stands in their condition without a man. It looks like you're the only man available. I'm afraid you're going to have to sit this game out."

"What about Junior? Why doesn't he sit with them?" I countered, hoping the ball, by some miracle, was still in play.

"Because he's the umpire this year."

Mama started laughing. They do that a lot. Daddy says something that's not at all funny, but Mama laughs anyway. She took a long drag off her Salem. She struggled up from the table and walked over to the sink. She turned on the faucet and waved the cigarette underneath the water. She tossed the soggy butt into the garbage. She looked very pleased. "Well, I'm going to go get dressed. Emory, pick up your father's breakfast dishes when he's through."

And with that, she waltzed out of the kitchen. Daddy swished some coffee around in his mouth. Then he grinned at me, like all of life was one big lemon-colored joke.

So I'd struck out. And as you can imagine, I was in none too good of a mood. There I was, sitting in the wooden bleachers of the Flagler Ball Field between two pregnant ladies. There was Daddy. Out on the field. Throwing practice balls, wearing his Charlie Looney and the Rockets band shirt, acting like he was a big hero.

31

I cracked my knuckles, partly because I knew it irritated Mama, and decided to try to ignore the ballplayers if I could. But there wasn't much else to look at. Clouds and sky and sun and the Tiama water tower. It sat out in a field just north of the ballpark. Recently the city had painted it white and written on it in blazing red letters PRISON CAPITAL OF THE WORLD. And on the very tip-top of the tower was a cross made out of water pipe. They'd painted it red too. When they did that with the cross my mama said, "Stupid sons of bitches. Mixing religion and justice. As if they can really compete with St. Augustine."

I let out a big long huff, hoping that Mama and Eudora would sense my unhappiness. They did, but it didn't get me anywhere. "Emory, you might as well just sit back and enjoy the situation, because it sure as hell isn't going to change," Mama said.

That made me mad, but I knew better than to smart off, so I said, "I'm burning up."

And she said, "Well, we are too."

Because of the bad mood I was in, I thought, At least you two have some protection. They were both wearing big floppy hats. Mama's was white and had a polka-dot scarf bandana around the brim. I looked up at it. The sun almost made the cloth glow. I shaded my eyes.

Mama was sweating bad. The color in her cheeks seemed to seep out with the sudden appearance of new sweat beads.

"Mama, are you all right?"

"Yes, honey, I just need to keep drinking this water," she said.

I slipped off my tennis shoes and decided to try to forget I wasn't on the field. I looked at the crowd. People were joking and shouting back and forth. Some were drinking beers, others Cokes. Popcorn and hot-dog smells mixed in with Mama's and Aunt Eudora's perfumes. I knew a lot of the kids, but I didn't want to talk to them since I so desperately didn't want to be one of them today. Mama said, "Here come the convicts." They were jogging out onto the field like they were a bunch of major leaguers, like their pictures were on baseball cards and not post office walls. But their dugout told the real story. Three prison guards stood watch, double-barreled rifles resting in their arms. A long time ago when I was little, I had asked Daddy why those men stood around with guns, and he had said, "For just in case." I looked at the prisoners for familiar faces—convicts who had played last year or maybe some I'd seen when we took that prison field trip. There were a few new ones, but the greats were back. Ezekiel, he was a colored man doing thirty years for rape or armed robbery, I don't know which. He was a top-notch slugger. Daddy said he probably could have played major league if he hadn't gotten in trouble. And Weezil Smith, he was a tiny, pale white man. But damn, he could run. Bobby Schaeffer had worked in the shipyard until a few weeks before the game. Last year the low-down scum had played for the Free Men. Made their only home run. Everybody said that was why he got himself thrown in the city jail. Just in time for the game. Daddy said he bitched and moaned for months that the Free Men was all just a bunch of losers and he would never play for them again. So about a month before the game he starts getting in trouble. Overparks right in front of City Hall. Doesn't pay the ticket. Flies forty in a twenty-five-mile-an-hour school zone. Doesn't pay the ticket. Gets drunk down at the pool hall. Breaks up chairs. Breaks a pool cue. Rips the felt right off a table. What's the city going to do? Put him in jail. Just like he wants. You know the Prisoner Selecting Committee had to love it. I watched him especially close. He was grinning from ear to ear, just trying to make the Free Men eat dirt.

Then Eudora interrupted me by putting her red-painted fingernails on my sunburned leg. She said, "Emory, put this on Aunt Eudora's shoulders, will you?" She pulled one of Junior's white handkerchiefs out of her purse and dipped it in Mama's paper cup of ice water. She wrung it out over my feet. The cold water felt like needles as it hit my hot skin.

"Jesus, Eudora," Mama said.

Eudora did not acknowledge my feet or Mama's comment. "So I don't know what to do," she said as I put the wet white square over her shoulders that were slowly turning pink. "Junior says I can't call him Junior anymore. He keeps screaming his real name is Burl, which it is, but Lord, after all these years I'm supposed to remember to call him Burl?"

"Well, it is his real name, Eudora. Give a sick man his peace," Mama said.

Eudora shook her head. Her eyes clouded. "Oh, Rose, you just don't know how bad it is. The other morning, he was in the bathroom for what seemed close to an hour. I kept saying, 'Junior, baby, you all right in there?' He kept saying yes, but I didn't believe him, so I finally just busted in on him. My God, Rose, he was bleeding. Bleeding out his butt. Turned the toilet water red. That disease is just eating him up."

I couldn't believe my ears. I couldn't believe Aunt Eudora was saying something so private and so horrible in public. I looked around to see if anybody had heard. No one was looking at us, but maybe that's because they was shocked too. I couldn't figure out how anybody could bleed from that place.

I looked at Mama to check for disbelief, hoping she would tell Eudora to shut up, but no. Mama says, like she's unaffected, "So, what in the hell is he doing umpiring today?"

"He insists he ain't sick. He keeps saying he's getting better and that the only thing that makes him feel bad is me fussing over him."

Under my breath I whispered, "Jesus Christ."

But I was too loud, or else Mama's ears could hear ants crawl, because she said, "Young man, if I hear you say that again I'm going to pop you right in the mouth."

I couldn't believe how thoroughly my favorite day of the year was turning to shit. I dropped my head between my knees. I wiped sweat out of my eyes. When was this game ever going to start, I wondered. But I got my answer right then 'cause Mr. Hollis who owns Hollis Car Repair said very importantly over the loudspeaker, "Everyone please stand for the National Anthem."

So we all stood up and Mama completely embarrassed me by holding onto my shoulder like I was the only thing keeping her on her feet. But Eudora was worse, because, while Mama kind of hummed along with the record, Eudora sang real loud. She especially cat-screeched the "rockets' red glare" part. And I swear the people in front of us were laughing.

When it was over, Mama said, "Eudora, you've got quite a voice," and she nudged me and said, "Go get me another glass of water,

34

Emory. Here's a dollar. And get yourself a cold drink. Eudora, you want a Coke?"

"A large," said Eudora.

I took the money and started to bolt down the wooden bleachers. Mama's voice trailed behind me: "And a bag of boiled peanuts. And don't run."

But I ran anyway. My minor act of freedom during an absolutely rotten day. I was breathing hard when I reached the Coke stand, but not so hard I didn't recognize who was standing in front of me. George Lewis. Mr. Lewis's son. Played in last year's game. "Hey, George, how's it going?"

He turned around. He was taller than me, and I was put off to see a thin scraggle of hair above his lip. "Hi, Emory."

"I thought you'd be playing in the game today. What happened?" I asked. Casual.

"My fucking old man said no way. Said not with them fielding an all-star team."

"Tough break."

"Yeah."

He turned away from me and ordered two hot dogs and three Cokes. I looked out at the field. Tiama's mayor and the three wardens were tossing out game balls.

I heard Junior shout, "Play ball."

George Lewis walked off without saying good-bye, and for some reason that made my day a little better. I gave Old Man Harris my order. As I reached up for the cardboard carrier he had put everything into, I said, "Hot damn. We're finally going to have a ball game."

Mr. Harris grinned. He had only two bottom teeth, as far as I could tell. "Here you go, young man. And don't let your mother hear you talk like that."

I grabbed the carrier and walked off. But before I got too far away, I noticed a Coke cup laying upside down. Perfect. I poised my foot above it and slammed down. Bull's-eye. The cup popped like a cap gun. Glares and sneers. Good.

The prisoners were up first. I hurried back up the bleachers as fast as I could go, but making sure I didn't spill our cold drinks.

I sat down next to Mama just as she yelled, "Knuckle-ball the bastard!"

Everybody in the stands started laughing. Daddy waved his cap, like he was proud of her.

Eudora said, "Rose, you're embarrassing me."

Daddy was the catcher. At the plate a big man, with arm muscles bulging like hams, stretched the bat over his head. He wore a gray T-shirt, the same shirt all the prisoners wore. On the back of their shirts, in big black letters, was spelled PRISON ALL-STARS. I think the prisoners looked better than the Free Men, as they were all dressed the same.

Mr. Hollis said, "Up to bat for the Prison All-Stars is Luther VanDiver. Mr. VanDiver is a guest at the Tiama Federal Penitentiary, serving six years for wire fraud. He is a native of Tampa, Florida."

People clapped and cheered while others booed. Some of the men whistled. I stomped my feet.

Tippy Garcia—he owned Tippy's Bar—threw a spinner. Luther VanDiver swung the bat hard but missed. Junior called it a ball. I think I saw Daddy shoot him one of his don't-fuck-up looks.

Junior looked tinier than usual, standing there in his white short-sleeved shirt, so close to ham-arms Luther. He was taking this umpiring real seriously. He even had a brush in his back pocket to wipe off home plate.

"Don't Junior look sweet," gushed Eudora.

Tippy Garcia, with the help of Junior's questionable calls, walked Luther.

The crowd hissed.

The sun grew brighter, sharper.

Daddy threw down his mask and walked to the pitcher's mound. He spit a wad of chew juice and then talked very seriously with Tippy Garcia. Their faces almost touched.

The prisoners had two outs by the time they made a run that first inning. That in itself was amazing, since Junior kept calling strikes balls.

I could tell Mama was tensing up about it. Finally she blurted, "That husband of yours doesn't know a damn thing about baseball."

36

Eudora didn't say a word. Acted like she didn't hear it. She shaded her eyes and looked out at the field as if a big pitch was coming up, but in fact the two teams were switching places.

The bottom of the first went fast. One. Two. Three. Out. Out. Out. Daddy didn't even get a chance at bat.

"Damn, this heat is starting to get to me," Mama murmured.

It wasn't until the fifth inning that the Free Men even got on the board, and by that time the prisoners had scored four runs. Daddy hit a single off Ezekiel Williams. And Jeff Brewster—he'd just graduated from high school—hit a homer to bring them in.

Mama jumped up and down and yelled, "I love you, Charlie!" Then she grabbed her stomach and slowly sat down.

So it was four to two, All-Stars, as the game headed into the sixth inning. I figured if I was playing we'd at least be tied.

Bobby Schaeffer was up to bat. He hit a double. As he slid into second, Joe Haley grinded his cleats into Bobby's base-grabbing hand. People whooped. The bald man sitting in front of me shouted, "That'll teach him."

Schaeffer clutched his hand as the next batter, VanDiver, came up. I felt a little sorry for Schaeffer, even though he deserved it, after the way he'd gotten into prison and all. I was staring down at my toes, realizing that the tops of my feet were most likely going to blister, when I heard the sound that all good ballplayers love. The solid smack of a perfectly hit pitch. I thought it would be a homer, but instead the ball sailed into left field, fell directly into Abe Pachini's glove, and bounced right back out again. VanDiver made it to first. Schaeffer hot-tailed it past third. We were on our feet. Schaeffer was stretched out flat as a road kill when Daddy tagged him out, his bleeding hand a good two inches from the base.

"Safe!" shouted Junior.

"What the fuck!" Daddy screamed. He threw off his mask. He grabbed Junior's shoulders and shook him. "Are you fucking blind or just stupid? Out! Out! The man is out! I tagged him a fucking mile from the base."

"Throw the umpire out!" I screamed.

The crowd booed and hissed. But Junior just stood there like he was listening to a preacher. He didn't look angry or scared. He looked calm, as if all this uproar had absolutely nothing to do with him.

"Oh, hell," Daddy said. He let go of Junior with a shove.

Schaeffer grinned and waved his bleeding hand at the crowd as he jogged into the dugout. The next prisoner came up to bat.

Mama didn't look at Eudora at all. She just said, stony and firm, "I've got to get out of this sun. I don't feel too good."

"You want me to go with you, Mama?" I asked.

"No, I'll be back in a minute. I'm just going to the bathroom. You stay so you can tell me what happens."

Mama looked cute, walking down those bleachers, one hand on her belly, the other groping shoulders, that white hat bobbing on her head. I watched her instead of the field, and I thought it was going to be fun to have a little baby brother or sister to fool around with. She was standing on the bottom bleacher and suddenly, just as if the life had flowed right out of her, she dropped.

Fast I was on my feet and bounding down the steps, but I couldn't get to her. A crowd already swarmed, thick and immovable.

"Mama, Mama!" I heard myself scream.

Then another voice, "Out of my way."

I believe that was Daddy.

I pushed and shoved and dug my nails into people so they would move. Finally I broke through. Mama was lying crumpled on the grass. Her eyes was closed and her skin looked pale gray.

Daddy was on one knee beside her. He held her white hat, crushed and dirty, in his hand. He looked up and saw me. His face swept into a huge angry blaze. He tossed the hat to the ground. He grabbed and shook me. Harder than he'd shaken Junior. His hands were vise grips around my arms. I knew he was about to hit me. He spit, "How come you let this happen, boy? How come? You were supposed to take care of her. Look what you've done here."

A hand reached in and pushed him away from me. "That's enough, Charlie," Junior said. "You just take care of Rose."

Junior patted me on the back. "You all right, son?" he asked.

I didn't answer. I just stared at Daddy, daring him to look me in the eye. But he turned chicken. He stared at the grass. "Where's the goddamn ambulance?" he said.

I knew I was going to start bawling. I pushed through the crowd. "Where in the fuck do you think you're going?" Daddy yelled. I ran. I ran past them all. Ezekiel Williams. Luther VanDiver. Weezil Smith. Bobby Schaeffer. Their faces blurred into one another behind my tears. I ran as fast as I could. Out of the park. Down Shell Drive. Past my school. To the ocean. To the ocean. Faster. Faster. Faster.

As I ran I thought, "I'm not ever going home."

Rose Looney

Here I sit at my kitchen table, watching my coffee grow cold, knowing with every pore of my body that when Charlie comes home tonight he's going to want to touch me. And what will I say? What will I do? Will I giggle like I did on our wedding night and feel like his touch is setting me free? Will I do what I've done for sixteen years of marriage: let his smile and sweet-talking apologies melt away any resistance, any anger? I have no idea. The only thing I'm sure of is how different this last fight was from all the rest. The rules had been changed. The stakes had been raised higher than I ever dreamed possible. Now even the sunlight that splashes into what I once thought of as my cozy kitchen seems brutal. I spent last night at Eudora's, but I can't stand that again. So what do I do tonight after suffering through a wordless meal and an hour or two of TV racket? Once the covers are turned down and the bedroom light is switched off and he gropes at me with hands I once adored, will I say, "Get the hell away from me, you son of a bitch," and do so confidently, not wavering, knowing that his touch isn't freedom but sweet poison?

I actually could do a lot with my day. I could pick up the broken water glass that I threw at Charlie two nights ago. It didn't hit him. Instead it hit just beyond his head, shattering against my yellow walls, leaving a shadowy whiskey stain that only a new coat of paint will hide. When I was first married I chose yellow for my kitchen, because I was so young and naive. I told the man at the paint store, "I'm going to paint my walls with sunshine." What a joke.

Or I could get off my dead butt and mop the floor, or put the broom that Emory had threatened Charlie with back in the closet. Or I could even go in and straighten the living room. I could empty the crumpled cigarette packs and the ashes and the half-smoked Salems from my kidney-bean ashtrays—the ones with all the tiny mosaic tiles that I glued in myself. I could straighten the lampshade with the picture of the fighting bulls on it. Charlie knocked it cock-eyed after Emory punched him. Or I could walk in there and do something harmless like dust. I could dust the family pictures I have set out so proudly on the TV console. I could straighten the oil painting—a seascape—that I bought at Woolworth's three years ago. It looks just like the Atlantic Ocean with gulls and sea oats and sand dunes and everything. But two nights ago, when I put my hands to my ears to block out not the shouting—that was already over—but I guess the memory of the shouting, I accidentally hit it with my elbow. And it crashed to the floor but nobody heard it. Yesterday it was back on the wall, crooked. I don't know who did that.

Then again, I could just sit here and try to imagine my living room with its beautiful white stucco. That's what I liked most about this house when we bought it thirteen years ago. We'd scrimped and saved for three years. I'd even held out grocery money—unbeknownst to Charlie—so that we could stop living in cramped, noisy apartments. This was the fourth house we looked at, and the minute I stepped inside I fell in love with it. It didn't have paneling like most of the other small two-bedroom houses we could afford. No. Somebody had bothered to stucco the living room and both bedrooms. The pure, clean whiteness of those rooms made me feel better off than we really were. But now when I think about my lovely living room, the walls are splattered with blood. Not much. Just a little. Like sea spray. And I don't know whose blood. Maybe mine, maybe one of theirs. But most likely Charlie's.

Of course if my life was still normal what I might be doing is humming around my kitchen baking Emory's favorite: sugar cookies. Even though he was growing as tall and handsome as his daddy, he still wasn't too grown-up for an after-school snack. But there wouldn't be any Emory walking through that kitchen door. There wouldn't be my son—who was now taller than me—tossing his books on the kitchen counter and heading straight for the refrigerator to drink the milk from the carton even though he knew I'd tell him to get a glass.

Emory was my only baby. After he was born I said, That's it. One is enough. I'm not like a lot of women—I remembered the pain of labor long after it was over, like it was branded into my soul. So my diaphragm became my talisman, my little charm that would ward against any more kids. But it didn't work. I got pregnant again anyway. Years later. And despite the memory of my first labor, I wanted that child. Once I became pregnant the thought of a baby crawling around my kitchen floor made any labor pain well worth it. But in a horrible, sinister kind of way the talisman was potent after all. Because I miscarried, and that pain was far worse than childbirth.

I need to get a handle on this. I need to understand what really happened in this house between my child and my husband. I'm sipping cold coffee. The afternoon sun is beating through the kitchen window without any wind to stir it. I like sitting here because all I can see is the yard, and not that damn penitentiary across the street. But I'm in the full sun and I'm sweating and I know heat rash has probably started to turn the inside of my arms a spotty crimson. But I refuse to check. Instead, I stare at my dust-covered pot of plastic daisies that sits in the center of my kitchen table. I know that if they weren't plastic they'd be long dead. I have a funny urge to sniff them—as if they might actually give off a scent. But I know all I'd get is a nose full of dust. So I refrain. Instead, I touch a harsh, faded plastic petal and consider the possibility that I should have trusted Charlie. Maybe after I'd found lipstick on his shirt for the umpteenth time—deep plum is a color I never wear—I should have just ignored it. Maybe after he phoned and said he'd be working late again and after I drove past the car lot and saw it was empty, I should have just said, That's a man for you. Maybe I should have just eaten all my pride and ignored the fact that Mary Sue O'Connor sidled her grocery cart up to mine at the A&P right as I was choosing a baking hen for dinner and said, "Rose, I don't mean to gossip, but Tom was at the car lot yesterday delivering the new lavender business cards Pauline DuPree ordered and he said your husband and Miss DuPree were on awfully friendly terms."

And I said to her, "Why, Mary Sue, what should be so remarkable about my husband being on friendly terms with his boss? Perhaps wandering minds see only what they want to see."

But deep in my soul I knew she was right. I got home and started putting two and two together. Again. I saw through all of Charlie's excuses. I even imagined him heading over to Pauline's for a quickie every time he said he was going out for a quart of milk. I figured it started even before I lost my baby girl. It wasn't the fact that I hadn't been able to bring his baby to full term. I figured he'd been cheating before that.

After one full water glass of Jack Daniel's I decided that from the very day we got married he had been untrue. And after two full water glasses, I decided the only thing left for me to do was get him to admit to me that he was a no-good, cheating bastard. And if he didn't admit it maybe I'd kill him. And if he did admit it maybe I'd still kill him.

I was horribly worked up.

So when he finally did walk in the back door, the kitchen door, wearing his jaunty hat and his beautiful charcoal-gray business suit, I didn't say how do you do or kiss my butt. I threw my third glass of JD at him. Which, of course, he ducked, so that it hit my nice yellow wall, thus the whiskey stain. And then he straightened up— his six-foot frame filling my vision—and started to laugh.

Then he took off his hat, removed his coat, and loosened his tie and said, "Rose, how the hell are you."

I'm not sure what all I said to him. But I gave it to him full blast. The shouting was horrible. And with Charlie and me it's always an easy transition between shouting and shoving. In fact, it's like time speeds up into one furious, barbed ball. So before I knew it I'd ripped his new white shirt. And it seemed like just seconds had passed when I found myself being shaken so hard I thought my spine would snap. "Shut your mouth, Rose Looney, slam it shut right now!" Charlie was screaming.

That's when Emory came out of his bedroom and pulled the broom out of the closet. He swung it twice—warning swings—and told Charlie to take his "goddamned hands off my mother." Which he did. So I ran into the living room, but Charlie ran after me. And I think it was then that I shouted at him, "Now I know why your mama abandoned you. Now I know why she walked out the first chance she got. Because you're bad seed."

That's when he backhanded me. Busted my lip. And that's when Emory jumped over the back of my blue upholstered couch and stepped in between Charlie and me. And he didn't give Charlie a chance to back down or to get in the first punch. He hit his father full and square in the face. Blood spewed and I was afraid Charlie's nose was broken. And I screamed, "Oh my God, Emory, go get some ice." Charlie stood there looking amazed—not angry, more like shock. He didn't put his hands to his face. He stood very still and let the blood flow. And Emory slumped down on the couch, put his head in his hands, and bawled.

So I went in and got the ice and put it on Charlie's face. He winced and walked away, down the hall. I put the ice to my own lip and then touched Emory's curly blond hair, but he waved me away. The silence was as violent as the shouting had been. I didn't know what to do so I did something dumb. I went into the kitchen and started a pot of coffee. But right as I set the pot on the burner somebody spoke. It was Charlie, in a very calm voice, calling, "Emory, I want to see you in your room. Now." I wanted to run in there, separate the two of them. Make it all okay again. But I couldn't move. My legs were like crumbling concrete. Scared, petrified. I just stood there watching the coffee percolate like it was my own blood, because I was convinced that the fighting would start again. That Charlie would raise his fist to Emory.

But what happened was worse than that. They were in Emory's room all of fifteen minutes. And then I hear Charlie in the living room. He has switched on the TV. I hear Rob telling Laura he can't possibly accept a raise if Buddy and Sally don't get one too.

43

And then Emory walks into the kitchen. He doesn't look like a boy blossoming into manhood anymore. Instead he looks scared, like the little kid who would fight back the tears after skinning his knees. But he says, his eyes peeled to the floor, "He said I should be the one to tell you. He's going to call Uncle J.W. We think it would be a good idea if I went down to Lake Okeechobee, spent some time with him. I'll just sugar-cane it for a while."

I said, "No, Emory, you can't leave me."

But he just turned his back on me. He just turned away and went to his room.

So at that moment I'm no longer thinking about being cheated on. My fury has now turned on the prospect of losing my son. I go in to Charlie. He's laying on the couch. No more blood. His nose is swollen but it's all right. And I say to him, "Please, Charlie, don't send our boy away. He's sorry. I know he is. He won't do it again."

Charlie put his hand on my hair and stroked it. He gently touched my lip. He said, "Now Rosie, the boy and me have decided. It's for the best. He needs to know what working for a living is before he comes back in this house and raises a fist at me." He said it kindly, so reasonably, like he was explaining why he wanted black car mats instead of white.

I shook my head. "No, Charlie, I won't allow it."

Charlie sat up, grinned. "Rose, you're not involved. The boy who thinks he's a man has decided." And then Charlie got up and went to bed.

So two days later I just sit here in my empty house, without a son, knowing that Charlie will be home tonight. Knowing that I put my son on a Greyhound bus headed for Lake Okeechobee and some god-awful sugar-cane farm yesterday. All because I stood up to Charlie about the wrong things. I stood up to him about his cheating when I really didn't have a shred of evidence. But I was too weak to stand up to him about my son. A speck of anger starts to break through my numbness and I think that come hell or high water I'll get the evidence against Charlie. I'll prove to myself and him that he was lying to me. That he was cheating. And how do I know this so well? I think I've always known it. I've never trusted him. I close my eyes and a picture of my mother comes to mind. I'm eight years old and Mama is beautiful even though she's so sick with fever, so close to dead. She whispers in my ear, "Your daddy did this to me."

It wasn't until ten years later that I discovered what she meant, that I learned what syphilis was. I was living in Richmond, having run away from our Grundy home three years prior, due to Daddy's horrible temper. When he got drunk he liked to beat me. So I found myself getting a job as a countergirl at the drugstore's soda fountain. Uncle Mason sent notice to me. In a short note he spelled it out. Your daddy is dead. Syphilis. You probably know it had been eating him away for years.

Finally I knew what Mama had meant. Daddy really had killed her. Injected her with death as they were making love.

I never let anybody get close to me after that. I just stayed stony. Alone. Afraid of night and day and everything in between.

But then I met Charlie. I'd come down to Florida thinking a single woman would be able to survive better in a gentler climate. I was sitting on a bench in St. Augustine, looking out at the bay, when this motorcycle racket started behind me. I turned around. And there he was. Atop this monster cycle. Charlie Looney the cop, in his knee-high black leather boots and his sharp, close-fitting uniform. He whipped off his helmet and flashed me that drop-dead grin. Above the rumble of the cycle he drawled, "Howdy, miss, I hope you're having a wonderful day." And then he sped off. But I saw him again, and again, and again. And soon I didn't have any other thoughts except for those that involved the strong, gentle, kind Charlie Looney. He seemed my haven, my salvation, my knight riding a roaring cycle who would take me in his arms and keep away all the pain.

I get up from my kitchen table and glance at my red-rooster clock that ticks so loud you can hardly ever forget it's there. It is just past four. Charlie hates that clock. He keeps asking why don't I throw it away and get a new one. I say because I like it. I glance at the broken glass in the corner. My impulse is to go ahead and sweep it up. To put my house back in order. I know if I do this Charlie will know I've started to forgive him. But I don't know what else to do. Where else do I go? So I walk over and pick up my broom. I look around at my yellow walls, my sunshine walls, and it hits me that I'm in a prison. I laugh out loud. Yes, that's exactly it— my house is a prison. But as I go over to clean up the glass, I realize I don't know who built its stifling walls—me or Charlie.

Soleil Marie Beauvoir

In the sugar fields we have this song. Somebody sings, "Mambo Beauvoir, will Erzulie visit us tonight?"

And I ring back, "If you are lucky, Erzulie visits you every night."

But this is just my talk, you see. Because Erzulie, the spirit of love, she's a real good lady. But never to me has she given a favor. Never to me has she said, Now's the time to break up this girl's loneliness.

So I just sit in these fields and work in these fields and play *mambo* to the other workers. And always I say nice things and do good deeds for my *loa*. But sometimes I say to myself, It's not enough, no.

Tonight I journey all by myself through a land so thick with cabbage palm and mangrove and cypress and more, just to make an offering to Erzulie. Maybe to discover what sound, what flower, what body is missing from this life of mine.

Erzulie, yes. The love spirit, and I mean, she is wild. Since so many of us long ago began dressing in Catholicism, we married Christ to our Voodoo. You know her, the Virgin Mother Mary: The whites don't know it, but she is Erzulie, yes. And believe me, she can be crazy. When Erzulie mounts you, sex, yes, it's everywhere.

But sometimes the worshipping is not enough. Sometimes it's the results that I want to see. And then sometimes, after a long night filled with the drums our *loa* love—after that rum is gone and after the holy candles have burned their last dance, them—I say to myself, Soleil Marie, why not leave these fields? Why not take your body and your *loa* and your good sense to another place?

'Cause, see now, I don't care for Uncle—J.W. is what the white men call him—or really for the work. I could go to the cities, get a job, live in a house built from brick walls, not wood. I'm a young lady. Very strong. And my friends say I'm pretty. So I know I could survive out there.

But then a voice—it floats in my spine like a clear pond—it says to me, These fields, these swamps, they are a part of you, Soleil Marie. It's then that I think hard about the mystery: Some moments in day and night I'm not a field worker slaving to make some white man's money grow. No. I am a bird and what flows in my bones is swamp water. And my mama and papa, no longer are they dead. No, they are voices that rise out of the swamp mud, mist floating between the palmetto leaves, spirits whispering in the fog during twilight hours. They fill me.

I don't have no mirrors to look at myself so that I know the truth. I don't have dollars clinging to my pockets to tell me what is and what isn't. I just have these voices, and these fields, and my *loa*. So for now, that is why I stay. Not because I'm dumb. Not because I can't be nothing else but a field flea, as Uncle calls us.

Hear me now. I know things even other *mambos* do not know. My Haitian mama, she too was a *mambo*, she married a Seminole, Papa. He taught her all the Indian ways. And they taught me. So I know it all.

For instance, see, to kill my enemies, I know how. A feather from a swamp bird, ibis or eagle, like that—I send it in the night to my enemy's house. I lie down and dream, giving it instructions. I send it there, it rides on the winds until my enemy is drunk with sleep. My feather, its quill is a needle, yes. It pierces my enemy's neck vein and fills with his blood. If death is what I want, I send my feather every night until no longer my enemy has blood. But this bloodsucking, I have had never to do. For this I thank all my gods.

And some of the ways Papa taught, yes, they keep us alive each day. Why do none of us ever get snake bite? White people, they die every day if they live where we do. It was this promise Papa's people made to the snake spirit. We don't ever kill a snake, not one, and we live. But we kill one, watch out. The agreement is off. The snakes, millions, they will slither up our legs as we sleep and strike a million times the skin closest to our hearts.

So no, Mr. Big Shot Uncle, I'm not just a field flea. And even though I have some longings and loneliness in this heart of mine, I've got what people like Uncle will never have. I've got so much more than what the dollars can do. So much more than what just a faint nod at a few saints can do. Because me, Soleil Marie, I've got the passion.

And it is this passion that tonight causes me to leave my little stilt house and wander deeper into the swamp. Erzulie, that sweet lady, has been so heavy on my mind. She's calling me. Trying to talk to me. I know if I listen right that maybe to do away with my loneliness she will.

So I move like silent water through my pine and palmetto. The glades, they are alive tonight, humming with frogs and acacia and wild crying heron. The good moon is full, easing my way and warming my machete.

Along the way I stop at a cane plant. And I say, "This is what Erzulie is needing." So I cut her a piece of cane. In my skirt pocket I carry three magnolia blossoms and a handful of sugar-cane tassels.

When I reach the pond I study what I see. 'Dillo tracks in the sand—mama and baby. In the distance I hear the quick, splashing sounds of a 'gator making a kill. But me, I am not afraid, because I know these kills are life-giving. I take the flowers from my pocket and to the pond I toss them—a sweet offering for Erzulie.

Then under the moonlight naked I become, and I step into that pond. I float among the lily pads, watching the stars wander the black sky. And I say inside myself, Erzulie, spirit of love, tell me what it is I'm supposed to be doing.

And I get bold. I say to her, Erzulie, since I'm such a good *mambo*, maybe a lover you could bring to me, maybe somebody to ease me when I get lonely.

I need to make her happy, so just as a breeze whips over the pond, I put that cut cane to my lips, and from it—for her good sake—I sip its thick, sweet milk.

48

Junior Jewel

I always hated the nickname folks around here gave me, yet for most of my thirty-six years I was bridled with it. Before I felt the full burden of my illness, I enjoyed strolling downtown. I would stand under the white porticoes of the plaza and watch the Negroes mill about. As the scent of oleander and bougainvillea lingered in the sea-salt air I would ponder what my ancestors did. I would think about how in order to strip the Africans of their dignity the slave owners first stripped them of their real names.

Now as I sit in this cluttered living room—a place that offers no hint of fresh air or blossoming tree—I wonder if in their freedom the Negroes, like myself, have a yearning to crush the titles which define them: the names imposed upon them by strangers.

My good mother picked out my real name far before my first gasping moments on this earth. How odd it is that a name she held so dear never stuck. And how odd that as my final breath lingers close and unyielding, I should contemplate, with such rigid attention, my true name. In lucid moments of day and evening, I allow myself the luxury of drifting back into my name, floating in it as if it were a clear, deep stream. I swim and float and some days I drown, but the drowning is good. I drift and sink like a free man, praying that the rushing current will heal me.

Today I have drifted from my bedroom and the putrid sheets of my deathbed. For the first time in three weeks, I am sitting in my living room, trying to pretend I do not smell or ache. I often wonder if the smells that cling to me while I'm half alive will remain after I'm dead, like noxious ghosts.

I thought of my stinking bedsheets when I awoke this morning, when the first whiff of the new day was myself. My wife, Eudora, was not stretched out like a fine feather beside me. She has not slept with me for many days. Once the pain became fierce, once even the light touch of her floating hand caused a dull ache to rise demonically in revolt, she left our bed.

It makes me sad to admit I was relieved. She misses the "personal times," as she calls them, for she is still a vital woman, healthy and full of sex. But as for me, I am just trying to hang on. Pleasure, large or small, does not interest my bag-of-bones body. And to think that once her little hands melded us into a single bird, that we flew with one motion through her body!

Perhaps it is a lingering memory of lust and passion, coupled with the absurdity of my shriveling self, that spurred me to leave my bed today, despite the effort and pain.

I sit in my royal-blue recliner; a pink-and-white lace doily graces each arm. I've always loved this recliner, ever since I saw it on the showroom floor at Ward's. Today I sit in it, and it feels like a huge lap whose comfort is fleeting, for the child in me knows that soon I must crawl down.

I watch my baby girl play on the floor before me. With her small hand she spins the toy wheels of her fire engine. Her hand stops and she stares into space. She waves at something I cannot see, and for a moment I think I should struggle up and look out into space with her. But something pulls my mind down and plunges me back into the cold, comforting waters of my memories.

I sit in this dark, beige-colored living room, surrounded by the things one accumulates in a life. A Daytona Beach souvenir plate hangs on the wall by the front door. We bought it on a visit three years ago because Eudora had said Daytona was even more cosmopolitan than Jacksonville. A vase on the TV tray glitters with a million tiny seashells that have been painted luster pink. I had seen Eudora admiring it in the window of a shell shop down at the beachfront. So five years ago for our wedding anniversary I gave it to her. Nature scenes—moose, bald eagles, otters, and the like—pictures cut from magazines, hang in brown plastic frames above the TV. They cover almost the entire wall. Eudora said she cut them out for me because she knows how I love trees. Then there are the two huge table lamps with gold-colored harlequin bases and chocolate-colored shades shaped like triangles. They rise like albatrosses at either end of our small wicker couch. Eudora bought them at a yard sale several years back. I don't know exactly when. She cooed for days about how beautiful they were. I never knew how much she paid for them, but for weeks she swore, "Sweetheart, they were a steal. An absolute steal," as if she suspected that I didn't care for them but that their economy would silence me. I could never bring myself to tell her I much preferred natural light in the daytime, subdued lighting at night, and a room without much clutter. And then I think, There is so much I never told her.

My little girl toddles over and I can see that she wants to crawl into my lap, but I know the pain will be horrible, so I do a terrible thing. I reach out and touch her head, and I say, "No, no, Luella. Not now. Daddy can't stand it right now." Although she can't understand my words, she senses my meaning. She stops and leans against the footrest, watching me with her huge brown eyes, studying me like I'm not her daddy but a wounded bird she has found outside.

I shut my eyes to this, and in my mind I whisper, Remember, little girl, who your daddy was—that he was Burl Junior Jewel. For a moment I think I hear the surf, but then I realize I'm listening to my own waters. And I'm drifting back, floating past this room, and past this illness, and I'm back at the plaza porticoes, and the scent of oleanders overtakes me, and I'm thinking once again about my name. I'm thinking about the times in my life that my name mattered. I see my father and mother. I imagine the pride they felt at bringing life to this earth. I believe my parents took great care in naming me. It is my awful luck that I did not come home to my true self until too late.

Actually, I view my name as a present my father gave my mother. Father, Eustis Jewel, gave Mother a beautiful cedar chest as her dowry. "This will hold all the precious clothes you will make for our child," he told her. I know this occurred, for when I was a small boy my mother often told me this story.

The cedar chest was encased, emboldened, and made beautiful by a rich oak veneer. My mother marveled at the veneer's many designs. She liked to say, "Look, it's like the art God paints on butterfly wings."

My father assured Mother it was the finest veneer available.

51

"Carved from the most choice and delicate burls North Florida oaks have to offer," he told her.

My mother murmured the sound over and over. She must have been beautiful, in her organza dress, kissing the word that was to become my name. Burl. Burl Junior Jewel.

The Junior was in honor of my father's father, for that was his given name. If he had a middle name other than Junior—that word that counts only with the federal government and those with whom you are most intimate—no one ever knew what it was. And I, like the grandfather I never met, would go through my life called Junior Jewel, or J.J. by my more vulgar friends.

I remember well the day I held my mother's hand in the butcher store. I was six, far too old to be holding her hand in public, but I had never been in that hideous place of foul-smelling dead flesh.

"This must be Junior," boomed the red-faced German who rested his clasped hands across his blood-splattered apron.

"Burl," my mother corrected him, for she tried a long time to make my name stick. "His name is Burl."

"Oh, baloney," the butcher's fat cheeks puffed out. He smiled and reached into the display case. It seemed as if from thin air a blade appeared, glittering in his thick hands. I believe that before my eyes had time to blink, he had sliced through the fat slab of head cheese. He wagged the meat off the end of his knife as he leaned across the counter. He offered it to me. "Here, Junior, my boy."

Not looking at my mother but glowing at me with his massive head and intensely blue and ice-white eyes, he boomed, "Why, a burl ain't nothing more than a wart on the face of an oak tree."

So after that I was officially and forever Junior Jewel. I signed my checks that way. When I asked to enter the Catholic faith, I was baptized that way. When neighbors dropped by with visiting relatives, I was introduced that way.

That's how it was until recently. Now I correct anyone who calls me Junior, even my wife. "Burl, Burl is my name," I tell them. I tell them not because I am mean or stubborn or fanciful— a fault I have been accused of my entire life. I insist upon my true name simply because death has a way of bringing a man home, making him be who he is supposed to be, despite himself.

I have these thoughts as I sit here in my living room, my feet propped up on the footrest of my recliner. It is hot, very, very hot. The heat causes my comforting dream waters to evaporate. It forces me back into the elusive but painful present. My baby girl, Luella, is no longer at my feet but has gone back to the window. She and her little drooping diaper. It hangs like a sad white cloud around her chubby thighs. Her funny state of dress does not matter, for Luella is not at all self-conscious yet. This is a phase I will never experience with her.

I am coming to terms with such things. She is standing on her tiptoes, gripping the yellow tile windowsill with such force that her tiny fingers are turning pale, edged darkly in red. My daughter is craning her baby neck in order to see the sky, I believe.

Luella can be a sullen child, given to long periods of halfhearted crying. Rarely have I heard her cry loudly, with gusto and anger, like most babies. She cries silently, her body shaking as if all the sadness of the world were welled up within her. If she does make a noise, it is a haunting noise that I sometimes hear in my sleep and in the early morning when the doves begin to stir the breaking day.

Dolls do not interest this child. Vehicles do. Toy trains, planes, cars, semi trucks. If it can careen across the floor as if in great escape, my child will throw back her pale face framed in brown curls and laugh. It is a giggle as pure as crystal. These past few months I have lived for that giggle. And for that face that searches the sky, that stares endlessly, fascinated, into an unknowable blue depth.

As for me, that blue depth recedes into black, and it is frightening. I do not know my daughter. What is it she sees? Some days, as the tiny blue pills prescribed to me so conscientiously by my doctor begin to take effect, I imagine that in that wide, gaping, endless mouth of blue, my daughter sees my death. I imagine she sees me floating, a speechless, sightless daddy drifting just beyond her minuscule grasp. To her I may already be dead. Or perhaps I never lived. Maybe she is not yet old enough for me to live. There I am— floating, floating. And even in real life, in real time, in this room crowded with dime-store whims and yard-sale treasures, I am denied, through pain, the pleasure of holding her. I want to reach out to her and say, "Come to Daddy, come to Burl," but I cannot, for the aching no longer ebbs, not one iota, with the downing of blue pills, torn pieces of my baby girl's blue sky.

Rose Looney

The Jewels have always been better off than Charlie and me. I don't mean so much so that they are in a different class than us. They struggle to put meat on the table and clothes on their backs just like everybody else. They seem to ride upon an air current above it, that's all. I have thought long and hard about this. I have wondered how Junior, through these years of oppressive days and sweltering nights, could retain his refined manner of speaking and those gentle, almost effeminate mannerisms.

As I understand it, and I cannot swear to this for it comes from Eudora's big mouth, Junior's father owned a fairly lucrative logging concern in Pensacola. His mother was a schoolteacher who taught him all sorts of things a boy usually does not know. For instance, Junior can recite poetry.

How Junior came to lose the family fortune is not so remarkable. He is a drinker and a gambler. He lost most of it before he ever met Eudora. Which brings me back to why Eudora and Junior always seem to float while Charlie and I sink deeper and deeper into shit of our own making. Junior's vices are far smaller than Charlie's. Junior loves the juice. Bourbon. He can't indulge much in his other vice, for if you do not own money, what fun is there in gambling? So he goes on these awful jags. It is the only time Junior doesn't come home. He's never with another woman. In a town like Tiama, tales of other women spread like wildfire. No, he goes to the groves. He gets wild out there, under those tall oaks. He suffers terrible redbug bites because he passes out naked on lumpy mattresses of Spanish moss. Eventually he wanders home and cries. Eudora, maybe because she doesn't have the backbone I sometimes have, cradles him in her arms, just like he was a little baby. She runs her needlelike painted nails through his dirty matted hair. He puts his head against her flat breasts and sobs, as if he is truly hurting, as if he saw something in those groves so horrible or so sad that living becomes a tragedy.

Despite the fact that I believe Eudora would let a hurricane whip her like a dog before she'd gain the sense to come in out of the rain, she is truly having her troubles now, and in this I find no joy. I have, however, thrown myself into Junior's problems—maybe because I'm a good friend or maybe because it gives me something other than Emory to think about. But even Charlie shows sympathy. Two days ago, in person, he gave Junior a carton of Pall Malls. Junior is not supposed to smoke, but it's one of the few joys available to a dying man. I say to hell with the doctors. Give the man his peace.

They say that in a time of crisis a person's true character shows through. And this is certainly true of Eudora. The poor woman simply does not have the constitution it requires to care for a dying man. So every day and many nights I go and sit with Junior. I am his nurse. Charlie hasn't given me any trouble about this yet.

Actually, say the doctors, Junior should be in a hospital. But the closest one is up the coast in St. Augustine. And even if there was one in Tiama it wouldn't matter, because Junior wants to die at home. "I want to die in my own bed, looking out of my own window at the oak tree I planted with my own hands," he tells everyone who visits.

Well—I say let him. What are they going to do in a hospital that I can't do, besides stick him with needles? And whatever flows through the needle's barrel and into the vein won't cure the cancer. It just inflates the bill.

Take yesterday, for example. I went over around noon. I buzzed the buzzer but Eudora didn't answer the door. So I let myself in, and there she sat—dead-faced—in Junior's blue recliner. She was not floating. With arm muscles tense, she hugged his soiled T-shirt. She looked at me but neither her eyes nor her mouth registered as much as a hello. It was as if that T-shirt was the only thing in the world she knew about. She held it against her. She caressed it. Then she buried her face in it and cried without making a sound. I wanted to rip it out of her hands, but I didn't have the heart for it. My superstitious side knew that the T-shirt, the way she caressed it, resembled too closely a death mask. I turned away from her.

Luella was sitting in the middle of the floor screaming because of her dirty diaper and empty stomach. I bent over and kissed her cheek. I said, "I'll deal with you in a minute." Luella is a problem for me. After I lost my baby I wanted nothing to do with Eudora's child. I could barely see fit to walk over to her house, because Luella seemed a reminder of all that I'd lost. But loss took on new meaning when Emory went away, when Charlie won the argument by playing the biggest card we had—our son. One way I try to get over my Emory-pain is by loving Luella. I change her diaper and feed her and talk to her just like the godmother I'm supposed to be. And Lord knows, that is not an easy thing to be, because the child is awfully fussy.

I pinched Luella's cheek and handed her my keys—which is one of her favorite things to play with—and then quickly walked to Junior's bedroom. I opened his door and caught my breath. About two weeks ago he began losing control of his bowels. And the smell was worse than slaughter day. He looked at me and his lips stretched into a pale streak across his colorless face. It was a gesture of shame and apology. Because I knew he deserved his dignity I looked him straight in the eyes. They flashed a recognition—a hard, cold blue.

In my biggest voice I said, "Burl," because that is what he wants to be called these days, "don't you go anywhere. I'll be back in a minute to deal with you." I winked at him. I closed the door.

Eudora was frozen and still sinking. Luella was still screaming. I snapped up the phone and called Inez Temple. "Inez, if you've got nothing cooking this afternoon I could use you at Eudora's, my dear."

Inez is a Negro woman who is as good and honest as the day is long. I met her way back when Emory was just a toddler. She was my baby-sitter. Eloise Carpenter, a neighbor who has long since moved away, recommended her. By the time I found Inez I'd gone through six other sitters, all of whom were lazy, dirty, uncaring, or all three. But not Inez. She took to my son as if he were her own child. No, to this very day I trust Inez implicitly. So as I stood in Eudora's house wringing the phone cord in my hands—my nerves starting to snap due to Luella's crying—it didn't surprise me that Inez didn't ask why or huff or offer any shade of an excuse. Quick as a bee she said, "Be right there."

I changed Luella's diaper, her screaming all along. I checked on Eudora. I put my hand on her sunken shoulder. "You all right, honey?" She didn't answer me. But she did meet my imploring eyes, so I knew that maybe something was going right.

Inez showed up with sweat beads glistening like pearls on her high, dark forehead. Her yellow-and-orange skirt was typical. Inez always dresses in bold, beautiful colors. I envy her that. She looks like some kind of huge, exotic queen in layer upon layer of bright color. My friendship with Inez is not something I make a big deal of around Charlie.

At the front stoop, she gave me a big hug. "Rose Looney, just look at you. All your troubles and you're helping like this."

For some reason an urge to burst into tears took hold of me. But most times I have far too much pride to cry. So I nailed myself down by getting real businesslike. I walked inside and said, "Inez, if you take the child, I'll take the mother."

"That's a deal any day of the week," she said. Without a moment's hesitation she picked up one-year-old Luella and supported her on one hip, and then balanced a grocery bag of canned food on the other. "This baby needs to eat," she declared.

She kicked open the screen door and walked over to my house. This is a gift Inez has: she can walk into any room in any house in any part of town and immediately understand a situation.

The house no longer seemed like it was teetering on the brink of disaster, since there wasn't a screaming baby around to jar the ears. I looked down at Eudora. She was helpless. It made me mad. But I am not one to act recklessly in the face of another person's sorrow.

"Eudora, you need some sleep and you need to get out of this house," I told her in my don't-argue-with-me voice. "You'll feel a lot better with some rest."

I took the T-shirt from her wringing hands and put it on the coffee table. "Come on, you're coming with me."

As I helped her out of the recliner, she looked at me with the same shame in her eyes as Junior did when his stench billowed over me. "It's okay, honey, you're just tired."

I'm not sure if Eudora used her own feet to get to my house. I felt like I was carrying her, and despite her bony frame, the woman was heavy, as if sadness had caused the hollows of her body to fill with rocks. When I opened my front door, there was Inez, rocking a sleeping child. She nodded at me to indicate all was well. Eudora looked at Inez and the child and then at me. I knew she was going to start her crying again so I looked away. "Thank you all so much," she said.

As I guided her down the hall to my bedroom, I said, "Eudora, girl, you just need some sleep. That's all that's wrong with you."

I reached over to turn down my once brightly colored peacock chenille spread, but she said, "No, I don't want to be under any covers right now." She just laid down on top of the spread, shoes and all, and I told her not to talk and held her hand and watched her eyes close. I waited a few minutes—until her breathing turned steady and deep. Then I slipped my hand from hers. I walked back to her house.

My next goal was to get Junior cleaned up. So I filled a two-gallon plastic bucket with warm soapy water, and then Eudora's big soup pot with clear water. This would be my rinsing water. I put Billie Holiday on the record player because she was one of Junior's favorite singers. Junior loved jazz. I opened the bedroom door. I knew he was appreciative of the music even though he didn't say so. I talked about this and that as I changed his soiled sheets. The price of tomatoes has gone up. Maybe I'll plant a garden next year. Amos Kirk is smoking cigars in City Council meetings again. I tried to be very gentle, for I knew moving him to one side and then the other caused him severe pain.

58

Before I put fresh sheets on the bed I washed the shit off him. Immediately I was sorry I had taken care of Eudora and Luella first. Perhaps if I had cleaned Junior earlier his waste would not have hardened on his skin. He kept his eyes closed as I scrubbed. I didn't blame him. I wrung out the washcloth and shimmied some Ivory soap into its rough surface. I made smooth arcs of white on his butt. Billie Holiday's voice sounded like crushed red velvet: "I wished on the moon for something I never knew."

Junior's naked body was so thin I believed I could see through him. I believed his bones had lost all resistance and could be manipulated like rubber toys. I saw them shrink like light in a room when the door slams shut.

I saw his heart. It was not a glistening red beet, pumping with the assuredness of a rising sun. No, it sat hard and stubborn against his ribs, a tiny, stiff pebble waiting to die.

I saw that his ligaments and tendons, those bands that tie muscle to bone, ached beneath the strain of forcing together a body that now wanted only one thing: to disappear.

I sang with Billie, "A sweeter rose. A softer sky." I set down the washcloth. "An April day"—I walked over to the window—"that would not dance away."

I pulled open the thick green curtains. I was shocked to find the windows closed. I opened them. Fresh air overtook the room as if it was furious at being kept out for so long.

I looked at Junior. He was staring into the branches of an oak tree. Years ago, with his own hands, he'd planted that tree. Now its limbs, thick with Spanish moss, rustled just beyond his window.

"I wished on a star to throw me a beam or two." I cupped my hands and dipped them into the cool, clear water. Junior's eyes continued to look past me and into the lacework of the crisscrossing branches. I held my hands a few inches above his chest.

"I begged on a star and asked for a dream or two." The water trickled from my hands. It splashed onto his skin. I watched the water flow, and then again I plunged my hands into the pot and again let the water splash.

I did this until I knew I had soothed him. I looked at his face.

His eyes were still scanning the world beyond my shoulder, and although he didn't smile, I believe firmly that somewhere inside himself he did.

I don't know why I did what I did next, but I couldn't stop myself. If it was wrong, may God forgive me, because I intended it with all sweetness. I bent over and kissed those lips that were nothing more than a dry scar sealing his dying face.

When I straightened up, I saw his hands—frail, shaking hands—slowly tracing the bathwater rivers that rolled across his fleeting body.

Soleil Marie Beauvoir

No, believe it I could not. With no mercy the hot sun beat down. It was the kind of day when I say to myself, "Soleil Marie, fly out of these fields. Fly now." But you know, that's when I saw him. Uncle's Boy.

See, I had heard about this Uncle's Boy. When he first showed in the fields, everyone's mouth rattled about the white boy cutting cane. But me, not had I seen him until this sun-flooded day. Because Uncle, see, had had me working for some time—borrowed help— on another white man's farm.

But now I was back in my fields, working, yes, and dreaming my flying dreams. I had raised my face to the hot sun. On mean days like this one I wanted to know the sun—to feel it full—so that I would not be scared. I stood so still, letting the heat beat on me. And when it was enough, and I was full, I opened my eyes and looked across those fields. Green leaves and black bodies moving together. But beyond that, far off from all of us, I saw him. Alone. Fighting with himself and the cane, like he was without happiness. Chopping, chopping, chopping.

So me, I stopped my machete swinging. I didn't care what anybody might say—I wandered closer. So close I could see him good.

But far enough away that he didn't know he was in my sights. And this is what I saw: Blond hair. A body, yes, but more. There were green eyes that I watched. And there was muscles straining with the machete, but he was a worker without grace. A worker without the knowledge of when to hold back and when to give. As he struggled with that blade and sweet cane, his eyes hooded, and I thought, Snake spirit. But when he throwed back his pretty face and passed fingers over his lids to clear the sweat, I didn't think at all. My body, though, began making plans of her own, she.

So it was then I decided to do some of my own seed-planting. For many a day I would pass by that boy. Nothing much. Just a walk. Just a stirring of sand. My people, none of them talked to Uncle's Boy. But to them he didn't either. Like he was not in our world. But that was just a lie my scared sweetness told to himself. So past him I'd fly. Not looking. Not speaking. Just enough.

I cannot say how many days before my seed-planting took on water. But to know that it happened is good enough, yes. In my fields I was, my mind filled with a clear, white space—a good way to work when the job is no good—and my eye caught on a color. Fast I quit moving. Without barely blinking, I saw between the fingers of the cane leaves. Uncle's Boy, squatting he was. And he was staring at me! Oh no, I don't think he knew I had caught onto his little piece of action in the fields, but I thought, Finally I have gathered some myrrh with my spice. I dropped my machete to my side. The white handkerchief I wore around my neck, I untied it and wiped across my sweating face. To please him, I drew it down my neck, across my chest. Even I sighed. Then I turned away to strengthen his wanting me, and also to hide that smile of mine.

Because my ears are always listening to the spirits in these fields, I almost always can hear the rhythms of love or hate. On that day the *loa,* all afternoon, talking to me they was, saying to me, "Time to move closer. Time to feed the crop."

So I waited until the sun filled the fields with cooling shadows. The machetes had fallen so silent and still, and my people was gathering at the well. Uncle's Boy was by himself. His fear splashed all over that pretty face, leaning against Uncle's white bus—the one that brings my people here from the cities. I said to myself, What

61

sadness, what fright fills my Uncle's Boy! So I dipped my tin cup into the water and drank until just a little river was left. Then I began my art, my life, my Voodoo. I spit into my tiny river at the bottom of the cup. And into that I poured some more water. And then like the good *mambo* that I am, I walked over to the scared boy, who seemed to be desiring to be back on his Uncle's white bus and headed out of here. To him I said no words at first. I just stared into his wonderful, sunburned face. I watched the colors in his eyes dance from dark to light, so that I knew, yes, that behind the pain was a goodness. I held out my Voodoo, my cup of water and spit. "Here," I says to him, "this you need."

He blushed—a shy boy—but he took the cup. And I could see so plain that his hands were just now beginning to harden over the blisters he'd carried for months. "Thanks," he said, in a voice that flowed from some uncomfortable place inside him. He took a sip.

I smiled at him. A nice friendly smile, yes. But what I said was, "No. You have to drink it all."

He giggled. Nervous as a cat, him. But I didn't let up. My stare kept on and so did my smile. No choice did he have. He put that cup to his lips and tossed down the holy water, me watching his Adam's apple shiver as it was cooled.

Then he handed to me our cup and smiles and says, "How's that?"

I let my eyes mingle into his. With every drop of water and blood flowing in my body I says, "Much better."

Charlie Looney

It's a hell of a note when two men become better friends in death than in life. But as I sat across the street in my black Chevy convertible, tucked in the nighttime shadows of the Palm Breeze Grocery, waiting for old candy-ass Lackly to leave his funeral home, I was prepared for something just like that to happen between Junior and me.

Yes, sir. Sitting there all alone. Cool as a cucumber because a breeze was coming in from the east. Blocked from most views because the grocery was on one side of me and the World War II Memorial Park on the other. Just considering what life had dealt Junior and what it had dealt me.

You might say that when Junior Jewel was alive he and I worked from an understanding. I had always figured him for a mama's boy. He'd always figured me for a wise-ass.

Maybe we were both right.

But as I like to say, death levels things out. Friends. Equal friends. Let's let bygones be bygones, and all that two-bit tripe.

That's why I was sitting there cozy in the Black Beauty—watching an occasional car drive along the boulevard—waiting for my chance to rescue Junior. Now wouldn't you call that a friend? I'm just a fellow waiting to grab his dead buddy so he can be buried decent. Just a little job to do. Just snatching him from the claws of a government that says Junior can't be buried in his backyard, where he wanted to be buried. They claimed Junior had to be stuck in a regulation plot in a regulation box in a regulation cemetery. Forget it. All Junior wanted was to spend eternity underneath that old oak he'd planted years back. It was my evening's mission to ensure that occurred.

Checked my watch. Ten-thirteen. I wondered what in the hell was keeping Lackly in there so late. I mean, what could be so demanding about his job, for Christ sakes? And then I thought, My man, maybe you don't want to know. Some things are better left alone. Hell's bells—I guess it takes all kinds.

I popped open my glove box and pulled out the brown bag Rose had packed for me. Saltine and mayo sandwiches. She hadn't forgotten the can of Vienna sausages. I'm no French gourmet or anything, but I sure do love to eat. I flipped open my pocketknife and slit a sausage in half. I put that sucker between two crackers. I took a bite, and cracker flakes dusted down on my T-shirt. I reached for the beer on the dash. Hell. One mouthful left. What good was a cracker sandwich without a cold beer? I slugged the brew down and tossed the empty into the backseat.

Didn't have a handkerchief or anything, so I wiped the pocket-knife on my shirt and then cleaned my fingernails with it. I thought about how funny it was that Junior's final exit would be via the Black Beauty. I mean, here I was, owning a car that glowed like the moon and sped like the wind, and Mr. Big Shot Junior wouldn't ride in it. I kept the fenders so clean and polished you could eat off them. The black hood stretched far enough out in front of you that it seemed to go on for miles, as if its steel body were really made of ribs and muscle and bone. Riding around with the top down, a guy could imagine himself to be king of the world—free of troubles, beyond tears—a knight streaking through town in a car that performed like a champion steed. That was my fantasy anyway. And Junior knew it. He knew this car was my haven, my idea of how right everything in the world could be—that it made me feel powerful and correct. That's why he would never ride in it: he never wanted to admit that I could be just as morally righteous as he was. My tastes in justice and cars may have been different than his, but he wouldn't even acknowledge I had such notions.

Checked my watch again. Three minutes later than the last time I looked. I tested the edge of my knife. Not that I was going to use it or anything. I just liked to make sure it stayed sharp.

Then I heard what I'd been waiting for: a slamming door. I slid down in my seat and took everything in. Pat Lackly, dressed like a fag in his white Italian suit and white suede shoes, jumped over the car door and into the driver's seat as if there were movie cameras around to record his stupidity. He fired up the Corvette. He spun out of the parking lot. Never did even look my way.

I waited until his taillights had become pinpricks in the distance, then got out of the Black Beauty. I dropped the knife in my hip pocket and grabbed my porkpie hat off the backseat. As if I was minding my own business, I crossed the street and walked around to the back of the parlor, which was hidden from the street by a hedge of Australian pine. I checked out the window screen. It was in that window only by the grace of God. I pushed on one side of it. The other side popped out. The building itself was a whitewash clapboard. The windows were the easiest to get in and out of. Hurricane windows. The only time you couldn't budge them is if you'd painted them shut. I was counting on Lackly's fancy ways. They paid off. The window slid open—no gummed paint.

The window was about waist level, so I just hoisted myself in. The room was pitch-black, and it smelled. Chemicals, like a doctor's office. There may have been stiffs right where I was standing. "Jesus Christ," I said. If I moved left or right, I might fall over one. I'm a grown man but, I don't mind telling you, I felt uneasy.

Light. I needed light.

I patted myself down until I found my matches in my back pocket. As I struck one, the room took shape. In front of me was a stainless-steel table. It was deep, almost a tub. Thick rubber hoses connected to it and led into floor drains. I saw the undertaker's tools. Saws. Blades. Scalpels. And everything seemed to dance due to the flickering flame. I'm telling you, this was creepy.

The match singed my fingers. I threw it to the ground and struck another. Along the far wall were supplies. Big bottles of pink fluid crowded the shelves. I moved in closer to read the labels: they all said "Everlast, The Embalmer's Friend."

Jesus, I could see Lackly in here with his white suit and white shoes, pumping dead, naked people full of pink Everlast. I laughed out loud it was so damn funny. I lit a cigarette. The smoke helped block the chemical odor.

"Junior, where in the hell are you?" I asked.

I'm not superstitious, and I don't scare easy. The rabbit's foot I take with me when I fish is just habit. Nevertheless, my job would have been easier if I'd known exactly where Junior was. But I don't shuck off challenges. I'm not a coward. I'm a no-good son of a bitch, but I'm not a coward.

The cigarette offered a speck of light, but it was the best I could do in a stinkhole situation. I held it in front of me like a candle. Slowly I eased out of Lackly's hatchet room.

As I walked down the hallway, I noticed the sound of my feet on the carpet. Kind of like a muffled thud, but there was nothing I could do about it. I stopped at a door on my left and squinted my eyes, craned my neck. By now I was adjusting to the darkness.

I could make out the rows of church pews and the stage where the bodies rested during services. But nothing there, no bodies.

A few feet ahead, on my right, was a pair of swinging doors. "Hot damn," I said.

I took a full breath, swung open the doors, and stepped into the room. It was colder than February. If I hadn't been so scared I might have exhaled and seen my breath. I felt the wall for a light switch because the darkness just wasn't going to do.

The overhead flickered on.

Bingo. There he was. Junior Jewel. My friend. In his gleaming casket, fresh and cold as a red snapper.

Now he wasn't alone in the room. Mrs. Batemeyer was there too. But my foremost concern was Junior. I guess I was a little shocked. Jesus, he was just laying there, white and puffy. But I walked closer anyway. "Hello, Junior. Hello, Mrs. Batemeyer."

Eudora had done a good job picking out Junior's casket. The lining was tuck-and-roll red velvet. Plush. Comfortable. Too bad he wasn't going to need it.

But Lackly had done a terrible job on him. He'd forced Junior's lips into an attempt at a grin. Junior never grinned that way. And his hair. It was parted down the middle instead of combed off his forehead. "Don't worry, buddy, we'll fix you up when I get you home," I said.

I glanced at Mrs. Batemeyer. Now I have to admit, Lackly did okay by her. Her lining was peach. It reflected off her skin, making her glow. Her hair was perfect, in that big bun on top of her head. Her lipstick matched the peach in the casket. She looked as if she was just taking a nap.

Then I figured out what else was wrong with what they'd done to Junior. "Jesus, Junior, they've got you dressed up like a fucking preacher, in a tie and a going-to-the-bank-to-get-a-second-mortgage suit." I decided I'd be doing my friend a favor if I adjusted his tie.

I flexed my hands a couple of times. Touching a dead man. The thought kind of drifted through my mind and caused my toes to curl, if you know what I mean. I counted to ten. Then gently, like I was touching an innocent woman, I loosened the tie. Using my thumb and forefinger like crab pinchers, I unbuttoned his top button.

"Well, good buddy," I said to him, "it's time for that ride you never counted on. The Black Beauty awaits."

Then something happened I'm not very proud of. I realized Junior was not going to get up on his own and walk out. I was going to have to wrap my arms around him. I was going to have to hug this dead man. My dead friend. I didn't want to. The thought of doing it was revolting. I mean, I'm being honest here. And in my favor, not many men would have had the guts to even be standing in that room. And obviously, I couldn't change my mind. I wouldn't give Rose, Eudora, nobody that satisfaction.

Junior's face was bluish. I poked my finger into his chest. It was hard, ungiving. I touched his arm. His belly. I felt his ribs underneath that suit coat. I looked at how his hands were hopelessly clasped together as if he was praying or worrying. And then, in addition to everything else I was feeling, I got tickled by the whole situation.

Junior, my longtime friend and foe, was helpless.

I could do anything to him, for the first time in my life, and he couldn't be superior to me. And all that was required of me was to wrap my arms around my friend and carry him out the window.

I drug a folding chair over from the corner. I stood on top of it. I positioned myself into a deep crouch. It was a wrestling move I'd learned years ago. I slammed one arm across Junior's thighs and shoved another behind his back. I yelled like a banshee as I pulled.

Junior gave at the waist. He leaned up two, three, maybe four inches. Then the son of a bitch—probably because of all the shit Lackly pumped into him—farted.

"Jesus fucking Christ." I jumped. I pushed against the coffin to regain my footing, but only succeeded in kicking the chair out from underneath me. As my feet touched the floor, I found myself face to face with Junior. The stupid grin. The sunken cheeks filled with Everlast. The high, white-powdered forehead.

"God damn," I screamed. I took him by the shoulders and did what I should have done when he was alive. I shook him hard. I shook him for the embarrassment he always caused me. I shook him because he so calmly smiled back at me, mocking me. I could hear his soft, sissy voice. "You failed, Charlie. You made Rose lose that baby. You let her go to the game. Go ahead and blame Emory. Send him away from home. Take from Rose not only her unborn baby but her half-grown son. You're wrong, Charlie. You're always wrong."

I thoroughly and fully hated Junior. I grabbed his face with one hand and shook it. "I should have killed you, Junior Jewel."

Nobody was going to mock me from the grave and get by with it. Not a dead baby, not a dead Junior, not an absent son. I twisted and tugged, paying no mind to his ironed suit and manicured hair. Out of the coffin he came, heavy and ungiving. I dropped him on the red shag carpet. He was pitiful, in that stupid suit, motionless on the rug. Grinning.

Eudora, the dumb broad, had stuffed his unfeeling feet into a pair of wing tips. Junior had wandered through most of his life barefoot. Now he was to spend an eternity in shoes. I started to laugh.

"Come on, asshole, we've got a date." I pulled him to his feet. I slid the porkpie off my head and planted it on his.

He was heavy, but I managed to drag him into the embalming room. "This is where Lackly pumped that glow into your cheeks, Junior. Say good-bye." I pushed him halfway out the window. I scrunched up beside him and slid out. Touching him no longer bothered me. He was just the same asshole he'd always been.

I left him half hanging that way while I ran and pulled the Black Beauty around. Now I admit I didn't act responsibly. Once I got him in the car I should have driven him straight home and buried him under his damn oak tree immediately. But as I was positioning him in the car, being careful to dip my porkpie over his eyes, I remembered that three nights ago I had left an almost full bottle of Jack Daniel's under my front seat. And along with that remembrance came an irresistible urge to drive Junior to the beach and enjoy a quick drink. After all, a man has to have some fun, and I was performing an awfully large favor.

I turned over the engine. "Just listen to that idle, Junior. Sweet as a purring babe." I revved it. "Hang on, Junior." I swung out of the parking lot and onto Atlantic Boulevard.

The ocean was just a couple of blocks away. We tooled past the surf shops and the snack shacks that offer up good beach fare: fried shrimp, hot dogs, and beer. I drove down the beach ramp, and I tell you, the smell of that ocean was, is, and forever will be intoxicating. "Man, just breathe that in, Junior. Nothing like a big dose of ocean air to get your heart beating again."

The hard-packed sand hissed beneath my tires. I parked facing the Atlantic. I turned off the motor. I counted on no one being out there this late, and I was right. We were alone. Just me and Junior. The stars twinkled overhead. I took a long swig of juice.

"Want some?" I joked. I felt good. Relaxed. It was a powerful feeling, knowing I had total control. Knowing I didn't have to share my liquor and he had to ride in my beautiful car. He wasn't going to be able to stare at me with those brown, droopy eyes that always seemed on the edge of laughing at me. No. He was at old Charlie's mercy. Charlie—his good, dear friend.

I drank my Jack Daniel's. I watched the surf crash and recede. I listened to the squawking gulls whose wings occasionally flashed white and moved on. I leaned back and breathed in the ocean air. I felt the juice begin to settle in, to sink into my bones like a good, sweet ointment. I watched a shrimp boat—its nets up like dark wings—a couple of miles out. I loved that sight. Shrimp boats. Salt air. Freedom. I thought about home. I knew Rose and Eudora were there waiting on us, but they could just wait a while longer. I do that a lot—keep Rose waiting. Actually, I know this little secret about Rose that she'd probably prefer I didn't. Seems like no matter what I do, she always forgives me. Eventually. Except maybe not about Emory. I think she may hold a grudge concerning that little portion of our history. But she'd get over that in time too. I knew she would. I said out loud, "You know, Junior, I had to send him away. He'd gotten a little out of hand, and so had Rosie. But it will all work out."

And then I thought, Well, that little father-son episode is just water under the bridge, or was it a burned bridge? I couldn't figure out which. But it certainly shouldn't ruin this lovely evening. I glanced at Junior. I drank some juice. The moonlight dispelled any hint of dead-man's-blue from his skin. "Hell, Junior, you'll be all right. Just taking a little nap, that's all you're doing," I said.

The most wonderful thing about ocean air is the way it provokes a man to think. How it just cools off the mind so it can get up and wander. The danger in all this, of course, is that sometimes your mind wanders over to areas of your life you don't want or care to think about—when your life's unpleasantness just pops up to the surface out of the absolute blue yonder. It's like having a bass on the line, and he's running you deep, and it's fun, and then he begins to give up, and the only way you know it is that the bobber bounces back up to the surface like an announcement that all the fun is over. That the little fishy fucker has given up. That's exactly it.

Well, I looked at Junior's pitiful burial suit and at his tie I'd so graciously loosened, and one of those dreaded bobbers sprung. The Fourth of July—three or four years back. My band, the Rockets, we had played at the Jax Beach bandshell, about fifty miles up the coast, the day before the Fourth. We played Bob Wills, Tommy Dorsey, a mix of all kinds of songs. Our only rule: The songs had to be toe-tappers. If you couldn't swing to it, we didn't play it.

This woman was there. A looker. You know the kind.

Well, she was sweet on me. I don't think it's anything I did in particular to cause this. But I *am* the bandleader. It's a responsibility. Women like that.

We were on break, and this gal, she had the biggest bullets you ever seen, comes on to me. Puts her arms around me, the whole bit. What am I supposed to do? I act nice. Polite. I am a showman. But that's where it ended. She wasn't my type. Too easy. Other things on my mind.

I go home. Like a damn good husband.

The next day, the Fourth, Rose inspects my band shirt. Of course, what does she find? Lipstick. Not on the collar—on the breast pocket. She suspects I've been having a fling with Pauline—the hot little girl who owns the car lot—which is a situation that is none of Rose's business. She accuses me. Shit. Maybe it was all the Jack Daniel's we'd been drinking, I don't know. But the more she yelled and cried about me with another woman, the madder I got. But not at Rose. At Junior. I mean, I hauled off and backhanded Rose because I'd had enough. The woman has a foul mouth when she's drunk and mad. But it was that weasel Junior who really had me riled.

See, there wasn't ever the possibility that Mr. Perfect would step out on his wife. I was getting shit—in this instance for no reason—and Junior was next door, innocent as a baby's butt. At the time it seemed crystal clear to me. The source of my troubles was sitting one house over. Well, I said to myself—Rose's crying stabbing my thoughts like a blade—I'm gonna fix you, Mr. Perfect.

Being as half cocked as I was, I marched into my bedroom. I got my gun from the bedstand drawer. I marched out of my house and over to Junior's.

He opened the door. Looked at the gun. Looked at me.

Now get this. "I'm going to kill you, you son of a bitch," I said.

But old Junior, he just spoke soft and calm: "Charlie, I want you to go home and apologize to your wife for calling her those ugly names you called her. After you do that, take a shower, eat some supper. Then you, Rose, and the boy come over. We'll walk down to the beach and watch the fireworks."

Then the crazy motherfucker took the gun from my hand. He emptied the chamber and handed it back. "See you tonight," he said.

And then he shut the door right in my face.

Man, oh, man. I tooted my car horn twice. I shook my head, amazed at the recollection. "Those honks are for you, Junior. I salute you, buddy, for not letting me kill you, and thereby saving me from going to jail." I reached over and repositioned the porkpie on his head so that it was at an angle. It endowed him with a kind of going-downtown-to-see-the-ladies look.

"Junior," I said, "you and me have had quite a history together. Hell, man, the first time I ever saw you, you was prancing around like a kid right out there in that very same Atlantic Ocean." Yes, indeed.

I took another swig of juice. I closed my eyes. I listened to the surf roll and recede, roll and recede. The ocean was never quiet, the waves were never still, but it always made me feel so damn

71

peaceful. On a night like tonight, when there weren't any people out to mess things up, you could hear the sea unfurling in peals all the way down the coastline.

I guessed I was doing all right by Junior—honoring his dying request to be buried under his oak tree and all. As far as I could tell, he had carried on with this damn strange tree-love his entire life.

"Yes, sir, Junior buddy, you loved your silly trees."

Way out on the horizon I spotted the lights of a tanker and then, out of nowhere, sounding like ages away, a foghorn cried. It was one of the saddest, most beautiful sounds a man could hear. And I think it provoked a memory. It made me think about before Junior got sick, when he disappeared from home—due to his tree-love— three nights straight. At the time I thought, Well, finally the man is showing some balls. Out having a little fun. Well, of course not. Eudora had blubbered at me endlessly to drag him out of a grove near the St. Johns River. He'd done this before. Not for three days or anything. But on occasion he'd go out to the woods behind our houses for extended periods of time, say four or five hours. But this was the most extreme incident. He was fifteen, maybe twenty, miles from home. Told me later he'd hitched a ride with a logging truck. So I went out there. Had to go in Eudora's rattle-trap jalopy due to Junior's hardheaded, mean-hearted refusal to ride in the Black Beauty. And sure enough, I found him. No stolen weekend playing cards or squeezing on some woman. Just stinking drunk and crying about how much he missed his dead daddy. Crying like a baby. Mosquito-bit. Redbug-bit. A mess. He kept pointing at the trees.

"See these oaks," he slobbered. His hair stood out straight because he endlessly pulled on it. "Their roots travel deep, and their branches reach far into the sky. They're much wiser than you or me, Charlie. They know more about the world than the two of us combined."

He always talked hocus-pocus bullshit like that when he wandered off.

"Well, no more hocus-pocus tree-love for you, Junior, old buddy." I looked over at him. The stars lit his face real soft. I started to get horrible sad. I found myself hoping that his tree-love had been a two-way street. "I think they loved you back, my man," I told him.

And you know, it was a possibility. I drank more juice and thought about the time tree rot had swept through the whole area. At least twenty oaks in town died, but not the one Junior planted in his backyard. I had watched him from my kitchen window. He piddled in his backyard for hours on end, caring for the sick tree like it was human. Every day he'd be out there cutting small strips of bark. He'd smell it. Then he'd poke at it with his fingers, just like Doc Weddle did to his wrist before declaring him dead. He'd put both hands on the trunk's fresh bare spot. I swear, I think he talked to it. But by God, the tree didn't die. 'Most all the others did.

Yes, I imagined old Junior, standing by his oak, sniffing it, poking it. Tree-love. "Junior, my man, you are something else. You know that?" I said.

I fished in my shirt pocket for my pack of Camels. I lit a match but the sea breeze blew it out. I tried it again, with no luck. And again. Finally, on my fourth try—with my head down by my dash to guard the flame from the wind—I lit up.

I settled back in my seat. I held the bottle up to the moonlight to make sure I still had a few good, strong slugs left. Then, out of nowhere—like a lightning strike on a clear day—a picture of my son Emory flashed in my head. Let's be honest here. That's not a picture I wanted to see. And then I thought of my brother's sugar farm. Emory'd been down there close to a year. The hard work was doing him good, I told myself. It was beating down that superior attitude he'd developed. I saw Emory raising his fist to me. I shook my head. I gazed down the coastline. Toss that image right out of your tackle box of bobbers, I told myself.

But then, like he was my frigging conscience, I heard Junior's voice. I mean, he wasn't really speaking—of course not. But in my head, he was nagging me. "Charlie, number one, he's your son. Number two, he's just a boy. Number three, you need to bring him home where he belongs. And number four, you shouldn't ever lift a hand against your wife, ever."

Jesus, that made me mad. I mean, when you get down to brass

tacks, what did Junior know? I work hard for a living. I don't just put clothes on my back. Rose's pretty white skin is covered because of my labor, not hers. Seems to me that gives me the right to do what I want without being nagged about it. And besides, how in the hell could Junior understand what a man like me goes through? Making a living and juggling my talent. Putting bread on the table and still playing music. The son of a bitch. I thought, He never was subjected to the bullshit I had to live through. By the time I was five years old my mother had me on a St. Augustine street corner crooning and dancing for tourists. The sound of change hitting the earth, thudding beneath my melody. Sometimes the sound creeps into my sleep. *Look at that cute little barefoot boy dance. Just listen, what a beautiful voice! Dear, throw him some change. Maybe he'll buy a pair of shoes with it.* And the laughter. The woman's beautiful fucking face and her laughter.

"See, Junior, I carry the burden of talent. I'm a talented man trapped in a world that doesn't understand me. Not my wife, not my son, not my dead baby, not you." *Listen to me; I'm your mother. We'll go inside together. I'll stay at the counter and talk to Mr. Buker. You walk down the first aisle. Stuff your pockets full. Make sure you get some canned meat. Stop when I say, "Come on, Charlie. Mr. Buker doesn't have what we need today."* Mama the thief. I did most of her stealing for her. I danced for her. Sang for her. Stole for her. Kept her in food and perfumes. Then she waltzed out of my life like a scented breeze. *Charlie, this is Clayton. He's Mama's new beau.*

"Junior, my man, you don't know shit. You never did. You never will." I kicked back and laughed. "But tonight, I'm going to teach you one thing. Have fun, you bastard."

I fired up the Black Beauty. "Hang on, asshole," I screamed. I gunned the engine. The wind whipped through my hair. The pork-pie flew off Junior's head. I executed three perfect doughnuts. The sand spewed up from the tires and flew in our faces. I raced the coastline. Faster than the birds. Angrier than the waves. Salt water splashed up under my car and onto its exquisite paint job. But I didn't care. "I'll wash you tomorrow, baby," I yelled.

It was a clear shot up the coast for two, three miles. Safe, isolated.

No motels until farther up. When I saw the first motel lights twinkle closely, I spun hard. A half-turn. Junior fell onto my shoulder. "Shit, man, sit up." I pushed him back into place.

We were having fun, I just knew it. The radio blared. I sung loud and clear. A song for each one of those assholes who'd ever laughed at me. And one for Rose and even the boy. If Junior had been alive, he would have sung too. I would have made him. He would have drunk from my bottle and laughed out loud. He would have begged me to push the Black Beauty even faster. I would have taught him at least that. And in my heart, I would have forgiven him for all his stupid ways.

I drove up and down the beach until my bottle was empty. I sucked the last drops and threw the bottle out of the car. I stopped the engine. I got out. I pulled off my shirt and jeans. I waded into the cold, black surf. The stars twinkled on the water in soft streaks. I splashed my hand around in it. A game. Catch the starlight. But the starlight moved, refusing to rest or stay steady long enough for me to hold it in my hand. I tried one, two, three times, but it always moved. Again and again. I pounded the water with my fists. The stars exploded. And then, Junior's voice—it cracked through my mind. Something he'd told me months before. We'd learned how sick he really was. I visited him and said straight to him, "Junior, buddy, I'm really sorry."

He had looked at me with those eyes that seemed to know everything in the world. "It doesn't matter," he said. "It just doesn't matter."

I slammed the water. I imagined I shattered the damn coward starlight. "Fuck you," I screamed. "Fuck the whole damn world." I dove beneath the surface. Black. Cold. Safe. I thought how nice it would be to hold my breath until the black, inky silence seeped from the water and into me. I tried to stay down. With all my power I thought, Stay down, stay down, stay down. No noise. No light. No sensation except being tossed by the current. I took water into my mouth and down my throat. I gagged. Then, like an idiot, I popped to the surface, sputtering and spitting. A human bobber. The bass had given up. No more tension on the line. No more nothing.

75

Wiped the salt water out of my eyes and looked around me. Shot a glance at the Black Beauty. Not a damn thing had changed.

Junior was still in the front seat. He was still unmoving and irritating. And I was standing in the ocean—colder than a New York pig—the stars still playing with me, riding the water's skin, bumping against my chest.

I headed for shore. I stood wringing wet and cold. I pulled my clothes on over my soaked body. I looked out at the horizon. I looked back at the car. The stars, the very same ones that had fucked with me in the water, now reflected off my hood. Their light bounced off and illuminated the pale, still face of none other than Burl Junior Jewel. I leaned close to my friend. I pulled open his lids. I stared into his deep, glassy peepers. "It did matter, you son of a bitch, and you know it."

I let his eyes shut and then got into my Black Beauty. "Come on," I said. "It's time to get you home."

Patrick Lackly

I had been dreaming a completely bizarre dream. I was over there, in Europe somewhere, in a museum. It wasn't a particular museum—more like a conglomeration of all the great ones. My dear mother was there. Mother, who is a bustling sixty-four years old, lives with me. And I love her dearly, but she knows absolutely nothing about art. Yet in this dream she was a connoisseur. Dressed in sky-blue pedal pushers, a tattered man's dress shirt, a straw hat, and pink flip-flops, she was expounding upon the masterpieces, revealing their secret implications via Freudian psychology. A crowd flocked around her, and as she spoke each great work came alive—literally. Monet's water lilies would suddenly shoot across the pond as white-necked swans glided and preened among them. A da Vinci Madonna removed an apple from her ample drapery and began to enjoy lunch. The baby Jesus stood on his tiptoes swatting at the apple, but he couldn't reach it, so he threw an absolute fit. His mother just laughed. Michelangelo's David began some sort of interpretative dance—a little number that combined ballet with African influences. This dream was a delight— the kind you hope you never wake up from. But just as Mother was about to explain the Oedipal forces shaping David's dance, an awful clatter started. It grew louder and Mother grew fuzzy. I fought it, but it was no good. The ringing telephone had intruded upon my dream and my mother's finest hour.

It must have been four-thirty or five o'clock. I considered just letting it ring, but I was already roused. I groaned and groped for the receiver. I pulled it over to my chest. Who would be calling us at this time of the morning?

Finally I managed, "This is Lackly."

"Mr. Lackly, I'm so sorry to trouble you this early. I know I woke you up, but we've got an emergency down here."

Miss Inez Temple. My cleaning woman. Predawn, on Mondays and Wednesdays, she cleaned the funeral parlor. Friday afternoons she cleaned my home. She was a woman for whom I felt deep respect, for I had seen the way the white countergirl at Woolworth's attempted to degrade her. And I had seen the snickers and stares of the bigots in town as she glided past them in all her startling colors. But no matter what a person did to Miss Temple, her dignity remained unsullied. Unfortunately for me, as this morning would progress, that would be a detail I would forget.

I was having an awful struggle waking up. I think I growled, "Emergency?"

"I don't know how to tell you this, Mr. Lackly, except to tell you straight out. Burl Jewel is not about to be found in this funeral parlor. I know it sounds amazing, and I haven't one thought under the heavens as to what in the world is going on. But this is the Lord's truth. His casket is here, but there is no doubt about it: Burl himself is gone."

"You mean we've had a robbery? Is the hi-fi still there? What about the Del Vecchio print in my office?" I heard my own voice, but it was as if it was not connected to me. It was as if a portion of my brain was still at the museum watching my mother talk about the ego and the id and phallus worship. In my sleep-fringed state, I could not make complete sense out of what Inez Temple was saying.

"Not a robbery, Mr. Lackly. A body-snatching. A good old-fashioned body-snatching."

This phone call was becoming more bizarre than my dream. "Is there any evidence of breaking and entering? Did you notice anything out of the ordinary?" I asked.

"Yes."

"What? Like what?" I grumbled.

"Cracker crumbs. Sprinkled like dust on Burl's casket. Goodness, this is awful, Mr. Lackly."

Awful. A woman given to understatement. As my mind grew more alert, the horrible magnitude of Miss Temple's revelation began to be apparent.

"Are you sure nothing is stolen?" I asked.

"What are you saying to me, Mr. Lackly? Of course something is stolen. Burl Jewel is stolen."

She could be exasperating. I was now fully cognizant of the fact that Burl Jewel was missing. I was attempting to pin down the motive. Surely something else must be gone. Valuables. The hi-fi. Paintings off my walls. Lab equipment. My mind was sluggishly wading through the possibilities.

"Mr. Lackly," she interrupted, "I don't believe anything to be missing but the body. Now you can call that unimportant if you're half asleep. But maybe you ought to wake that body of yours fully and get on down here. This is trouble."

Of course she was right. But it's not every day that someone steals a body from my parlor. It wasn't just that I was half asleep. Whether I was waking or dreaming, this scenario made no sense to me. Why would anybody steal a body? My mind lurched and chugged. Miss Temple had to be wrong. They stole something of importance and took the body to hide the fact. No, that couldn't be right. Why would they risk getting caught by being burdened with a corpse? And Miss Temple was extremely efficient. She was probably exactly right regarding no valuables' being stolen. Perhaps it was a hoax. Some children playing a prank. But my God—children moving a dead body! Very unlikely. And then I remembered something from *Perry Mason*. Mother and I loved that show. He always asked his clients, "What enemies do you have?" So I asked myself the same question. I tried to think of one person who despised me so much that he or she would commit the sacrilege and crime of body-stealing. No one. Not a single, solitary individual. I was an honest businessman. I provided a good service at a fair price. Nobody *hated* me. But then I thought, Oh—maybe they do. Lackly's Funeral Parlor was the only parlor in town. Most towns have two, one for Negroes and one for whites. Imagine—segregated dying! But Tiama was too small to support two mortuaries. Some Negroes elected to use Mr. Washington's services in St. Augustine. But most figured that was too much trouble. They came to me. It's a service I've offered quietly, because to get on the wrong side of the Klan can be a business's downfall. But you've got to do something really blatant—like the café downtown that let Negro patrons sit at tables right up front by the windows. They shut it down within a week. But what I do nobody sees. Why should they care? I knew, however, things in Tiama had been different lately. The rumor mill had it that Klan activity was stepping up. I can't remember a time when people were this tense. Wasn't it just two days before that Wally Jenkins, my barber, had said to me very quietly, right as he was trimming my sideburns, "I hear the sheriff has told them they can do all the beating and harassing they want—just so they don't kill nobody."

That had to be it. It was the only explanation that made sense. It was the Klan's way of saying to me, "Stop burying them, or we'll bury you." How tidy. Steal a body the morning of the burial. The hysterical wife—first she swoons. Then she calls the sheriff, calls the newspaper editor, possibly goes before the City Council to demand an investigation into yours truly, and before you know it I'm not burying anybody—Negro or white. And my mother is on my case like a bat out of hell.

That thought certainly snapped me awake. "Miss Temple," I ordered, "you are not to do anything. Do not answer the phone. Do not open the door to anyone. Do not leave. I will be there in short order."

79

I groped around my room in the predawn darkness. I threw on my robe over my pajamas. No time to bother dressing. I didn't see my tennis shoes anywhere, so I just slid on my old green flip-flops. As quietly as possible, so I wouldn't wake Mother—she certainly didn't need to know about any of this—I shut the front door and didn't turn my headlights on until I was out of the driveway.

As I drove to the parlor, I made decisions. I wouldn't call the sheriff. I would just take the warning in stride and never service another Negro client.

I pulled into the parlor's back lot so I could not be seen from the street. I unlocked the back door and then locked it securely behind me. I knew exactly what I had to do. As abhorrent as it was, I had no choice. I'd have to lie to Burl Jewel's family. I would behave as though his body remained in my parlor. As though the coffin that we would lay into the ground later that very morning contained his body. But first, I would have to either cajole or scare my friend Miss Temple into silence.

It was the only way.

"Miss Temple, where are you?" I called. I walked into the hallway. "Miss Temple?"

"I'm in here with Mrs. Batemeyer," she called.

I burst through the double doors, and there she was. Dazzling as always. I secretly envied the way she dressed. Colors from head to toe. Of course, most people could not get by, dressing that way. But on Inez it looked stunning. A large woman, by most any standards, and more—she was tall, regal. If I, by some freak occurrence, were transformed into a colored woman tomorrow, I would want to look just like Inez Temple. Coils of purple and yellow fabric on her head. Always her head was covered. I don't know of a soul who'd ever seen her hair. And swaths of beautiful yellow cotton on her body. She was a queen. Somewhere in her lineage—maybe a great-great-grandmother, or a distant cousin—royalty existed. It was one of those instinctual things I just know. And sometimes, after my third or fourth brandy of the evening, I'd even entertained the thought of asking Miss Temple to dinner. But of course, I was always aware that the idea was only a fantasy.

I stood there looking at her and tried not to be too kind. "Miss Temple, what on earth is going on here?"

She waved an arm at Burl Jewel's empty casket. "See for yourself. A casket as empty as the day is long."

"What time did you get here?" I brushed past her and stood between Mrs. Batemeyer and the empty casket.

"My usual time, Mr. Lackly. Five in the morning."

"And you're saying that Burl Junior Jewel's body was gone when you got here?"

"Of course that's what I'm saying. There was no body-snatching taking place while I was here. You know better than that."

I turned away from her. I had to think. But she said, "Mr. Lackly, what is going on here? I've told you what I know. When I got here the body was gone. Every stitch of him. Now why this attitude toward me? We ought to be calling the sheriff and letting Mrs. Jewel know her husband is missing."

"The sheriff!" I shouted. And then I told her my suspicions. I laid it on the line. Clearly. Logically. I knew she'd go along with me. It was the only thing we could do.

But no. Not Inez. Instead she simply blazed with indignation. She shook her head incredulously. She started spouting phrases like, "Evil begets evil" and "We must put these criminals behind bars" and "Stopping the Klan begins with you, Mr. Lackly." She sounded like a politician running for office. The entire time, she looked me straight in the eyes, and I wanted to glance away, but she held me. She possessed a natural power that was overwhelming. She planted her hands on her hips and closed her eyes once—very slowly, dramatically. It was a gesture so certain and so righteous. If my own well-being had not been in such clear peril, I would have been swept away. But I had to remain steadfast. I had to hold out against Inez Temple. She was attempting to force my hand with her stubbornness. I was simply going to have to do something bizarre—something fundamentally awful—to force her into cooperating with me. But before I could, she said, "And besides, Mr. Lackly, your plan just won't work. You can't have a funeral with no body. There's no way to hide that fact."

"Well, Miss Temple," I said, "you're wrong about that. Closed-casket ceremonies are not uncommon, and"—I looked at Mrs. Batemeyer—"we do have a body. Someone who is a widow and childless, no living relatives to speak of. At eight I will place a call to Mrs. Jewel. I shall tell her that as owner and director of Lackly's Funeral Parlor, I must insist that her dear husband have a closed-casket ceremony. I will appeal to her sympathies: 'Burl would have wanted it that way. He would have wanted people to remember him not as the emaciated shadow in the casket but as a happy, vital member of our community.' "

Inez was sharp. She perceived the rest of my plan before I could utter it. "You mean to tell me you are going to put Mrs. Batemeyer in Burl's casket? You plan to bury her in Burl's grave! And what do you plan to do at her funeral? Bury an empty casket, I suppose."

I know this was difficult for Inez, and while I was glad she was catching on so quickly, she was also beginning to get on my nerves. Why couldn't she simply cooperate with me? It was in her interest as well as mine. I tried to maintain my patience. I explained that by our actions we were hurting no one. I explained that if one of Mrs. Batemeyer's old cronies questioned the closed casket, I would politely reply that I was fulfilling the dead woman's wishes.

"No one gets hurt," I said. "Mr. Jewel's family is spared the trauma of his post-death disappearance. Mrs. Batemeyer spends eternity in a lovely burial plot, even if it's not the one she chose when she was alive. And I get to keep my job, and consequently so do you." I stroked Mrs. Batemeyer's hair and looked at the dead woman appreciatively. Inez simply had to understand that my dishonesty in this instance was hardly more than a white lie.

But of course, why did I ever think I could persuade a woman who was as strong-willed as Inez Temple? She bantered at me, "Don't you think you better consider the consequences of your actions, Mr. Lackly? I'm saying *consequences*!"

Inez stepped up to the foot of Mrs. Batemeyer's coffin. Her eyes— so wide and lovely—flashed with that wonderful, but ill-timed, righteous anger.

I adopted an icy tone. "My good sense, Miss Temple, could save us both. I like you. In fact, I consider you a friend. So none of this

82

is easy for me. But Miss Temple, the survival of my business depends on this. I must insist you go along with me." I was imploring. Begging.

She looked at me with such contempt that I truly felt ashamed. But as I've said, I believed I had no other option. "Never," she said. "As long as the sun rises and sets on this earth, I will never go along with such foolish acting."

I turned away from her. Away from her gaze that seemed to strip me to the bone. What was I going to do? How could I shake her? I heard her moving around behind me. What in the world was the woman doing? Looking for clues? Leaving to go call the sheriff? I knew I had to act quickly. I gathered my resolve. I became steel. I turned and faced her gaze. I had no choice.

"Threats," I said, "as unkind as they may be, at times are useful. So listen closely to this one: If you breathe a word to anybody— the sheriff, Mrs. Jewel, a roach as it crawls across your windowsill— I will ruin you. I will not want to. And I will agonize over it forever, but I will have no choice. I will say your words are the vomit of a nigger woman's crazy mind."

I looked down at Margaret Batemeyer. I was an actor whose performance could mean life or death. But the lines were not written. I had to ad-lib. And I had to be good. "I'll say you stole the body, Miss Temple. I'll say you are some sort of witch." My mind whirled in an effort to choose the right words, invent the awful scheme. "I'll say you are some sort of Voodoo queen. That you do things with these dead bodies."

It was then that I had a stroke of genius. I needed a visual aid. I took Margaret Batemeyer's still, overpowdered face in my hands and began to manipulate it. I arched the eyebrows. I opened the lids. I pushed the sagging flesh into two bulbous cheeks. I opened her mouth and then stretched her painted lips into a garish, silent scream.

"Miss Temple, I'll have to fire you. I'll bring the sheriff in here, and some TV cameras, and show them what you have been doing to these poor departed souls. And I'll say you stole Burl Jewel's body for an evil Voodoo rite. And I'll say, 'Look at what she did to poor Mrs. Batemeyer here.' I'll say you were probably going to steal her body too, had I not come in here and caught you in the act of some bizarre ritual."

Inez raised her arm into the air, her palm open, as though she were taking an oath. "God forgive you, Patrick Lackly, God forgive you."

What was wrong with her? Why wouldn't she simply cooperate with me? I ignored her invocation of a spiritual power and correctly pointed out that if she didn't cooperate—and if I accused her of the crime—she'd be thrown into jail and I'd retain my business, because the Klan would figure that I'd done them a favor. "They will have a nigger-woman Voodoo queen on their hands who snatches bodies. You'll never work in this town again," I said. I was so angry, so desperate. It was as if a new person emerged, a stranger—I had never before in my life behaved so horribly. "In fact, I'll make it so bad the only way you'll be able to stay in Tiama is if your new address is the state pen."

I searched Inez's face, but I saw no signs of cooperation. She was hard. And unreasonable. Maybe she simply knew that I could never follow through on my threats. I was a disaster. I looked at what I'd done to Mrs. Batemeyer. It was shameful. My impulse was to push her face back into its peaceful repose. I wanted to shut her eyes. I wanted to let her rest, even though I knew that notion was ridiculous. But truly, what I'd done to her made her look undead, tortured. Her blank, marblelike eyes stared up at me. She was screaming damnations at me. She was no longer Mrs. Batemeyer, the town's most beloved librarian. She was a ghoul. I felt myself begin to crack, to become completely frightened. I looked away from her. I prayed, Surely my actions have been so outlandish and horrifying Inez will now do as I ask.

But the woman remained steadfast. Never have I met someone who could stand so thoroughly on principle. "First off, Mr. Lackly," she said—and she actually shook her finger in my face— "don't you set your dirty, filthy hands on that poor dead woman unless you mean to put her right again. Second off, I'm going to get to the bottom of this. Your threats do not mean squat to me, and the Klan does not frighten me. Furthermore, you're acting like a foolish, selfish brat. And I won't be a party to it. Third off, I quit. I will not work for a coward."

She spun around and, with a grandness I have witnessed but a few times in my life, she walked out the door.

And so there I was, alone, as foolish and scared as I have ever been. I looked at Mrs. Batemeyer. It was chilling. Her wide-open mouth seemed to mock me, curse me. I looked at my hands that had turned her sweet old face into a hellish mask.

That was, I believe, my life's lowest moment. I am accustomed to handling the dead. Understand this: I am a scientist. I embalm bodies so that they will last forever. It is a noble profession. I placed both my hands on Mrs. Batemeyer's face. I know it was because I was so shaken from those early-morning events, but my hands simply didn't seem to work properly. Her flesh was ungiving, stiff, reluctant to go back into its proper place. It was as if the corpse truly had turned against me. I felt that I actually had transformed Mrs. Batemeyer into a monster from hell. I pushed and molded and pushed and molded until finally her face regained a bit of its former dignity. I looked at the palms of my hands. They were stained with the dead woman's makeup. At my core, I knew I had committed a supreme profanity. I fled the room.

I ran into my office with its beautiful green brocade wallpaper. Mother had picked it out. Occasionally she has good taste. I entered my private bathroom. I threw open the medicine cabinet. Band-Aids. Haley's M-O. Hairspray. Rubbing alcohol. It was a silly gesture—Mrs. Batemeyer had no germs—but it seemed precisely appropriate at the moment. I uncapped the alcohol. With it I cleansed my profane hands. But as I watched the cold, clear anti-septic fill each of my cupped palms, a chill settled over me. My plan had not worked. Inez Temple would not keep her mouth shut. For that, however, I could not blame her. It was because of my cowardice and the Klan's horrific hatred that I had lost my maid, lost my friend, and possibly would lose my business.

I returned the alcohol to its shelf. I walked over to my desk and flicked my Rolodex open to Eudora Jewel's card. I would phone her from home. I would continue behaving as if Inez would come to her senses and stand by me. I had been good to her. A good employer. An ear easily bent. I took note of Mrs. Jewel's number. As I exited the parlor and locked the back door behind me, I practiced what I would say. "Mrs. Jewel, believe me, this is the way Burl would have wanted it. As dignified in death as he was in life—a closed casket would accomplish that, Mrs. Jewel."

Inez Temple

Been weeping ever since it happened. Since the dawn that saw Burl Junior Jewel's body disappeared. But not weeping how you think. Not weeping because of the disappearance. That was all a fluke. A charade tragic and comic.

The Lord moves in strange ways, my Bible tells me. So I accept the twists and turns of my life, accept them without complaint.

I clean houses. You can tell a lot about people by the filth they build up 'round them. You gain secrets about them. You understand their souls by studying the rubble strewn or ordered on nightstands, kitchen tables, waxed or unwaxed floors. But like a good preacher, a decent doctor, the secrets stay with me. Not to be blabbered 'round town. Not to be held like a hammer against their heads.

But sometimes a recitation, a testament, is in order.

It was a beautiful spring morning that followed Burl Junior Jewel's disappearance. As I stepped out of the funeral parlor—madder than ten gamecocks in a pool of mud, all because Pat Lackly was trying to play me for the fool and he should have known better— I paused. I looked at the lilies I'd planted all along the length of the building. The sun, just beginning in the day, filtered through high morning clouds. People who are late sleepers miss this light. It can turn the ugliest man into, for a few moments, someone grand. That's what it did for my lilies. Yes, they are always pretty. But the gentle light turned them prettier than you can imagine.

"Good morning, little missies," I said. Beauty has a good talent at taking off anger, you see. I got in my car and, instead of driving over to Eudora Jewel's or the sheriff's and babbling about a missing body, I thought, Go home, Inez Temple. Think about this. Not seeing it all. Go think on it. Go figure the missing pieces.

I drove through my neighborhood. One thing about Negro neighborhoods. People always out. Friendly. People sit on their porches. Stand outside visiting. Nod at you as you drive by. Some white areas, goodness, they're like graveyards. The mayor's neighborhood, for example. I clean his house. But it's a moneyed neighborhood full of Cadillacs and columned houses and sodded yards. But it seems the more money, the bigger the houses, the dimmer the life. None of them sit on their porches jawing with the breeze. Sometimes when I drive through the rich neighborhood, I get tickled. I think of them behind their big oak doors, just counting their money. Over and over. Nonstop. It's hard to imagine them possessing any real joy.

I believe there is a seed of God in all of us and in everything we do. That's why I keep my house in order. Freshly painted. Every spring it gets a coat of white paint. And every spring I change the color of my wooden shutters. As I drove up and my shutters winked light blue beneath the strengthening sunlight, I knew, come next April, I'd do them lavender.

I got inside and said, "Hello, Mr. Pecker." Mr. Pecker is my parakeet. I named him such a thing out of pure innocence. See, he likes to peck at his image in the mirror. Peck and peck and peck. All day long. That's what that little bird does. His name does not mean a single other thing, although I've friends who giggle and attest otherwise. Mr. Pecker squawked a greeting. Good company, that little bird. I walked over to his cage and stuck my finger between the bars. "Hi, pretty baby. You're Mama's pretty baby."

He hopped over and beaked my fingertip. Didn't hurt. Just a little pinch. His eggplant-colored eye studied my face, I was sure.

"Yes, and you love me too," I crooned. I wiggled my finger around so that I could rub right behind his little yellow head. That bird ate it up. Baptists say animals don't have souls. I know better.

That's why I became a Catholic. St. Francis, now that man, God bless him, understood that animals possess souls.

"Well, Mr. Pecker," I said—I took my finger out of the cage— "I suppose Burl Junior Jewel's soul is where it should be, even though his body is not."

Mr. Pecker's wings flapped bright and sudden. He flew up to his high-most perch and shrilled in quick clips, admiring himself in the mirror I bought for him the very day I brought him home from Woolworth's.

I kicked off my shoes and left Mr. Pecker to his own devices. I went to the kitchen to brew myself some tea. I heard Tigerlily meowing at the back door. She was a stray mama cat I took care of.

"Okay, okay," I said. I poured some milk in her bowl and let her in. She swirled once around my ankles and then settled at the milk. I loved her orange fur. I'd seen that exact same shade in the sky when the clouds were just right so that they reflected not just invisible light but strong fire colors.

I fixed myself the tea, and this time made it with condensed milk, an energy-giver for sure. I walked back to the living room and turned on the fan. I sat in my favorite chair, a rattan with red pillows. It was situated by my big living room window on the east side. From there I could look out on my elephant ears and crocuses in the side yard. It felt good to be off my feet. I watched the steam rise from the tea, and then the fan rotated just right so that it blew the sun-filtered swirls away. I gazed out the window. A mockingbird squawked, acting like a blue jay up in the wax cedar. I knew that meant a cat, probably that sneaky tom I named Bluenose, was prowling round.

I sipped my tea. I began to try sorting out the morning's awful events. A stolen body. A funeral man who was kind and gentle acting suddenly insane. None of it made sense. I mulled and fretted. I thought about how my grandmama had insisted life wouldn't give me such trouble as I had experienced that morning.

My grandmama, she was a wise woman. She read the caul on my face the morning I was born. Said the fact that I had a caul at all marked me special. Said I was born wet and bloody and squealing, and that she held me in her two huge hands and laid me "like a whisper" on my mama's belly.

As she told it, I was born just as dawn was breaking, so she neared the candle close to me. She gasped, "Why, Rebecca"—that was Mama's name—"this child has a map to her soul on her pretty little face."

I know this story as sure as I know there's stars overhead. Being poor moneywise, we had but only one bed. I'd be tucked between the two of them—Mama and Grandmama—pushing my skinny legs against theirs and playing with their hair. Then I'd plead, "Come on, Grandmama, please. Tell my caul story again. Tell me what its map said."

Often I call upon the memory of my mama and grandmama, for they are strength-givers in death and life. So I sat pondering Burl Junior Jewel and invoked my grandmama's words. "You will know things fast," I said out loud, but in my heart it was Grandmama's voice that spoke. "Truth will come easily because, child, shiny buttons will never blind you. Wolf cries, crocodile laughs, snake words shining like pearls will never blind you. But my grandbaby, even though you may never be blind, you may not always know what you see."

I let the words linger in the air. I willed that they behave like a salve and heal my confusion.

As I stared out my window, I watched a lizard sun himself on the elephant ear. I thought, A riddle to start off my life with. A riddle I come face to face with in the form of an empty casket and a frightened man playing with a dead woman.

Maybe Patrick Lackly was right. Suppose this was a setup by the Klan. Seemed like if that was the case, they had us both trapped. I've tried long and hard to believe that the evil never wins out. That the evil will eventually eat itself up and leave us good people alone. But goodness gracious. This time there were too many hidden cards—the people who stole Burl Junior Jewel, Patrick Lackly's capacity to turn into rotten meat, the likelihood of the sheriff believing a white business owner over a Negro cleaning woman, the law's obvious tendency to turn a blind eye to the Klan. And then there was the matter of my courage. Where was it? I tapped my fingers on my armrest. Deceit marring such a nice day.

It was then, my mind rolling over possibilities, that I heard a car door slam. Sounded like it was in front of my house. I looked out my front window. Walking on my yellow step-stones, making sure she didn't stomp on my grass, came Rose Looney. Now, I like Rose Looney. She's regular folk, you know. But what in the world was she doing walking up to my house? No, I didn't wait for her to reach my porch. I threw open my jalousie door.

"My, my, missy. What a surprise!" I said. "You all right? That husband of yours didn't do something stupid again, did he?" I asked, and held the door open wide. Rose was a smart woman. From the first time I saw her, years back at the Coquina Motel, it amazed me that she married the man she did. I'd seen the situation a thousand times, didn't matter if the couple was black, white, or polka-dotted. The woman would be head and shoulders above the man, but him and his groin—they would control her like a bad spell. That's one reason I didn't give squat for men in a personal way.

"Inez, he has done something, but this time he wasn't alone," she said. She patted my arm and then said, "Sorry to come by so unannounced."

Now do I say something or do I stay silent? Best keep my prolific mouth shut for a while, I decided.

"Come on in. Sit down and I'll pour us some tea," I told her.

She looked well. Tired, but that was Rose's way. She sat on my couch and took in the room. I shot to the kitchen.

"You have a real nice house," she called out.

I poured two cups of tea in china given me by one of my cleaning clients. Since Rose was company, I decided against using my big, sturdy, everyday mugs. The china was ivory-colored, with pretty blue birds painted on it. A bonus for loyalty, the old white woman had said.

"You never been here before, have you?" I said as I came back to the living room. I handed her the tea. "It's not much, I mean the house. But you know, Rose, it's mine. One of the few things somebody would have to work like the dickens to get away from me."

She eyed my china cabinet and its pretty glass. "Inez Temple, how did you get all that beautiful stuff?" she asked.

"Worked for it. I didn't buy it from a store, don't get me wrong. A client gave it to me, but it was an earned gift. Long ago my mama told me, 'Don't you take any handouts, girl. Never. People will use it against you. Take what's yours, what you've earned, and leave the rest alone.' "

"Sounds like good advice to me," Rose said.

Tigerlily jumped on the couch. She sized up Rose, who danced her hand across the cushion, bait for Tigerlily. "You sure are a better housekeeper than I am. This place is neat as a pin." Tigerlily pounced, and Rose jerked her hand to her chest.

"Doesn't this cat try to eat your bird?" she asked.

"Not as long as I feed her," I said, and Rose started laughing. "What is it the Bible says about the lamb laying down with the lion? You know that lion must have had a full belly."

Rose grinned but didn't speak. She rubbed Tigerlily's neck. Sounds became noticeable, loud. The tin whir of the fan. The snap and flap of the breeze-blown curtain. The comforting chug of Tigerlily's motor.

"Well, Rose, I suspect this is not just a social visit," I ventured.

"No, Inez. You're right about that." She kept her eyes glued to the cat. "Eudora and Charlie, they didn't think I should come over here. But I had to. I just couldn't stand you believing Junior's body was stolen."

I let out a deep sigh. Another hard twist to cloud or clear up the day. "Tell it to me, Rose."

"It's just that sometime early this morning, probably about the time Charlie drove in the driveway with Junior, I remembered you clean at the funeral parlor. Then I got all shook up."

"Wait a minute. You mean to tell me your husband stole Burl Junior Jewel's body?"

"Of course. He had to."

"What do you mean, 'had to'?"

"Eudora and I made him, so that Junior could be buried under his oak tree. You know, it's illegal to bury somebody anyplace but a graveyard."

"Oh my God. You stole him. Who all knows about this?"

"Just the three of us and you. But like I said, we hadn't counted on you knowing. We figured it would be Pat Lackly who discovered the body was gone, and we knew pretty well what he would do. Either he'd never tell us it was gone, so he could save face, or he'd tell us and we'd ask him not to pursue it, out of respect for the grieving widow. But then I realized it was your morning at the funeral parlor. We had no idea what you would do."

"Well, where in the world is Burl now?"

"In Charlie's old Coast Guard trunk, buried where he wanted to be buried."

"You put his body in a trunk!"

"Inez, we didn't have time to build a coffin, and there was no way we could steal Junior *and* that monstrosity Eudora got carried away with and bought."

My, my. I decided these people were crazy, even though I had to admire their convictions. "So what are you going to do about the services at the funeral parlor today?"

"Oh, we're going."

"You're going. Well, I hope you all are good actors, because you're going to need to be. You've got Mr. Lackly in the biggest nit I've ever seen him in. Threatening me, and—oh my God, Mrs. Batemeyer. Rose, he plans to bury Mrs. Batemeyer in Burl Junior's plot."

Confusion knotted Rose's face, and then she began to giggle. "Are you kidding me? We thought he would just bury the empty coffin. We have created a drama. How funny!"

"Funny!" Lord have mercy. "There is nothing funny about it. Bodies need to be properly recognized. I can understand what you did for Eudora's husband, but at the same time you've wronged Mrs. Batemeyer."

"Inez, I wish that wasn't going to happen to Mrs. Batemeyer, but look at it this way: She's doing Junior a favor. And let's be realistic. They are both dead. They don't know where they're buried. We really did all this for Eudora. She's the one who'd go through the rest of her life hysterical because Junior wasn't under his damn tree."

People do not understand that the spirit lives on. That you can wrong a dead person, just like you can wrong the living. But I knew lecturing Rose on this point would be a waste of my breath. A person has to come to this on her own. I sat back in my chair. I shut my eyes, trying to glimpse at some peace. "So what is it you would have me do?"

"Inez, you know I like you, respect you. I'm sorry you got caught in all this. But can you just keep it quiet, not tell a soul?"

I nodded my head yes, but I kept my eyes closed.

"And one other thing."

"What is it, Rose?" I opened my eyes.

"Eudora wanted me to ask if you could come over and watch Luella while we go to the fake funeral."

Oh my goodness. "What time?"

"Can you come over in about an hour?"

"Is that little girl ever going to know where her daddy is really buried?" I asked.

"Inez, I guess not. I mean, we broke the law. Eudora made a choice, and it included lying to the child. No way out."

"Okay, Rose. I'm doing this because I like you. It wouldn't really do anybody any good if I spilled the beans. But goodness, don't you realize this lie is going to ripple for generations? Didn't you all think about that?"

The sunlight filtered through my windows and hit Rose full and sharp in the face. She was a beautiful woman, but lots of pain was gnarled in that face. It occurred to me that she could probably use a good cry.

"Inez, what were we supposed to do?" she whispered. "We thought we were doing good."

I leaned forward and patted her hand. "Thank you for telling me, Rose. At least Burl Junior is where he wanted to be."

Rose eased Tigerlily off her lap and stood up. She looked out the window. "So you'll come over?"

I got out of my chair. I put my arm around her shoulder. "You tell Eudora not to worry about a thing. I'll stay quiet. And tell that little Luella her godmama's coming to see her."

Maybe most people would have left it at that. They would have been satisfied knowing where Burl Junior was. They'd sleep tight because there wasn't a raving band of white-hooded body-snatchers roaming the night. But not me. No. After Rose Looney's visit, my confusion was swept clear, and in its place brewed an uneasiness. The type of uneasiness that seeps into your bones and refuses to be flushed unless you do something grand. A grand action. Yes. That's what was in order.

So after Rose left, I whirled through my house. Straighten the doilies. Dust the crucifix. Fluff the pillows. Feed the bird. But in my head, of course, I was planning, planning, planning. It became clear to me that, of all the clowns in this body-snatching parade, the one who would be most truly hurt by it was the most innocent one: little Luella.

And then of course there was Patrick Lackly. What a child that man was. I thought, Inez, now call that boy and set him straight. I guess I should have been angry at him. But everything he'd done was acted out of fear. He didn't mean any of it.

I dialed his number. When he answered, I said, "Mr. Lackly, you need to sit yourself down in your chair and relax. Because, see now, nobody stole Burl Jewel's body because they were out to harm you. Most likely you're the last person the Klan cares about. That body was taken to help Burl. That's all I can say about it. Don't ask me any questions. You just know it's all okay. Don't call the police. Don't say a word to anybody. It will just get some good-meaning folks in trouble. You hear me now?"

He sputtered on the other end. Then he got out this weak, "Why, of course, Miss Temple. Whatever you say."

And then I said to him, "And two other things, Mr. Lackly. One, please don't ever act so foolish around me again. And two, I take back my resignation."

"You don't know what this means to me, Miss Temple," he said,

94

and I thought I detected a quivering voice. "Thank you. Thank you."

I considered pushing for an apology, but then said, Oh, why? It would not have changed anything.

I hung up the phone. And as I got ready to go see Luella, I pondered the possibility that Mama and Grandmama were two beautiful, transparent souls looking after me. In fact, I pondered it so hard that I heard Grandmama's voice clearly waft through my mind. "Child," she whispered, "shiny buttons will never blind you."

When I drove over to Eudora's, I was not alone. I had my Bible and my rosary and my plan and my faith. Armed with these and my good intentions, I entered her house.

Rose was friendly but vague, as if she was badly fatigued. Charlie, in his white short sleeves, nodded at me but did not speak. Which was fine with me, because in my book that gentleman had a bunch of growing up to do. Eudora was in her mourning clothes. By nature she was a fragile woman, but now with all the stress she was really shaky, yes ma'am. Plus the doctor had prescribed some silly pills for her, so she was glazed. Eudora I can take or leave, but I saw her in that condition and my heart went out to her. I did not hesitate. I put my arms around her. I said, "You know, the good Lord loves you and Burl and your little girl. Everything's going to be all right." But I'm not sure she even heard me.

And nothing, not a word, was said about the body-snatching.

The three of them, they seemed to huddle in a clot as they moved out the door. Silent and tired and not understanding their actions, but bound together in grief, they climbed into Charlie's black car.

As soon as they were gone, I eyed the diamond of my plan. I hugged her to my chest and then put her in her playpen.

I hurried out to my car to retrieve my Bible. I walked back into the house and said, "Little girl, we're going to say good-bye to your daddy right."

I lifted her up out of the playpen and searched in my pocket for a lemon drop. Whenever I babysitted her, we played this game. A kiss for a candy.

We walked through the kitchen to get to the back door, and Lord, it looked like every soul in Tiama had brought over food. I always thought that was one of the strangest of customs. Bringing over food to a woman who's far too upset to eat. But it was all there: sweetbreads, fried chicken, deviled eggs, cole slaw, meatloaf. I decided that when Luella and I got done, I'd come in and put some of it away in the refrigerator.

We stepped out back, and what I saw amazed me. Charlie had gone nuts digging. He'd make no kind of graveyard man. He must have dug a fourteen-by-fourteen-foot plot. If anybody in town became suspicious, this sight would be the capper. As obvious as a brewing storm.

"Come on over to the tree, Luella. We've got some talking to do." Now this was a sweet child. I have no idea how much of what I said she understood, but I believe it got in her brain, to be remembered and contemplated one day.

She toddled over to the tree. She pushed her palms into the freshly turned earth. "Weeee," she squealed, sifting the dirt through her chubby little hands.

I knew getting her undivided attention would be impossible. I decided to move on. I opened the Bible and withdrew the rosary I had placed in its pages. I made the sign of the cross and then said, "Luella, the soil that you're playing with is the soil that carries the soul of your daddy." A good start. I liked it.

"You may not remember these words, and I won't be able to remind you of them, but I pray the good Lord will see it proper to instill in you a love for this place. Maybe in his wisdom he'll coax you to love this tree the way your daddy did. And maybe, if that happens, you'll come to realize who your daddy was, and how deeply he loved you."

Then I thought I ought to witness as to her road ahead, so I said, "Luella, dear, you are going to have some lonely times. You're going to wish you knew your daddy. You're going to wish you knew what it felt like to sit in his lap. Each time you do a good feat, you'll wonder if he would have been proud of you. You'll wonder what his voice sounded like—if it was kind, gentle, gruff, or tired. You're going to wish you had a daddy to help you through those dark, confusing times of youth. And Luella, you'll be mad at him. You'll be angry because he left you, and you'll wonder about his true nature. But baby girl, listen to Inez: As you grow to love this tree, so will you grow to know and love your daddy."

I looked up at the pieces of sky that lingered in Burl Junior Jewel's beloved oak branches. I said, "Bless this man, Jesus, because he was righteous and just, and he loved his family."

A piece of scripture floated through my mind. Out of Matthew, I believe. When I was little my mama made me memorize a Bible verse every night. And this one came to mind, and I thought it fitting because it was sweet and gentle. I hugged the Bible to my chest and knelt down in the earth. I looked straight at Luella. Dirt caked her from head to toe. Her wide brown eyes shadowed serious as I reached out and grabbed her hand. I recited, " 'For where your treasure is, there will your heart be also. The light of the body is the eye: if therefore mine eye be single, thy whole body shall be full of light.' Yes, sweet Jesus. In the name of the Father, the Son, and the Holy Spirit. Amen and amen."

I kissed Luella's little forehead. I thought we'd done pretty good. "Now it's time to get some flowers on this grave," I told her.

I considered making her move out of the dirt, but she was already filthy and she wasn't hurting anything. If I'd thought ahead, I would have brought some plants from my own garden to plant for Burl Junior. But I was just going to have to move some from the flower bed by the house. If Eudora squawked, I'd replace them. But for everyone's sake, she couldn't go on with a big bare spot that screamed crime.

So Luella and I, we worked hard. I pulled out the gardening tools that were stacked underneath the back porch. I'd dig up a marigold or pansy, being ever so tender with the roots, and Luella would run it over to the grave. This was going to end up being a real nice garden. I was patting myself on the back for having such a wonderful idea. I decided that my next trip over, as a gift, I'd bring an azalea. I'd leave a spot smack-dab in the middle of the plot for it. A meditation garden, that's what we were creating. The oak would provide just enough shade to keep the azalea from burning up in the summer sun.

We put in ten plants total. The garden needed more, but we ran out. It was just going to have to be an ongoing project, and I kind of liked that idea. I was hot and sweating, and we both needed showers. But we had done some good work. I said, "Luella, just look at our labor. We have done good, little missy."

I turned on the hose and drank from it. I offered some to Luella, and she giggled as the spray hit her lips. I turned off the faucet and attached the hose to the sprinkler and then turned it back on. Delighted, Luella started running in and out of the swirling water. The dirt on her became little mud rivers. She looked like she was having so much fun. I just joined in. I should have known better. A woman of my size running around like a fool. I ran after her. My clothes were wringing on me, and we were laughing like two in-love hyenas.

The sensation of the sun and water and all the running made me feel my childhood again. It was back with me, in a flash. There was no difference between Luella and me. We were experiencing the same joy. She ran out past the sprinkler, and I ran after her.

But I didn't see the rake. It was a good, sturdy rake. The kind with iron prongs. Every other prong stuck out about an inch farther than the ones in between. My sights were on that precious little girl. I ran, but it seemed like out of nowhere my feet were all tangled up. It was the rake handle. I tripped on it and fell forward. I saw those iron prongs coming at me. I tried to twist away, but I didn't twist enough. I was falling, and not a thing to do about it. I landed hard, head forward. The prong, the one on the very end, I believe, ripped directly through my eye. Not my lid, no, because I kept my eyes open. It tore only the eye. I watched it tear. I mean, I saw how I was headed toward that iron finger, and how I seemed incapable of avoiding it. I saw a bright flash of light, like a flash fire, and then I saw only black.

Now, I don't remember any pain. I remember sound. I remember the sound of crushing and tearing. It was inside my head, and the sound—it too had a color—it was all black and torn with fire.

And I remember that little girl crying. Hers was a loud, long wail.

So of course, you know, they couldn't do anything, those doctors, about saving my eye. It's clouded, and blind, and my lid hangs half shut over it. But that's not what bothers me. It's the weeping. It cries all the time, a steady stream down the right side of my face. Oh, sometimes it's not much, just a trickle. But some days it's heavy, like real tears. This is mysterious. I've watched closely, but there's no accounting for the heavy or slim days. I'll keep watch, though. Seems that if I could just get a pattern to it, I'd find out it was all for a reason. It pains me to think of the other possibility— that God just blinded me on a whim.

Patrick Lackly

A light rain had begun to fall as they lowered Burl Junior Jewel's casket into the earth. I looked up at the sparsely clouded sky. I thought, Good-bye, Burl, wherever you are. And then I considered the body inside the casket. I considered Mrs. Batemeyer. Even the thought of Inez Temple's keeping silent about this affair did nothing to wipe away my guilt over toying so with the dead woman. I watched my assistants as they began placing the flower sprays around the burial plot. If I'd been a religious man, I might have asked someone, somewhere, to forgive me.

Mockingbirds
and Goldfish

Soleil Marie Beauvoir

The night I planned to ask Erzulie to bless my intentions toward Uncle's Boy, right, I was nervous. Too nervous for a *mambo*. Every person who brought me flowers and food so that the *loa* would be pleased and have good times with us, I made them leave all everything at my door. I wanted to be alone, just me and my thoughts of Erzulie and Uncle's Boy.

I picked three people I knew the *loa* had their sights on, and I said to them, "Fix everything. The candles, they must be in their right places. And the machete, make it sharp."

Then I gave the oldest one, he may be a *houngan* one day because he is able to know things, David, I gave my last bag of flour and some good white sugar, him.

"Tonight draw Erzulie," I told him. "Make her pretty." He grinned at me real big, for maybe he even knew what was up.

I sat on my porch and watched each move they made in the clearing in front of my house, everything my people did. But I was hidden because my house has tall legs, and the afternoon shadows grew over me like moss.

My dog sat with me. She rested her big head in my lap and was serious, she. This dog, yes, knew the depths of the water I treaded in. I rubbed her ears with my thick hands. It gave her pleasure. Pleasure this dog deserves, she works hard. In my sleep the dog guards me, see? She paces, paces all night at the big black gate, the opening to my dreams. This way I sleep forever without nightmares.

When the drummer began the rhythms that would first call our *loa*, all of me, my soul and my body, eased up and got happy. I listened to each beat, I felt the pull of changing rhythms. I remembered Haiti, the stories told me. Mama longed for the kind of drummers she grew up with. In this sugar field we have only one, but yes, he is good. But what it must be like on the island, five,

103

six drummers all beating like crazy, as if their fingers held the warm pounding hearts of the *loa*.

Imagine what I say now. The new ones, the workers just here from Haiti, they say the head honcho back there, Papa Doc, he does terrible things. Like he told everybody, with his big mouth, that he practiced Voodoo, yes. Now they say he does something called antisuperstition campaign. Rumors fly like eagles. No more drums, the eagle says. If he wipes out drums he wipes out Voodoo. I think that Papa Doc, he worships dark spirits. Best to leave Haiti, I tell the new ones. Good they're here.

But I sat in my house, me, on my porch, hidden from most white people because the house, it was in the middle of the cane fields we worked. And I was happy because I had at least one drummer, and he was good. It wasn't long before the night blacked out the sky and my body started its little sway. I thought about what had happened earlier that day. It was cool—dew still shimmered on them cane leaves—and Uncle's Boy walks up right behind me. I act like I don't know this, just a little game. And then he says, "Hi." And I turns around and says, "Hi." And he says so fast he barely breathes, "Would you like to get together some night this week? You know, sort of hang out." It took—believe me—all the steel in my body not to grin. Like I don't care I says, "Sure." And I tell him the way to my house and says to him, "Tomorrow night would be good." And then he does this thing: he looks around to see if anybody is watching. Not a soul. So as sudden and soft as lightning on a sunny day, he kisses my cheek. I'm so surprised I can say no words, which doesn't matter because he walks away fast as a rat.

But that kiss didn't blind me. There can be no loving without Erzulie's blessing. Believe me, yes, that would cause a kind of trouble no body needs.

I looked down at the clearing, the place where I would please Erzulie. A few people was dancing. Some, they were drinking and smiling and talking in whispers. Everything looked right. The candles were right, in a circle around the big stone. On the stone, like a beautiful painting in a white man's church, was David's flour-and-sugar drawing of Erzulie. Lots of work he had done—she wore earrings and smoked a cigarette. The drums, they were beating so sweet. And I say, Now, now's the time.

So I walked down my porch steps, and when my drummer saw me, I think he made a fast rhythm. I gave my greetings to everyone, say about twenty people. They closed in 'round me, all their faces gleaming with heat and excitement, and I thought, Let's not keep Erzulie or Uncle's Boy waiting.

My people were giggling and shuffling their bare feet. The machete laid like a piece of moon, shining, sharp on the stone. David, he could work good, you know.

I picked up the blade and raised it north, east, west, south. David stood by the stone, watching what he should do next by reading the words in my eyes. To his chest he hugged a wire cage painted pure white, and in it was a squawking chicken. Without any spoken word passing between us, David unlatched the wire door and grabbed that chicken.

The chicken's eyes, they seemed huge, like spirits was already in him. So I took the bird from David. Yes, I stroked him—at least I tried hard. We don't kill what doesn't want to go. But this bird, he was ready to join the *loa*. I was good, from long ago, at holding chickens still. I know some *mambos*, give their *loa* a bull. They fondle his balls, and some of the people, they suck the balls so the bull is very happy as it becomes a god. But as for me, I've only given chickens.

I raised this one to the four corners. And again, I took up the machete. I was fast, but still I felt the bird's stiff bones pop under the force of my killing blow. This bird, I was right, was full of *loa*, for its blood squirted on my white dress and probably on my people, the ones who were near.

I let the head stay where it was, on the stone. Its big yellow eye looked up at the stars. I held the dead bird over Erzulie's picture. Those last shivers of the bird's life, I don't know, maybe they excited me. I splashed its blood on Erzulie's white image and I spoke to her. I told her I would give her every pleasure. I love you, Erzulie, I told her, more than any other *loa*. I told her she could have Uncle's Boy with me. That we would love him together, yes.

Then Erzulie, she began to slowly mount me. Some *loa* grab you fast. One minute you walk with only yourself. The next minute you are a horse ridden at the *loa*'s whim. But this time no. Erzulie tingled through me. Teasing me. Not taking me fully.

"Give me the rum," I ordered.

Somebody, I don't know who because Erzulie was shading some of my mind, handed me a fat jug. I stuffed the bleeding end of the chicken neck into the jug and squeezed. I made blood go into that rum. I pulled the chicken out and threw it. It landed next to its eye-swollen head. I lifted the jug to my lips because Erzulie, thirsty she was. I drank until she was happy. Then Erzulie told me to share it.

"Everybody drink," I shouted, but the voice wasn't mine. It was hers, heavy and full of heat.

The drum music, oh, it was good. It made Erzulie fast and wild, yes. She was forcing me to walk up to dancing, sweating men and rub my hands all over them. The kisses, they were fuller than flower blossoms. But Erzulie that night, maybe because she knew Uncle's Boy would be a treat, she seemed to want women. They were all so pretty. Their breasts, they pleased her most. She danced and danced, she pushed me against the ladies. With my mouth she nipped on their ears.

I remember this. I remember the body of the one Erzulie liked the most, but who it really was I cannot say because Erzulie was filling me quick. And when a *loa* mounts you all the way, you can't remember nothing because you're not you. You're *loa*.

But the one Erzulie desired most, was a woman, she, that is fact. We slid and rolled our hips against each other. And Erzulie, she is so sly, she tricked our dancing, moved our feet, guided us to the stone.

I only remember slices from then. The sweet sight of the lady's skin, her nipples, I think. I see Erzulie make me push the lady against the stone. I see that her body covers the sugar-flour-and-blood picture of Erzulie. I think that I'm frightened, that this bold move will anger Erzulie. But really, it was what she desired, yes. Because in that very second Erzulie mounted me with all her hot fury. And you know, I remember nothing after that.

Erzulie had stolen my mind and had good fun.

I woke the next morning in my house, on my mattress, by myself, not knowing what I had done. But that trickster Erzulie. She left me a clue about her deeds. I threw back my blanket and looked down at my body. I caught my breath and said, "Hail Mary full of grace." Because sugar, flour, and blood, they glowed like coins all over my dark skin.

Emory Looney

You see, I knew that sliding out of my bedroom window in the middle of the night would be the second act of manhood I ever committed in my life. My first act occurred when I knocked the shit out of the man I used to call Daddy. I suppose he thought sending me down here to my uncle's sugarcane farm not only would get me in line but would ensure that he stayed alive. I would never have really harmed him, I don't think. It's just that the last time he backhanded Mama I decided that enough was enough.

I'm none too happy about the way things turned out with my father. If I were to be really honest, I'd say I wish I'd never slugged him and it's too bad he's not a different kind of man. But of course, I'm never really going to say those words, especially to him. Shit. It's over with. I don't have a father no more and he don't have a son. Time for me to move on with things. I've got to live. I suspect that one day I'll forget he ever existed.

Maybe the end of our father-son relationship was supposed to be. This is the way I see it. Things come in threes, right? I believe that. That's why it's so clear to me that my manhood would walk up to me in three stages. Maybe there was no choice about me slugging my father. My mother always calls me wild, but really I'm organized. Take this manhood stuff. I see it clearly; it's all mapped out. One, I break loose from my father. Two, I figure a way out of this house and into Soleil Marie's arms. Three, I cross the bridge: I make love to Soleil Marie.

Now, my plans for Soleil Marie weren't immoral or anything, because I was head over heels. Call it love at first sight if you want to, but the moment I saw her I knew she was special.

The first thing that attracted me to her was her collarbone. I spied it one day as I was kneeling down between plants, out of sight, to get a rest. Between the leaves I saw only a part of a woman. I saw from waist to neck. I saw beautiful skin stretched out, sweaty and gritty. I never saw the face. Until a few hours later, that is. See, this is how it was: I didn't have a single friend anywhere in the world. J.W., he made me go to school. I wanted to just quit but he said a diploma meant something. He never said what that something was. So there I am, a high school junior on a special work program, which meant that I went to class in the mornings and was home by one so as I could work in the afternoons. I hated math and English and my teachers and the other kids because everything and everybody was strange, and I made friends with no one. Not the kind of friends that matter, anyhow. And in the fields who was I supposed to talk to? With the exception of J.W.'s men, I was the only white guy out there. So I just stayed off to myself, angrier than hell at my daddy because of what he had done to me. And deep down I was the kind of lonely that makes your bones actually ache. So when Soleil Marie took it upon herself to walk up and offer me some water, it was like a fresh breeze blew by. There was something sweet and gentle, yet wild, about her. I had looked at her eyes and down at her collarbone and back at her eyes. When she handed me that old tin cup full of water and smiled at me, it was the first time in months that I thought about something other than how miserable I was. Every day after that we'd talk a little, and then some more. She liked to talk about her dog, so I always started off with, "How's that old hound of yours?" But that's all we had—bits of conversation out in the field. Finally I just had to have more, even if my uncle found out. Early one morning—while most of J.W.'s men were still nursing their coffee up by the tractor shed—I walked straight up to Soleil Marie and asked if it would be all right if I paid her a visit. Thank God she said yes.

Escaping from my uncle's house wasn't too difficult. I didn't dare risk using the front door, though. J.W. bolts it crossways with a pine two-by-four and locks it with a combination deadbolt. I don't know what he's so scared of, with him being out here in the middle of nothing. I asked him once. He just sucked air through his teeth. He looked at the ground and back at me. Then he said, " 'Gators."

No, I knew that an escape out my window would probably be the surest way to get out of the house without waking J.W. I waited until the snores that filtered through the bedroom wall thumped into my room as steady as rain. Then, using only the moonlight to guide me, I pulled on my clean jeans. I picked out my new shirt. It was blue and white and had pearl snap-buttons. I wiggled my feet into my boots that had a nice design like snakeskin on them. It was those boots that almost did in my evening. I popped out the screen, no problem. I pulled it into my room and propped it against the wall. I had planned to slide right over the window ledge and into the evening, but it was a longer drop than I'd imagined. From my butt to my feet, I dangled out the window. There would be no quietly touching my feet to the ground. I had to jump. To me— and this is probably only because I was so nervous that my ears exaggerated everything—my boots hitting the earth boomed like a shotgun blast. The sound beat in my lying ears. I stood there frozen, scared that Uncle J.W. would wake up and pull me back into the house by my hair. Uncle J.W. is old, maybe forty or fifty, but swinging a machete all his life in his cane field has made him stronger than most his age.

So I stood still, not even breathing, until I was sure my escape had not roused him. I stepped away from the house and walked behind the shed where the old school bus is kept. Uncle J.W. picks up the migrants from other farms or from the cities in that bus. It's the bus that carried Soleil Marie here.

The thought of her, my soon-to-be lover, made me shaky and happy. I realized that if someone had told me twelve months ago that I would be standing on the edge of an Okeechobee cane field, stars shining overhead in a big black sky, I'd have said, "Bullshit." If someone had told me that I was going to walk through that cane field in order to come face to face with my third act of manhood, and that act would involve a pretty little colored woman, I probably would've busted that someone right in the face.

See, I've always done what people told me to do—until my first act of manhood, that is. My folks would tell me not to take up too closely with coloreds; I never brought any of my colored friends home. Mama would tell me to take out the trash: every morning before school I took it out. That son of a bitch I used to call Daddy told me not to hang out after school at Bobby's Pool Hall, because that was the coloreds' pool hall: I never went, though I wanted to, due to the fact that men and boys lost and gained fortunes there.

Yes, it was a place of good luck. Whether you won or lost, you left feeling good about yourself. Trust Eugene Barker, he was a nigger friend of mine, he told me that white people were always welcome in that pool hall. He said that as long as white people were welcome, it would be a place of good luck, but if one ever actually entered the hall and won a game, then the good luck would vanish. You see, I wanted to visit that pool hall bad, but I never did go.

Now I can do as I please. I stood at the edge of the field and felt good about that. It was near harvest time and the cane poles rose eight or ten feet into the sky. I looked at their leaves shaped like sabers. I saw the tiny flowers that formed the tassels. The wind blew, and the field made music; the cane leaves rubbed against one another the way crickets rub their legs together. And yes, their sound, the crickets and those leaves, was the same.

As the field song grew, a smell grew with it. It was the same smell that had shook me out of a sound sleep a couple of times the past week. It was the smell of sugar, and it was so sweet and strong it caused a picture to crawl up in my mind. It was the picture of a woman. I don't know what woman or why my mind chose her, but there she was, pregnant with a rising belly. As the belly got bigger I imagined the smell of the sugar cane grew stronger. It grew so strong the woman was finally compelled to have her baby. Of course, I didn't see that part. I just thought it was nice that my mind worked that way, that I would think of the field giving off scent and of a happy woman about to have a baby.

I decided that was a good thought to set out with. I headed due north, straight through the fields. I was not sure how far I had to travel, but Soleil Marie had assured me that due north would bring me to her doorstep.

110

As I walked, my mind shot over to what I knew about sex. Not a damn thing. I saw myself as I had been a lot lately, out in the shed, my pants down around my ankles. A mayonnaise jar stuffed with fresh liver. Humping. Humping. The picture of the blonde in the hot shorts torn out of J.W.'s *True Detective* tacked to the wall. What a stupid sight.

I felt a little ashamed. To keep up my courage I saw Soleil Marie smile at me with that pretty face and say, "Honey, it's okay. The past don't matter. It's just you and me now."

I picked up my pace. But not for long, because I discovered that walking through a cane field at night is not nearly as easy as walking through it during the day. I conjured thoughts of what could be lurking in the field. Diamondbacks, for instance. Or panther. 'Gator maybe. It was beginning to dawn on me that Soleil Marie's directions were not really very complete. What if I veered easterly? What if I came face to face with a damn 'possum? What if Soleil Marie was just having fun with me? Maybe she sensed my sexual inexperience, and this was just a big joke.

If I was to complete my mission, I was going to have to think of something besides Soleil Marie not being for real or what could be hiding behind the next plant. I tried to turn my mind back to the day I first stepped foot on this farm.

That day it was hot, and I was angry. The farm was nothing but one flat, endless, boring blanket of gray soil. Stubble stuck out from the field like ugly, dead arms. And I thought, This is what my first act of manhood has brought me. I get to live in a godforsaken hole swinging a machete sunup to sundown beside a bunch of the craziest and prettiest niggers I'd ever seen. Haitians.

For some reason my thoughts made me pause. Maybe it was remembering how dead the fields looked when I first came here. At the risk of sounding sissy, they looked kind of glorious right then and there with me standing in the middle of them. I stopped walking. I looked at the plant next to me. It was tall, taller than me. I took one of its leaves in my hand. I felt its smooth surface. Suddenly a kind of pride about my work burst through. My hands had blistered and cracked during the summer months due to J.W.'s frenzy over weeds. When I had swung that machete, hours on end,

I was never happy. I had thought, What harm can a few weeds cause? The only harm was that they might take over one or two plants, and that meant J.W. would feel a tiny pain in his bank account. Big deal. But here I was, touching this cane leaf and feeling good about it. Maybe my weed-chopping had helped this plant live.

I moved on. I walked with giant steps through the field I had helped grow. I was tired, but I walked strongly because I knew my third act of manhood was near.

I guess the only explanation for what happened next is what the locals around here call swamp fever. Oh, it didn't last long. And it was sudden, like a chill that grabs you in the middle of the night and shakes you out of a sweet, sweet dream. There I was, walking along like a real man, when a heron let loose with one of those lonely, strange cries they have. It sounded like a mating whoop, and it was so close and clear that goose pimples cropped up on my arms. I wondered if J.W. knew there was a pond out this far, but my wonder was snuffed out, because in a split second, before my very eyes, I saw a flash. If I had bothered to think about it, to pause and decide whether it was maybe just heat lightning or my imagination, maybe I wouldn't have acted so foolish. But no, my mind jumped. The fever rose. Wildfire, I thought.

Holy shit. At that moment I knew one thing. A wildfire in a cane field is like dousing a live match with gasoline. I ran. Reeds whipped past my face, stinging my eyes. I squeezed my lids shut and kept zooming. I was a madman running for my life. I imagined the blaze was gaining on me quickly, flicking its fiery tongue at my boots. I thought I heard the awful sound of living things crackling beneath the weight of deadly heat.

Many a night since then I have wondered, Why me? Why did I get a sudden case of the fever on the most precious night of my life?

But also many a night I have counted myself lucky, for the fever carried me out of that field. Yes, call me a liar, that's okay, but this is the God's truth. I ran and ran, so convinced that I was trapped in the middle of a firestorm. With clenched eyes, I zigged and zagged and zigged and zagged until I no longer felt the sting of whipping reeds.

That night was strange, for it seemed that out of sure death I tumbled effortlessly into the safe, cool comfort of a clearing. As soon as I ran breathless and scared out of the fields, the fever evaporated from my brain. As it lifted, I realized there was no fire, that I had been tricked. The fever had caused a momentary lapse of good sense, like a diseased wind that meddles with your well-being and rolls on.

I opened my eyes and tried to calm my jolting breath. I looked out across the clearing. It was then that I had my vision. Or should I say, my first vision.

Oh, it wasn't a pure vision—reality was mixed in with it—but still I saw it. The real part was Soleil Marie's house. It sat about a hundred yards across the clearing, a wooden shack on stilts with a huge screened-in porch on all sides. The screen was tearing off in places, and immediately I knew that I would come out here in the light of day and fix it for her.

As I pondered that thought, another gust blew up from the fields. Maybe it was because my ridiculous sprint had left me pooped, I don't know. But when I let the gust blow over me, I relaxed. Just for a few seconds I shut my eyes and breathed in the field's weird smell. Then it happened. My mind saw better than my eyes.

In my brain I saw the fields. Now believe this: The fields danced. I mean it. All those plants swayed and swooned as if they had a life all their own. I tried to shake it off and see for real again, but then my mind switched pictures. It showed me my Sweetness, my Soleil Marie. She stood in the middle of the clearing. She was smiling and she held a candle. The flame danced like sure, wild wings in the yellow-flecked irises of her eyes. Even in my vision, I was in love.

I slid my eyelids open and checked the field. No fires, no dancing, no Soleil Marie. Shit. If I hadn't known better, I would have sworn I'd been standing out behind J.W.'s shed for two or three hours smoking hooch and guzzling Jax after Jax. That would have explained all this. But sometimes, you know, life isn't so simple.

This was one of those times.

I headed toward the shack and wondered if all guys as they are about to achieve manhood have visions. I wondered if this vision stuff was a kind of secret happening that men are not allowed to talk about. As I bolted up the shack's rickety wooden stairs, I developed my thought. I suspected that once I had tamed Soleil Marie, that once we had ridden each other into the passions of my manhood, all of the evening's visions would be wiped from my mind. Poof. Gone. Never to be remembered again. That way I could go about the business of being a man without worrying that I would reveal any masculine secrets.

I stood on the top step and paused. I ran both my hands through my hair, tucked my shirt more neatly into my jeans, and checked my fly. I began to realize I was nervous. Well, already I'd had a hell of a night. I remembered one of my mama's favorite expressions. She likes to say, "My nerves are shot straight to hell." For the first time I understood what she meant by that.

Shot straight to hell, yes, but I couldn't let a detail like that get in my way. I wasn't about to turn around and walk back through those fields without having shed my skin first, so to speak. I stood there quiet for a second, looking out over the cane. This is it, bud, I said to myself. Then I knocked on the screen door.

Nothing could have prepared me for what I saw next. My Sweetness walked out to the porch and opened the door, as if it was a normal night. And she was beautiful, really. She was smiling, just like in my vision. Her white cotton dress was tied at each shoulder with little white strings. It took me like one second to stare at those naked shoulders and memorize them. Beautiful. Beautiful.

"Hi," I said, and I grinned at her. "I made it."

"You didn't get lost, did you?" she asked. She talked with a real light tone, and all her words, even though they was sometimes jumbled, seemed perfect. I wondered how a colored girl who grew up whacking cane could say all her words so much better than me. It's not that it made me jealous, no. But I'd be lying if I said it did not shake me.

I stepped onto the porch and stuffed my hands into my jeans. I felt suddenly and completely like an idiot. Was I supposed to sweep her off the ground and kiss her? Should I have brought her something from J.W.'s house? Bread, grapes, some wild flowers? I didn't know. I'd heard that people's nervousness takes annoying forms, and this I believe, for out of nowhere a hiccup curled in the back of my throat, ready to pounce if I tried to speak. Soleil Marie stood in front of me, her hand toying with her bead necklace, waiting for an answer about me getting lost.

"No," I managed to croak. "Due north—they were good directions." Then I clenched my jaws tight. Trap the fucker, I thought: the hiccup had become my enemy.

Soleil Marie touched my shirt. Her fingers did not match her tiny voice. She had worker's hands. I looked at the callused, chapped fingers. They looked sore, and that hurt me. But worse than the hurt was this kind of guilt that began to swim around inside me. Where it came from or why I had it I did not know, but I didn't like it.

"You must be tired, it's a long walk, no?" she said. She stepped up to a wobbly cypress side table. In the center a candle glowed, and I wondered why I hadn't noticed the candle right off, after having that vision and all. An old tin bowl gleamed in the candlelight. She looked at that bowl and back at me.

"I hope you don't mind," she said to me. "Back home we have a custom, we always wash our hands in candle water before we go inside our homes."

Of course, I obliged her. There were all kinds of flower blossoms floating in the water, and it came to mind that J.W., when he wasn't calling the migrants "field fleas," referred to them as "those weird niggers." But what could be wrong with dipping my hands in water mixed with a few flowers? I boldly stared at her face as I shoved my hands into the bowl. My Sweetness was so pretty in that dancing light. Her skin was a soft color, kind of the deep brown of a horseshoe crab.

If my used-to-be father ever found out what I was about to do, I figured, he'd kill me. But used-to-bes don't count. I hadn't picked Soleil Marie to be my first lover because she was colored. No. But I have to admit, when I thought about how angry my old man would be if he knew about this, I wanted to laugh.

Instead, because I didn't want to break the mood, I forced myself to calm down. So what happens? The damn hiccup blurts out of my mouth. Embarrassed? You bet. I jerked my hand out of the water. I knew my face was probably the color of my imaginary field fire. But you know what she did? She acted like she didn't hear a thing. Her expression did not change or nothing. She wrapped my wet hands in the skirt of her dress and dried them.

I couldn't control myself. I pulled one of my hands from the soft cotton folds and touched her hair. I wanted to love her, right then and there. I thought about how easy it would be to untie her strings and run my tongue along her beautiful collarbone.

Soleil Marie held my hand and walked us into her living room. Actually, it wasn't just a living room. It was like the whole house. You know, my parents don't have much money, but we are rich compared to this girl. No running water, no toilet, no bathtub, no electricity. The guilt that had bubbled up when I noticed her cal-lused hands was back. "This is where you live?" I mumbled.

"Sometimes I live here. Sometimes in the camp. Mostly I'm here." She picked up a plastic jug and poured what looked like water into two jelly jars. She offered one to me.

"Thank you," I said. I looked around the room. I was, once again, feeling dumb. But I was curious too, because this room was like nothing I'd ever seen. It wasn't evil or rat-dirty or anything. Unique, I'd say.

I guessed right off that Soleil Marie was Catholic, because on the wall was hung one of those crucifixes. Stuck behind it was a couple of dried palm fronds that curved 'round Jesus's plastic body.

There wasn't much furniture. Only a few tables. And candles shaped like swamp animals, panthers, 'gators, and such burned everywhere.

Shoved between some of the candles were empty Coke bottles. Well, they weren't exactly empty. They were full of water. A few looked like they had food coloring in them—you know, what ladies do to liquor bottles in their houses to make them red or green or yellow? But these weren't fancy bottles. Just Coke, and some of them had herbs floating in them.

Strange stuff. The curiosity alone helped ease my nerves. Soleil Marie's special concoction did the rest. I took a gulp from my glass; I was happy for a drink of water. Jesus Christ.

I coughed but managed to keep the liquor down. After the first shock wave was over, whatever it was spread out across my chest, and hell, it felt good. Warm, calming.

"It's not the best rum in the world, but it's the best we do out here," Soleil Marie said between giggles.

She was a little girl, but she was a woman too. And as I watched her delight at me half choking to death, it dawned on me I knew absolutely nothing about her. Her age. Her dreams. Why was she out here all alone? Why did she do farm work when she could manage in the city?

I was thinking these questions as I watched her move across the room. She stopped in front of the only thing, besides the floor, a man could sit on here, a mattress. It was shoved up against one wall and was piled high with pillows. No sheets, though, but so what. She stood by it and rubbed her hand up and down the lumpy, stained surface like an invitation for me to sit.

My many questions disappeared, because I learned all I needed to know about her in that instant. Her desire. She wanted me. I could feel it.

I took another slug of liquor and walked toward her. I traced my finger along that collarbone that stood like a jewel above her tits. Her eyes looked boldly into mine. I said to myself, This is it. But something inside me wouldn't let me just hop on her. I guess my mother had instilled something in me. A respect of sorts about women. This was a discovery, for in all my daydreams about Soleil Marie, I never once bothered to make small talk. But now, out here, when it was the real thing, I tried.

"Don't you get lonely out here all alone?" Then, like no big deal, I sat down on the mattress. I drank some more.

There was a trunk next to the mattress. It was cluttered with a slew of potted plants—like herbs. I sat my glass on it and wondered what in the world she kept in there.

She snuggled up next to me and talked as if she was as comfortable and cool as a butterfly. "Lonely? No, not me. The camp, it's about a mile east. Not a long walk. I'm there a lot, but this house, the work it brings me, it's my inheritance."

Now, who in the hell would believe they had inherited a shack in the middle of nowhere on property that wasn't theirs? Silly woman, I thought.

"Inheritance. Sweetness, that can't be. My uncle owns all this.

He may not know your shack sits out here, but it don't matter. He owns it anyway."

Then she did something that was spooky. She looked at me with half-closed eyes and said, like she was a queen, "Nobody, no human, not your big uncle or even the president's uncle, owns these swamps. They may think they do, but that's just because they think money is power."

She stood up and got the plastic pitcher full of brew. She stood over me, close and hot. I watched the liquor gurgle out of the pitcher and into my glass. She started to set the pitcher on the trunk but put it on the floor instead. "But it's okay," she continued, as if she had never paused. "Your uncle has to do what he's doing, and with him gritting his teeth all the time, yes, because his happiness and sadness is all he really owns."

I grinned at her. I felt full of myself. I pulled her down beside me. "And what do you own, my Sweetness?"

"You," she said. Then she giggled like she was twelve, and I decided she was an uppity and childish woman, and I liked that.

She took a long pull from her glass and winked at me. Her eyes were small; they shined. "You have beautiful eyes," I said.

She pressed her rough hand against my neck and stroked me. "Are you happy, my Uncle's Boy?" she asked.

"Uncle's Boy!" I laughed. Her wild-ass way of talking excited me. A picture of that son-of-a-bitch former daddy flashed in my head. He would have punched any woman black and blue who had called him somebody's boy. But I am not my daddy's son. I emptied my glass and cupped her hands in mine. I sang out, "Soleil Marie, Soleil Marie, what a funny and pretty name, my Soleil Marie."

"Funny name, no." She stuck her thick pink tongue out at me and then, honest to God, she licked my cheek. She kissed my ear. I held her close to me as she whispered, "*Soleil* is French for 'sun.' Do you want to see the sun, Uncle's Boy?"

With one hand I pushed her back on the mattress. I gazed at the wild, mean woman who would make me into the man I had always wanted to be, and here she was calling me boy. But it was okay, because behind her wicked tongue was a tender voice. I looked at her, from her bare feet to her head. Despite the gnat bites and scratches that made it obvious she was a field worker, her cinnamon-colored skin looked soft and glowy. She smiled. Her teeth were perfect white buttons set off by the prettiest face I had ever seen. "Sun Marie," I proclaimed, "you are the light that brightens my day."

Then I kissed her. God. And again. Her tongue knew what to do, and mine followed. She arched her long neck like it was an invitation to explore, so I traced its curve with my tongue. I followed the snaking necklace down to where her dress hid her tits. It was weird, for I moved as if I'd done this all before. You know, like an animal that gives birth for the first time; she don't know what's going to happen but she knows sort of what to do. I pulled the string, and the only one who knew my hand was shaking was me.

Whether Soleil Marie had done it before was really no concern to me, although I suspect that she had, because as soon as I untied her straps she wiggled free of me fast. She stared down at me with eyes that had shifted from sweet to wild, but still they were beautiful. Before I could reach out to touch her, she whipped the dress off over her head. Instantly I understood just a little bit more about the bridge I was about to cross. Some men say they like to look at naked girls, and of course I do, but Soleil Marie was different. I looked, you bet, every curve and mound. But more than that, I listened, for this perfect body glistening in front of me could teach me many things, all kinds of tricks and motions. I started at the bone that had called to me from between cane leaves. My hands moved fast—tits, belly, thighs—for I wanted to feel all of her in one great moment.

This was love. I knew it. I stood up. I was going to take her in my arms and love her good. But damn, she was fast. Like a hummingbird swooping for nectar, Soleil Marie unzipped my pants and held my joint between her two small hands.

I gazed down at her. A kind of ecstasy began to take over as I drank her every feature. The wet petals of her mouth. The soft round ridges of her cheekbones. The moon-kissed circles of her eyelids. I touched her hair like it was gold, and her beautiful slanted eyes seemed to flutter over me.

I'm not sure how long we were like that, staring at each other,

119

drinking each other in, kissing and giggling. But I know this: When we fell back on the mattress and joined together, that's when I had my second vision. We moved, she and I, like the tight body of a great bird. Say I'm crazy, go ahead, but we flew. Soleil Marie was the wings, and me the darting body.

She was so sweet and slow. I shut my eyes. Below us swayed the dancing fields. Their sweet smell ruffled through us as we dipped and soared through a sky made beautiful not with stars but with candlelight.

Yes, we flew fast and deep, and when we came I recognized the sound of our flight, the sound I had been listening to from the first moment I had plunged myself into another person and become a man. Whether it was a part of my vision or cold, tough reality I do not know, but it was the song of the lonesome heron that I had heard when I was lost in the fields, and it tumbled clearly and fully out of the parted sweet lips of my lover.

Inez Temple

Oh yes, I was a tired woman that night. I'd done three cleaning jobs that day. Plus earlier in the evening I'd visited Mrs. Jackson, who wasn't feeling so well. I'd taken her a big pot of lentil stew. That's one of my specialties, you see. So I was quite content to finally be off my feet. I was sitting at my kitchen table shelling some peas. I had the radio on, listening to some young Negro man from New York City talk about economic empowerment. My bad eye was awfully bothersome and my good eye was sore from doing the work of two. It had been months since the accident, but I wasn't adjusting well at all to this half-blindness. So I sat there listening and shelling—all with my eyes closed.

I was almost done with the shelling when it happened. The young man on the radio was saying something to the effect that us Negroes had to take control of our own economic and political destinies.

And right out loud, as if I was talking to somebody, I said, "You know that's right." But I'd no sooner got out those words as when I didn't hear the radio anymore. And the dark blankness behind my lids disappeared. I'm saying to you it was replaced by the strangest sight—just like a movie playing in my eyes. But what I saw was beautiful. It was swampland filled with mangroves and the like. And I didn't see them, but I was completely aware of that swamp being filled with mysterious animals. And then the land changed into something less wild—a sugar plantation, and I swear I could smell the sweetness wafting above that tall cane. And suddenly I was in the middle of those fields. I was standing right in front of this pretty dark-skinned girl. But she wasn't normal like you or me. She glowed. I swear. From inside out she was shining with the prettiest light you ever seen, like a thousand burning candles flickered inside her. Then she opened her mouth, and I thought she was going to speak to me, but instead out came this strange, low, lonesome cry. And the next thing I knew that pretty girl wasn't a girl anymore. The candles had burned away her real skin, and now she was a bird—a heron, I think. I reached out my hand because I had the most honest urge to touch her, but before I could she rose from those fields just like she knew what she was doing. Her wings spread out like great velvet hands across the sky, and a thousand other birds rose with her. And then I became aware that I was not alone. I turned my gaze from that amazing sight in the sky and looked at the fields again. Sure enough, there stood a boy. I didn't see his face, but I felt exactly what he was feeling. It was a joy as pure and perfect as cold spring water.

And then, just as fast as it started, it shut off. My eyes saw only black again. No more fields or bird women or joyful boys. I was back in my little apricot-colored kitchen. The young man wasn't on the radio anymore—they'd switched to playing some kind of bebop music.

I shook my head. I said, "Missy, those pills that doctor gave you for your eye is making you see things."

Straightaway I set my peas to the side, marched myself to my bathroom, and flushed those green-and-yellow capsules right down my toilet. I said, "No more of those things for you, Inez Temple."

121

Then I went back to my shelling. But one thing you can be sure of: This time I kept that eye open.

Rose Looney

I read somewhere about crazy people. About how some of them—especially women—when they've gone off their rockers will spend hours a day washing their hands. That's exactly what I reminded myself of. The weather was oppressively hot—high nineties—and the Atlantic was chock-full of tropical storms that could blossom into hurricanes at any moment. The more I listened to talk about violent storms, torrential rains, the greater the urge grew in me to clean my house, as if I could impose order where there was chaos. So that's what I was doing, even though it was so hot I thought I might melt.

So far I'd cleaned out Emory's closet. This was a feat in and of itself because I hadn't stepped a foot in his bedroom in over a year, not since the argument. The memories were just too awful. It just hurt so much to miss him the way I did. For a while all the mess with Junior kept me preoccupied. But after he died and Eudora calmed down, all I had to face was an endless string of miserable holidays and empty hours without my son. Oh, I'd thought about going down and visiting. I'd even asked Charlie to let him come home for Christmas. But all Charlie would say was, "Not until he apologizes." All Emory would say was, "I'm not coming home until he's not there anymore." So there I was—stuck between them, neither one willing to give an inch and me seemingly helpless to do anything about it.

But lately I'd been building up to something. I'd been trying to figure a way to win. I'd been telling myself, Rose, face the dirt. See it for what it is. But try not to see it where it doesn't exist. Then maybe you'll know what's what.

That's as far as my philosophy had gotten. But already it had

122

helped me garner my courage. It enabled me to open that shut door and walk into Emory's room. Once I did I went straight to work. I threw away old sneakers. I hung up shirts. I found a cigar box full of old school supplies from when he was in elementary school— broken pieces of crayons, chewed-on erasers, unsharpened pencils. Back in a corner I found a belt I'd given him one year for Christmas. It must have fallen off a hanger or just gotten lost in the general mess. Suddenly I was scared that he'd outgrown all his clothes and that he didn't have a stitch to wear on that crummy little sugar farm. I'd have to send him a clothing care package. That's all there was to it.

Then I looked around his room. The baseball bat propped against the desk. His Mickey Mantle wastebasket cluttered with the same trash that was in it the day he left. A pile of old seashells on his bookcase. The crazy blue curtains with the white jets that I'd sewn myself. It occurred to me that those curtains needed to be washed— all the dirt from all these mean days and nights had to be gotten rid of. I pulled them down. I stared out his windows but saw nothing except the cold, ugly walls of the prison across the street. They shimmered in the sun like a mirage, and I thought, Wouldn't it be funny if that's exactly what it was—if that granite monstrosity was just our imagination. I breathed in deeply, but my lungs filled with nothing except hot, steamy air. I thought, Jesus, Rose, that air is so hot it could burn your lungs. And then I was overwhelmed by the realization that a house across the street from a prison was the most horrible place in the world to live. Breathing became difficult and I felt like I might faint, and somewhere way in the back of my brain I had this fantasy to become a guerrilla fighter and burn down that prison.

But instead I walked away from that window and laid down on my little boy's bed. I hugged his curtains to my sweaty body and thought if I cried I'd feel a lot better. But I couldn't. I just laid there lost and fretting, my mind meandering from one silly item to the next. I thought about this report I'd heard last night on TV. It was a special about hurricanes. Sam Cato, the Channel 4 weather-man, he said that hurricanes—despite all their fury—don't have any control over what direction they move in. They're like a stone in a stream, he said. They're at the whim of the air currents that push them from one place to another. All that destructive force and not a mind of its own. And it dawned on me that maybe those storms weren't unlike Charlie and me. We just kind of let our emotions or our liquor or our old ghosts spur us to some horrible action without ever thinking about the final consequences. Big old blustery Charlie and Rose Looney being pushed around by our own fears, our own devils. Somewhere in all these strange thoughts I knew there was a decision to be made. But for the life of me I couldn't figure out what it was. And I said to myself, Well, Rose, maybe things will change for you. Maybe this weather will kick up a big old storm that will wipe your slate clean. And then again, I thought, probably not.

So I got up from Emory's bed and with his curtains in my hands left his room.

But this time I kept the door open.

Charlie Looney

Just trying to unwind. That was all. Sitting in the dark, cool shadows of Tippy's Bar. Enjoying the first jolts brought on by my ingestion of a Tippy Torpedo. One part beer, one part champagne, one part Wild Turkey. Let me tell you, that is one fine drink. Causes hair to grow in places you'd never suspect. Background noise buzzed in my ears—the rumble of the jukebox, the clatter of balls breaking across the pool table, the snorts and stamps of the usual after-five crowd. Some blonde kept playing "Your Cheatin' Heart" over and over and over again. I loved that song. It spoke to me, you know? Hell, a great song. I sat there sucking down my liquor, singing along with Hank real softly, and considering the two pieces of paper tossed on the bar in front of me. Two folded-up pieces of paper, I might add. Because, see, I had what was scrawled on them memorized. Some babe, I don't know—I think her name was Sally—came up and rubbed against me. "Hey, Charlie, want to dance?" I waved her away. I just kept considering the two pieces of paper because they presented to me a huge dilemma.

The paper on my left was the kind housewives write grocery lists on. A flimsy piece of paper. Yellow. Small. A rectangle. At the top was a red-ink picture of a woman pushing a grocery cart. In block letters, like a yellow-pages ad, were the words MY GROCERY LIST. Then her handwriting. *Sweetheart, have a nice day at the lot. Hope you don't have to work too hard. I'm fixing us a nice dinner for tonight. Love you, Rose.*

I closed my eyes and sniffed. The smell of the paper on my right was intoxicating. Lilacs. Pure, unadulterated class. Lilacs. The type of aroma that gives good men hard-ons. The kind of paper that feels good to touch. Easy on the eyes with its soft lavender color. Gold embossed flowers curling down and across its edges. And the hot, red imprint put there just for me—a set of full, juicy lips. Pauline's lips. *Coquina Motel. Tonight. Eight o'clock. For the fuck of your life.*

So there it was. Pauline or Rose? Pauline or Rose? The question of the century. I mean, see here, the dilemma I was in put me in the position of being a son of a bitch. I could not please them both and remain Mr. Nice Guy. No way. So what was I going to do? Why not just go out and have fun? Raise a little hell? Come home when I goddamn feel like it? I'm the bread-earner—a man who always does what he wants. Yes, sir. And if you believe that, you'll believe I've got a gold tooth in the back of my mouth worth fifty million dollars.

I caught the bartender's eye. Tippy Garcia's son. Young. Wet behind the ears. But he makes a damn good Torpedo. "Do me again," I said.

I fingered the lavender paper and considered Pauline. Pauline DuPree. Five years ago when I walked onto that car lot and into her air-conditioned office with its lavender eyelet curtains, she looked up from her desk and said, "Honey, turn around, a full circle."

Then she said, "You want a job?"

Oh, right from the start I knew the two of us would end up in the sack. I just didn't suspect how quickly it would happen, and of course, who could have imagined the style of our lovemaking. Hell blazes hotter when we get it on.

Maybe that's why every time I've tried to quit Pauline I've failed. It's embarrassing to admit a woman has power over you, but God damn it, Pauline has me in the palm of her soft little hand.

I remember the time I told her it was over. I pulled up my trousers and zipped my fly before she could grab me again. "That was it, Pauline. Our last time. I'm going straight now. I can't do this no more to Rose."

"You'll never stay away," she told me as her blue eyes narrowed into snake slits. "You need what I've got. You have to feel what I make you feel, or you'll do something dangerous, asshole."

And I stood there and took it from her. I let her call me asshole with that superior look on her face. And I crumbled. I didn't walk out that motel door. Instead I got down on my knees and with my tongue gave her goddamn feet a bath.

Jesus, I could be a crazy son of a bitch. I downed the Torpedo in two gulps. I ordered another one. And I thought, Why not blow off Pauline tonight? It's not like it would hurt anything. See now, Pauline was an independent gal. Business owner. Single. Saw me and whoever else she wanted to see. Interesting woman. And it wasn't like we were having some raging, passionate affair. That would have meant I was cheating on Rose. And this wasn't cheating. This was just keeping one foot off the bed and on the floor—for freedom, see. With Pauline there wasn't any moaning and complaining about, "How in the hell do you expect us to pay the electric bill this month?" and "How much money have you poured down your throat over at Tippy's?" and on and on. There was just a kind of free, hell-raising fun. No big deal. A dip in the sack. A few hours with no responsibilities. Zap—a new man.

But shit, Rose'd call it cheating. She's a black-and-white woman.

I threw a George Washington on the bar. I considered taking my two notes with me but thought it best if they ended up in Tippy's trash. I picked up Pauline's lavender paper and held it to my nose. Lilacs. Unbelievable. I tossed the paper back down on the bar and commenced to finishing my drink. And it was then that this thing happened, see. I was just sitting there minding my own business, considering my situation, when Horace Taylor—he owns the Tiama Singer Sewing Machine Retail and Repair—came walking through the door. And when he opened that door a big old breeze whipped through with him and carried Rose's note off the bar and onto Tippy's polished terrazzo floor. I looked at the bar. That beautiful lavender paper stared up at me—all by itself. Singular. Isolated. Alone. Well, suddenly, with the opening of a door, life was as clear as a glass-bottom boat. The Coquina Motel it would be. I'd just have to do a little covering with Rose, that was all.

I picked up Pauline's note and slid it down my breast pocket. I made my way back to the pay phone. I dropped the dime in the slot and dialed home. I caught my reflection in the mirror. I pulled my comb out of my back pocket and ran it through my hair.

Old Rosie answered after two rings. "Honey baby, I'm really sorry," I started out. And then I told her about how I had to drive into Jax Beach to deliver the contracts on a station wagon some deli owner was buying for his business. Sounded completely plausible to me. And it was only half a lie. The guy had come in today looking at wagons. I knew I'd get one of two reactions from Rose: a tongue-blistering like you've never heard, or complete and total belief. But she surprised me. She said in a calm and reasonable voice, "Charlie, I have no idea whether you are lying or not. I did a lot of cleaning today. I even went into Emory's room and cleaned it. And it made me do a lot of thinking. Be careful if you're lying to me, Charlie. Not because of what I might do to you, but because of what the lie will do to you. Now, I've got a nice roast in the oven. It'll be here when you are. It's up to you."

I think that was the damnedest thing I'd ever heard out of her mouth. But I went with my gut reaction. I said, "Now Rosie, of course I'm not lying. As soon as I'm done with this I'll be home." I hung up the receiver and headed out the door.

But her strange words played in my mind again. I began to consider the fact that I could lay lower than the lousiest hound. But why dwell on the negative? I dropped it.

When I got in the Black Beauty, I threw back my head and let loose with a Charlie Looney howl. I started down the road and thought, This kind of freedom is a wonderful thing.

127

The sunset was putting an orange glow on the world as I flew down A1A. Only a few cars out. A good chance to enjoy the ride. I loved A1A. A skinny line of highway snaking past palmetto rushes, swamp, and the Intracoastal on the one side, sand dunes, sea oats, and the ocean on the other. Along the way the dunes would suddenly level out. No trees, man. Not a one. No scrub either. It was in those naked spots a man like myself could see the Atlantic winking fast, flirting—a blue flash and nothing more. It was beautiful.

Traveling A1A made me feel like an astronaut flying through space. Yes, sir. Like I'd just left Cape Canaveral on my own private rocket ship. Just me, old Charlie Looney, flying by the seat of my butt up the East Coast.

I'd been traveling maybe ten, fifteen minutes when I decided to have a beer at this fish-camp bar I knew about. I took a dirt road west off A1A. It wound through the brush and over dunes. A wooden bridge that was only about a foot above the inlet creaked under the weight of the Black Beauty.

When heavy rains, hurricanes, and the like whip through, the bridge washes out. Old Man Potter and his wife sit in their stilt house, stranded, happier than hell, cut off from civilization, watching the water flow underneath their fish-camp shack. They say that when it floods, Potter just opens a window and throws out a line. Must be a pretty good life. Just fishing all the time. And a good woman. I could get used to that. Then I thought, Well—*maybe* I could get used to that.

About five cars were pulled up at the bar. I parked between a pickup and a Harley. A neon JAX BEER sign glowed in the window. The jukebox was blaring Jerry Lee Lewis. He can play the keyboard, but his voice is nothing compared to mine. I can croon it, more like that kid Presley. Better yet, Marty Robbins.

The joint was packed. I checked out the action. Mainly old salts, and a biker and his old lady. In the corner, underneath the fishnet with shells stuck in it, sat a couple of darkies—spooks, niggers, coloreds, Negroes—whatever they're called these days. Seems like every time you turn around they want to be called something different. Don't know why they don't leave well enough alone. Always bitching about something. Seems to me they've got it pretty good.

Ought to stop moaning before they fuck up and make somebody really mad.

I walked over to the bar and pulled up a stool. Mrs. Potter wobbled over. Jesus. She had to be in her seventies.

"What's the story with the darkies?" I asked.

She shot me a look and then studied the bar. She wiped the space in front of me, and it wasn't even dirty. "Don't worry, Charlie. It has already been explained to them that they're welcome to have a drink but their place is not at the bar. The corner only. They know that. They don't bother nobody," she said, and then she flopped a ticket pad down on the bar.

"Hell, I didn't say they were bothering anybody. I just wanted to know if they were regulars or what." The broad was getting bitchy in her old age.

"Dear, you here to eat, drink, or what?" She studied me through her butterfly-wing glasses.

I shot her a big old smile. "Mrs. Potter, I'm here to see your pretty face." I put my hand over hers. She broke out in a giggle like she was a fourteen-year-old debutante. "And while I'm at it I might as well have a Jax draw and two deviled crabs. No, make that three." I winked at her.

Her old face crinkled into a million smile lines. "Oh, you, stop that." She giggled. And then she pulled me a draw.

The biker and his old lady were arguing about whether Galveston or Daytona was a better biker town. They were just having fun. Sucking on some longnecks. Even though they were disagreeing, they seemed to really be enjoying one another. Like the fact that they had something in common to disagree on made them closer. Both were tattooed. The gal had sort of a green rose on her forearm. Not a very good job, I tell you that. That tattoo could not have been done by a professional. I saw something on the biker's forearm, but it was hard to make out. He twisted, reached for his beer. The tattoo wasn't a picture. It was a bunch of jailhouse scrawl. I made out "We the people . . . " Now what do you make of that? A dirtball biker with words all over himself. Man, the world was full of the damnedest things.

Mrs. Potter slid my deviled crabs across the counter. "Thank you, sweetheart," I said. I split open the crabs and poured a good, thick stream of Tabasco down the center of each one. Nothing better than a well-made deviled crab. One of the finest meals on the face of God's green earth. And then because I'd gone and thought about great meals, Rose popped into my mind. She'd probably spent all afternoon cooking me that pot roast. I hated feeling guilty. But I guess I didn't hate it enough.

I paused from my meal and stared dead ahead. A mirror hung on the wall, behind the bar, straight in front of me. In the mirror was the reflection of the two coloreds. I think maybe they were married. Definitely they were sweet on one another. She was laughing and looking at him like he was the biggest deal in town.

Amazing stuff. I mean, I didn't want to stare. Not at all. But see here, the colored girl was pretty. And acting like most women do when they've got the hots for somebody. Making eyes. Smiling like they've got some big female secret us males are just dying to be let in on. Femming and fawing and making the man feel all good. It's a wonderful thing, this male-female stuff. I suppose it does not matter what corner of the earth a man journeys to—if he's worth even half his salt, he'll find love. We have to. It's the way we're made.

I turned 'round. The colored girl was looking at her man with her head tilted, her eyes sparkling, like she was seeing a beautiful dream, like this guy was some kind of salvation for her. I was drawn to those eyes of hers. You know the kind I mean—big and innocent even though they see everything. I checked out their hands for wedding rings. No. They were clean. No rings at all. I turned back 'round. Maybe they were married and were just too poor to spring for the gold. Or—now get this—maybe they were just like baby Pauline and me. Grabbing some fun on the side just to prove they were fucking alive, or something like that. But I didn't like that thought. I wanted them to be married. I wanted them to really love each other. I chowed down on the deviled crabs. Maybe there was some poor colored woman somewhere nearby crying over her cold pot roast and her empty house and her no-good husband.

I looked at my watch. I had to get out of there. Had to beat it down the road and see Pauline. Then I considered the fact that it wasn't too late. I could turn around the lie and just go back home. I looked in the mirror. I wanted just one more glimpse of that pretty colored girl. I scanned the mirror. Catch the reflection. See that happiness again. Hell. They were gone. Didn't even hear them go. No sign of either one of them. That was a disappointment.

Threw a buck on the bar. "Mrs. Potter, don't be cheating on me while I'm gone. You keep a place safe for old Charlie, you hear?" I teased.

She blushed and waved me away. Women never change. Even when they're eighty years old you can make the world okay by just sweet-talking them.

I stepped outside and looked at the sky. The sun had set. Only a few stars were out, because clouds were banking in off the ocean and the wind was picking up. I admired my Black Beauty shining like a monster under the stars. That car made me feel like a rich man, it did. It was the perfect machine. Pistons never failed. Gears never dragged. Could outperform any hot rod driven by any slick-haired, wet-eared kid Tiama could offer. I jogged down the stairs. I smelled rain. Sure as shit, it was going to rain.

In the car, I thought again about the possibility of turning it around and heading home. But I'd come this far. And hadn't the wind sweeping Rosie's note off the bar been a sign? Sure it had.

So I steeled my resolve. I looked at the rain-threatening sky and thought it was a good thing I'd had the sense not to put the top down. I gunned the engine. I flew down the dirt road. Every once in a while the Black Beauty and I indulge in a game of chicken. I know it's dangerous, but it's also a testament to good luck, good fortune, and good wheels. It's like a drug high without the drugs. "Here we go, baby," I purred. As I neared the blacktop, I stepped on the gas. I kept my sights straight ahead, resisting all urges to look left or right. I zoomed out onto A1A, and the speed forced the Black Beauty into a spin. I burned rubber as the world whirled. I laughed good and full out loud, and then straightened her up like an arrow. God damn, smooth as silk—not even a near miss, not another car in sight.

"Hell's bells, lucky again!" I screamed at the top of my lungs as

I barreled down the road. I was alone, and at that very moment, I liked it that way. Just me and myself, except for the occasional flock of pelicans skimming the dunes.

The more I drove, the clearer it became that I had miscalculated how long it would take to get to the motel. With God as my witness, I have no idea how this happened. I knew A1A like the back of my hand. I must have read my watch wrong back at Tippy's. I had been worrying about Rose, I'd been drinking Torpedoes, eating deviled crabs, doing this and that. What can I say? I fouled up.

It seemed like years later when far in the distance, I finally spied the red neon VACANCY sign. I took the Black Beauty up to eighty. Minutes could mean a lot in this situation. I tightened my grip on the steering wheel. "Hold on, Pauline, I'm coming," I said, like my words were going to run on ahead of me.

I steered the Black Beauty into the motel driveway. The glow of the neon reflected off my hood. The sign gave off a constant static buzz, as if a fly was trapped in the curves of its smooth letters, getting zapped again and again.

Driving slow, I looked into each cottage window. See, we have this signal. Pauline always puts a plastic lilac in the window. Our secret language.

I pulled up next to her Caddy and saw the lilac in the cottage window closest to the beachfront. Looked at myself in the rearview mirror. I was none the worse for my journey. I got out of the Black Beauty. The wind was whipping in off the water. It blew sand in my eyes. I had to shade them and let them tear up to clear. I leaned against the Black Beauty, covered my eyes with my hands, and tried to gather my thoughts. The smell of rain was even stronger: it would start soon. It was going to be a hellacious storm. I felt queasy. Fuck. A case of the nerves. I patted my breast pocket to make sure I had my cigarettes on me, then took a deep breath and walked up to the cottage door. The wind was whipping at my shirt. I knew what I had to do. That door wouldn't be locked. I swung it right open and walked in.

The room was pitch-black. I couldn't see a damn thing, but she was there. Old Charlie could smell her—yes I could. Lilacs. The smell filled the room. This was her little game. Find her in the dark. But nature betrayed her. Lightning slashed through the room for a second, maybe less, but long enough for me to see her. One moment stolen. Like a dream. She was standing by the bathroom door in a purple negligee.

"Hide-and-go-seek, I found you," I said, and walked over and grabbed her. She started laughing, and I wrapped her in my arms. She was soft and warm. We kissed.

I was enjoying just standing there smooching on her when she pulled just a little away. "You're late, you son of a bitch," she whispered.

I felt her breasts. I imagined they were full of milk. To drown in warm Pauline DuPree milk—that would be something.

"Now honey, I'm a busy man. I have things to do."

"Yeah, Mr. Big Shot, like what?" She pushed me away and flipped on a lamp.

She was so beautiful. She'd made herself up just right for me. A big hairdo. Her black eyebrows painted on like arches, I loved that. Damn lovely woman.

I began unbuttoning my shirt. I grinned at her. "Woman, you could not imagine some of the things that weigh on my mind. Political concerns. Social concerns. Fucking-you concerns," I said, and we both laughed.

"Well, I'll just have to make you forget all about those first two, won't I?" she said.

And even though she had a wonderful way of flirting, because her flirting wasn't cute—it was sex-filled—my attention kept being diverted from her because of the rain. It was loud. Coming down hard. I didn't say anything for a second. I just gazed at Pauline and listened to the rain pelt the windows. The wind was howling crazy just outside the motel door. A good old Atlantic downpour. For one split moment I imagined being out there naked in that wind, being blasted with blowing sand.

I shook off the image. I decided that Pauline was one of the most beautiful creatures on the face of the earth. She wasn't the best. Rose was the best. But she might have been the prettiest. "You ever think about us, Pauline? About us ever being something more than this?" I reached for her.

She laughed her naughty little giggle and put her arms around my neck. "Hell, no. You and me, Charlie, we're like a couple of fireflies. We go on our merry way 'most all our lives, but then something happens." She traced my lips with her finger. "We see one another and a spark flares in us. Temporary. That's all we are, Charlie. You not feeling guilty again, are you?" she asked, and with her question came her know-it-all tone.

So I decided to let it drop.

"I've missed you, woman," I said. "You stayed away from the car lot all day. What's the deal?"

She picked up a pack of Salems off the dresser. She lit one like she was a movie queen and then offered me a drag. "Absence makes the heart grow fonder," she teased. "Plus I had business in St. Augustine today."

"What kind of business?" I asked. I reached out and played with one of her beautiful curls. But as I played, my hand froze. Her hair reminded me of that colored girl's. Jet-black and stiff.

"My business is none of your business," she said, and winked at me. She had that talent, twisting words. And it seemed like everything she said was soaked in sex.

I heard a pounding on the windows, and I jumped.

"Easy," she said. "It's just the storm. Hail, I think."

"I'm easy, I'm easy," I said. But something was happening to me. And it wasn't just guilt either. It was like a slow-dawning, slippery realization that I just might not be into this. That maybe tonight I really didn't want to lie. I decided to do my thing with Pauline and get out of there. Not hang out. Head on back down the road.

I got undressed and in the sack. And Pauline was like she always was. A hellcat. But I didn't care. I just didn't care. Pictures of Rose kept floating through my mind. I took Pauline in my arms. Nothing backed off. I kissed her. The rain and wind howled louder. I held all Pauline's purple self, all her perfume. I decided holding her was like holding a butterfly, trapping it, making it flutter in my hand. I kissed her and kissed her. The rain pounded the jalousie window. The perfume was drowning me. The smell—sickening, overpowering. She tasted bittersweet, a lilac in my mouth. And you know, it was like I wasn't even there. I just kept seeing Rose's face. Rose's face. Looking calm and honest. And then a weirder-than-hell thing happened. I started thinking about that colored girl back in the bar. It's like I could hear her laughing. I swear to fucking Christ. She was in my head, smiling and preening. Flirting with that man of hers. Being her pretty colored self. Being completely focused on him. Nakedly, honestly loving him. I wanted to run out of the room. I wanted this whole ordeal to end.

And then, there was Pauline saying, "Honey, what is wrong? Well, honey, you've bit your lip clean through."

And I didn't have any idea what she was talking about. But I knew I had to get out of there. Get the faces out of my head, get the voices out of my head.

"Here, put this on your lip." It was Pauline shoving a washcloth filled with ice at me.

I pulled on my clothes. I guess I said good-bye to her. I just don't know. I hit the door, and the rain stabbed me like knives. I was having to fight the rain and wind and sand to get to the Black Beauty. It took my full strength to pull open the door. I struggled, as if I was trapped in the madly beating wings of the storm, just to get inside the safety of the Black Beauty. But I made it. I grabbed ahold of the steering wheel like it was an anchor, and pulled myself in. But the rain was blowing inside the car. The wind whipped in all directions, forcing the car door to stay open. I summoned every ounce of muscle that clung to my frightened bones and began to pull the door shut. But in an instant the wind shifted like a devil dance. The wind slammed the door. I had nothing to do with it. Here, in my own car, I was helpless and cold and soaked to the core. My teeth started up their involuntary chatter, and a pain stung me. I looked in the rearview. My lip looked busted. Jesus—I had bit it myself.

I knew I had to get home. It was the only place I had. I started the car and tried to find my way out of the motel lot. But the wiper blades couldn't keep up with the rain's crazy pounding. Sheet after sheet. No way could I drive in this. But no way could I go back into that motel room. What the fuck was wrong with me? I stopped the car under the neon. I closed my eyes and put my head back. I felt my lip. It throbbed beneath my shaking fingers. The rain hit my hood like it was trying to beat it in, and my head swirled with pictures. That colored girl smiling, winking at her lover. That colored girl raising the beer bottle and drinking, but keeping her eyes on her man. That colored girl reaching over and placing her little hand on top of his. I covered my eyes. And this strange thought floated through me. I thought, Why couldn't I ever just be honest? Thunder cracked and the wind moaned like some kind of angry, hurt bird. Even with my eyelids closed I knew that lightning was firing up the whole stinking world. And then I had another crazy thought: Maybe the only place in the universe it was storming was the Coquina Motel.

And I was completely and mercilessly afraid. Old Charlie was an isolated, two-bit coward sitting in the middle of a storm in a motel parking lot. I saw Rose, worried and sad, sitting at our empty supper table. I saw Rose looking at me with her steady Irish eyes. I saw Rose struggling to be good to me, to be honest with me. But more than anything, I saw Rose trying to trust me. It's the one thing about her that always made me the maddest—her distrust of me. But who in the holy hell did I think I was? Why should I demand she trust me? Just because I was Charlie Looney? Hell, I'd never given her one minute's reason to trust old Charlie. And the more she loved me, the more I treated her like shit behind her back. Maybe I never believed I deserved for her to love me. Maybe, with every tick of the clock, I've resented being loved. That sure was a hell of a thought. One I had no idea what to do with, but a hell of a thought. Every pore of me wanted to get back home, to steer that car right back out on that highway and head home. But I might as well have been paralyzed, because I wasn't going anywhere. I was trapped in nature's storm and my own.

I opened my eyes and stared past the neon sign into the black distance. "Rosie," I said. "Rosie." I was gentle with the perfect sound that formed her name.

But I wasn't sitting at our kitchen table to hear her say, "What, Charlie? What's going on?" All I heard was the thunder echoing across the sky like a long, sad, ancient scream.

Rose Looney

The air in my kitchen was thick with the scent of the apple pie bubbling in my oven. It was a scent that suggested domestic peace, happy homemaking, perfect children, and all that other malarkey.

Well, believe me, the smell of that baking pie belied my situation. Yes, my life was a hell of a mess. I'd taken account of all the evidence. No doubt about it. My husband was having an affair with Miss Pauline DuPree. My son was growing up without his mother or his father. And me? I was in limbo—attempting to find a way to pull my family together. All I knew was, I had to stay steady. If I flipped my lid I might lose again and blow my family even further asunder.

I opened the oven door and closed my eyes to the heat that bellowed out. I lightly tapped the golden crust. I'm notorious for burning pie crust, but I was watching this one like a hawk. It was as if all my bandaged pride and pain was mixed in with those apples—hard apples that would become tender and weak as they cooked—so weak, I hoped, that when the pie was done, the apples would melt in your mouth.

It may sound hysterical, but at that moment I figured that if I burned that pie, my life was finished; I would just give up and stop trying to turn a nightmare into a happy home.

I shut the oven door and checked the clock. I'd give it five more minutes. I heard the dull buzz of Charlie's razor. I was wearing my pink dotted-Swiss dress. Its full skirt had two huge pockets. That's where I'd hidden my secret weapon: Emory's letter. I picked up my glass of iced tea and swirled the cubes around. I tried to imagine my son's face, but all I could see were the pictures of him I'd glued into my photo album. Every time I saw him, he was trapped in a square, held down by four black corners.

Charlie's razor droned. I took out the envelope and studied it. Emory's handwriting was improving. Big *o*s and long *t*s, as if he were confident. I withdrew the letter and read it again, even though I nearly had it memorized.

Dear Mama,
Sorry I haven't written in a while but I've been awfully busy. Believe me, a sugar-cane farm is a full-time operation, and J.W. relies on me a lot. So that's why I haven't done much writing. But I thought I ought to let you know I'm okay.
Big news is, I guess, I've been seeing this girl for a while. You'd like her. She's stubborn like you. And she's got a real pretty name.
I imagine you and old what's-his-name would hardly recognize me—I've really been growing. Thanks for sending me the cash—it comes in handy keeping me in clothes. J.W. says I grow overnight. He gave me his old razor. Went out and bought himself a new one. Said I might as well own it since I was always using it. He's a real character.
With graduation just a few months away, I've been thinking about my future. I'm not sure what I want to do. I know you're proud about me getting my diploma—that was real nice what you said in your letter. But please don't plan on coming down here as I'm not going to be in the ceremony or anything. I hate stuff like that. And as for presents, money would be better than, say, a tie. But like I was saying, I don't know if I'll stay down here. Get a real job. I don't know. The army looks kind of good.
Anyways, I'd better go for now. And remember, you and me, we are still family, no matter what old what's-his-name does. Hope you're okay.

Your son,
Emory

Sometimes I'm too dumb for my own damn good. I should have put my foot down when Charlie sent Emory away. Yes, I should have acted—I should have let Charlie leave rather than lose my son. But no, I let Charlie's hot wind burn me to a crisp. Now somebody else was giving Emory his first razor. "I imagine you and old what's-his-name would hardly recognize me." And his first girlfriend. No telling what kind of trouble that can cause. And all that talk about his future, and his parents are nowhere in it. It was as clear as air to me that all I had left of my son was the letter I held in my hand. But this is the way I'd been thinking ever since my eyes first skimmed the neatly written words: Don't just lay down and take it. Do something. Scheme and plot.

I tucked the letter back into the safety of my pocket. I checked the clock. I pulled on my heat mitten and opened the oven door. The apple filling was boiling up through the holes I'd pierced in the crust with a fork. A few drops had splashed onto the cookie sheet and were burned a deep brown. But my crust, it looked perfect. I thumped it with my unmittened hand. It sprang back firmly, with good shape. The crimped round edges were so precise the pie looked store-bought. I closed my eyes and breathed in a good, clean smell. This pie would hold its shape when cut, I just knew it.

I felt like a fool, but when I opened my eyes they glazed over with tears. And I thought, Yes, I know I'm right. Somehow, some way, we'll salvage a family out of this mess.

I spent most of the afternoon protecting the pie from Charlie's damn fingers. He has this terrible habit. If it's a pie or a cake, he just has to stick a hole in it. He jabs my beautiful baked creations with his index finger and then sucks off whatever happens to stick to him.

"Don't you dare lay a hand on that pie, Charlie. It's for tonight, when we get home," I told him.

"Come on, Rose, just a taste," he teased me. He was standing dripping water onto my freshly waxed floor. The water splattered like little transparent balls on my linoleum. I looked up from my floor and eyed his skinny legs, egret legs that poked out below the white towel wrapped around his waist. My eyes flew to his face. I could tell he was attempting to smile, but it hurt. We'd not been speaking much since he came home with that busted lip. Said to me that he bit himself. And he said how sorry he was he came home late but that he got caught in an awful storm. Said he loved me more than anybody in the whole world. How stupid does he think I am? Not waltzing through the door until midnight. The lip swollen like a melon. I know what it was. It wasn't a storm. He wasn't out on business. He'd probably taken Pauline to some joint and gotten drunk. Ended up fighting with somebody. That's it—another bar-room fight.

But to tell you the truth, what made me even angrier than him sneaking off with Pauline and not coming home for dinner that night was the simple, pure fact that he lied. Now, as he looked at me, trying to smile, that lie stretched between us as big as the ocean that was but three blocks away from the very kitchen we were standing in. I wanted to say, "Does it hurt? Does that busted lip remind you of your lie every time it throbs?" But no. He was going to suffer through this one, not me. I'd stay quiet, but this time he'd be the one to hurt.

Without a word, I'd let the lie swell like a storm tide between us. And just when the undercurrent grew so strong it could sweep him away, I would gather my strength. Power garnered through patience. I'd toss out a lifeline to my floundering husband. I would reel him in. And because, despite himself, he had maintained some semblance of a conscience, he would know, in every pore of his body, that he owed me.

I wiped my hands on my dish towel and then slid them into my luxurious pockets. I pressed my hand against my son's letter. My lucky letter. I smiled. I sensed the tidewaters rising.

"Charlie, after all these years I think I might have finally cooked a perfect crust. The thought of you poking it full of holes is not pleasant." Then I winked at him, just like old times, just as if he hadn't given me some of the most miserable moments of my life.

I was surprised, but he didn't respond. No smart-assed retorts like, "You never complained about me poking you before." In his bare feet, butt naked except for the towel, he walked over to the oven, where I was standing. He looked at the pie and back at me. For a split second I thought he was going to grab my face. Slap me. But no. He reached out his hand and caressed my hair. Haltingly. Gently.

I looked at his eyes. There was a time in my life when I would stare into them and feel safe, as if they presided over all that was beautiful in the world. That was years ago. Since then I'd gotten use to seeing bravado, meanness, or some kind of extreme sensuality I couldn't quite explain.

Yet this time it was none of those things that I saw. I saw fear in those eyes, my Charlie's eyes. I don't know where it came from or why it was there, but by God, this time I was going to be smart; I was going to reach past myself and become a part of his fear.

Then I was going to manipulate it.

Charlie had his heart set on marching in St. Augustine against that colored preacher they nicknamed "De Lawd." According to some, the preacher was coming in to cause trouble. As for myself, I planned to withhold my judgment until I had more information. Maybe the man was okay. I've always contended that the color of a man's skin has very little to do with what's inside him. But around Charlie I contended that very quietly. Nevertheless, Eudora, Luella, and I were going to watch the men march. Charlie had bought a Dixie flag, which he promptly attached to the car antenna, and had gotten a haircut for the occasion. We were sure even TV cameras would be there.

Charlie didn't want Eudora to go. She drives him crazy. "She's going to have that big damn mouth of hers flying the entire way to St. Augustine," he griped.

But I didn't have any choice in the matter. As soon as she read the newspaper headline CITIZENS PLAN MARCH TO PROTEST CIVIL RIGHTS LEADER, she was at my back door asking me what I intended to wear.

Now, no matter what other faults I may have, I'm tasteful. I dress for the occasion. This is not something that came easily to me. I had to cultivate it. I read magazines. For instance, I subscribe to *Wisdom*. They run interviews of people with lofty minds—artists and writers. About three issues back they interviewed that famous Spanish artist Picasso. I don't care much for his painting, but you have to admit the man is smart. So that magazine is for my mind. For fashion, I study the models in *American Homemaker*. You may say, Why not read *Vogue* for fashion? That's a joke. Those models look like damn two-ounce fools. If I waltzed down a Tiama street with some of those clothes on, they'd run me out of town on a rail. No, the women in *American Homemaker*, they're realistic.

Unfortunately, Eudora has never bothered to school herself as I have. And her perception is off. At thirty-nine, she dresses like she's twenty-one. I think it has something to do with Junior being

141

dead. It's as if she can't wait to get her hands on another man, and she thinks the way to accomplish it is to dress like a damn whore.

Now, I'm not being too rough on her. There I am in my sprightly, yet properly mature, pink dotted-Swiss, which also hides the few pounds I've gained over the years. And what does Eudora come through my door wearing? A skintight orange dress that has no straps. No straps. To a protest march. My God. That little girl of hers was dressed more like a lady.

"Jesus fucking Christ," boomed Charlie when he walked into the living room and got an eyeful of Eudora. "What kind of dress have you poured yourself into?"

Instead of responding, Eudora busied herself with her daughter's nasal problems. She pulled a Kleenex out of her purse and covered Luella's nose with it. "Come on, Luella, blow for Mama," she coaxed.

I probably should have kept my mouth shut, but hell no. "Eudora, is that dress new or did you own it fifteen pounds ago?" I asked.

She wiped her daughter's nose as if it had no nerve endings, which of course sent the little girl into a wailing fit. Eudora opened her purse and studied its contents, so she didn't have to look at Charlie or me. I saw her face tighten as if an invisible hand had pulled taut a drawstring, and I knew I'd gone too far.

"Eudora, you look just fine. Don't worry with us. We just like to tease you," I tried.

Eudora pulled herself up. The slumped shoulders unfolded into a correct posture. She turned a defiant and angry face to me.

"This dress cost me almost thirty dollars. I drove all the way to Jacksonville and back for this dress. This dress has style and class, two things you all obviously know nothing about. I am your friend. Therefore, neither one of you had better make fun of me tonight. Or you will regret it," she said. Then she tossed back her head, like she'd really told us off.

"Come on, Eudora," Charlie growled. "Rose said we were just joking."

The last thing I needed was a pouting Eudora on my hands, so I walked over and put my arm around her chicken-thin shoulders. "Hey, we're going to have fun, just us girls. Charlie's going to walk down the street like a big shot, and we'll find the TV cameras and stand right in front of them. The whole damn world will know we were there. Hell, we'll be a part of history," I said. And for good measure I pecked her cheek.

I felt her shoulders relax. She patted my hand and giggled. "You're right," she said. She posed like a fashion model, head high, arms akimbo. "We are going to have a great time. And I'll be there, maybe in the middle of a riot, glowing in my beautiful orange dress."

Charlie grinned at me like he and I were, once more, the conspirators we were in our youth. As if we were the two laughing young lovers making fun of the world—and getting away with it—believing nothing would change, believing we would always be in charge.

I touched his hand and said, "Let's go." He put his arm around me like I was his pal, like I was a buddy he played ball with. It was then that I realized Charlie did not know that our conspiracy—that bond we had darkly created by breaking all the rules—had stopped being fun years ago.

We had suspected the march was going to be a big deal, and we were right. TV reporters and men strapping big cameras were all over downtown St. Augustine. The evening was warm, the breeze gentle with hibiscus, and people were laughing and excited. We could barely drive through the streets it was so crowded. Charlie kept honking the horn like he was wading through cattle. But my God, we were lucky, because we managed to park right across from the Old Slave Market, right where all the action was to take place.

"Look, Charlie," I said. "They're trying to rig up a flag next to the Civil War monument."

The Old Slave Market was teeming with white men in white shirts. The entire plaza seemed unreal—more like a Hollywood set than a park in the middle of town. At one glance everything looked sort of silly and festive. But there was a violence underneath the laughter, that's for sure. The men who were crowded around the monument were shouting directions, none of which seemed to be working. That monument had always made me sad. It honored St. Augustine's citizens who'd fought for the South. It had each dead soldier's name engraved in the silver-gray granite. Surprising to me, many of the names were Spanish. Toward the top were the words OUR DEAD. And then: *They have crossed the river and rest under the shade of the trees.*

It was a beautiful monument. But I didn't know how they thought they were going to manage to fly a Dixie flag on top of it.

Charlie laughed. "Crazy motherfuckers, but more power to them."

He pushed in the car's lighter. "Now Rose, Eudora, Luella, I want you all to stay in the car until I get back. There could be trouble tonight," Charlie ordered as he tapped his Camels against the dash.

"The car, no way. We're going out there with the action," I countered.

"Rosie, absolutely not. We don't know what those hyena-faced niggers might do. All three of you are not to step one foot out of this car. If you do, you'll walk home," he said.

Eudora said, "My God, look at all these people. And policemen, they're everywhere. Ain't this exciting! Charlie, do you think the Klan is going to be here?"

Charlie rolled his eyes. "Eudora, there's one thing about the Klan—what they do you don't see. They're back-alley fighters."

There were an awful lot of police. And even with the carnival-like air, there was also something dangerous about these white back-slapping good old boys. "Charlie, are you sure you ought to be doing this? You could get knifed or something," I said.

"Nobody's going to knife me. I'll kill the son of a bitch first. Now you all stay put and lock the doors," he said, a cigarette clenched between his teeth.

"Hello, Charles, my man. Looks like we've got us a protest march shaping up." It was Foster, a St. Augustine police officer. He was bent over so that he was eye level with Charlie. He offered his hand.

Charlie shook it and nodded his agreement. "Hello, Mr. Policeman. So what do you think, going to be trouble tonight?" he asked.

Foster laughed and straightened up. He fiddled with his massive black belt, which was like a carpenter's apron cluttered with the tools of his trade: billy club, cuffs, gun. "Well, Charles, seems to me that depends on two things."

"And what's that, Foster?" Charlie was getting nervous. I could tell because he was sliding his hands back and forth along the steering wheel.

"Depends on how much shit you white boys try to dish out and how much shit our darkies intend to take. Ain't that right, Charles?" Foster tapped the roof of the car and then, without waiting for Charlie's response, sauntered off.

"Whose side is he on?" snapped Charlie. "That's just great. Now we've got nigger-loving cops." He got out of the car and slammed the door shut. "Stay put," he ordered, and then he was gone, swallowed up in that monster crowd.

"Have you ever seen so many TV cameras! And look, I got us something. I picked them up at the drugstore." Eudora opened her purse and pulled out three tiny Rebel flags. "One for you, one for me, and one for you, sweetheart." Luella grabbed her flag, and Eudora said, "Now you wave the flag, sweetheart, right out the window, when the men march by."

Luella was giggling and repeating, "Rebel flag." I held mine in my lap and looked at the crossed bars and stars. It dawned on me that behind my excitement, which was probably due to all the TV cameras, I really didn't know what I was doing here. I didn't fear colored people. I didn't go to bed at night scared they were going to run us white people into the Atlantic Ocean. "You know, Eudora, maybe all this is wrong. I mean, I wouldn't tell Charlie this, but what's wrong with colored people having the same rights as we do? I've got some colored friends I'd much rather sit across the table from than some of the white trash I know."

Eudora's eyes were aglow. I hadn't seen her this excited since before Junior died. She acted this way when they'd go dancing on New Year's. "Oh, Rose, you know what the scientists say. It's been proven, they just ain't as smart as us. That's all. I like some of them, just like you, but I can't say I want one teaching my baby girl arithmetic."

I looked out at the crowd. Police sirens were wailing. Across the street, between the Old Slave Market and the wax museum, a line of horses mounted by police officers fidgeted and neighed. I wondered if the police horses thought differently, lived their lives differently, than the horses that usually filled the streets around St. Augustine, the ones here for the tourists. Day in, day out, horses drew carriages filled with camera-laden goo-goo-eyed tourists. And the colored drivers in their top hats pulled on the horses' reins and adjusted their blinders and gave them water and accepted tips from the white tourists. Every one of those drivers was colored.

Someone passing the car shouted, "Nigger, go home." I clenched the stupid dime-store flag in my fist. Suddenly I wanted to tear it up. I wanted to head back to Tiama and forget that my husband was out there behaving like a damned fool.

But I was stuck, so to get rid of my frustrations I started in on Eudora. "Listen to me, Eudora. You mean to say that Inez Temple is not as smart as the two of us put together? And if she's so dumb, why do you let her baby-sit Luella for hours on end? Maybe the coloreds are even smarter than us. That's what I think. Maybe they will take over the world, and maybe they should." I sat back in my seat, completely furious with myself and the whole stupid crowd.

"Oh, honey, don't you ever let Charlie hear you say that," said Eudora, but she wasn't concerned with me or my words at all. She had pulled Luella over to the window and was pointing out people and horses and policemen. "Look, Rose, I think they're starting," she said. "Go on, Luella, stick your flag out the window. Wave it. Wave it at the crowd."

More sirens sounded, and I saw a sea of faces, white faces, coming down the street. Suddenly the car filled with a white light. A television reporter was shoving a microphone at Eudora.

"We're on TV, Rose, look. It's a television camera."

"Do you ladies mind if I ask you a few questions?" the reporter asked. He pushed his glasses up the bridge of his nose. Two huge, wild-looking guys were on either side of him, watching the crowd, ready to fight. They were bodyguards. Hired protectors. I wondered who in the world would want to do harm to the reporter. And then I thought, That's an easy answer. The Klan doesn't like answering questions or having its horrible acts exposed.

"Yes," I snapped at him, "we do mind."

"No, go right ahead," oozed Eudora.

Luella stood on her mother's lap with her body hanging out the window and waved her flag. The marchers paraded past the car. Their feet sounded like one long muffled scream against the cobblestones. I couldn't take it. "Luella, child, you stop waving that flag," I said.

A marcher with black hair and pitted skin stopped and patted Luella's head. He laughed and grinned into the camera. He had a crazy shock of hair and some teeth missing. He looked like that cartoon coyote who's funny until he blows up the bird. I shivered. And he purred, "Luella, you just keep waving that flag. Now don't you stop, you hear me?"

Luella giggled madly and Eudora squealed, "My God, he knew her name. He knew your name, sweetheart."

"Why did you ladies come out tonight?" asked the reporter, in his confident broadcast voice. But he was sweating so bad that I knew he was scared to death or from the North—or both.

"Because we're crazy," I said under my breath.

Eudora smiled like a diamond. As if she'd been training for this moment all her life, this half-baked woman was transformed into the essence of poise. My blood boiled. She didn't look at the reporter. She stared right down the barrel of the camera. "We're here fighting to preserve our way of life, a beautiful way of life, not for ourselves but for our little ones, like my little Luella here."

The light snapped off and the cameraman focused on the marchers. One of the bodyguards patted the reporter on the back and said something to him. I couldn't make it out, but I was sure it had to do with how completely stupid Eudora had sounded. Then they waded into the white-shirted ranks of the marchers.

I don't know how many protesters there were. Maybe a few hundred. All men. And many of them—like Charlie—had come in from surrounding towns. I couldn't really understand what their point was or what they hoped to accomplish by walking around downtown. Somewhere in the crowd somebody started singing "Dixie." It caught on and soon all of them were crooning the tune, not like it was the beer-drinking song that it truly was but as if it

147

was sacred. As if they were a bunch of Irish tenors singing a beautiful love song. And Eudora joined in. She waved her flag alongside Luella's. In a high, shaking voice, she sang, "In Dixieland I'll take my stand, to live and die in Dixie." A gentle sea breeze blew, rustling the palm fronds and causing the riggings on the sailboats in the harbor to ring like wind chimes. Eudora turned around to me with tears streaming down her face and said, "Oh, Rose, it's beautiful, ain't it?"

"It's about as beautiful as my fat butt," I growled.

It wasn't long after that that Charlie stuck his head in the window, grinning like a jack-o'-lantern.

"We're showing them now," he announced, and then he was off, like some sort of phantom irritant.

I watched silently as the procession headed up tiny Charlotte Street. Luella and Eudora grew bored with the show and played patty-cake in the backseat. The marchers must have zigzagged up Charlotte and then down St. George, because before long they were back at the Old Slave Market. Somebody began addressing them, but I couldn't make out the words, and actually I was relieved about that. I had already listened to enough stupid, meaningless words in my life. But Charlie was there. Yes, sirree. As if him marching around downtown St. Augustine with a bunch of other idiots was going to make a difference. He actually thought he could stop time, make things stay the same forever. Jesus, he should have known better than that. Charlie, the man who turned a promising marriage into one battle after another. The man who sent his son away without a second thought. He was, I decided, down in the deepest regions of himself, a destroyer. So why did I love him? Why did I put up with a tattered, pitiful excuse of a home life? I no longer had any answers. I sat there twisting my hands, thinking how much fluff all my highbrow family-reuniting ideas were. I heard Luella blow a kiss to Eudora and tell her, in that tiny baby voice of hers, that she loved Mama. I stretched out in the front seat and rested my head on the car door. The wind ruffled through my hair. I felt my dress pocket to make sure Emory's letter was still there.

"Getting tired up there?" asked Eudora.

"Yes, ma'am. I wish he'd get over here," I said. A few people milled about on the sidewalk across the street, but most of them were gathered at the Old Slave Market. I shut my eyes and thought about dozing off but knew it was impossible.

Eudora and Luella were reciting, "Fee, fie, foe, fum, I smell the blood of an Englishman," just as a woman's loud, razorlike shriek sent me bolting upright.

Eudora yelled, "Oh my God, that young man has a gun! There, Rose, by the wax museum."

People scattered like roaches in light, and some hit the pavement. Just yards in front of us, frozen in a stance right out of the movies, posed a handsome young man. I will never forget his face. Black Irish, that's what I think he was. High cheekbones, fair skin, a black mustache, and black, wavy hair. His maroon shirt was open at the collar. Sweat glistened, and his eyes flashed. He waved the pistol in the air. He shouted something, but too many sirens and voices were wailing for me to make anything out. Then he started to shoot. I don't think at anybody in particular—more like he was shooting the sky full of holes.

"Oh my God, he's shooting!" screamed Eudora in delight. Luella jumped up and down.

"Fools, get down." I came up over the seat and pushed Luella behind it. Eudora flew down over her. I slumped down in my seat so that my head was hidden from view. I heard the hooves of police horses pound against St. Augustine's ancient cobblestones. The only safe place was probably within the three-hundred-year-old walls of the fort that loomed giant and dark against the bay. St. Augustine, the city that had been burned time and again by the English and occupied and abused by the Yankees during the Civil War. Only the Spanish and the southerners had treated her right, and I thought, Tonight that's no longer true.

"Is he dead? Did he kill anybody? What's going on?" asked Eudora.

"How in the hell am I supposed to know? I'm not going to get my head shot off," I snapped. "Now where in the hell do you suppose Charlie is?"

"Don't worry, baby, we're okay. Bang. Bang," Eudora told Luella.

"Bang. Bang. He's got a gun, Mommy. The man has a gun," squealed Luella.

"He went that way." I heard a voice rise out of the confusion beyond the car. This was like being blindfolded in a riot. Which way? Which way was he going? Where was Charlie?

A gust blew through the car as the driver's door swung open. The three of us huddled still and frightened. Even little Luella remained quiet. Someone got in the car and the door slammed shut. I kept my face hidden behind my arms. The car seat smelled of booze and tobacco.

"Well, ladies, a bit of excitement tonight." I looked up: Charlie, sweaty and self-important.

"Oh, you!" I said, and the three of us girls burst into giggles. I slugged his arm.

"We thought you were the guy shooting the gun," I said. "You about scared the living pee out of us."

"Now you all stay down. We don't know where that crazy son of a bitch is. I'll get us out of here in no time." Charlie started the car and steadily beeped his horn, then drove slowly through the confused crowd. I slumped in my seat, but not so far down I couldn't see what or who we were driving through.

A cop blew his whistle and pointed at Charlie. He shined his flashlight into the car. "Where are you going?" he asked. He was young. I'd never seen him before.

"We're trying to go home, sir. Trying to get out of here so you men can do your job," Charlie said kindly.

The cop said nothing, but he waved us through.

We sped past the fort and the old city gates. Past the old Huguenot cemetery where Protestant victims of a nineteenth-century malaria epidemic were buried. I remembered the story as to why they were outside and not inside the confines of the city gates. Only Catholics had been allowed burial within the city. All others were required to take their dead someplace else, as if even in death equality didn't exist. And I thought, Maybe nothing ever changes.

Then I said, "Charlie, where in the hell are we going?" He should have taken the Bridge of Lions over to the beaches. We weren't even going in the right direction.

"I'm just driving around until the crowd back there breaks up. Just a little cruising," he said. And I didn't argue, since he was the driver.

But maybe I should have, because before I knew it Charlie had gotten us right smack-dab in the middle of colored town. And I started to say, "Charlie, what do you think you're doing?" But instead I shut up and took notice. Ahead of us on the oak-lined street was a bunch of parked cars. Normally I'd just figure it was a church service. However, under the circumstances, I knew something bigger might be up.

Charlie slowed down. The crickets chirped loud and full. Then another sound began to break through. As we got closer to the church, it grew crisp, clear. It was a man's voice. A colored man's voice. And I knew what I don't think the others did: It was *his* voice. And I can say this: It was beautiful—full and soft but also strong. And for some reason my mind filled with a picture of an orange tree just bursting with fruit.

"Charlie, listen," I said. "It's De Lawd. I know that must be him." On the corner behind a wrought-iron fence was a freshly painted wood-frame church. The yard was well tended. Wisteria and verbena flourished beneath the tall oaks, and wild rose crawled and curled up a white wood trellis. A sign hung over the doorway. In neat, hand-painted letters were the words NEW SALEM PRIMITIVE BAPTIST CHURCH.

"Stop the car. I want to hear," I insisted.

"Jesus Christ, Rose. Why do you want to hear that troublemaking colored?" Charlie growled.

"Because he's important, Charlie. And besides, then you can tell all your buddies about it. You can exaggerate and tell them you went inside and punched him or something."

My husband snarled up his face, but he stopped the car. Luella was tired and fussy. She began to cry.

"Goodness, Rose, this is nonsense," bitched Eudora.

I ignored her. I jumped out of the car, unlatched the iron gate, and walked to the side of the church. The window was wide open. I peered through the screen. I could see everybody, hear everything. Colored men and their wives, balancing pretty little children on their hips. Old coloreds stood alongside young coloreds, and sprinkled throughout the congregation were a few well-dressed white folks. Up near the front was Inez Temple. And sitting next to her was none other than Pat Lackly, the funeral parlor owner. People wafted hand fans painted with pictures of Jesus, or wiped their sweating faces with handkerchiefs. It occurred to me how very stupid our protest had been. These colored people weren't hanging out in the streets, watching us make fools of ourselves. They were in church. They didn't give two flames in Hades for our fanfare, even if we had gotten all the TV reporters up and down the coast to come take our pictures. We had been too cowardly to protest here, in their midst. It was enough to make me ashamed of every white man and woman who had agreed with our "protest march." Enough to make me angry at myself for going along with Charlie's childish hatred.

I raised up on my tiptoes to get a better view, as Charlie walked up behind me. "You're a crazy woman," he whispered.

"Shhh. Listen to them," I said. Men and women, boys and girls, they were swaying back and forth and answering the preacher De Lawd.

I pressed my face into the screen—I wanted to get a good look at him. He was younger than I'd imagined, and there was something about him I liked. I think it was his eyes. They looked gentle. Peaceful. Like they saw past this world. His sweet voice rose up.

"I hear they are beating you," he sang.

"Yes. Yes," came the answer, as pure and sure as a church choir.

"I hear they are cursing you."

"Yes. Yes."

"I hear they are going into your homes and beating you."

"Yes. Yes."

Then his voice trembled like a cymbal, and I was enthralled. "Some of you have knives, and I ask you to put them up. Some of you may have arms, and I ask you to put them up. Get the weapon of nonviolence, the breastplate of righteousness, the armor of truth, and just keep marching."

I was amazed. The people, solid and unified, cheered De Lawd. He was telling them not to be violent, not to shoot guns, and they,

152

with one voice, cheered, "Yes. Yes." They clapped their hands and stomped their feet. They hugged one another, and De Lawd looked on them from behind that rickety pine pulpit, and I decided those words that poured from his sweet face were healing words. This man wasn't preaching hate. He wasn't a troublemaker like everybody had been saying.

Charlie groaned. I shot him a look, immediately mad at him. His face had gone chalk pale, as if he'd just been hit solid and hard. I thought it was because De Lawd wasn't a monster after all, and Charlie had figured he was going to have to do some explaining to himself. But his gaze was so fixed, so strange. Something else was going on. Maybe he was surprised to see Pat Lackly there. I looked in the direction of his stare. The pine pews were filled, as were the aisles. Charlie seemed to be looking off to the right. Inez and Lackly were up front on the left, so it wasn't them he was shocked by. Most people were standing and clapping their hands. Some were accentuating the general excitement with amens. Since their backs were to us, it was difficult to tell who was who unless you knew them real well. But then I saw this colored man next to a white woman. I thought, That's it, Charlie thinks there's some mixing going on. I looked back at my husband. He sure appeared stunned. I looked back at the colored man, a young buck. Actually, I've always found colored men attractive in an exotic sort of way. The white woman's brunette hair was done up in a bouffant. I strained on my tiptoes to get a better view. Sure enough, they were holding hands. I watched, fascinated. They were just two strangers I was spying on, until they turned to each other. They smiled, and she reached up and gave her buck a kiss. Right on the lips. My heart swelled. Suddenly I was no longer aware of anyone else in the New Salem Primitive Baptist Church. Not even De Lawd. Because the woman doing the smooching was Pauline. Pauline DePree kissing a colored man in front of my Charlie. What sort of wonderful God would be so kind to me, I thought. I wanted to dance, to jump up and down, to laugh deliriously, but I knew better than that. The colored man gazed down at her, just like he was in love. He withdrew something from his shirt pocket and touched her face with it. A plastic lilac.

The ride home was quiet. Eudora and Luella dozed in the back-seat. Charlie stared stonily ahead, driving, wrapped in the black silence of A1A. I engaged not a soul in conversation. Let the tide-waters rise, I thought, but when I heard the words in my head, they were spoken not by me but by De Lawd.

It was time for me to be the all-consoling, all-understanding wife. Never was there a better trap. There would be no "I told you so." No "Now maybe you'll grow up and behave like a decent husband." I had bigger fish to fry.

As we drove into Tiama, I broke the silence. I softly put my hand on Charlie's thigh. "Sweetheart, when we get home, why don't you carry Luella in for Eudora. That way the poor child won't have to wake up."

He nodded his assent, but he didn't say a word. I do believe he was shaken to the core. The streetlights along Beach Boulevard dispelled some of the evening's shadows. I could see Charlie's face clearly now. Weariness or shock or both had deepened the age lines. His face muscles were so slack I imagined they might slip right off his bones, and I had to look away because my face was itching to burst into an ear-to-ear grin.

We pulled up in front of our house and Charlie shut off the ignition. I looked across the street and, because the moon was hidden by some clouds, the prison appeared unreal—almost like a shadow. I shook Eudora gently. She woke up looking like her true self: dazed and tired. I watched as Charlie gathered little Luella into his arms. Briefly a memory flashed in my head. The baby girl I'd lost. She would be Luella's age. My little sweetheart who never even had a chance at life. I started in on an old refrain: If I'd just never gone to that ball game that hot summer day, if I'd just stayed home, if I'd just taken better care, if I'd just— I battened the memory back down. I fished my house keys from my purse. Some things are best never remembered or reconsidered, because they are unchangeable and forever painful.

But not my Emory; him I could do something about.

I unlocked the front door and entered my home. I tossed my purse on the couch, kicked off my shoes, and headed straight for the kitchen. I put on a pot of coffee and then moved my beautiful, perfect pie from the kitchen counter and placed it smack-dab in the middle of the table. Pie plates, forks, server. I took down two shot glasses and pulled the Jack Daniel's bottle out from behind my baking utensils. My secret stash so Charlie don't drink it all.

The front door opened. "I'm in here," I called. He mumbled something, and then I heard him go into the bathroom. I poured the shot glasses full of liquor. I poured the good, strong coffee into our cups. Be calm, I told myself.

I sat down at the table and lit a cigarette. I jiggled my foot, a nervous habit. I felt to make sure Emory's letter was still in my pocket.

The toilet flushed. The bathroom door squeaked on its hinges. "Come on in and have some pie," I called.

The man looked beat, just beat, as he sat down. "Well, that was quite a night," he said, but his tone was kind of like that of a whipped dog. He poured his shot of Jack Daniel's into his coffee. "Thank you, Rose, this is good," he said.

"Well, let's see if my prediction about this pie is true." I picked up the knife and poised it over that lovely tan crust. Then Charlie Looney surprised me. He touched my hand.

"No, let me. I'll cut it," he said, and the words were almost gentle. I handed him the knife and his hand trembled. I put my hand over his. My little silver wedding band had held up through these years. It still shined. I looked him in the eyes, but his gaze was on our hands. "It's going to be okay, Charlie, I promise," I whispered.

His jaw set tight, and he nodded. I watched, fearful, as the knife's tip disappeared beneath the crust. Swiftly Charlie had cut two nice triangles. I slipped the pie server into the pan. I lifted the piece. There she was, a firm, golden apple pie. "I did it, Charlie. It's not falling apart or anything."

"Your pies have always been fine to me," Charlie said. He was trying to be nice, and I was pleased.

I broached the subject. Softly I asked, "You still going to work at that car lot?"

Charlie set his fork down. He put both elbows on the table. He looked down at the pie. "Rosie, I didn't know how to tell you this, but I quit the lot two days ago. Been scoping things out for the band. I'll book us more jobs, and if things get rough, I don't know. There's another car lot in town."

Two days ago. Well, that was news to me. Welcome news, but still I wasn't very pleased that he hadn't told me. "Why'd you quit the car lot?" I asked, struggling to keep the knives out of my voice.

He took a deep breath and looked off into space. I knew when he spoke his words would be dripping in irritation. But no. Instead he just sounded tired. "Honesty, Rose. I decided I couldn't be honest and work there."

I had no idea what that meant. Since when did my husband acquire a sterling conscience? So I said, "What, did you and Miss DuPree have a fight?"

"God damn it, Rose, it had nothing to do with Pauline and everything to do with you. So get off my back about it. Okay?"

He looked like a little hurt boy who was confused but still trying to behave despite himself. I almost felt sorry for him. But hell, he deserved it. I felt like God, on my behalf, had kicked him right in the balls. But I knew now wasn't the time to rub it in. I had to stay focused. I had to get this conversation back on track.

He finished his pie in about three mouthfuls, but I said to myself, Don't nag, don't push. "More coffee?" I asked.

"Sure. The pie was great," he said lamely.

I poured the coffee and filled the shot glasses. "It's sure good to be home," I said casually. "You and me, Charlie, age is catching up with us. It's like, with a snap of the fingers, we're not spring chickens anymore."

Charlie managed a smile. "Oh, we'll always crow," he said.

But I didn't respond. I just sat there and stared at him, steadily, steadily. I looked at his bruised lip and then into his green eyes that had lost their bravado. If he'd been his old self he would have yelled at me, slapped me, knocked over the table, something. But he just sat there, taking it, drowning in it.

I reached into my pocket and withdrew Emory's letter. With all the strength I had in me, I threw out my lifeline; I tossed the letter

156

onto the table. "That's from Emory," I said. "Our son, our one and only child. It's time, Charlie. I'm calling Emory home."

Charlie looked at the creased envelope. He moved his hand toward it, but then stopped. He looked away from me, out the window, but I knew he couldn't see anything; it was too dark.

Then, in the quietest voice I'd ever heard Charlie Looney use, he said, "Thank you, Rose. You're a good wife."

Emory Looney

I knew if J.W. ever caught me he'd kill me. "The niggers don't come in the house." That was like the first rule he issued when I showed up here. But what he don't know won't hurt him—that was my motto. That's why it was a complete and thorough source of joy for me to see my Soleil Marie's pretty little feet propped up on J.W.'s coffee table. Every so often she'd wiggle her callused toes or rub one mosquito-bit foot with the other. Or she'd take her feet off the table and retrieve the *TV Guide* from underneath the couch where J.W. kept it hidden. Then she'd stretch out again, each bare and dirty foot silently announcing that Soleil Marie behaved—much to J.W.'s outrage, if he had known—as if this rambling old house belonged to her.

But see, despite my thrill at Soleil Marie's presence in my uncle's house, I really wasn't taking a risk. J.W. had gone fishing with Earl Reynolds. I knew he wouldn't be back until dark, and by then Soleil Marie and me, we'd be gone. We'd be at the Dog Days Carnival in Clewiston, riding a carousel or eating cotton candy or kissing behind a rusty hot-dog stand. In my pocket were tucked the keys to J.W.'s jeep. Underneath my arm was curled Soleil Marie. In my wallet were two crisp tens I'd earned with my own two hands. All of which added up to the ingredients for a perfect date.

Unfortunately, however, Soleil Marie had this thing about TV.

157

Oh, I understand it, since she was poor and strange. But ever since I first snuck her in the house, I had a hell of a time getting her attention away from the boob box and centered on me. She loved the commercials. "Plop, plop, fizz, fizz. Oh, what a relief it is," she'd sing loud and off key. In no time at all, it seemed, she knew the words to the commercials' songs, and sometimes she'd even speak along with the actresses. That's a spooky memory, if you ask me—being able to see a commercial once or twice and then have it memorized. And right off, before I even showed her where J.W. kept the *TV Guide* hidden, she knew where it was. Her hand went straight underneath the couch and pulled it out.

We were watching the *Afternoon Matinee,* "brought to you by Big Thirteen, your station that cares." It was a movie filled with people dressed in fancy clothes, drinking champagne and such. Some lady with her midriff showing waltzed around this stage, first shaking her shoulders and then her hips and then everything, and all the while she kept a towering basket of fruit balanced on her head.

"Now how come that fruit doesn't come tumbling down?" I wondered.

Soleil Marie arched an eyebrow at me. "Women where my mama comes from, we carry anything we want, yes, on our heads."

"Oh, you do?" I knew she was bullshitting me. "Like what? I bet you couldn't carry any fruit basket on your head."

Soleil Marie loved being challenged. Her eyes lit up like firecrackers. Her feet flew off the coffee table and she stood up. She surveyed the room. In a pile on the floor next to J.W.'s recliner was a stack of old *American Sportsman* magazines. She picked up all that she could carry and rose like a queen. She placed them on her head. She began to walk. She was the Statue of Liberty with a tower of magazines as her crown and thin air for a torch. She glided across the room. A movie-star smile spread across her face. She spun around. Miss Lake Okeechobee, my beauty queen, stopped in front of me. She pursed her lips and slit her eyes—the way actresses do when they are trying to be sexy. Then she let loose with a shimmy. It was a good one too. But the magazines fell to the floor like lead-filled ducks.

In between our laughs, as we picked up her mess, I said, "Come

158

on, Soleil Marie, we need to finish our Cokes. We're never going to get to the carnival at this rate."

Right then this commercial came on that she knew. She patted the magazines into a neat stack as she watched the tube. The actress looked like the all-American mother—the kind who never yells at the kids when they fight and scream and cry and smear mustard all over her draperies. Soleil Marie brought on this high voice and mimicked, "Oh, please, Mr. Smith, help me. How can I ever get the stains out of my husband's collars?"

Then she cast a sideways glance at me. "Your mama, she's like that?" she asked.

"My mama? No. My mama is hell on wheels. Except when it comes to the son of a bitch, and then she's got all the spine of a wet dishrag."

"Son of a bitch—you mean daddy? Your mama won't stand up to your daddy?"

Soleil Marie was always trying to do this to me, to pry into my family business. "Yes, I mean my daddy." I was in none too good of a mood to talk about any of that stuff now. I wanted just a fun afternoon. I didn't need for the son of a bitch, even when he was two hundred miles away, to make me miserable. I stood up and went over to the TV. "Now come on, Soleil Marie, you've got five more minutes of television time and then we're going. Don't you want to go to Clewiston?" I started switching channels. The TV flashed out different shades of light as I whipped through the stations.

"Stop, stop, stop," she blurted out like a BB gun. "Walk back to that other channel. What you just passed."

"The one we were watching?"

"No. Walk two turns back."

"The word is 'go,' not 'walk.' " I flipped the channels. A picture blossomed on the screen.

"There. Going on there, now what is happening?" she asked me.

I stepped back. I studied the scene. I wasn't really sure. An ocean of people, colored and white, but mostly colored, filled the screen. It was a demonstration of some kind, for sure. The marchers carried neatly printed signs, not last-minute sloppy jobs. I read some of them out loud: " 'We march for jobs for all now!' 'We demand

159

voting rights now!' 'UAW says: End segregated rules in public schools.' " I wasn't sure what "segregated" meant. I read another one: " 'We demand decent housing now!' " That one got me. Decent housing. For like two seconds a picture of Soleil Marie's house flashed in my mind. No toilet. No real kitchen. Just walls and space. I turned the sound up.

"They are calling it the March on Washington," the announcer said. "Organizers estimate that more than two hundred thousand persons have marched to the Lincoln Memorial—one hundred years and eight months after the Emancipation Proclamation. It is important to note that, despite this tremendous sea of people, thus far there has been no violence."

"My people," Soleil Marie said, "marching for good lives, them?"

"Yes, ma'am, that's what they're doing."

"Uncle's Boy, sit down," Soleil Marie said like her life depended on it. "To see this I need."

My Sweetness looked at me with a face filled with amazed confusion. "What is this Emancipation Proclamation?" she asked.

"You don't know about *that*? President Lincoln and the slaves and all that. You don't know about it?"

"And who was going to teach me, Uncle's Boy? Your uncle while I bundle his cane? He's going to tell me about freed slaves, me?" She pulled her hand away from mine. Boy, she could get angry fast.

"Jesus, Soleil Marie, I'm not putting you down or nothing. I just want to know about you." I set my gaze to the TV and was half tempted not to speak to her because her tone had made me mad. But then I thought, Emory, that's kind of childish: getting mad just because she was. So I tried again. I said, "You mean that after you were born and old enough to walk and all that, you went to work in the fields? You never went to a schoolhouse where they taught English and math and history and all that stuff?"

Soleil Marie looked down at her work-beaten hands, those hands that should have been smooth and pretty like the ladies' hands on TV. And then she burst into tears.

Great. Now I'd made her cry. I could be a fool sometimes. Why hadn't I figured out on my own she'd never been to a real school? Here I was, a brand-new, big-deal high school graduate, and my

Sweetness hadn't been to school a day in her life. What had I been thinking she was doing while I'd been spending my mornings at Okeechobee High? Hell, she'd been making money for J.W. I thought about those other migrant workers. How they built make-shift tents out of old cloth in the fields so their babies could play in some shade. I thought about the ten- and eleven-year-olds. How they were out every day working beside their parents. I had never once given them any regard. I had been so tied up with hating the son of a bitch and figuring out ways to get past J.W. that I had been utterly and totally oblivious to the people who were, when you got right down to it, my coworkers.

I couldn't believe how stupid I'd been. I glanced at my Sweetness. She wasn't crying anymore. She just sat staring at that wave of people on the tube. I touched her face, but she kept her eyes swung far from mine. "Why, Soleil Marie, I bet you can't even read."

"No," she shot, tough, like her insides were filled with nails. "I can't read your white people's newspapers or your white people's books. But I know more about those fields and swamps, more than you'll ever dream about, Uncle's Boy." She tossed the words, and her eyes stayed away from me. She pouted her lips out.

Now, since leaving Tiama and the son of a bitch, I had begun to discover some things about myself. Most important, in this in-stance anyway, was my tendency toward action. I hated to admit it, but J.W. may have been partially responsible for that. When we'd eat together he'd spear his catfish with his fork, then hold it in midair. He'd wave its breaded body at me. "Action, Emory, is everything. If you don't like something, act to change it. Take me, for instance. Born butt-poor, but I acted. I acted through hard work, and it brought me this cane farm."

J.W. with his breaded catfish was on my mind as I leaned over and kissed Soleil Marie's cheek. "Listen to me, Soleil Marie." Suc-cess through action. "I'm going to teach you to read." I plunged on before she had a chance to shoot something mean at me. "Now this isn't nothing to be ashamed of. Take me, for instance: I can't add my way out of a paper bag. But reading is different. You've got to know how to do that. Like these colored folks on TV. Why, every one of them can read. That's why they are out there demonstrating. They want"—I was getting lost—"they want to read even better. Why, hell, you'll catch on in no time. Before you know, we'll be sneaking up in old J.W.'s bed while he's out fishing. We'll be between the covers and you'll be reading the Sunday papers to me."

"From Uncle's bed I'll read to you?" The gleam was back in her eyes. She loved being devilish.

"Hell, yes. We'll read all about all this freedom you folks are getting."

Soleil Marie was okay after that. Convincing her to let me teach her to read had been only a matter of phrasing it correctly. We stayed on the couch like that for a while, watching the march, me holding her hand. Sometimes I'd tell her bits and pieces to help her understand—like I explained about Lincoln signing that piece of paper setting slaves free. I spoke quiet, though, because when a person reveals something deep about themselves, a secret nobody else knows, well, they're vulnerable. Soleil Marie was a woman swarming with pride. Secrets don't come gracefully out of those kind. But now I knew something about her that said a lot. Not even being able to read. Working her hands until they bled for my fat-cat uncle, and she couldn't read.

I watched the events unfold on TV. A colored man with a ringing voice spoke to the massive field of people. I hadn't paid much attention to all this civil rights stuff. I mean, at that point, I never knew if things really changed, nor did I really care. I was all wrapped up in my own problems. Civil rights, for all the few seconds I had thought about it, was something that concerned people far removed from me. But suddenly, with my Sweetness's revelation, what these marchers were trying to accomplish took on new meaning. I looked at her. Glued to the TV. I brushed her cheek. "Come on, baby, enough of this. It's almost four o'clock. We'll think about it all later. Let's go to Clewiston."

She nodded her head okay. I went to turn off the TV, but I just couldn't. I decided to let that colored man's voice fill up J.W.'s house. I imagined the voice washing away every shadow and filling every glass and mug. In my heart of hearts I wanted it to press against the house walls like a tidal wave, and I wanted J.W. to walk in the house and be overwhelmed and beat by it.

Soleil Marie brushed my hair off my forehead as I stood at the front door getting the keys out of my pocket. I imagined the colored man's words rushing in watery, foaming waves over the couch and bed and curtain and hi-fi. As the deadbolt clicked into place I heard him: "I have a dream."

Soleil Marie Beauvoir

Carnival. Uncle's Boy, he wanted to go so bad to this, it meant so much to him. But you know, if truth be told, it mainly scared me. I mean, I can survive anywhere. But every person on this earth has a place she'd rather be at. Me, yes, I guess I preferred my fields and swamp. But I was paying the cost of pleasing Erzulie so well. I'd gotten Uncle's Boy. Now I had to do things with him I not always wanted. Like Carnival.

Before I snuck up to the Big House, spying through the palmettos to make sure Uncle was gone, I lit two candles. I lit one for Erzulie. Keep her happy. I lit one for *loa* Papa Legba, for good times. He was a party man, yes.

Now, my Uncle's Boy, I love him. Pretty as the sun that boy. And excited. To talk to him someone would have thought Carnival was important. They'd think, "Oh, Carnival. Must be mystery, love, good times, like Feast for the Dead." But knew better, me. See, many times I watched, I studied these things when I passed through the cities. Cities always have like a big party. Lights, people, music, food. But never once does the people think, "Souls, they are here. I beat this drum, I blow this horn for my passed papa or sister or aunt." No, believe me, this they never do.

What was up I didn't know. But the morning of Carnival, when I was lighting those candles, these two mockingbirds, you see, they

163

flew from the skies, rested on my porch, watched my hands they did. I looked at their bodies. So pretty, shaped like swollen arrows. To them I said, "Welcome." Who these birds were I didn't know. But mockingbirds don't fly up every day and watch me light candles, no. So I said to myself, Soleil Marie, something could be up. A breeze blew through. I sucked in as much of the clear wind as I could. I wanted it to sit in my body. Swirl through, find my heart and my bone, I told the breeze. The two mockingbirds right then, lifted wings through the air, them. Then I knew. I opened my mouth so the breeze could leave. Believe me, yes, I felt the sign was definite. Change was coming.

It was these things I considered as Uncle's Boy put me in the jeep and carried us to Carnival. Maybe the change had to do with what Uncle's Boy and I saw just before we left the Big House. This man was on the television, with skin like mine. They kept calling him a king—which confused me because he talked like he was from America, and here they don't have kings. But he stood before what seemed like a million people. And in a voice that, really now, was a song, he tells them that people like me, important we are.

He was talking with some words Uncle's Boy had to explain to me because sometimes, yes, my language is not so good. But I got the man's message. This I did. He talked with a good, full hope that me and all my people could be happy one day.

Now true this is: I love my fields and my animals and my Uncle's Boy, but there were things to think about, yes. Like this, I thought: We are loving these fields all day so Uncle can rest in the Big House, and he don't even let us use a real toilet. We have to walk far and go behind a tree. That means we lose work time. That means he can hold back some coin from us. I grew kind of mad at myself. Maybe Uncle needed some earful.

I wanted to know the nature of everything the man on TV said. You know, like it is when your eyes are closed and you bite into a ripe, pink plum, you know what that fruit be. You know its color and its feel. You know its juice and its flesh. You understand it from the inside out without even having to open the eyes. That's how I wanted to be with the TV man's words. So I says to my

Uncle's Boy a desire I'd been wanting. I says to him, "Teach me to read, Uncle's Boy."

Yes, these thoughts were lightning before my eyes as we flew in the big jeep. My Uncle's Boy turned on the radio so loud I'm sure the clouds could hear it. But yes, I kind of liked this music. This guy was singing this song about the night having a thousand eyes. And I thought, Yes, that is true.

"Who is singing?" I asked.

"Bobby Vee," my Uncle's Boy shouted back. He knew everything, no, about music.

Bobby Vee. Bobby Vee. I would try to remember that name.

Uncle's Boy, he liked to drive with a hand on the wheel and a hand on my knee. I patted that hand that was resting on me. The wind whipped hard on our faces, but that is a feeling I like. I pushed my face into the wind, my eyes stayed open wide, sometimes tearing. The glades, I watched them thicken into firm land. Swamps floated past like watery clouds, and the palmettos clustered out bigger and bigger until no more was there swamp. Just highway and concrete. And then not too far off, above the oaks and palms, I saw it. Pink, green, and yellow dots. Carnival. The dots moved across the sky. I watched, trying to see each one by itself, not wanting to let them bleed into one another—the bleeding is an old eye trick. Important it is to see a thing's own pattern, not let the eye trick confuse one dot for another. As Uncle's Boy drove closer, I saw the dots were colored light bulbs screwed into a huge wheel. People sat in bright-colored swings that hung from the wheel. Fun they was having, yes. I could see some smiles.

"Soleil Marie, that is a dandy of a Ferris wheel and we are going to ride it," Uncle's Boy said. He parked far off from other cars. Scared of Uncle, that's what he was. Somebody might scratch the ugly old jeep. "Now I want you to be careful. Gypsies work these carnivals. They'll steal you blind faster than you can blink."

"Gypsies?" I liked the music in the word. It sounded not thick and solid like American words. It sounded, no, like a music burned with spice.

"Yeah, you know. Those thieves who wear lots of scarves and look like dusty ni—"

165

My Uncle's Boy fast stopped his words, stopped just like one of those gypsies stole his voice.

"Dusty what?" I asked.

His face blazed real dark. "Nothing. Just forget it." Then my Uncle's Boy, he jumped out of the jeep. He walked to my side. This is something he taught me. A gentleman, he claims, always opens the car door for his lady. Me, I first thought, See, this is stupid. Here I sit like Mrs. Zombie, not moving, until he opens the door. But now I like it. I'm not a zombie waiting for the open door no more. Now I think, Queen Soleil waiting for the good man to behave with kindness.

He opened the door, but no offering of the hand like usual. No, instead, those eyes of his, they shifted left, right. There was no choice. On my own I got out of the jeep.

I would have put this in my mind, pondered it 'round and 'round, except for this place. This Carnival. It could enter the mind and blow all else away. You see, there was music. Not like my drum music. Not even like Bobby Vee. This was high music, touching the upper body. Made the brain think happy things. See, the drums, they touch the low body. They make the hips rumble. It is the body and the sex and the soul the drums please. But here, at Carnival, the music was like wind blowing its way through a tin pipe. And everywhere was these noisy little children dressed in shorts and tiny cotton shirts. And their parents looked just the same, but bigger and drained. Everybody was hungry. It was like food danced in every hand, was jammed into every mouth. Uncle's Boy had to tell me the names of the food, because the way I live, my people and I have never to eat like that. Cotton candy—it was stiff balls of color just like the same, yes, as the light dots on the big wheel. Then there was corn done to many ways: popcorn, corn dogs, corn fritters.

"We're going to eat good tonight, Sweetness," Uncle's Boy said. He grabbed my hand. He started up to a trailer painted pink and yellow. A banner—red, white, and blue—draped across the trailer's whole side.

"See that"—Uncle's Boy's pointed—"that banner says 'Tickets.' "

I glared at the word. Glared at each and every letter. I wanted

166

to never forget their order. See, a good student is what I would be, learning every word. I stood there, yes, glaring at the word, and then a nest of little children, they walked us by and two of them— girls—they put their grimy hands to their mouths and giggled as they looked. Three of the others pointed fat little fingers at Uncle's Boy and me. The tallest one, he had brown hair cut so short I could see his brain skin, he yelled, "Mama, Daddy, look. That man's holding a nigger's hand!"

Fast, like I was shit, Uncle's Boy dropped my hand. "What, what?" I asked him.

"Soleil Marie, don't start. This is not a good place. Just walk to the ticket booth like no big deal." Then my good man, my Uncle's Boy, he walked away from me. Straight to the booth he went. Not waiting for me, not touching my skin the way he so always does. I wanted to hit him. But then my eyes, they looked around. A string of white men there between me and the trailer. They was sneering at me over pink and blue clouds of cotton candy. Quick, like a bee sting, I shot to Uncle's Boy's side.

In his hand he wiggled a string of tickets so long it reminded me of my dog's tongue when hot and thirsty she is. We walked into the crowd, away from the sneering whites. "Now listen to me, Soleil Marie, we're going to have to cool it while we're here. You understand? No touchy-feely until we get back to the jeep." My Uncle's Boy, he looked kind of nervous, and I says to myself, This sweat on his forehead, this is not heat sweat but nerve sweat.

"I'm not scared of these stupid people," I said, in my queen voice. But as I said it, eyes, I could feel a thousand of them from everywhere, staring at me. It was like we was wearing flaming clothes sizzling so bright and hot that they caused the crowd's eyes to be burned into us. I looked at him and smiled, but inside me, yes, I was angry. I sang to him real quick, sweet as sugar, "The night has a thousand eyes." I laughed, but Uncle's Boy, miserable he looked.

"I mean it," he snapped. Jaws like a 'gator, I thought. I wanted to push him, push that whole "nigger" idea, push him for not being my grand man. Why didn't he, my Uncle's Boy, tell those people

167

wrong they were? But see, many voices I have. Another voice inside me spoke. Calm down, Soleil Marie, it said. Just keep that sweet smile on the face.

So we went on. Uncle's Boy bought me a corn dog. Hot paper, that's what I thought it tasted like. Uncle's Boy ate it like that boy he'd never eaten before. "Good stuff," he marbled, his mouth full of hot paper.

"Tell me when you want to do something," he said in my ear as we walked, people's eyes still on us. But less concerned was I growing with their stares, and more with what I saw. All these trailers painted in beautiful colors: pinks, greens, reds, yellows. Flower colors. And all blinking with light bulbs. On one was painted a big woman, big. Except a beard she had. I caught my breath. See, I know about these things. Probably this happened. Probably her parents dead. Probably she never saw them to the other side the right way. She probably made the dead parents angry. So, pop, one morning awake she is. And to the mirror. And there, her parents' hurt and anger growed all over her face, a beard.

We moved on. I tried to make sure I saw every sight, smelled every smell. But the smell, mostly sawdust it was. Then screaming I heard. I turned.

"It's the House of Horrors," Uncle's Boy said.

"House of Horrors?" I heard shrieking. The house was painted with evil *loa*. Black magic, yes.

"Yeah, you know, you ride through there on one of those little cars and they scare the shit out of you. Come on, let's go in."

Now this I could not believe. These people, no wonder they were mean. Only sick, bad things come to people who play with the evil *loa*. I turned from the sound and the horror house, but what do I see? The trailer side painted with a snake. A huge snake, fat, with bad *loa* eyes. A man with red hair and beard and a hat stood on steps that entered the snake pit. "See the largest snake in the free world. It will amaze you, thrill you. See the snake that weighs over three hundred pounds. You will never be the same." That was it. A snake spirit in the face of evil. Snake spirits on their own, not bad are they. But these people, they had this snake in prison, and right across from the *loa* house. These people playing with darkness.

They were conjuring the evil. I had to take care. I bent down and grabbed as much dirt in my two hands as I could. I threw one handful on Uncle's Boy for protection. Then threw one on me. "Run, you got to run," I screamed.

Through the crowd I flew. So scared I was the evil was on my heels. I saw the sneering and surprised faces blur past me, all one long sneering face they became.

"What in hell has gotten into you?" I heard Uncle's Boy, his voice flying up from behind me. I felt his hand grab my arm. The force—him pulling me to a stop and me struggling to go on—it caused me, my whole body to jerk around. "What are you doing?" He shook my shoulders.

"Your eyes are blind," I said. "You never saw the evil back there. You just never saw."

Uncle's Boy did that thing he does when he's confused. He wiped his hand over the face, his. Then the top teeth bite into the lip on bottom. He let out a big breath and looked away. Three seconds. Then he turned back to me. "Okay, Soleil Marie, let's just go to the midway and ride the rides. No more bearded ladies or horror houses or anything." He touched my arm, but didn't my hand hold. We walked in the direction of the big wheel.

"You ever ride rides at a carnival before?"

No, I shook my head.

"Well, we're sure as hell not going on any where you could flip out on me again," grumbled him. He started to beat his shirt, there where I throwed the protecting earth.

"Don't," I ordered. I made my eyes firm, the voice loud. And my Uncle's Boy, he stopped.

The midway, as Uncle's Boy called it, beautiful it was. Not like those trailers painted with evil. Here it was all rides, studded in colored lights. People's hair flying as they swung or spun through the air. Smiling, giggling faces. "This is more like it," I said to him. And him, he grinned real big, like I had pleased him.

"We can ride as many rides as your heart desires," he said. So I took them in. I studied each one, seeing how much fun they would be. But my eyes always drifted back to the big wheel.

"That one," I said. I pointed at it. It traveled through the sky.

The sky—its blue and white clouds—was beginning its slow walk into night, but the wheel just traveled on, in place. Spinning, going nowhere, while the sky walked into shadows.

"The Ferris wheel it is. You aren't scared of heights, are you?" he asked.

"What do you mean?"

"Like when you're high up in the sky. Does it scare you?"

I laughed at my Uncle's Boy. "Didn't you know, Uncle's Boy, at night I fly."

He narrowed his eyes. "Witch," he says. Then a smile.

As closer we came to the wheel, the bigger it towered. Excited I was. Uncle's Boy handed a young dirty man wearing an apron our red tickets. This man, he stunk. He looked at Uncle's Boy. Then he looked at me. A scar, red and thick, stretched from his brow down across the cheekbone. There was this lump in his one cheek. He held up our two red tickets. I looked at the hand, his. A round stub was where his little finger should live.

He spoke to my Uncle's Boy. His leg jiggled. "You and her want to ride on my ride?" He grinned, but I knew it was not friendly. His teeth, brown-stained they were.

I smelled trouble in the wind. My Uncle's Boy seemed to grow bigger. "You got a problem with that?" he said.

The man laughed. "Hell no, pal, it's not me with the problem." Then he spit this wad of tobacco juice, right in the sand by my feet. He kind of bowed and waved his arm out wide. "Be my guests," he said. Uncle's Boy glared at him. But we got in the little blue swing anyway. The man, with that same smile stuck on the face, he locked us in.

He looked my Uncle's Boy straight in the eye with a face red and explosive like a sore. "Have a nice trip, nigger-lover." He stepped back. That grin it was a scratch across his face. I watched his nubbed hand reach for the yellow stick that moved the big wheel. Lots of people, they were already in the other seats, giggling and excited.

"Motherfucker," Uncle's Boy said.

"Gypsy?" I asked.

"No, just a stupid damn redneck."

170

I looked at the man. He looked back. Music, that high music, blared. I didn't say it loud. But I moved my mouth clearly, so he could see my words. "Stupid damn redneck motherfucker," I said. His face, like the sore it was, exploded, and the big wheel, it jerked into its circle walk.

Up we went, slow at first, our little blue swing rocking gently. Uncle's Boy and me, we held hands. It's like Uncle's Boy felt there was no cause to be hiding our love when we were in the air. Plus the redneck, mad he made Uncle's Boy.

We curved up into that sky and I said, "Oh, look, over there." I pointed east. "The night's first star."

It was then Uncle's Boy brushed my cheek with a soft, swift kiss. "Happy first star, Sweetness," he said.

I was kind of loving this, you see. Up, up, up, and then down, down, down. The happy music almost sounding like rain on my good tin roof. As we flowed down to the earth, I thought, Yes, this is exactly like it is for birds, all kinds of them, when they land. The earth rushing up like a sweet hand to touch the face. I looked at this man, the angry bad one, when we traveled past and began climbing back up. But I thought, This was a webbed man. No happiness. No kindness. Gripping those yellow gears the way people grab sticks when they is going to beat a man with them.

"Trouble is in that man," I told as we swept past him and swayed up, back up, into the night sky.

"He's just an asshole," said my Uncle's Boy.

We must have made five, six circles through the air when our big wheel stopped. My face must have showed me scared, because Uncle's Boy, he said, "Don't worry. The ride's over. They're just letting people off."

Now this was true, for every few minutes the wheel would jerk into a motion again, and we would walk just a little bit more through the sky, toward the ground. I huffed big and long. I could have stayed up in that air forever. Our one, tall walk through the sky, gone it was. Now we only felt the jerk and tug of start and stop while the angry man let people off the ride seat by seat.

The last people to be let out we were. With my soul I know the

171

angry man planned it that way. My Uncle's Boy, he says to me, "Now don't say anything to this guy when he lets us off here. Just get up and walk. Okay?"

Uncle's Boy. Sometimes he talked to me like I was three years old. Those people in the seat before ours, three giggling girls, they were. And hairdos just the same. Stiff long hair that flipped at the ends. One of them blew a bubble as she stood up. Her friend popped it and then smiled, like she was smart for popping that gum.

The angry man, he stepped back to his yellow stick and we moved down. Uncle's Boy left my hand alone, and me—I felt sorry the ride was over. The angry man, that leg of his jiggled again. He pushed the stick all the way to the back of its oily yellow box. And we jerked hard. I caught Uncle's Boy by the arm because shocked I was. No more gentle circles in the sky. Suddenly we were swift, flying, flying. Like each little swinging seat was in hot flight after the other. I looked down. So many people, but they were shrinking into midgets as we raced up. I saw the sneer, like he was an evil mud-eater, on the angry man's face. The breeze blew hard through our hair, like the jeep breeze that made my eyes tear. I looked at Uncle's Boy. He was staring at me with confusion in the eyes. But then we both, the two of us, laughed sudden, hard and so good. As we flew back to the ground, the sneer on the angry man's face grew huge and monsterlike. But he was a monster without an enemy, because fun this flying race was. People started to gather near the big wheel like little clumps of lily pads. Staring up, pointing, some waving. When we flew past close, I could hear some of their words. "Make them go faster." Then another, "That's enough, you'll make them sick." But we was determined: the angry man, he was not going to win.

"Whoopee!" my Uncle's Boy shouted.

For me, I closed my eyes and let my body take full sense of this trip that took us nowhere but up and down. I was that feather, my papa's feather, flying through a breeze thick with the smell of corn dogs and cotton candy. The wheel raced on like the angry man was never going to do nothing to stop it, like my Uncle's Boy and me might be flying forever on the angry man's ride. The crowd, in my mind I saw them as wingless souls coming to beg Uncle's Boy and me to give them some flying lesson, they grew.

Uncle's Boy said, "Jesus, everybody in this place is looking at us."

Then the wheel, without no warning, began to slow. Nervous I became, thinking we might have to run through that smiling, hollering crowd.

"When he lets us out of here, we'll just act cool and walk straight north, toward that hot-dog stand and out past the rides straight to the jeep. Don't lose me, but just keep walking. Don't stop to talk to nobody. Don't look anybody in the eyes." My Uncle's Boy, quite a boss man he could be. But his words might as well stayed in the mouth because the ride, see, it was not over. This angry man, foolish and full of himself as could be, he thought he was scaring us. He thought if he just kept us in the little blue swing we might start shouting or panicking or crying. What a fool that angry man was. He slowed down the big wheel enough that he edged it up, up, up. And then he stopped it, yes he did, when we was hanging at the highest part of the wheel. Then he wiped his hands together, like an honest work he had done. He throwed back his head and laughed. Then that angry man, he walked away.

So what, in all this land, was we to do? We looked down at all of Carnival. Its lights twinkled happy and sure in the warm night air. It looked like its own city, yes—full and bright and dirty and busy. I said to my Uncle's Boy, "This is beautiful, no?"

"That son of a bitch. I wonder where he thinks he's going." My Uncle's Boy, rubbed those hands together, his. Then let loose with one of those pretty smiles. "But it is kind of nice."

I decided to watch everything, you know, the way the eagle does. I turned my head one way, turned it the other way. I saw that sign, the one I knowed. "Tickets," I said, and pointed at that banner my Uncle's Boy first showed to me.

"What?" Then he followed the line of my finger. "Well, hell's bells and cockle shells, that's right. Tickets. Now let's see. That sign made of lights, over there by those horses. It says 'Hot Dogs.' The first letter, it's an *h*. 'Hot,' " Uncle's Boy said, and he breathed hard on the *h* as he said it.

"Hot."

"Good. Now over there, to the right. 'Kiddie Rides.' "

"Kiddie Rides." My Uncle's Boy, a good teacher, him. He made me think of each one of those sounds, like each letter was a note of music. I tucked it in my mind. I said each word as its own song. I knew soon, in my swamp house, I would by the light of my candles put those notes together to form longer songs, whole sentences. Soon I would read, and then I would know all everything those whites in the city knew. No fooling with Soleil Marie.

We was sitting there, happy, holding hands, me learning the words "House of Mirrors," when the visit happened. The second visit of the day, yes. The Carnival breeze was blowing by. Trying to say "mirrors," I was. Then those mockingbirds. The ones from the morning who watched me light my candles. Yes, I swear to all my gods it was them. They flew past, above Carnival and its lights and its tiny people. First one, then two, those mockingbirds perched on our little swing right down by our feet. Oh yes, they did. Not for long, no. But they were there, and me and my Uncle's Boy, we shut our mouths, because shocked were we. I looked at those birds. And they looked at me. And then everything changed. I felt my body rush into a warm, golden place, like I was dipping my whole self, my body and soul, into a lily pond near my house, one that the *loa* love. And then I knew. My mama and papa—their souls for some reason had taken shape. This day, from morning until night, out of the swamp muck Mama and Papa had come to be with me. But why? Had I angered them like the bearded lady had angered her parents? Was something wrong with one of our *loa*? Was it a warning? Maybe sickness or death sneaking up in the night? But none of these thoughts did they click. But then I said, Stop. I shut down my brain. I said to myself, Listen to them. Listen to your mama and papa looking like these mockingbirds. And I did. And in no time what I heard was my own body. With these closed eyes of mine I saw inside myself. And I saw that no longer I was alone. And never was I to be alone again. I saw that there was a baby happy and gurgling inside me. Swimming in circles in my belly like keeping in step with the big wheel, my baby was. The *loa* was very pleased with me, they must have been to give me this gift. I

174

opened. The mockingbirds, those parents of mine, gone they had flown.

"Did you see that?" My Uncle's Boy said with that same voice he uses when we watch people on TV throwing funny balls, running down long green fields.

I took the hand, my Uncle's Boy. I held it against my soft, growing belly. I fingered the veins that crawled underneath his skin. "Oh yes, Uncle's Boy, I did see."

Emory Looney

It was three days after I took Soleil Marie to the carnival that the letter came. I had been in town, running errands for J.W. I'd copped a Jax out of the refrigerator and downed it. Nothing like a good cold beer to cool a man off. J.W. was off somewhere. Probably out tinkering with his new tractor. I decided to stretch out on my bed for a few minutes, maybe steal a few z's before he thought of something else for me to do. I walked in my room and there it was. On my bed. In its airmail envelope. Mama always buys the airmail jobs even if she's just mailing a letter to St. Augustine.

Shit, I said under my breath. But it wasn't that I was angry or nothing. It was just that, well, getting a letter from home was always like walking into a dark room. Even if you'd been in the room a thousand times, the possibility for something disastrous waiting for you was always there. I thought about just not opening it, acting like I never got it. But hell, it was from my mama. I couldn't do that to her. I flopped on the bed and tore open the envelope. On the back she'd drawn three X's. Three kisses for her son. The letter started out easy enough. Everything was fine. A new drugstore was opening up on Beach Boulevard. Randy Jewitt got thrown in jail for drunk and disorderly. Eudora was starting to see lots of men friends. What was poor little Luella going to do? Then came the zinger. *Emory, dear, I know this may be hard for you to believe, but your father has undergone a real change. He's not like he used to be, Emory. He's not angry all the time anymore. He's treating me good. I know a lot has happened in the past, but believe me, son, your father loves you. We want you back home. Soon. Now that you're done with school you can come home and get a job. I know this is a lot for you to take in at once, but it's best for all of us. We can be a family again. Your father is going to talk to J.W. in the next week or so and make the arrangements.*

I couldn't believe my eyes. Here I was, making it on my own, even if it was in my uncle's house, and they were going to tell me I had to move back home? Who in the hell did they think they were? I looked at my crumpled-up pillow, and in my mind's eye I saw it as my daddy's face. With my hand balled up like a fist of steel, I pounded and pounded that pillow into pulp.

No son of a bitch was going to make me go home.

Rose Looney

I love autumn in Florida. It's like, just when we're all about to wilt from the summer heat and humidity, God cracks open the freezer door. The air churns with a freshness, and everyone and everything perks up—crisp and lively. I know that in other places, like up north, fall is a season when things begin to die. But not here. In Tiama it's a time to be renewed, a time when nature and humans gain a second wind. So of course it was my hope that Charlie and me, the two of us together, would also gain that second wind.

And because I was trying so hard to make that happen, I found myself standing before my vanity mirror one lovely October evening studying my figure. Suck that gut in, girlie, I told myself. I breathed in and watched as my belly became just a tad less noticeable beneath the smooth folds of my black satin skirt. Charlie and I hadn't been out on a date in years. Even tonight wasn't a real date. I mean, we weren't going to be able to snuggle close in some candlelit bar, playing footsie and flushed and giggling due to how we hoped the evening would end up. That was in the premarriage days. No, we were too old for that stuff. This date was a bit more practical. He was playing at a club on the beach. But he was taking me with him. After eighteen years of a rocky marriage that at times seemed to be sanctioned only by hell, even going to the 7-Eleven together could be classified a date. At least if you were desperate and crazy about the man. And I was.

It was a cool night, and I had all my windows thrown open. I was aware of a rhythm created by the gusting breeze and my drapes. The drapes would balloon like sails and then deflate, go limp, smacking against the wall each time. I would have to spray my hair with that extrahold stuff I bought downtown and put on a scarf to prevent my hair from being blown to hell and back in that wind.

I opened my makeup drawer. I kept my slim tubes of lipstick turned upside down, their labels showing. A small attempt at order in an otherwise teeter-tottering life. I studied the options. Tango Red, Pink Passion, Sweet Melon, Crazy Coral. Their names sounded like tropical fruit drinks offered in ritzy hotel bars.

Through my window wafted the light, tripping music of Eudora's wind chimes, and then I heard two sets of laughter. Hers and one of her many men friends'. The one currently occupying her front-porch swing (he was by no means the only one who sat out there with her, copping feels like there were no neighbors for miles) was a guard at the prison. She'd nabbed him, no doubt, by sitting on her front porch in almost no clothes.

I'd watched her. She knew those prison guards across the street had a clear view of her. She'd reach into her iced tea and pull out an ice cube. Then she'd rub it from the tip of her chin down to her cleavage. Behaving like a wildcat in heat. Junior would turn over in his grave if he knew.

I pulled my glance away from the window. It was a damn shame, but it seemed to me she was a woman who just couldn't survive without a man. When she didn't have one hanging around or didn't have any prospects, she'd mope and drink beer out of a plastic tumbler all day, thinking none of us knew it was beer. Like we couldn't smell it, right. But then some fool would catch her eye and the chase would begin. The ice cube down the cleavage repeated over and over until she'd caught him. It made no mind what he looked like or how old he was or what he did for a living. Only his gender mattered. As soon as a new one was hooked, gone was the down-in-the-mouth Eudora. She'd perk up fresh as an orange blossom. It was no secret to her or anyone else that I preferred the moper to the wildcat. At least during the moping periods, that little Luella wasn't subjected to a string of men waltzing through her house.

But Eudora wasn't my problem tonight. No, sir. I looked at my orderly rows of lipsticks. I chose Tango Red. It would show up good in a dark bar, and the color seemed to put a little bit of blue in my hazel eyes. I slid the color onto my lips and heard Charlie rummaging around in the kitchen. Probably fixing a ham sandwich. He says he always gets hungry about midway through a gig. In my mind's eye I saw him sitting at the kitchen table, being ever so careful not to let the mustard squirt onto his new white western shirt. I'd put a lot of work into that shirt. Inez Temple had sewn the shirts for the band, and I had done the sequin work. In red sequins across the back of each one I had sewn *Charlie Looney and the Rockets*. Then down at Woolworth's I'd found the perfect thing: red sequin appliqués in the shape of rockets. I'd kept the appliqués a secret from Charlie. I sewed them on the shirts one day when he'd gone fishing. It about blinded me—doing that close work all in one sitting. But it was worth it. Charlie just beamed when he saw them. Said that hell, his band was going to look better than Hank Williams's.

My red lips looked perfectly good. I smiled at myself in the mirror. Tonight we'd make a nice-looking couple. Of course now, nice-looking was a far cry from hunky-dory. I mean, for instance, I believed that Pauline DuPree was really out of the picture. Pauline DuPree standing in that church kissing a young colored man. That's what did it. It jolted Charlie. But jolts don't mean the leopard has changed his spots. Who's to say there weren't a thousand Pauline DuPrees out there? Who's to say Charlie hadn't become just more wily about the fool things he did behind my back?

I leaned close to the mirror. Actually, maybe I had on a little too much Tango Red. I blotted and looked at the stain left on the tissue. Two red lips. Oh, how many times I'd seen that telltale evidence on Charlie's collars. Damn me, no matter what I did or how old I got, it always came down to that: Does Charlie really love me? What's real and what isn't? What matters and what doesn't? I crumpled the tissue in my hand.

Then I grabbed the can of spray and gave my hairdo a good shellacking. It would take a Mack truck to rearrange my curls now. I rummaged through my bra drawer until I found the red silk scarf Charlie had given me for my last birthday. He had said it was the color of my temper. Not tonight, though. Tonight it was nothing more than the shade of my lipstick. That was all. Nothing else.

As I walked into the kitchen, Charlie looked up from his almost consumed sandwich. He wolf-whistled, long and loud.

"I'm not letting you out of my sight tonight," he said.

He grabbed me around my waist and then buried his head in my chest. I couldn't help it, I had to beam. I saw myself. I saw how we must have looked kind of silly like that. Me, with my head arched back, beaming. Charlie nuzzling my breasts. Lord, like a couple of eighteen-year-olds.

The Bonfire. God only knows what moved Sam McAlister to name it that. Since it was right on the ocean, I always thought it should have a more appropriate name, like the Castaway or the Ocean Breeze.

On the outside the place was all done up in neon. Red and blue flames flickered up in the neon brightness, and underneath the flames, like they were burning in hell, were little yellow bulbs that spelled out BONFIRE LOUNGE.

Spotlights with red, yellow, and green filters illuminated the palm trees and palmettos. On either side of the front door neon flames licked the side of the building, and in the grass next to the walkway two gas torches burned day and night, rain or shine.

From a passerby's point of view, the place was definitely a showcase.

Inside, the decor was a cross between what I'd call an African and a beach motif. Jungle masks hung beside fishnets studded with seashells and starfish. On one wall was a mural, painted by an artist from Jacksonville. It was an ocean scene: white sand, waves, sea gulls. But peeking out from behind the palm trees were natives painted up in exotic fashion and wielding African shields.

Now all this may sound fantastic, but the main draw was not the mural or the fancy neon flames. It was the phones. On each and every table sat a red telephone. If somebody sitting at another table caught your fancy, you just rang them up. Each table had its number prominently displayed in silver glitter on the back of its chairs. And every phone had a red light that lit up when its number was dialed. McAlister said he got the idea when he went to San Francisco a few years back. He said several of the nicer bars were done up that way. Charlie, the minute he caught wind of McAlister's plans, claimed the phone bit was a million-dollar idea.

Our plan for the evening was that one of the other band members, the drummer, Bubba Fletcher, would bring along his girlfriend. That way we'd both have somebody to sit with, even though we didn't know one another. Bubba, ever since his divorce, had gone through woman after woman. Charlie and I tried to remember all their names, but there had been just too damn many of them. So it was bad on my part, but I figured there was no need to try really hard to get to know this latest one, since she'd probably be around only a few weeks or so.

Charlie and I stood just inside the doorway, touching hands. We surveyed the room. It was early yet. The clientele was still tame and was composed mainly of older couples out for a few drinks and some conversation. The single crowd wouldn't start coming in until nine or ten. Bubba and what's-her-name weren't around yet.

"How about over there, that booth near the stage," Charlie said.

Charlie walked slightly behind me. He kept a hand on my shoulder as we zigzagged toward the booth. I loved it when he did that. Oh, I know it was a small gesture, but that hand on my shoulder, guiding me through a public place—it was an announcement that we, in some measure, belonged to one another. It made me pleased as punch.

Mockingbirds and Goldfish

I slid into the booth and Charlie set his guitar case on the stage. Then he scooted in beside me. He held my hand. He acted like I was the most wonderful woman in the world. Maybe that's why I stayed with him. The lows were horrible, but God, the highs sure were good. "Two Rob Roys," he told the waitress, who wore nothing but a black leotard, fishnet stockings, red high heels, and devil horns.

He lit a cigarette for me and then one for himself. He talked, the cigarette bobbing between his lips—a knack I never could master.

"Rose," he said. He squinted as the smoke curled up into his eyes and wafted over his wavy blond-but-graying hair. "I love you, woman. And I always will."

Well, that was quite a statement. Charlie was good at that. Saying something as if you'd been talking about it for a while, when really you hadn't. What he did, I think, is he'd think about it, work himself up over it. And then blurt out a defense or an argument or a bold opinion. It often left me openmouthed.

He drew hard on the cigarette and then palmed it. It looked so small in his big hand. I noticed how callused his fingers were due to his guitar strumming. He held the cigarette up by its filter and studied its fiery, glowing tip. Then he said too sharply, "Don't ever forget that." I mean, he said it like if I forgot it he'd beat me.

But this was just my husband's way. I don't think he could help it. He talked rough, but there was something so vulnerable there. From the core of his spine to the hair on his chest, he was a walking, talking, breathing glob of insecurity. Why, all the bravado, the yelling, the beating, the womanizing—it was all a cover-up. A grand scheme to make people believe Charlie Looney knew who in the hell he was and what he was doing. I was no longer fooled.

The waitress brought our drinks. She leaned over as she set them in front of us, and in my mind a picture flashed of what Charlie probably would have done had I not been there. A dollar bill down the cleavage, a slap on the ass. But not this time. This time his eyes watched the drinks as they appeared before us. He threw a buck down on the table. He said, "Keep the change." The waitress hobbled away in her too high shoes.

I reached over and hugged him. In his ear I whispered, "Charlie Looney, there isn't a thing in this whole damn world you should be afraid of."

He tossed back his head and laughed. He flashed me that drop-dead smile and said, "Woman, you ain't kidding."

So until Bubba showed, we drank and talked aimless, chatty talk. It was all gloss and no pain. No arguing. No underhanded accusations. No talk about Emory or his possible homecoming.

And even though we didn't actually discuss Emory, I couldn't keep him totally out of my thoughts. My son refused to return our calls. J.W. was proving to be noncommittal and an asshole. I know at least three weeks must have passed since I sent Emory a letter telling him to come home. I would just have to get in the car and drive down there. I saw myself in Charlie's black car driving south, breaking all traffic laws. On the seat beside me was a bundle of brand-new clothes—jeans and shirts and even a nice leather belt with the name *Emory* carved into it—a kind of coming-home present. Then I realized I didn't even know what size shirts my son wore anymore. All those shirts hanging in his closet were probably too small. Probably, hell! Two years is an eternity in teenage years. The fact that he'd been gone that long was too much for me to think about. I had to act—no, believe—that the phone calls and letters and god-awful birthdays and holidays occurred within the span of a few months. That was it. Emory was gone on a little vacation. He'd be home any day. I looked around the bar, at the smoke rising from cigarettes, at the couples nuzzling and laughing and drinking. I pushed my nails into Charlie's hand. It was a good way to kill the rising pain.

You know, after you've been married so long, your partner sometimes knows your thoughts. Charlie was saying he decided the band would open the first set with some soft dancing music. I must have looked a million miles away, because Charlie patted my hand. "Push those goddamn thoughts away, Rosie," he said.

"Sorry," I said. I pulled the ashtray closer and flicked my cigarette. I pulled up the cuff of Charlie's shirt to get a look at his wristwatch. "It's about time for your boys to show up," I said.

"They'll be dragging their asses in any minute now," Charlie said. He waved his hand in the air, like somebody hailing a taxi. From about three tables away, the waitress saw his flailing arm. She didn't move. She just looked like, "What in the hell do you want?" Charlie held up two fingers and then flipped his pinkie through the air fast. Bar code for another round. Occasionally he'd run into a waitress who didn't understand his little system of signals.

I'd say to him, "Charlie, just order in English so she'll understand."

And he'd say, "Baby, if she's going to succeed in this business, she's got to learn." He'd look at the waitress in question and move his hand vertically through the air, like he was pulling on a light cord. That meant he wanted a draft.

Before long, Bubba and his date showed. And I must say, this Theresa Shaw looked like jailbait to me. Charlie and I exchanged knowing glances. Theresa seemed scared stiff of all of us, and I swear to God I think she had a pimple or two. I thought, Great— I've got to sit here all night with this kid who doesn't know her butt from a hole in the ground. We exchanged hellos, and the next thing I knew, the bass, piano, and steel players were crowded around the booth and Charlie was kissing me on the cheek and saying he'd see me after the set.

So there sat Theresa and I—her looking like she wanted to be swallowed up into thin air and me checking her out as if her life was my business.

"Theresa, would you like a cigarette?" I asked.

"No, ma'am," she said as she played with the lace collar on her shell. "I don't smoke."

She immediately looked guilty. And I thought, Jesus! Bubba Fletcher, what have you done now?

Then I heard my husband's voice over the mike. I looked at the stage. A floodlight illuminated Charlie but kept the rest of the band in semi-darkness. Damn, he was handsome. A little age had done nothing to dampen his good looks. I loved that big, solid Irish face.

"Good evening, folks," he said. "I'd like to welcome you to the Bonfire Lounge." As smooth as glass. The salesman who could sell a fire extinguisher to a fish. "We will be playing for you some toe-tapping, leg-jiggling, hip-swaying swing. So be kind to your waitress and spicy to your partner, because I am Charlie Looney and we are the Rockets!"

The lights came up. The band hurled into "Great Balls of Fire" with Charlie doing lead vocals.

The dance floor immediately filled with jumping and bopping bodies. I winked at Theresa. I think a tiny smile slipped up on the corners of her mouth.

"Is this the first time you've heard them?" I shouted.

She nodded.

"They're good," I told her. She didn't shout anything back. She just looked like she hoped I would figure out what she meant. She had these big blue eyes framed by long brown lashes. She was skinny, like she'd break if a good wind caught hold of her. She was just a baby. A shy little baby wearing a pink shell and a too tight skirt.

"Relax," I told her. "Enjoy the music."

She sort of half nodded. I turned my attention back to the band. I thought about what Charlie had said: "I think we'll open up with some soft dance music." I laughed. "Great Balls of Fire" was about as far as a person could get from soft dance music. He couldn't stay on a settled-down course if his life depended on it, I thought, utterly amused. And then the ramifications of my thought seeped a little further into my brain. And then I wasn't so amused.

But I felt better just as soon as the song was over, because Charlie, in his voice like velvet, said, "We're going to slow it down a bit with a soft, sad favorite."

Then he started his croon. "Lock, Stock, and Teardrops"—a bluesy little number, but the way Charlie sang it, it had heart and guts. Jessie Hawkins made the steel guitar talk as my husband, his eyes half closed, his lips so near to the mike I think they touched it, sang the song that at times in my life, I swear, I could have written. It was all about hurting your lover to the core but then expecting forgiveness. One of you threatens to leave, but the other knows it will never happen. It's as if your love is so sad it paralyzes you.

Jessie let loose with a long solo, and my husband swayed back and forth to the music, his eyes now shut to the world. An ash fell from my cigarette onto the table, but I didn't care. I kept watching

184

my husband, the man I loved. I was mesmerized, wrapped up in the spell he cast. Then he slid his eyes open and looked straight at me. He winked. A sudden lapse in the beer-swilling pain he projected onstage. So he was playing all along, crooning like he cared about that song, like he felt it. But did he or didn't he? I had no idea. Maybe he was just an actor in the lights, milking the audience for all it was worth. He plunged into the second verse, as heartfelt as the first, and the room seemed to sway within a smoky haze.

"You love him very much, don't you?" It was Theresa. She speaks. Jerking me from my daze.

I sipped my drink. I looked at her innocent face. "Yes, I suppose I do. How about you?" I asked her. "How'd you meet up with somebody like Bubba?" I wondered if she knew that what I meant was, What in the hell are you doing with somebody old enough to be your daddy?

"I met him at the 7-Eleven in St. Augustine."

"At the 7-Eleven?" Most likely at the candy rack, I thought.

"Well, not exactly at the 7-Eleven, but at Sims Television next door. They have one of those colored TVs. They're really neat, and Sims keeps it on all night, right in the front window. My daddy says it's good advertising to do that, but my mama says it's an awful waste of electricity. Anyway, some nights we go down there to get a Coke at the 7-Eleven. Then we watch the color TV through the window. It's really good. Have you ever seen one?"

"A color TV? Why, yes," I lied. "So tell me, you were on the sidewalk outside Sims Television watching the color TV, and what? Bubba was there too?"

"Oh, yes," she said. She played with the strand of artificial pearls at her neck. "I mean, I don't know what he was doing in St. Augustine, being he lives here in Tiama and all. I never asked. I guess I just assumed it was to see the color TV. Anyway, he was there, and about five other people from town. He started talking to my dad, and the next thing you know he was talking to me." She leaned forward and sipped her Cuba Libre through her straw. Then she punctuated her explanation with, "We hit it off real good."

The waitress wobbled up. "Another round?"

"No, just two Cokes," I said. She looked down her long nose at me. "It's a momentary slowdown," I explained. She forced a smile—the kind with no teeth, just upturned lips—and then limped over to the table next to ours.

"She's not going to make it all night in those heels," I said, and I nodded in the direction of the waitress. Theresa looked down at the shoes, but her face stayed pasty.

"Theresa, how old are you?" There, I'd done it. Just gone straightforward and asked.

She took it as a challenge. Her face toughened, and she tossed her straight hair off her shoulders. "I'm eighteen, and don't you tell a soul."

I shrugged. "I'm not going to tell. But do yourself a favor." I lit a cigarette. A delay device I'd learned from Charlie. She looked at me like she was expecting the worst and was bored by it. I exhaled the smoke in her direction. "Don't ever make love without a rubber. There's lots of ways to walk down the aisle, but with a baby isn't one of them."

The waitress set the Cokes down in front of us. Theresa looked like I'd slapped her with a twenty-pound bass. There was a stirring of the maternal in me. But I decided to call it tough. "Can you be a dear and bring us both a shot of Jack Daniel's?" I said to the waitress.

Theresa didn't know what to do with me. She sat there petrified, I believe. So I made conversation. "My husband is a handsome man, isn't he? See those shirts? I don't know if Bubba told you, but my friend Inez Temple sewed those shirts. And I sewed on the fancy sequin lettering on the back. I think I might have a talent in sequin lettering, if I say so myself."

"Rhinestones," Theresa muttered.

"Pardon me?" I asked. The waitress set down our shots.

"I really like rhinestones," Theresa offered. She was trying to be nice. I kind of felt sorry for her. "Because they aren't gaudy or nothing, no matter what you put them on."

I held up my shot glass. "Well, Theresa, to rhinestones, then."

Her uninteresting face lit up a little. She tapped her shot glass against mine. "To rhinestones." She smiled, and then we both slammed down the Jack Daniel's, letting its fiery sweetness soak us.

That's how the evening progressed. Charlie would play a set and then come sit with us. He'd put his arm around me, and he'd smile a lot. Then he'd rub his forehead like he was nervous. Theresa and I got on better the drunker we got. She told me a story about how her daddy once had this dog that could catch freshwater bass in its mouth. He'd dive right down into the water and come up with a flopping three-pounder. But once a storm came up on their lake while the daddy and the dog were out fishing. A swell tipped the boat over. The dog drowned. Theresa finished the story with tears in her eyes, saying her daddy hadn't caught a bass out of that lake since the day the dog died.

So I told her about the way Charlie does not look at anything but the newspaper when he gets up in the morning. He reaches over the pages and dumps the cream and sugar into his coffee cup without ever once looking. But one time, as a joke, Emory moved everything around. He put salt in the sugar bowl and ketchup in the creamer. I told her how Charlie took his usual huge swallow and how he spewed that god-awful mixture all over the kitchen. But there Emory and I were, doubled over laughing until we both almost peed in our pants. My story was not nearly as interesting as hers. But it wasn't as tragic either.

And then Charlie made one of those grand gestures he was so good at. It was close to the evening's end. Theresa and I were sitting in our little booth singing along with the band. Sometimes we'd pick up the red phone receiver and dial a table and then hang up. The waitress was barefoot and her devil horns were askew, tilted, so that they looked like bull horns. Charlie held the microphone with both his hands.

He said, "Folks, have you all been having a nice time tonight?"

"Yes!" everybody shouted.

"And you've been dancing all night, haven't you?"

"Yes!" they yelled.

"Well, we're going to do something a little different. I'm asking you all to sit this one out so that I can have a dance with my beautiful wife."

Everybody started clapping. Some of them whistled.

I could have gone through the floor.

187

"Mrs. Looney," my husband said, "can I have this dance?"

He stepped off the stage and offered me his hand. What could I do? I was so flustered, but so thrilled too. Never had he done something as grand as this. I stood up. Theresa leaned across the table and patted my hand. I heard some woman at a booth behind mine say, "Oh, how sweet."

The music swelled, and Charlie took me in his arms. Oh no, it wasn't a slow song. It was what Charlie calls a swinging waltz. The kind of song that keeps your feet moving and your body gliding. Bubba was doing the vocals, but Charlie was singing in my ear. The song's key phrase was something about sugar-cane time, about two lovers walking in the light of a "sugar moon" during the harvest.

"Oh, Charlie," I said. We were gliding, looking into each other's eyes. I felt the song was his way of apologizing about Emory. Here he is, in a public place, where he's at his best—singing and entertaining—and he has us dance to a song he knows will make me think of our son, of us all coming together again.

"Thank you," I said to him.

He smiled.

And I saw a beautiful spark in my husband's eyes. It was the spark that caused me to fall in love with him that day he roared up on his police cycle in St. Augustine. It was the spark I tried to remember on those horrible nights when he didn't come home.

It was the spark I grabbed ahold of as we danced. We swirled and swirled among the lights and the glitter and the smoke. I kept my eyes glued to his, glued to the spark, fearing it might flicker. Yes, I stared at my adoring husband. And as I spun inside his sure grip, I murmured, "Please, Charlie, don't ever, ever leave me."

Charlie Looney

a It was a fine morning that found me barefoot in my backyard. Late autumn and not a cold spell in sight. Just a faint nip in the air that caused the sky to turn deep aqua—as if it was a fantasy sky that might crack if a bird flew too fast or too far. It was beautiful. My nice thoughts, however, got snagged on noise from next door. Eudora playing her Pat Boone album loud enough we could all sing along. But I decided not to let it bother me. I tried to block the music out. I sipped my first cup of coffee and took in the tiny world of my house and home. I thought that even though it was small—I mean, I didn't own a palatial estate or anything—Rose and me had done all right. We were getting older. Settling in. Making fewer mistakes. I'd shucked off some excess baggage, primarily in the form of Pauline DuPree. I'd decided to make an honest go of it. Get the Rockets going full-time. Drink a little less. Eat a little better. Maybe bring Emory home. Try to make things count in my life and not be so scattered. Behave—always and forever—like a good-hearted family man.

Yes sir, the morning sure was speckled with refined thoughts—mature thoughts. I downed an immense swallow of java and then looked across the fence at that grave-garden Rose, Inez Temple, and Eudora had gone crazy and planted on Junior's grave. A shower had passed through predawn. From the looks of it, I figured the rain had given Junior's azalea blossoms a few more days on the vine. I looked up at the sky. No clouds. Most likely no more showers. It was a perfect day for grilling, I thought. I decided if it was okay with Rose, we'd just hike on up to St. Augustine to Haney's Meat Market and get some fresh ribs. Barbecue them this afternoon. Everything in the world would be finer than the hair on a frog.

I walked back into the house. Rose, in her housecoat, drinking coffee at the kitchen table. She looked up and smiled.

"Hi, sweetie," she said.

No makeup on. A little sleep in her eyes. She looked real pretty. I just stared at her for a minute. Then I said, "How about you and me take a ride up to St. Augustine and get some of Mr. Haney's ribs for grilling this afternoon? It'll be just you, me, and a pack of pork."

"Oh, I'm sorry," she said, "but I promised Eudora I'd help her hem a dress this morning. She can't ever get the right length, you know." She paused and drank some coffee. She seemed to hesitate, and then she said, "Why don't you go on without me? I'll be done with Eudora by the time you get back."

I considered this suggestion. In fact, I considered it a good suggestion. I leaned over and kissed her cheek. "You need anything while I'm out?"

She looked at my face like she was trying to find some sign that I would really go out and do what I said I was going to do. Fear and trust were Rose's dual yo-yos when it came to me. But I believed in that saying about time: with time all that fear would go away. "No, no," she said. "We've got some baked potatoes and some corn on the cob. That should do it."

So I went into our bedroom and threw on a cotton shirt. Wallet and keys off my bureau. This would be just a short little trip. Nothing big. I blew Rose a kiss as I headed out the door. She looked at me suspiciously. "What? You're driving all the way to St. Augustine with no shoes on?"

I grinned at her. "It's Florida. You're not supposed to wear shoes."

"I love you," she said.

"That's good. 'Cause I'd hate to be on a one-way street," I joked. And I was out the door.

The Black Beauty gleamed in my front yard. The oleander reflected in her highly polished hood. Her spotless white leather interior flashed against that hard, dark exterior. I checked the sky again. Beautiful day. I decided to put the top down. I stepped back and admired her. Like that, topless, she really looked like a cruiser. I hopped in and turned her over, and listened to the purring engine. As sweet as mama's milk. I pulled out into the street and thought about how I had managed to keep her beautifully timed. I'd turned her into a powerhouse, stronger, with more pick-up than on the day I bought her. That car had a power that could defy us all, one that if I pushed could go, hell, maybe a hundred forty, a hundred fifty miles an hour. A perfectly tuned, perfectly timed muscle machine. I figured the Black Beauty was one of the few things I'd consistently done right by.

I drove down our street and checked out the prison. It seemed it never changed—like a wart on the back of your hand that you can't get rid of. I said to myself, At least I never saw the inside of those walls. I maneuvered out of town, stopping first for a six-pack. Then it was on to A1A. I passed the Coquina Motel. I noticed it for a couple of reasons. One, the neon wasn't lit up like a whore. I don't remember that sign ever not being lit. Didn't matter how fast a person drove past it, you could hear its god-awful buzzing. And if you drove up to it, to get to the motel office, it was eerie— those bugs getting electrocuted among its hot colors. But no, for some reason today it was not turned on. Maybe a death in the owner's family or something. Hell, that old motel had given me a whole bunch of memories. It was where I first made love to Rose as her husband. And it was where we first met Eudora and Junior. Didn't like Junior too much when I first met him. Had him pegged for weird right from the start. But this is how it is: The guy grew on me. Found it hard to dislike him after a while. And then, of course, it served as my hideaway with Pauline DuPree. Good old Pauline, who swung both ways, and I never even knew it until the night of our protest march, when I saw her kissing that colored boy. It really shocked me, I'm telling you. I mean, it was already over between us—I'd decided that much. But when you think you know somebody so well and then discover you don't know them at all— well, it shakes a man up, that's all.

Now as I came closer and closer to St. Augustine, this kind of reminiscing mood sprang up on me. And it didn't get any better once I was inside the old city walls. I got this big urge to just drive around and see the sights. Remembering this, remembering that. The alley behind the old blacksmith's shop. I'd won and lost many a dollar rolling marbles in that alley. The corner near the wax museum. The shorts. Jesus, I must have been only five or six. Tiny brown shorts. Bare feet. Dancing like a monkey. Knowing my dinner depended on it. Some of the tourists' nickels and dimes hitting my hot, dusty, dancing feet. What a childhood I had, let me tell you.

I drove by the old fort. Teeming with camera-hugging tourists. Back when I was a kid, shit, you could go inside that fort and wander around inside its damp, sixteen-foot-thick coquina walls— walls that just absorbed cannonballs and grew stronger—and not see another soul.

I used to study the walls. Especially in the prison section. I called it the dungeon. The chains and shackles hung limp from the coquina, but I was a kid, see. I had this imagination. I used to scare the shit out of myself in there, imagining it was haunted. I figured the ghosts of English and French prisoners were still chained up in there. In my brain they would beg for mercy from the Spanish soldiers. Then I'd hear a noise. A drop of water echoing. Drop. Drop. Or maybe the footsteps of gun-slinging, Spanish-speaking ghosts. I'd run like hell out of the darkness, into the blinding sun. I'd have to stand there, paralyzed and breathless, until I could see again, so that I didn't trip over a cannon and tumble over the side into the moat. But being scared was so much fun that I'd be back the next day, touching the dungeon walls, thinking I'd find evidence of their torture, like bloodstains hundreds of years old.

I perused the sights almost like I was a tourist. Past the old city gates and a crumbling ancient cemetery. Past a sprawling fruit stand where Yankees could buy citrus and ship it up north. Past that renowned tourist trap, the Fountain of Youth, where a slew of Indian skeletons were laid out in an open tomb. Ancient Indian burial grounds—I had heard tell that there was hardly a place you could walk in this town and not be walking on an Indian's grave. But at the Fountain of Youth the skeletons were lying there as if they had just settled down after a night of drinking, when something out of nowhere killed them all. Some guys who were planting orange trees in the Fountain of Youth Park discovered the skeletons back in the thirties. Bigwigs from that Smithsonian Institution flew down and dug in the earth for weeks. Evidence of our historical past, the local yokels tell the Yankees. Hell, what it is evidence of is how stupid the tourists are to pay cold, hard cash to drink spring water that will supposedly make them live forever while they gaze at some formerly spring-water–drinking dead Indians. As I drove past, I slowed to watch a plaid-shirted, sock-wearing grown man arrange his family of a wife and two toddler daughters so that he could snap their picture beneath the stone-buttressed arch of the park entrance. I thought, Well, hell, if Ponce de León believed the fountain bubbled with immortality, I guess some white man from New Jersey might as well be fooled too.

The park faded into a few oak branches in my rearview mirror. An urge to drive into dangerous territory began to push aside my more playful mood, so I took a chance and drove down Masters Drive to my childhood home.

The air clanged with all kinds of bird ruckus, and the salt-scented wind shifted into a homesick smell of rotting and renewing moss. I slowed the Black Beauty. The oaks and the moss shaded me from the sun. The old wood house was overgrown as ever. The tin roof. I always love that sound, rain on the tin roof. I stopped the Black Beauty. A shabby little house. But wholly unbelievable trees. Old, huge live oaks. Knotted limbs. Thick trunks. The house looked empty, abandoned. Had no idea who owned it. Maybe nobody did. Now *there* was a thought: A piece of property, beautiful and rotting, that didn't belong to a living soul. The porch needed repair. A fresh coat of paint, new screen. I could see the old goldfish pond through the thick foliage. It was built of coquina. About five feet 'round, and a foot deep. Mama had raised the biggest goldfish in there you ever seen.

Goldfish. They were part of it all. The ritual. After dancing for coins all day, I'd stuff the pennies and nickels into my pockets. One cent always went for a soft drink. I'd get home and she'd make me turn my pockets inside out. She'd take all the money for herself, not leaving me a thing. Nothing. Not one red cent. At least that's what she thought. But I always managed to keep one penny hidden from her. I tucked it in a hole I cut in the waistband of my shorts.

And when I knew she wasn't watching, I'd sneak out to the yard and sit on the goldfish pond's coquina wall. I think I loved those stupid fish. They had this beautiful color. And they lived in a cool place, swimming between lily pads as big as my grown fist. I'd snake a finger into the waistband hole and pull out my remaining coin. Then I'd say, "Goldfish, goldfish, make me rich."

I'd flip the penny into the pond. It would hit the water without a sound and then float, between water weeds and waltzing fish, to the bottom.

In my stupid little child's brain, I thought those fish would take care of me. I thought that all those pennies I'd thrown in there would turn to gold. Then I'd be a rich and happy little son of a bitch. And see here, to reinforce my fantasy, some days I'd walk on out there and throw them my penny, but all the pennies from days past would be gone. So I decided that the pond and the fish were magic. That those fish, yes sir, had swallowed the pennies and one day would return them as big balls of gleaming gold.

Then one morning I heard something in the yard. I forced myself fully awake. I peered out my bedroom window. And there she was. Mama. Bent over my goldfish pond. Struggling. Pulling out every one of the pennies I'd thrown in. She'd wipe them off one by one with her skirt and then drop them in her apron. I never forgave her for that. And I never threw another penny in the pond.

"You brats get back in the yard." My daydreaming slammed shut. I looked in the direction of the voice. Three little colored girls. Standing on the corner across from the Black Beauty. Laughing and dancing and then pushing and shoving to beat each other back up to the yard.

It was then that a foolish yearning came over me. I raised up in the seat far enough to get my hand down my pants pocket. I felt the spare change.

There it was. A couple of pennies, maybe more.

It was a childish thing to do, but so what? A little childhood reenactment never hurt a soul. I got out of the Black Beauty and trotted across the street. The asphalt was warm, but not hot, under my bare feet, due to the shade.

The old iron fence was rusted. Overgrown with crepe myrtle. Just like when I was three. I tried the gate. It wouldn't budge at first. On the third try it swung open with a lonesome cry. Probably not been oiled since Mama died. Grass was knee-high and mostly choked with sandspurs. I wished I'd worn my shoes. I kept having to pause, pull the spurs out of my skin and from between my toes. I heard something by the porch, in the brush. I got closer, trying— unsuccessfully, I might add—to avoid the spurs. I thought maybe an old raccoon had taken up under the house. But no. As I came closer, about five wild kittens skittered off.

The old house looked haunted, but I decided that was just because it was chock-full of memories. The windows to the Florida room were mostly busted out. Their screens hung stiff, crazy. A good pounce by a cat would bring them down. The place had always been nothing more than a tin-roofed dump cluttered with all the glass curios Mama and I stole from the dime store. Now it wasn't even that. It was just a shack that seemed to stare back at me. Then I thought, No, bud, that's your past staring back at you. If you don't care about things—old houses, wives, whatever—they fall apart. That's the way it goes.

I walked on over to the goldfish pond. My feet were starting to bleed. Just little trickles from being pricked. I stood looking down at my feet for a minute. Just couldn't bring myself to look in the pond. Didn't want to know that all the fish were dead. Then I said, Come on, man, don't be a jerk. You got change in that pocket just waiting to be tossed. Waiting for one more throw at good luck. I looked down at the lily-covered green water. The sun filtered through those huge oaks and speckled the water's surface with bits of light. I took a closer look.

By God, I saw movement. I thought my eyes were deceiving me, but they were as twenty-twenty as they come. First I saw one fish, then two. Must have been five or ten of them, all swimming like I'd never left the place. Fat and sassy and golder than gold. Some with white-rimmed mouths. They'd dart up and prick the water for air and then float back down. I thought, Jesus Christ, all the time spent when I was a butt-nothing kid hoping those fish would make me rich one day. I breathed in real deep and let the great mossy, damp smell of that overgrown yard fill me. It transported me back, you know? I was once again a snot-nosed kid just wanting some love and a full belly and dreaming of a magic pond. I pulled a fistful of change out of my pocket. I picked out a penny. I stood there, just like thirty-some-odd years ago. I closed my eyes and said, "Goldfish, goldfish, make me rich."

I opened them. I moved to toss the coin. But then I saw it. And then I thought, No, the shifting light must be playing tricks. I told myself to flick my wrist, skim the coin. But no, I saw it again. I held onto the penny. I put it back in my pocket. I sat down on the two-bit coquina wall. When I was three, this wall looked like a fortress, and now I was fearing my weight might crumble it. I pushed a lily pad. It sailed off, scooting others with it.

There, at the very bottom—I swear to Christ—winking up at me, was something small and round. I plunged my hand down into that cool water. The goldfish scattered. The weeds curled like snakes around my hand, my forearm. I couldn't get ahold of whatever it was because it was slick and slimy from the algae. I flipped it off the bottom with my fingernail and then grabbed it as it floated up. I was trying not to be excited. This, after all, was just some childish game. But I couldn't help it. I knew what it was, what it had to be. I brought it up and then slowly opened my hand. There she was: the prettiest one-cent algae-covered coin I'd ever seen in my life.

God almighty, Mama hadn't gotten every one of them after all. And no, it wasn't gold—it was better than gold. It was mine, completely mine. Something that I'd earned and kept and nobody'd managed to take from me. It seemed my mama had found a way to steal everything from me, herself included. But not this. Not this one little, lousy, good-for-nothing penny. Shit, I was happy.

I began to study it, wiped off some algae. For a minute I was afraid it was a joke. That some neighborhood kid had come over here and thrown it in. But no. It was stamped 1925. I shook my head amazed—the year I was born. I held up that little round piece of copper and marveled at it.

A scruffy orange-and-white cat—probably the mama of those kittens living under the house—approached, meowing. She had that look cats get: this was her territory, and I was the intruder. I bent down to pet her, but she hissed at me. Decided it was time for me to go, so I dropped the penny into my breast pocket and patted it, making sure it was safe and sound. "Bye, mama cat, take good care of your babies," I said, as I walked past her accusing stare and out of that trashy yard.

For a minute or so I just sat in the Black Beauty, thinking about what to do with the penny. It had been safe in that pond so long that it would be a damned shame to lose it now. And then I thought, Well, hell, who never loses a thing? Who is the love of my life? I'd give it to Rose. In fact, I'd go see Old Man Evans at the jewelry store. He could drill one perfect hole in it. Put it on a charm bracelet for her. But no other charms. Just the penny.

I drove over there. Evans was in. Older than the Mona Lisa. Sitting behind big glass cabinets filled with diamonds and gold. An easy mark is what he was. It's a wonder he hadn't been robbed all the way to doomsday. I told him what I wanted. Not a single muscle moved—not a frown, not a smile. I just said, "Evans, my man, I need a favor. And you're the fellow who can do it." I showed him the penny. He did not appear impressed. "And if you don't mind, sir, I want it on that charm bracelet over there." I tapped the glass countertop to make my choice perfectly clear. Sterling silver. Rose preferred it to gold.

The old man moved about as fast as curdled milk. I thought about going over to the butcher's and getting the ribs while Evans did his thing, but then I decided, Hell, no. I ain't letting this old guy out of my sight. For all I knew, a 1925 piece of copper could be worth something these days. If I wasn't watching him, I wouldn't put it past the old codger to pull a switch. I cleaned off all the remaining algae before handing it to him.

The high, tinny wheeze of the drill started up. It would have set my teeth on edge had it lasted any longer than it did. Evans had on these huge magnifying goggles. It was my bet that he wore them for almost everything he did. Jesus. He couldn't see. Might as well retire, I thought. Sell the joint and relax. Enjoy life a little. He started working with the bracelet. Fastening the penny on just right.

"You hear about that colored preacher?" he asked. "The one that came in here this past summer and caused all that trouble?"

I didn't answer him direct. I put both my palms down on his counter. I towered over the tired old man. But he never looked up. Just kept working. "What do you got?"

197

"It's not what I've got, it's what he's got. A cottage, Sixty-three Orange. On the island. He and the whole damn family. Little pickaninnies running around the yard. Don't know if he bought it or rents it. But he's there."

The old man held up the bracelet by one thin finger. Absolutely gorgeous.

"How much damage have we done?"

"Five."

"Five! Jesus Christ, that's robbery." I pulled the five from my wallet and tossed it on the glass counter. I plucked the bracelet off his finger. "Thank you, sir. You do fine work." As I hit the door, I nodded at him.

Now that was interesting news. Mr. Big Shot Nigger living in St. Augustine. Miss Pauline DuPree and her colored boyfriend's favorite preacher. I held the bracelet up in the sunshine. The penny hung from it like a jewel. "Yes, sir," I said. Rose had a birthday coming up. It'd be the perfect gift. I put it in my breast pocket.

I walked down the street and stepped into Haney's. The aroma of fresh meat. Pork, beef, sausage. It made my mouth water. I looked at all those different varieties of meats, and I wondered who'd rented the cottage to the colored preacher. This town had more colored-loving white people than I'd suspected. I ordered four pounds of ribs, then walked back to the Black Beauty, hugging the paper-wrapped meat like a football. I tossed it in the backseat and got in. The address was floating through my brain: 63 Orange. I decided to drive over there. Just see what was happening.

I made my way across the Bridge of Lions, tapping some nowhere rhythm on the steering wheel. I drove past a section of tourist-trap motels and then turned onto Orange. It was a quiet street with neat little rows of pink and yellow cottages. Nice autumn Saturday afternoon. People at the beach, at the movies, downtown. I slowed the Black Beauty. There it was—63—a little Florida beach house with a concrete driveway. An old blue Ford parked out front. Coquina in the flower beds. Shining white aluminum awnings. A rose trellis in front. Little neat azalea bushes hugging the little neat pink house that gleamed under the sun. Nothing out of place. Not one giveaway as to who lived there. Not a single detail that shouted, "See here,

a colored family lives here." This looked like any decent neighborhood in any itsy-bitsy Florida town. And then I thought, So,
what was I doing there sitting in my Black Beauty checking out this
house as though I might discover something important—as if I
might walk right up that concrete drive and tell Mr. Colored
Preacher Man to get the hell out of Dodge? I looked in my rearview.
A white woman driving a yellow Fairlane was coming up behind
me. She passed, but not before she shot a look at me as if maybe
I was casing the neighborhood. I looked back at the house. I saw
a curtain—most likely the living room curtain—move. A face appeared. I recognized it, I did. It was the preacher man himself. He
just stared out the window at me, his face calm, unafraid. There
was no hate there—not any—I swear to God. Just a mild curiosity.
For a split second our eyes met. And I thought, Jesus Christ, Charlie
Looney, who in the blue blazes cares where the man lives—he's
not hurting you. I jerked my gaze away. I pressed the gas.

As I headed back toward A1A, I felt just slightly like a fool.

Inez Temple

Now this is the truth: Mayor Edgar G. Collingsworth's
mansion was a house built, polished, and serviced by my
ancestors. Oh, I don't know if I was a direct descendant
of any of them, you see. But every inch of brick and mortar had
been put in place by slave labor. And they had done a fine job too.

That's one of the reasons I enjoyed cleaning the mansion. It possessed a legacy. Those ancestors of mine had lived, played, prayed,
and suffered among those marbled floors and wainscotted walls.

There is a Negro community up in St. Augustine named Lincolnville. Lots of slaves, once they'd been freed, settled there. Built
it into a thriving little community. I never, ever entered the mansion
without wondering how many of the folks who built this place lived
long enough to set their newly freed feet in Lincolnville.

Now Mayor Collingsworth was a rich man, yes indeed. But big dollars don't make for big brains. This was certainly true in his case. He used all that money of his to—among other things—cover up the beautiful work my people had toiled to create. Maybe if he hadn't been a widower he wouldn't have spent so much money on useless things. Maybe his wife would have bought expensive clothes and scents and such. But as it was, the mayor had littered nearly every nook and cranny, nearly every inch of wall, with the ugliest, highest-priced junk you ever seen. Gone were all those wonderful antiques. No more oak sideboards. No more mission clock to tick away the passing days. No more lace curtains to filter and soften that old harsh sun. No, ma'am. He'd done away with all of it. He was a big-deal modern man with all the junk to prove it. Now brass giraffes and overstuffed red furniture and heavy drapes with plastic backing and ceramic figurines of Martha and George Washington rubbled the whole place.

Well, my goodness, the old mansion was so cluttered visitors might not even notice the one true bit of history it managed to hang onto: the hand-carved ebony staircase. I'm saying, it was a beauty. But those visitors would be so busy trying not to trip over the horrendous wooden ducks that served as doorstops that they'd easily miss paying proper due to my staircase. And that is a crying shame, because all that carved ebony was much more than just a way to get up and down between the mansion's two floors. You see, those stairs were a marvelous, carved-out-of-blood storybook.

I wish I knew who carved the staircase. I certainly do. I think his name ought to be plastered in all the great art books right alongside Leonardo da Vinci and Michelangelo, because what this man created was a masterpiece, yes it was. See now, on each ebony step he had carved the faces of fellow slaves. Some of the faces were wide open, like they were finding relief in singing a good, clear song. Others were twisted in a kind of pain that no person on this earth should ever have to experience. But the crowning jewel was the newel. Almost as though he'd had a premonition of Lincolnville, he carved into the newel a black family—mama, daddy, and baby— standing tall, together, intertwined, inseparable as long as that staircase existed. I think that newel was an expression of everything that the good man had lost and all that he hoped to regain.

And every time I polished those stairs one of my prayers was that each and every one of those souls had made it to Lincolnville.

And it made me wonder what the mayor prayed for. Every night before laying his soft body down in his big, fat bed he had to walk up those stairs, and he probably never realized that he was walking on the faces of my people. I wondered if after his chubby diamond-ringed fingers ran along that banister rich with images of real folk doing some serious suffering he ever knelt in front of his bed and asked for any sort of forgiveness. I wondered if he ever realized that living right up in Lincolnville were the grandchildren of the people who built his fancy house.

Now, I cleaned the mansion three days a week, rain or shine. And I always started off with that staircase. My hands would begin to ache as I culled from that dark old wood its beauty. By the time I was finished, yes ma'am, those stairs gleamed and sparkled, out-shining those crappy brass giraffes, plastic clocks, and Mr. and Mrs. George Washington.

The mayor would cluck at me on his way out the door (off to some busy city meeting, no doubt, about something like should parking meters be changed over to nickels from pennies): "Miss Temple, you spend way too much time polishing. The kitchen needs cleaning. The bed isn't made. I've got city council members coming here for cocktails tonight. Can't you do something besides polish that rail?"

And me, I would look up from my prayers, and I would say, "Yes sir, Mr. Mayor. Don't you worry about a thing. Your house will be spotless." And then I'd go back to polishing the muscled body of a slave. And I'd hear the mayor grunt, and I would hold my breath until the front door slammed.

This one day, though, the mayor had been gone for about an hour. Still, I wasn't alone. His aunt from New York was visiting. Now this was an old white woman, and white women tend to show their age.

Mrs. Barthaleme Finster was no exception. Wealthy. Widowed.

A string of pearls around her neck. A white-powdered face dotted with vermilion rouge. And an absolute fascination of lines colliding, splitting off, and colliding again, beneath that carefully applied cloud of expensive, smelly, desperate dust.

So I was polishing. And humming to myself like I often do. And I heard her pounding her cane on the pink-veined marble floor. Now I'm not a bad woman, but I decided to ignore her pounding cane. I hummed a little louder. I polished the face of a female slave who hugged her baby to her breast, her eyes mostly shut, not in ecstasy but exhaustion.

Mrs. Barthaleme Finster, inheritor of land someplace in New York City, pounded that cane like she was beating a snake with it. It grew so loud that soon I was going to have to take on the volume of an entire church choir to drown her out. Then she started clanking a spoon against the side of her juice glass. And no, you may be wondering, she did not stop the cane-banging once she started with the glass-clanking.

That was it. A grown woman behaving like she had ants in her pants. I threw down my polishing chamois. I headed to the first floor and marched into the breakfast nook. She sat at that grand little glass-top table, dressed in silk and pearls, her face unfurling in wave after wave of red, causing her white powder to show up as separate gritty grains.

She stopped the racket but still looked angry, a little child with sand thrown in her pretty little face. That's what that woman was.

With hands on hips, I said to her, "My goodness, Mrs. Finster, what in the world is this ruckus all about?"

She waved her white linen napkin with the monogram EGC over the remains of her breakfast. The English muffin with orange marmalade had only been nibbled at. "Take it away," she snapped.

"Excuse me?"

"Take it away, take it away!" She shook the china plate so that the butter knife resting on it clattered.

Now this woman, with her mean-spirited sterling-handled cane, she was old. And maybe she even wobbled a little. But as sure as I know a bird from a bear, this lady could walk. And surely, somewhere along the way, she'd been taught some manners. Must have left those back in New York, I thought.

"Mrs. Finster, you got a broken leg?" I asked.

She raised her cane like it was a wicked-witch finger, and pointed it at me. Her eyes had paled so with age that I had no clue as to whether in better days they'd been blue or green. "Don't you get impertinent with me," she said.

I thought a second. I decided, I surely did, that she was spoiled nuts. I also decided I didn't have to put up with it. "Mrs. Finster," I said, "perhaps you don't understand. I am the cleaning woman in this house. I am not the servant, the slave, or the cook."

She opened up her mouth to say something, but then shut it. Her hand flew to her pearls, her little haven of safety. Then she said, "Oh, oh. I see." She rested the cane against her skirt and wrung the napkin in her hands. "That eye of yours. I noticed it the other day. It was clouded, but it wasn't running as it is today. No telling what kind of disease you have. You must see a doctor. We don't want the help spreading germs." She looked at me like she'd won a point or two.

She had. I hadn't noticed my eye of late. I touched my face. Yes, it had started its weeping again.

I said, "Mrs. Finster, you need not worry about catching any diseases from me. I've seen my share of doctors. It's nothing anybody can fix, and as sure as I'm standing here, you can't get sick from it."

I was very angry and knew I should leave. I turned to go, but then, with a voice crackling like aged paper, she said, "No, come back here. I want to talk to you." Her old face snapped with a look of triumph, of having figured it all out. She sat forward in the chair, as though about to offer a benediction. Her voice took on an edge, a brightness. "It must be awful being a nigger in the South," she said. "Tell me all about it. You can sit on that couch over there while you tell me."

I wanted to stomp her. I wanted to shake her so hard her perfect false teeth would fall out. But no, no. I knew the boundaries. I believed firmly the word to be mightier than the sword. I worked hard at keeping my voice in balance. Clear, not a quiver, less than a shout: "Mrs. Finster, being a 'nigger' in the South is like living in heaven compared to what it would be like to work for a foolish, vain, selfish person such as yourself. The kitchen is that way. I suggest you clear your dishes before the mayor comes home for lunch."

With what I considered to be a flourish, I exited the room. My bandana-wrapped head held high. My steps evenly paced, not a rush. Yes, my mama and grandmama always told me I had a sense of drama about me. It was a handy talent to have when facing anger.

I stopped to look at myself in the mayor's monstrous Louis the Fourteenth mirror that hung like a reflective beast in the long, curving hallway separating the central portion of the house from the private quarters, where nonfamily visitors never ventured. I moved in close to my reflection. My tears seemed a river. The skin below, a soft path that would soon be chapped if the crying didn't abate. I let go with my imagination for a minute. I saw my skin developing stones and rocks beneath the burden of these inexplicable tears. They forced my calm, steady tear-river into an uneven flow of rapids and whirligigs. A furious flood down my face. I laughed at the notion, I surely did. But one thing is true, the old woman had gotten to me on my weeping. That's probably why I snapped back so hard. Oh, now, the Lord knows that woman was wrong, speaking to me that way. She's not good folk. All taken up with her own skewed sense of propriety and standards. But I should have let her words slide off my back like so much dirty rainwater.

I went on back to my work, sometimes pausing to wipe away the cursed weeping. With my chamois I buffed and polished that ebony newel to a glow.

Rose Looney

 It didn't matter what I did—no matter how many pairs of socks I put on my feet—I just couldn't get warm. This was the worst December in memory. And if it didn't let up soon, all the orange groves south of here were going to be hit hard. A killing freeze. That's what the experts were predicting. It was just god-awful. So I got out from under my pile of blankets and off the couch and went and turned up the thermostat. Then I went into the kitchen and checked the time. It was eight forty-five, and Charlie had gone out in the cold and dark—in his shirtsleeves, no less—to do something. He'd been out there a half-hour already. I turned on the oven and opened its door. I stood there shivering. How could he stand outside when I was nearly frozen inside? I was getting worried, but I was trying not to go out and call him in. I kept telling myself, He's a grown man, he can take care of himself. Try not to be such a nag. So I stood there shivering, managing to thaw out only my hands while the rest of me stayed frozen. I kept listening for Charlie sounds. Footsteps in the backyard. A cough or a whistled tune. The back door opening. But instead all I heard was the rooster clock's loud ticking. Finally I gave up. I said, Baloney—I could certainly go out and check on Charlie without doing it like a nag.

I went and pulled on my old tweed overcoat. My feet barely fit in my slippers due to the three pairs of socks I wore. I looked like hell. Like some sort of washwoman. That's what cold weather does to me. I tied a scarf around my head.

So all wrapped up like that, I went out in my backyard. It was pitch-black. The moon wasn't out. Stars weren't out. It was just a strange and awful night. Black and cold.

Maybe he was out behind the trees. Surely he wouldn't have gone beyond the fence. It was just woods out there. And then a bayou.

"Charlie," I yelled.

There was no response.

My teeth began to chatter. The worry I'd been harboring started to rile me really bad.

I walked around to the side yard and made sure his car was still out there.

"Charlie, where are you?" I screamed.

And then I heard him, real close. "I'm over here, sugar."

"Where's 'over here'? It's freezing out."

205

"At Junior's."

Was he out of his mind, I wondered, or just drunk as a skunk? I looked into Eudora's yard. The back of her house was dark. She must have been in her living room watching TV. I heard a match strike, and for a brief second I caught sight of my husband sitting on the bench Inez had given Eudora after Junior died. But the wind picked up and blew the match out. I walked over to the fence. "What in the world are you doing, Charles Jefferson Looney?" I asked.

I heard my husband laugh. "Nothing to worry about," he said. "Just came over to take care of my old buddy, that's all."

Then Eudora's back-porch light came on. She screamed out her back door, "What in the world are you all doing out here? It must be below freezing."

I looked at Charlie. He was sitting there barefoot. He had a bottle of Jack Daniel's, but I don't think he was drunk, because most of the liquor was still in the bottle. He looked pleased as punch with himself. Junior's entire garden was covered up in the old sheets and blankets we kept in the toolshed.

"Why, thank you, Charlie. I'd forgotten all about the plants," yelled Eudora. "That's awfully nice of you."

"Just keeping things going," Charlie said. Then he smiled at me real big.

"Come on, sweetheart, you're going to catch pneumonia out here," I said. "We'll see you later, Eudora. Stay warm." I waved at her, but my eyes were on Charlie. He adjusted a blanket that was on one of the azaleas, and then he walked over.

"Aren't you freezing?" I asked. Eudora's porch light went out.

"Naw. It's just a little cold snap," he said. He opened the fence gate. As we walked back up to the house, he put his arm around me. He seemed as if his actions were most reasonable and normal.

Once we were back inside I couldn't take off my coat. I was just too cold.

Charlie stretched real big. "Hell, Rosie, your blood's too thin for this weather. That's all."

Then he said, out of nowhere, "You know, it's almost your birthday. Just a couple more weeks."

I grumbled, "Please, don't remind me."

206

He laughed. I remember how solidly he laughed. As if he was really enjoying himself.

"You want some coffee?" I asked.

"Naw. I think I'm going to watch a little TV. Maybe hit the sack early."

It was then I realized that he did look really tired. So I said, "How about I turn on the electric blanket and get the bed all warm for you?"

He kissed my forehead. He said, "That sounds good, Rosie."

So I took off my coat and stuff, and Charlie went and watched the tube. And I just went about things, you know? I turned on the blanket. I brushed my teeth. I washed my face. I heard canned laughter from the TV. It seemed like everything was okay. I remember hoping that Charlie didn't fall asleep on the couch. I decided to give him thirty minutes and then I'd go see what was going on. I got in bed. The sheets weren't yet warm, which of course caused me to curse. I started one of my crossword puzzles. I had this book: *One Hundred Crossword Puzzles*. I picked one in the middle because it looked easy. That's all I was doing. Just the crosswords. I finished all the easy across ones. It had taken me about twenty minutes or so. I tried number five down. "Where astronauts go" was the clue. Five letters. My mind checked out the possibilities. I ticked off the planets one by one. Mars, I thought, but that just had four letters. I was about to try Pluto—I mean, I was about to write it down in those little blocks—when this horrible noise stopped me. Never before had I heard such a sound. It was inhuman. Guttural, volcanic, dangerous, unworldly. The kind of noise demons and devils make in the horror shows when they're angry. I was so frightened I could not move. And it mushroomed closer and louder and all around me. I put down my pencil. Petrified, I listened. I made out the sound of a staggering footstep, and I thought, Oh my God, Charlie. I flung back my covers and ran out into the horrible noise. Charlie was holding himself up by holding onto the walls. His eyes were wild, like they saw every single thing in the world. And his face was purple, so purple. I ran to him. I threw my arms around his chest and tried to help him into the bathroom.

"Can you talk, Charlie?" I asked, but his eyes just stayed wild, and he looked past me, and he clung to me and to the tile walls. I think he was trying to get to the toilet, but he never made it. He let go of me. He grabbed hold of the towel rack, and he vomited into the tub. His body convulsed and knotted, like something was alive inside of him, violently trying to break out. I put my hands to my ears. I remember thinking, My God, he's going to vomit up part of himself if this doesn't stop. He's going to kill himself.

I grabbed a towel. He was still on his feet, still holding onto the towel rack. I wiped the vomit and sweat from his purplish face. His eyes began to roll back, and somehow—with God as my witness, I do not know how—I caught him as his knees buckled. I was not human as I half pulled, half carried him into our bedroom. I'm the woman who can't open a new jar of pickles, but I got him to the bedroom. I laid him on the bed. I remember exactly what happened. He looked at me, and he was already so nearly a ghost. His face absolutely drained of color. And then there was a flash—one quivering spark in his sweet and tortured eyes. And then he didn't move. And his eyes held no light. And there were no sounds.

Except for me. Me pounding his chest. Me massaging his heart. Me trying to beat it back into life. Just one more, two more pumps—anything. Me, leaning over my husband, pounding his heart, screaming, "Please, Charlie, don't do this to me. Don't die."

Soleil Marie Beauvoir

By now, my baby has been inside me almost four months. But barely do I have a rounded belly. Yes, I told this child, wait a while to show yourself. Stay light as a little featherless bird until the time is right to tell your papa. See, I had to prepare my Uncle's Boy so as not to frighten the man away. And I had to get all the right blessings too.

So with my baby floating inside me as silently as a little sparrow,

I headed to the lily pond of mine. The waters, yes, where the *loa* cooled themselves. Holy water, pure and simple. In my canvas sack, one I'd stolen from Uncle's shed, I carried all everything that I needed. Be it this way—people, never are they blessed with children unless the *loa* are pleased with them. And unless my parted papa and mama, unless they too were pleased with me. Now for this pleasure the *loa* give me, I must give them pleasures in return. Else I or Uncle's Boy or even my baby end up like the bearded lady at Carnival. Respect, see, doesn't end at the passing on.

So on my way to the pond I stopped at the special trees—the ones where *loa* often live. A palm tree, its brown skinny body snaked up through the sky—taller than all the others it was. This tree, it belonged to Damballah-wedo. A good and powerful *loa* is Damballah-wedo. *Loa* of snake and lightning. A major *loa* in this world's creation. He's been a friend to me through many bad times. And I know this, see, I know Damballah-wedo loves oranges. This I know, like everything else I know: I have *connaissance,* power-giving knowledge, knowledge of the *loa* and our ancestors.

I dropped my sack to the sandy earth. Twilight, she was coming on, filtering the palm's brown body with tender shapes of light and shadow. The weather was turning cooler and the wind less boiling, which was kind of a relief, you see. I unbuttoned the white blouse on me—as *mambo,* white is the only color I wear. Like that, my chest free, I pressed my body and my baby and our souls against Damballah-wedo's loved tree. I wrapped my arms around it and knew that inside that tough brown bark was a snake soul good and loving.

I closed my eyes. The cool sugar wind blew, and I knew my *loa* were with me. The palm swayed, a dancer, a lover. I held on tight. And I said to Damballah-wedo, I said, "Thank you for this child, serpent, serpent-o Damballah-wedo. Life-creator. I will bring this baby up in your ways, to love you, yes, like I do."

Then from the palm I let go. From the sack I pulled a candle full of ground bougainvillea root. With matches I took from on top Uncle's TV. I offered the candle to Damballah-wedo. In the earth I put it. I lit it. Its flame caught, blue and hot and white. I took an orange from the sack. I sank my thumbnails into its skin and I peeled. The skin I offered to the flame—it fired green sparks. And the orange, itself, that I broke into sections for Damballah-wedo, it I sprinkled around the candle, around the tree.

Damballah-wedo, pleased was he. The wind blew, and the fronds shook and rustled like clapping hands.

I said to Damballah-wedo, "You are welcome," and then I tossed the sack over my shoulder and walked on to the pond.

Sometimes, my people and me, and always at Christmas, we come here to this pond and celebrate Christ and many *loa*. We do our sacrifices. Because all the receiving is in the giving. Life for life. That chicken dies not in agony but in glory. It joins those on the other side and is nourishment. Yes, on the special times we all come to worship in the water. But me, because I am my people's *mambo*, and because I know I must stay close with my religion, I visit the sacred pond many times. See, peace is nothing more than a swimming fish.

Now I know that in this pond I am safe from bad snakes, because my papa's blood is in me and protects me. Plus Damballah-wedo knows me well. So even when I am floating out there in the middle of that pond, all alone, with nothing but the flowers I have offered the water and the *loa,* those water animals do not bother me. And never afraid am I.

So naked I became. I looked down at my little sparrow belly and marveled at how good my baby obeyed me. I tossed my clothes to the ground. And from my sack I pulled herbs I growed: garlic, fennel, palmetto root, azalea blossom. Of course, sugar. With these I made rich the water, and began my chanting, I:

> *Day is dawning in Africa and the cock crowing cocoriko*
> *Three Paters, three Ave Marias*
> *Damballah, who is leading the African who has left Africa*
> *Papa, who is the Seminole who protects the panther*
> *Mama, who is the Haitian who guides the good* mambo

Chanting I kept on as I entered the water. I put myself fully down there, under the water. And I knew they were all with me. Those who had passed on, happy that a new life was born in me. Mama and Papa no longer mockingbirds. Maybe they were tiny shooting fish. Maybe they were the blossoms stretched and wide open on the lily pad. Maybe they were just pure spirit filling the cool water. This I do not know. But they were there, mingling with me and the herbs I offered. I floated in that water. I placed my hands on my belly and I knew that soon I would be telling my baby to hide no more. Soon Uncle's Boy would know just how connected to me he was. At this very moment in my life I was happy, for me, Soleil Marie Beauvoir, was a rich woman.

I floated there among the past, with my future growing inside me, and thoughts of my Uncle's Boy filled my soul. I thought of his beautiful face that I love, and knew that what we felt for each other was much more than just sex hunger. There is a sweetness that runs deep in him. I thought of the times my hands would be so sore from all the field work and he would show at my house with store-bought cream that he'd rub in gentle until all the pain flew away. And when we'd just be quiet together, holding on, letting all the swamp sounds float over us like we was the only two lovers in the world, like we understood every living thing about the other without ever having to mutter the pain or the sorrow. One time he told me he loved my papa and mama even though he never knew them, all because they had me. And I says to him, "I love your mama and papa too." And he started to cry. Right in my arms, my lover cried. And it was then that I knew he wanted to see his papa again. That he really didn't hate him. But his hurt was so deep he never dared speak kind words about the man. I didn't poke the wound. Some things, as a woman, I know not to do. But as a *mambo*, I knew too that there would be offerings to make, prayers to be said, gentle urgings to be tried, so that my dear Uncle's Boy could find peace about his daddy. And now what a gift, this baby of ours. Maybe the child was the key to the bringing together. What grand-papa could not love his grandbaby! As I floated in the cool water, I practiced what I would say to Uncle's Boy. Tomorrow I would tell him. I'd say, "Sweet man, we're having a beautiful baby to-gether." And in this fantasy his eyes would light up so bright, and he'd hug me and kiss me and say he was going to marry me. And everybody, even his papa, would be so happy.

Mama, Papa, Erzulie, Damballah-wedo—I prayed to them all. I

prayed for completeness between Uncle's Boy and his papa. I prayed for the good health of the child swimming inside me. I prayed that Uncle's Boy and me would be happy together forever. But then something happened that was not good, no. The sugar wind blew strong across the pond, pushing my offerings like they were boats gripped by the hurricane. The water turned so cold I thought it would burn me. I understood that sign. My *connaissance* was sharp, a blade revealing meat beneath the skin. I saw an uncertainty in this water. An uncertainty I did not like. A dancing shadow Mama and Papa could do nothing about. I murmured three Hail Marys. I whispered, "Erzulie, do not leave me now."

I thought about my baby. About how, no matter what, this child would be strong and healthy, him. This child would be moonlight. Graceful and warm. A pebble completing the circle. I closed my eyes. I had to push the uncertainty away. And because I did not know what else to do, I chanted my chant again.

Emory Looney

I'd been loading the harvest all morning. We pile it on the trucks and drive it into Clewiston to be processed. I tell you, it was hard work. But seeing how this was my third harvest, and how J.W.—for all his faults—had taught me good, this year's crop was a whole lot easier on me than the others had been.

We were up and out in the fields early, just as dawn was breaking. Everybody was dressed in layers of shirts and some people wore knit gloves, because a cold front was rolling through. The change in the weather only served to remind me that my diploma was a few months old and I still hadn't figured out what it was good for. I was determined not to head home unless I could see my mother without *him* around. But I needed to decide my future. Did I want to work in these fields forever? If I left, how would Soleil Marie like living in the city? By now I thought I could never leave her. But then again, maybe I should join the service—honor, glory, John Wayne, and all that—and then I'd be gone from her for just a few months at a time.

I looked out over the fields and thought, At least we aren't harvesting in the summer. Don't know how people do that—like berry pickers. I stood leaning against the truck and did what I always did the first thing every morning: greet my Sweetness. She'd be bent over, bundling cane, and I'd go over and talk to her. But discreetly. Like it was no big deal. I didn't want J.W. blowing an absolute gasket. She was about fifty yards out. I headed toward her, nonchalantly, like it was no big deal.

I didn't know what I'd do if J.W. ever confronted me about her. I guess I'd tell him it was none of his damn business. As I walked toward her, I watched her work. Her hands were so graceful and her movements sure and swift, as if she was simply an extension of the sugar cane.

She looked up and flashed me that beautiful smile. We stared at one another good and long, because often looking at each other was just about all we dared do around the others.

Then Soleil Marie says to me, "Uncle's Boy, we need to talk. Soon."

So I said, "Okay. But I'll have to go to your place because J.W. will most likely be home tonight."

Already, even though the air was cool, Soleil Marie was sweating. I wanted to wipe her face off. I wanted to take that scarf right off her neck and dip it in some cool water and wipe it across her skin. "You okay?" I asked.

She nodded yes, but I wasn't so sure. "If you're sick or something just go on back to your house."

All she did was smile at me. And there was something different about her. I don't know what. I wanted so bad to reach over and touch her. Just her hand or her cheek. Right then and there she seemed radiant to me. And for a split second I thought that I should say to hell with J.W. and just give her a big old kiss in front of God and everybody. But I didn't have the nerve.

I walked on back to the trucks and to my work. Actually, I was

213

happy as hell. I had a good woman, and even though my future was uncertain, at least I was working. I got three trucks loaded before lunch. The migrants would go sit under trees and such at lunchtime. Mostly they ate bread and fruit. For a long time I thought that's what they wanted to eat. Then I realized that was all they had.

As for myself, every day I'd go to the house and eat good. Steak sandwich some days. Other days fried grouper. J.W. had this cook come in three days a week. She'd cook meals and put them in the icebox. All we had to do was heat them up.

So I was in the house, eating a tenderloin sandwich, washing it all down with a big glass of milk. I was planning to sneak a sandwich out to Soleil Marie. All I had to do was put it in my shirt. If J.W. asked, I'd just tell him I'd eaten doubles that day. But it was then that the phone rang. I should have just let it ring. I should have just walked out of the house and delivered the sandwich. But no, not me. Not conscientious me. I picked up the phone.

"Hello, Emory?" It was Mama's voice. And it was trembling.

"Hi, Mama, yes, this is me." My mind moved quick to make up an apology over why I hadn't responded to her letter about coming home, or why I hadn't called her. But before I could, she dropped the news.

"Emory, I want you to come home. You got to come home now." The big pause, but then she started again. The bombshell. "Charlie's dead."

I was blank. Not a feeling. Not one speck of emotion.

"Emory, are you there? Are you okay?"

"Yes, Mama, I'm here." I thought, What am I supposed to do now? Where is my concern supposed to fall?

"Sweetheart, I've got so much to do. I've got to go see Pat Lackly and I've got to get Charlie's suit pressed. I don't know which way is up. Emory, I need you. Please come home." She was crying hard and I knew it wasn't easy for her to get her words out.

All at once I felt trapped and alone and sad and angry. But I knew Mama might truly need me. "Listen, I'll catch the first bus back that I can. I'll be there soon. Is Aunt Eudora there with you? You're not alone, are you?" I asked.

Yes. That's all I had, concern for my mother. Nowhere in me

did I feel a thing for the son of a bitch. Only for Mama. I knew I had to go back. I had to make sure she was okay. It was like a new responsibility, like being man of the house. "How did it happen?" I asked.

But to that question I got nothing but an earful of tears. Amazing. The man had been no good to her, and here she was all broken up. Love, I supposed, could be a terrible thing.

I tried to calm her down, but nothing I said helped much. I hung up the phone and thought, What to do next? I figured J.W. had to know. He was in his bedroom watching the TV he kept in there. Every weekday he ate lunch in his room and watched *The Andy Griffith Show*. He didn't like to be interrupted either, so I stood outside and waited until I heard a commercial come on. I knocked on the door. There was a rustling of papers and then his gruff, "Come in."

J.W. was always sunburned. I think even if he never went out in the sun again, his skin would stay red. The sun had permanently and forever changed it. Even his bald head was freckled.

I looked at him and figured there was no other way to do it. Blunt and simple. I said, "I've got to catch a bus home. Daddy's dead. I don't know how. Mama was too shook up to tell me. But I need to see her through this."

J.W. was not a man who showed emotion. And even this, the passing of his brother, did nothing to shake up his round red face. He took another bite of his sandwich and chewed it like it was beef jerky. He drank his beer. He ran his hand over his shiny head. "Well, I guess you do have to go. But I can't. Harvest. Too much to do for both of us to leave. I'll have one of the boys drive you into town tomorrow."

Then he nodded. His signal our discussion was over. I turned to walk out. I heard Andy tell Barney that no, he couldn't go dancing in Mount Pilot because Aunt Bea had planned a big dinner.

"Hey, son." I turned around. "Son"—that was a first. J.W. didn't look at me but stayed steady on Andy and Barney. "I hope you'll be coming back here. You learned good."

"Thank you, sir," I said, not believing my ears. I shut the door behind me. All of a sudden I felt that too much was happening at one time. As soon as I had started feeling comfortable, like things were going my way, something pushed me off balance, uprooted me once again. I walked back into the kitchen. The steak sandwich I had planned to pilfer was sitting on the counter. I rubbed my hand over my face and wondered how in the hell I was going to break the news to Soleil Marie. I grabbed the sandwich and headed out the kitchen door. And even though I was walking upright on my own two feet, I felt like I was tumbling through black space, like the one thing that the earth did not possess was solid ground.

Soleil Marie Beauvoir

This baby, now, was making me sick. It needed to grow, so I whispered, "Go on, baby. Get fat, like a little dove. I'll tell your papa tonight."

To meet Uncle's Boy in the evening time was my plan. But to see him and feel good I knew I had to go rest. Lorgina Piet, a good woman, a hard worker, she said to me, "Soleil Marie, you go lay that body down. If you were white, you would be pale."

So that is what I did. When lunch break came, I wandered back to my house. On my mattress I laid, and my black dog, she laid with me so happy she was to have me home. I drifted off to sleep, that sugar breeze blowing over me, and my dog protecting my baby and me.

I slept so hard and deep—the kind of sleep that allows not a single dream to be remembered. I think I could have slept straight through the night to morning had not a huge crash of thunder shook my house. I woke to its rumble and the dog ran through the room, and I says to the dog, "Don't worry, that's just Damballah doing his thing."

I brewed some garlic-root tea. I ate three dates. When this baby comes, it will be dates that give me the strength to bring it into this world. I sat on my porch and drank my tea. The rain started. I watched it fall on the world around me, and I breathed in its smell. The smell of the earth just beginning, that's what the rain smell is, I decided.

Better I felt after finishing my tea and dates. I brought in a tin tub I kept on my steps to catch rainwater in. I washed my face in it. Then I set it out again. Rainwater is good for medicine. The right herbs in that water is a magic thing.

So I sat watching this cleansing rain and hoping my Uncle's Boy would still show despite the weather. Sometimes Damballah would throw a spear of lightning across the sky. I would catch my breath, so beautiful it was.

And sure enough, he did show. He walked all the way to me through the cold rain, and he was soaking wet. And I smiled when I saw him there in the clearing. But him, he walked so slow and cautiously. When he reached the top stair and stood in my doorway, this is what he says to me: "Sweetness, lie down with me. I need for you to hold me."

I knew something so bad was wrong. So very quietly I took him by the hand and into my house. I took off his wet clothes, and we laid down under my old red-and-blue-and-yellow blanket that my mama wove years ago, when she was just a girl. We hung on tight to each other and my Uncle's Boy, he just cried right out loud so hard.

His skin was cool from the rain. The swamp and the fields were quiet except for the storm sounds. It should have been romantic. It should have been a celebration with me telling Uncle's Boy about our secret: our baby. But all there was in all my house was sadness.

Finally, when I thought maybe he could talk, I says, "Tell me, please. What so bad has happened?"

With those teeth of his clenched, with as much anger as sadness, he says, "The son of a bitch is dead."

This was such bad news. I was hoping my Uncle's Boy would forgive his papa while the man still lived. That way the legacy would be good. No angry, hurt parents passing on to the other side. No enemies to torture you in your dreams. No sad memories clouding your every day. "I'm so sorry," I said to my man.

He hugged me real close. "Soleil Marie," he said, "I know this

217

sounds crazy because I hate him so much. But now that he's dead, it's like a part of me is gone. I'm so mad and so hurt. Why couldn't he have lived to be an old man, running around Tiama like a fool? Maybe we would have never spoken to each other again, but at least he would have been out there like some sort of goddamned anchor.''

I brushed his beautiful curls off his forehead and whispered, "You know, I think your papa loved you even though he did a bad thing. And I think parents, they sometimes do the bad thing just because they're confused. Maybe give up your hate, Uncle's Boy. Maybe in his passing you can find that love for your papa again.''

"I'll never love him, Soleil Marie. Never.''

Now how could I tell him he had to? How could I tell him that he was going to have a baby and for its sake he had to forgive his papa? How could I say anything to my man who was so tangled up?

So I didn't. Instead, I held my Uncle's Boy and tried to comfort his hurting. And sometime that night he told me he was leaving. He was going to Tiama, to his mama. And I know he had to go. I know this was a good thing because at least he was honoring one of his parents. So there was no telling him he was having a baby. I had to make sure he felt so free to go do what he had to do. But I clung on tight, and I says to him, "Please be coming back here. I don't think I can live without you.'' And then I did this thing I hate. I started crying. Just like a weak woman. In between my sobbing I says, "Uncle's Boy, you got more family than you know.''

He kissed me all over. He kissed my feet and my ankles and my belly and my face. He promised me he'd come back. "I'm not sure when, Sweetness, but I love you. I will be back,'' he says.

And then, in the morning, he left.

Hauntings

Luella Jewel

 The newest of Mama's boyfriends, he was sitting at our supper table. And he was doing all kinds of things. Like, he was talking to dead people.

Mama and him did this a lot. They'd give me hot tea to drink. Then them, both together, they'd stare at the bottom of the cup when I was finished. Their hands touching. My mama's skinny red lips would be shut but still smiling. Then they'd read the crud floating at the bottom.

This one day it was really hot. And I didn't want nothing hot to drink. But they told me I had to. Tea-leaf reading was what they were about. Talking to me about how I had the gift. That ghosts wanted to talk to the world through me. And see, I have this stutter. It came on me like about a year and a half ago (that's what Mama says). Sometimes when I talk I can't barely get my words out. Mama and this boyfriend said it was because of the ghosts. They said them stutters were the ghosts trying to speak. So they made me drink this scalding tea. To see into the future, they said. But this time, like I sometimes do, by mistake I drank the tea and all the crud too.

They were kind of mad.

But I didn't care. I slapped a mosquito off my arm. It was hot. Real hot. I just wanted to go in the front yard and play in the sprinkler.

But Mr. Switzer, that was his name, he said to me, "Well, little girl, don't you want to know the future?"

My mama, her bony fingers most of the time hurt me when they touched me because she was what my friend Leslie Ann Williams calls "a squeezer." She grabbed my arm. She brushed my hair off my face. "Of course my Luella wants to know the future. Don't you, dear?" The big grin this time.

Now, I know this Mr. Switzer was one of Mama's best boyfriends, but I didn't like him. I thought he was scary. It bothered me when he kept talking about how spirits was always trying to enter my body so as to speak to the world.

I liked Bobby Reynolds. That boyfriend was a guard at the fed. That was right across the street from us. He told neat stories and always brought me a cold drink. But this Mr. Switzer—nasty as a pig. Sometimes I wanted to kick him, bite him. But I didn't, because I knew I'd get slapped.

Mr. Switzer, he says to me, "Right here." And he pointed a long white finger at his bald head. "Touch my brain."

Was he crazy? No way was I going to touch his brain. "Wh-what do you m-m-mean?"

I walked backward, away from him. He was ugly.

He took his big glasses off his face and pointed at a spot on his head. "See this?"

It was a dent. Right there. On his head.

"What you're looking at, my child, is no accident, but an act of God."

My mama, she made a noise.

"Dear, why don't you tell Luella how you lost your skull? Luella, this is a good story. Sit down and listen to Mr. Switzer."

I wished with all my heart that my Aunt Rose was here. Because she, she always tells my mama, "Shit, Eudora. This is complete and utter nonsense. And for Christ's sakes leave Luella out of this."

But she never comes over when *he's* here.

Mama glared at me. "Sit."

I slumped over to the chair. I was *so* hot.

"Well, ladies." Mr. Switzer drank his beer straight from the can. Not like my mama. Hers was always in her coffee cup. The one with blue daisies. "I lost my skull, like I said, through an act of God. So that my brain would be exposed to the vibrations of this world and the next. Oh, to the average man I lost my skull to a traffic accident. But no!" He leaned across the supper table and pointed his glasses at me. "No! God caused me to lose part of my skull so that those who have departed from us can speak to me from the grave."

He touched his brain. "It's a steel plate. Acts as an antenna to the spirit world."

Bobby Reynolds, the boyfriend I liked, he told me that the fed was built on an old Indian burial ground. And that the prison was haunted by the leader of the Seminoles. Bobby called him Chief Wandering Lake. Then there was my daddy. He died when I was just a baby. And then Uncle Charlie. I didn't go to his funeral. Mama said I was too little. I was only three, but I remember Aunt Rose's red eyes from all her crying.

I looked at my mama and then at Mr. Switzer. He says to me, he says, "You know, child, children are naturally more receptive to messages from the dead than we adults."

My mama said, "Is that right? Well, Luella, go on, touch Mr. Switzer's brain. Who knows who will speak to us? Maybe President Kennedy. He hasn't been dead very long. Or even Roosevelt. Or maybe that skinny old Lincoln! Or maybe some long-dead ghost doctor who'll have a cure for that stuttering of yours."

I was so hot. And I was thirsty. That big fat Switzer staring at me. I didn't want my daddy talking to me. Dead fingers touching me. Maybe hurting me. What did dead people do when they came back? Maybe my daddy was a mean person. Maybe he was angry at me for him being dead and me being alive.

I jumped from the chair, and I hit my funny bone on the chair arm. But it wasn't funny. Nothing was funny. I looked at my mama. Her stupid smile. Trying to make me talk to dead people. Trying to make me listen to those dead, gray voices whispering, whispering, whispering. I looked at that ugly old Switzer-kitzer.

"I h-h-hate you," I screamed at him. "I hate you."

I ran to my bedroom. And then, because I was so mad, I slammed the door as hard as I could.

Rose Looney

My house is falling down around me. And I don't even care. What is a woman supposed to do about windows with broken glass? About a house that needs paint on the inside as well as the outside? About a toilet that runs all the time, even after I've shaken the handle?

I think these thoughts during my walk home from work. See, I don't have a car. I gave Charlie's Black Beauty to my son. I can't take the memory. Every time I looked at that car I saw images of Charlie. Charlie driving like a madman down A1A. Charlie up early on a Saturday morning polishing that car like it was a jewel. Charlie dead drunk and asleep in the car. Charlie honking the horn, imploring me to go for a spin.

What Emory has done with the car I have no idea. I never see him. He waltzed in here after Charlie died and then waltzed out. Like my life has nothing to do with him. Oh, once in a rare while I get a letter from him. Occasionally a phone call.

After Charlie died, I went to work. I had to. No life insurance. No pension plan. He never held a job long enough. So I inspect chickens. For the Florida poultry-processing plant. I make sure all the feathers are off and the skin looks healthy, not green, free of disease. It's about three miles from my house. Some days one of the girls gives me a ride to and from. But some days I'd just rather walk.

It is hot and humid. My uniform is sticking to me. I am but a block from my house, the prison trusties' farm to my right, when I spot the green Olds. Harry Switzer's green Olds, parked as pretty as you please right smack in front of Eudora's house. What a fool that woman is making of herself. An absolute fool. It doesn't matter that the man is from Jacksonville. Everyone in town knows he is married. His wife, so I hear, suffers from diabetes. A bad case of it. I hear it has just about taken her sight away.

Now, I have rarely approved of any of the men Eudora has shacked up with. But this Harry Switzer, what a case! His job is

224

to sell things—shampoos, floor cleaners, hairsprays, pots and pans.
A door-to-door man. That's how he and Eudora met. Showed up
at her doorstep one morning and didn't leave until six or seven that
evening.

Oh, I've watched it all. Saw how in the beginning he'd walk up
to her door carrying his trunk of what-have-yous. But soon that
charade gave way. In no time at all the trunk stayed in the car. In
its place was a crystal ball and a spray of flowers. Not even the
pretense of doing business. The man calls himself gifted. Says he
is a parapsychologist.

That'll be the day.

Yes, I met him once. And once was enough.

I peer into his car as I walk by. A tricounty map is on the front
seat. An empty peanut wrapper. A pack of Kools on the dashboard.
I find myself wishing there was something more in the car. Something that would incriminate him in the eyes of Eudora. Like maybe
a smut magazine left wide open. Or a note from another girlfriend.
Surely Eudora isn't the *only* fling. But nothing. Just an unkept car
and an odometer that reads 46,782 miles.

I walk past Eudora's house. I pause in the street and look at my
little place. No more flowers. One shutter is hanging by a thread.
Peeled, chipped paint. A rotting fence. But so what, I think to
myself. Who in hell am I going to impress by fixing it up?

I unlock the front door and then immediately open all the windows. The house is like an oven. I go into my bedroom to get out
of my sticky uniform and put on something cooler. The bedroom,
it is really nothing more than a changing room since Charlie died.
Maybe it is because he died in the bed, I don't know. But since the
night it happened, I haven't slept in that bed. And I never will.

I pull the rayon smock off over my head and drop it on the floor.
I catch a glimpse of myself in my vanity mirror. The mirror is
cracked near the top. I'd hit it one day with the broom. I had been
attempting to get cobwebs out of the ceiling corner and whacked
that mirror like it was a baseball. I'm surprised I didn't do more
than just crack it.

For a moment I stand there naked, staring at my reflection. I
mean, I'm naked except for the bracelet. I found it a couple of weeks

after Charlie died. It was buried in his underwear drawer. One penny on a sterling chain. Stamped the year he was born. Now what am I supposed to make of that? What was he doing with it? Was it for me? Was it a gift for me he just never had the chance to give? Or was it for someone else? Did Charlie stay unfaithful to me until the day he died?

I didn't have any answers. But I tell you this: When I found it, I put it on my wrist, and I've never taken it off. Not even when I bathe. I just let it haunt me. Dangling on my wrist like a question mark.

I look hard at myself in the mirror. Since Charlie died, I've sure let myself go. No more twenty-six-inch waist. No more size nines. I trace my finger along the scar on my belly—a reminder of my son delivered to the world via a cesarean. It is a scar that I've viewed alternately as a badge of honor and an embarrassment. An embarrassment because it is disfiguring. An honor because it is a reminder of how I forced Emory into the world with tremendous effort and love.

However, as I stare at the mirror and feel the scar's edges that are still rough after all these years, any romantic notions evaporate. It is just a scar. Nothing more.

I throw on my housecoat and go into the kitchen to fix some iced tea. I hear a pounding on my back stoop. I look out my kitchen window. It is Luella bouncing one of those brightly colored play balls. Her hair is pulled back tight in one long braid. God, she looks like her daddy. And by her actions she certainly doesn't take after that mother of hers. Luella is a tomboy. She stands up for herself and doesn't let people walk all over her.

I open my back door. "Hey, skitterbrain. You want to join me for some iced tea and some lemon cookies?"

She shrugs her shoulders, but I see a little brightness fire her eyes. "Well, come on in. But leave your ball outside," I say.

I watch as she sets the ball by the door and then sits herself down at the kitchen table.

"What's your mother doing?"

"I d-don't know," she lies, but very shyly. I feel awful about that

226

stutter of hers. My theory is that she stutters because Eudora provides her with such a crappy home life.

I pour us two tall glasses of tea and set a plate of cookies between us.

"Harry Switzer's over at your house, isn't he?" I sip my tea. Luella dunks a cookie in hers. She nods yes.

"H-he was t-t-trying to make me touch his brain. So I could talk to dead people. Like my d-daddy."

"He's doing what! Is that mother of yours completely out of her mind?"

Luella blinks her wide eyes. She sucks some cookie crumbs off her finger. Then she says, "Mama thought m-maybe President Lincoln would talk to me. T-tell me how to stop my stuttering."

I throw my hands up in exasperation. This is just too much. I refill Luella's tea and then mine. "Listen to me, young lady. I've been your mother's friend for years. I've stood by her in some of her roughest times. Like, for instance, when your father died. I was there helping her every step of the way. Why, even Uncle Charlie helped out. But something has gone a little wrong with your mother." I stop. I know I am treading on some dangerous ground. I have to pick my words very carefully. I want to help Luella, not scare her with my concern.

She grabs the last cookie off the plate. I retrieve the box from the kitchen counter and set out a few more. The poor little girl is ravenous.

"Luella, what did you eat for lunch today?"

She pops a cookie in her mouth and mumbles, "A peanut butter s-s-sandwich."

"Peanut butter. Is that all you ate? No corn, no green beans, no—I don't know—no applesauce?"

The little girl shakes her head no. I swear, some days I can't believe how unfair life can be. Here I sit, a person capable of being a perfectly good parent, and my only child refuses to let me mother him. And Eudora is blessed with this wonderful little girl, and she ignores her.

"I've got an idea." I pat Luella's hand. "How would you like to have supper with me tonight? And we can have a slumber party after that. Just you and me. After supper I'll pop up some popcorn and we'll watch TV. How's that sound?"

I know I kind of push it. I mean, I don't wait for her answer. But that's because I know what is best for her in this instance. Why, no telling what time Harry Switzer would be breezing out of there tonight. I jump up and go for the phone. "Now Luella, I don't want you worrying about anything I've said. It's just that your mother doesn't deal with all her senses when it comes to men." I dial Eudora's number. It rings five full times before she bothers to pick it up. I am so fed up with her just the sound of her voice makes me mad. "Hello, Eudora," I say as nice as I can manage. "I just thought I'd let you know Luella wants to spend the night over here tonight, and I've told her it's okay."

Then she asks me if I'm sure it is all right. As if she really cares.

"Of course it's okay. I don't mind at all. If you need us for anything just call," I say, but I am afraid I haven't totally hidden the edge of sarcasm in my voice. Knowing Eudora, however, she probably doesn't catch it.

I hang up the phone. I hear the thump, thump, thump of Luella's ball pounding the side of my house. I pick up her empty glass. She's eaten all the cookies but one. I sink my teeth into it, and while I chew I think about how nice it is to have a child in the house.

Luella Jewel

 My Aunt Rose, she told me to sleep at her house one night. So I did.

But I was scared.

I got to thinking about ghosts. About how dead people wanted to talk to me because I was a gifted child. I didn't want the gift. I wished ugly old Switzer had never told me about it.

So when I went to bed in Aunt Rose's big bed, I was scared for her to turn out the light. But I couldn't tell her that. I didn't want to be called a baby. She tucked me in the covers. She was big and always smelled salty. But I liked her anyways. She kissed me on the forehead.

"Sleep tight. Don't let the bedbugs bite," she said.

"After a while, c-c-crocodile," I told her. Then I said, "Aunt Rose, you aren't going to c-c-close the door all the way, are you?"

"Oh no, sweetie. I'll leave it open. And you just call me if you need me."

She turned out the light and left me alone. The bed seemed huge. Shadows moved everywhere. I wanted to turn over and sleep, but I was afraid.

What would happen if I turned my back? I made certain to keep my hands and my feet on the bed, under the covers. Ghosts could be hiding under the bed. Maybe flying around me, waiting for the one minute I was not looking for them. Then they'd swoop down from the ceiling and choke me.

I thought of Chief Wandering Lake. Maybe he was angry because of the cowboy-and-Indian days. Maybe he was out for scalps. Then I thought, No, he probably likes kids. Maybe if I have the gift I'll be able to wish for things and, poof, there they'll be. Like maybe he could help me with my math. Or like maybe I should wish for a new pair of tennis shoes.

I heard Aunt Rose making her bed on the couch. I saw the tail of a sheet rise through the air like magic. Then settle on Aunt Rose's couch.

The wind outside was making shadows in the bedroom dance. I pulled up the sheet to cover myself completely, except my face. And I said my wish but not out loud. I didn't need to say it out loud. Old Switzer says spirits can read your mind. So I just moved my lips. My wish was, Please, Chief Wandering Lake, give me a new pair of shoes. The kind with long white laces.

I didn't move a muscle. I didn't even dare breathe. Waiting, waiting for the shoes. But then I only got scareder. I thought, Oh, no. I thought maybe Chief Wandering Lake was bad. And as soon as I went to sleep he'd stuff my feet into my new shoes and tie the laces tighter and tighter until my toes, even my pinkies, could not move or breathe. And all my blood would be cut off from my feet. I saw Chief Wandering Lake—I mean, in my head, of course—leaning over my feet, and my laces were long as snakes. He had an ugly smile on his face. A devil laugh. And he was tying my laces tighter, tighter, tighter until my feet started to drop off my ankles.

And then the worst part happened. Mama has a picture of my daddy. It hangs on the wall in our living room. That's how I know what he looks like. I saw Chief Wandering Lake's face explode. And in its place was my daddy's. My daddy was coming back to haunt me—all because I had the gift. I saw him stretch those laces far over his head. I imagined him saying things like, "I'll teach you not to talk back to your mother" and "So how many boyfriends does she have?"

Then I thought to myself, No. Maybe my daddy's ghost is nice. Maybe he wants to help me. But I didn't want any help from a ghost. In my mind I saw the picture again: My daddy pulling those laces so tight my toes squirted blood.

A cat outside the window made some kind of growl. I froze. I saw the shadows in the room reaching out to grab me. I said forget it. I got hold of my pillow and jumped out of bed. I ran to the living room. Aunt Rose was sleeping. Snoring. I threw the pillow on the floor by the couch. I laid down.

But I didn't fall asleep for a long time. I laid there listening to Aunt Rose's snores.

And I listened for other sounds. Maybe whispers, maybe growls, from the spirit world.

Emory Looney

I was the new shucker at Pelican Bill's Seafood Restaurant on Cocoa Beach. That meant I stood behind the oyster bar, a white apron covering my blue jeans and my Pelican Bill's T-shirt, with a silver glove made of mesh steel on one hand. Its purpose was to protect my hand from both the sharp oyster shells and the oyster blade I used to force open the fish. The blades were kept so sharp that one slip, one out-of-control flick, could mean a slit wrist.

This was not a job I particularly enjoyed.

It was a step up from busing tables, though. And a whole lot better than the janitor job I had but one brief week. As a janitor, all I did was clean toilets and pick up trash at a shopping center. Never again. People eyeing you like you were trash, just because you had to pick up *their* trash.

I'd been at Pelican Bill's for three months. Been in Cocoa for four. Three months, that's the longest I'd kept a job since Daddy died.

I'd become sort of a traveling man. Me in the old man's car, driving from town to town, job to job, flirtation to flirtation. It was a stupid thing to be doing. I knew that. But it was also like I didn't have a choice. Seemed like no matter how hard I tried to get it together, I just kept spinning out. It had been over a year since I'd left Soleil Marie, and not a day went by that I didn't hurt like hell over it. I never meant to be gone so long. But nothing in my life was right. A lot of my time was spent talking to her in my head. I'd tell her my troubles and try to imagine the advice she'd give me. When I went to sleep at night—even if I was holding somebody else—I dreamed it was Soleil Marie I was holding. I had to get back there. I knew that. But like a nightmare in which you fall down and can't move even though the rattlesnake is gaining on you, I couldn't seem to gather enough courage to face her. I didn't know why. Maybe because I'd blown things with my mama, and my daddy's ghost haunted me continually. In a matter of seconds I could go from hating him to loving him and back to hating. It kept

231

me bouncing. And the longer I bounced and the longer I stayed away from Soleil Marie, the more I knew she wouldn't take back a bum like me.

So that's why I was hanging loose at Pelican Bill's, standing behind the oyster bar, looking out at the afternoon customers. Most were tourists. Sunburned and oiled. Hats on head, lots of jewelry. The men wore shoes with socks—even the men who wore shorts. It was a funny sight. And they seemed to treat seafood like it was some sort of delicacy. And they treated me like I was a circus attraction. *Watch that blade spin. See the man risk death as he dazzles you with his amazing shell-shucking.*

And I wasn't even that good yet.

But of course, I knew I would never, ever get that good either. Because what I had was an urge not to be the world's greatest oyster-shucker but to get back on the road. The itch had returned, and I had to scratch it. Had no idea where I might go. Maybe between lunch and dinner, or at sunrise, or in my sleep, I'd find the courage I needed to head south again.

I gazed past the tourist customers and out the windows. In the parking lot, in all her faded glory, sat the Black Beauty. Oh, she'd done good by me. She always got me where I wanted to go. But I'd mistreated her. I'd wait until she was almost drip-dry of oil before I'd refill her. I never performed maintenance on the car. I just waited until something broke before I fixed it. And also there was this thing about the Black Beauty: She didn't shine anymore. My daddy seemed to spend his each and every waking hour—when he wasn't raising hell—polishing her. Not me. Not once in all the time I owned her did I polish her up. Then of course there's the bumper. I got rear-ended by a cab one time when I was driving through Orlando. Squashed it in like it was cardboard. And getting bent up like that caused rust to set in. No way was I going to spend the money to get it fixed.

I remember when I got the Black Beauty. My mama was all grief-stricken over him dying. I tried to comfort her for a while. I told her I'd take care of everything, that there was no need for her to be sad. But nothing I said was enough. She stayed sad. She stayed wrapped up in the man who'd kicked me out of the house.

Then she said to me about two weeks after the funeral, "Emory, here are the keys." She held them up by their white rabbit's-foot keychain. "Charlie would have wanted you to have that car out there. I don't need it. I can't take it. It keeps too many memories alive. I know you'll take care of it the way your father would want you to."

And she put the keys in my hand and pressed my fingers shut over them. And she cried.

I could not believe it, no sir. Here she was, acting as though the man had loved me or something. Acting as though no bad blood had ever passed between us. It was then I knew I had to leave. There would be no being the head of the house. No being a babied son. Her love was all for him.

Three days later I left.

And I've not been back. But I have written from time to time. I'm not an unfeeling bastard. I'm just trying to get things together. Sometimes I think I'll just get in the car and go pick up Soleil Marie and take her home to meet Mama. "Here, Mama, meet my colored girlfriend, Soleil Marie." The shock on her face would be worth a million laughs. But she'd handle it. Eventually.

"Hey, are you in there?" It was Tracey. One of the waitresses. She was real nice. Pretty blue eyes.

"Oh, I'm sorry. Just daydreaming for a minute," I apologized.

"Well, don't let Bill catch you. He's in a shitty mood," she said. She pulled a package of saltines from her apron and opened them. It always shocked me when pretty girls cussed. "I need two dozen oysters, pronto," she ordered, and then popped two crackers, whole, into her mouth.

I nodded. I iced two platters. Just like the training manual said to do, I arranged the half-shells in two circles.

"Hey, what are you doing? No baker's dozens around here."

I looked at her. I was truly puzzled.

"The oysters," she said. "You put thirteen on that plate."

Like an idiot, I stood there and counted. Sure enough, she was right. I took one off. I fixed her second platter. She garnished both with red sauce and lemon. I watched her walk off, carrying the platters as if there was no way she'd ever, ever drop one. As if

233

accidents were something that just never happened to her. The sun on her blond hair, it made it shine. That hair of hers, I decided, was really beautiful. And then I had this funny hope. I hoped it wasn't bleached.

One of the busers, the new guy they hired after promoting me, he let down the blinds. One of the tourists must have complained about the afternoon glare.

I couldn't see the Black Beauty anymore. The lowered blinds blocked my view. And the sun didn't filter through the windows anymore, so it couldn't light up Tracey's hair. It was probably out of a bottle after all. Nothing is that pretty by itself, I told myself.

Over by the kitchen's swinging doors, Pelican Bill, in the flesh, was standing there. Watching me doing nothing. He was fifty-some years old, wore fat diamond rings, and told fishing stories to anyone and everyone who would listen.

I picked up an oyster, and despite all that steel mesh, I felt the stubborn shell give as I sank the blade in.

Soleil Marie Beauvoir

I'd thought that it would all be different, no. That in the cities I would find a fine job. And my baby would be dressed in pretty clothes. And even without my Uncle's Boy, my baby and me would make a happy life here in the city.

I had waited so long for him. Every day I lit candles and said prayers and wished him back. But none of them prayers of mine were answered, no.

Soleil Marie, I said to myself, the man has left you and he is never coming back. So why stay where the *loa* don't listen and the memories don't stop? I'd heard of so many of my Haitian people, living the life in Miami. So that's what I did. I took my baby in my arms and I left them fields.

But you know, it just proved to be mean. Take this room of mine,

234

yes. One little window. No breeze can squeeze through. I see not whole clouds. Just parts of them. And hot. It's like dying, it is. And many days the plumbing, it doesn't work. And the roaches and rats are plenty. And the food is not enough. And my baby and I are getting skinny. Oh, so skinny.

What am I doing? What for am I here? Those questions, yes, seem to be the only sounds inside my voice.

But at least there is my baby. Her color, yes, it is so pretty. It's like Uncle's Boy and me, our skin just melted together to make another skin, so much prettier than our own. And this hair of hers. No one has seen prettier. It is yellow, sun-bleached cane. Curls around her face. She is what I love now in this world. She is what I ask the *loa* to protect. Although this I must say. In the city, *loa*, not are they so powerful.

Judy is my friend who lives down the hall. To my room she would be very soon. She watches Charlité.

Charlité.

Charlité is my baby's name. I named her to honor Uncle's Boy's dead papa. This is the thought that came to me: Maybe, with my strong will, I can ease the man's suffering by naming his grandchild for him. I'd asked once of Uncle's Boy, What is your papa's real name? And to me he said, "Charlie." So, Charlité. See, this is one thing I'm sure of: Uncle's Boy did nothing to honor his papa's passing.

I was playing bird with Charlité when Judy knocked on the door. Holding our arms out like great wings, that's what we did. And then to swoop around the ugly room, saying "whooosh." Judy had on almost no clothes, because it was hot, no. She was a fat woman. A white woman. Judy Gabinski. But lots of boyfriends she had. I asked her how she got so many of them. She smiled real big, showing her one tooth off to the side to be gone, and she says to me, "Why, Soleil Marie, it's my personality."

But I know what it was, really. She kept marijuana in her room. Now this she never smoked when she watched my baby. To this I made her swear. But those boyfriends, they were there to smoke her drugs. She just gave them free to all the people who wanted. It was her way to be happy. She never guessed, this woman, that when the drugs were all gone, so would the crocodile friends be gone.

"Did you finish that homework I gave you?" she asked as she bent over to kiss Charlité, her boobs almost falling out the little halter top she liked to wrap herself in.

I handed her pages. *I moved to Miami because of my baby.* That's how the first sentence it began, my homework. "I am a good student, no?" I asked. I'd been in this city almost five months, and the first, the only person to be my friend, yes, it was Judy. And teaching me to read, she took up where Uncle's Boy dumped me.

"So, back in a few hours, I should," I said to her. This keeping my life tied to so many hours, it was not any easy thing. In the fields we just knew by the sun. And the work was hard, but so often it was steady, even. Here, I am tied to that Mr. Gibson, the owner of the Jupiter Motel. That's my job. I clean rooms, a maid, at the Jupiter. I'm either not fast enough for the man, or I'm too fast, or I clean too much, or I don't clean enough. Uncle, he just had us do the cane. We do it good, and he never complained to us. That much, yes, I must say for him.

Judy Gabinski, she worked five nights at this restaurant she says is famous, Wolfie's. This I cannot believe. I think my friend Judy likes to tell stories, to make things better than they are, you see. "Hey, ah, listen, Soleil"—Judy had a very funny way to speak. She says to me she was born in a city called Brotherly Love. She says all everybody speaks that way there. "I'm thinking about having you and maybe Rick over for spaghetti Sunday night. Do you think you can make it?"

Now this is an example, yes, of being tied to hours. I not only have to be at the Jupiter to please everything about Mr. Gibson, my Judy, she wants to plan all my free time too. But see what I do? I just nod my head. Afraid to make Judy angry. My only friend. Plus, see, it means some food. Good food.

I say my good-byes, I check to make sure my candle—only one candle these days because it is not like back in the fields, where I could make them so easy—is still burning. I kiss my Charlité. I tell her, "Now, who is your mama's favorite angel?"

And my baby smiles. She says, "Me, me, Mama."

I have to go past eighteen houses or buildings to get to the Jupiter.

I counted them one day so that no never would I lose my way. So many tall buildings, all in pretty colors, easy to get lost, yes.

It was early in the day, but already cars and trucks and buses. Everybody they honk and yell. It seems to me they are all angry. Not a soul happy, this I say to myself.

Finally, after walking, walking, walking, I get to the Jupiter. Walking in the city, on hot concrete, there's no joy like the walking on swamp earth.

I open the door to which it says EMPLOYEES ONLY. Inside it is cool. Air-conditioned. Uncle's Big House had this cold air almost all the time. I put my card that I have to write my name on every week into the big metal box. The box writes on my card the exact time, the exact hour and second, I come to work. It's like a *loa* that don't ever let you forget a damn thing. Its whole front is a clock. I punch in. That's what they call it. Punch in, like I'm hitting a body.

Mr. Gibson, he walks around the corner, so fast. Everything that man does is so fast. A rabbit in some life, him.

"Miss Beauvoir," he said, but the voice, it was high, like some kind of tension might explode through the mouth. A pencil, slim like his fingers, in his hand. His fingers, moving up and down the pencil all the time he spoke, like worms under the sun. "You are fifteen minutes late. Again. Now you know, I insist my employees punch in on time. You understand, don't you? I mean, your English is not *that* bad, is it?"

To him I could not speak. I put my eyes lower, not to look at his.

"Well, perhaps it is. Listen, Miss Beauvoir, I have just a small motel here. I have to work extra hard to keep up with the likes of the Deauville, the Fontainebleau. Cleanliness is very important in this business. My maids need to be punctual."

Punctual—a word I didn't know. I'd have to ask Judy. I looked up at Mr. Gibson, past the crawling fingers, his. But still to speak, no, it was not possible. I thought if I opened my mouth tears would fall out. It was with a good heart I walked here this morning. No meaning in anything I did to make this man mad. I nodded my head at him. He nodded back, then walked past me, like everything in the world was understood and written in blood somewhere that only white people and rich people could read it.

237

From the supply room and its gray walls I pulled my cleaning cart. I pushed it out into the big heat of the day.

I knocked at the orange door of room A. "Maid service," I called.

There was no answer back, so with what Mr. Gibson calls a skeleton key—not a good phrase, I wanted to tell him—I unlocked the door.

Whoever was being in this room was not checked out, because, see, the suitcase, wide open it was on the bed. But no one was home, so I began my job.

A big liquor-drinker, I said to myself. Because the wastebasket, full to the brim with bad-smelling bottles. A liquor called Wild Turkey. In the sink, there were three cans of Schlitz floating in water. Now this I've seen before. To ice the beer in the sink, but not let melted water run out. Probably too drunk to let the melted water out. They should just drink rum. Good for the inner sight, it is.

So a drinker I had on my hands, but what else did this person do?

I go to the closet. A good place to find answers.

U.S. Navy. That was what was in gold on a hat set so properly in the closet. And uniforms, so stiff and straight they must hurt to wear. And big shoes, thick, shining like cockroach shells.

Oh, yes. My dream was to go barefoot again, all the time, like back home. This wearing of shoes, like putting our feet in prison, no good it was.

I had to stop nosing and go to work. I moved the suitcase off the bed. To the suitcase stand I put it.

I changed the sheets, fast. I could do this real well. And I liked to snap the fresh white sheet in the air, letting it float to the bed. It looked so graceful. Free. It looked like a good place to sleep with that sheet flying down like a feather.

I straightened the wall picture. It was all ugly oranges, yellows. Flower petals that seemed, yes, to scream. This picture I did not like.

To dust the rooms when visitors were still there, this was a hard thing to do. Never did you know if you could move all their belongings, so many belongings, to one side, so as to make a clean space.

"Do your best," is all Mr. Gibson would say, "but don't do too much. Don't give guests the impression you were snooping."

So I go to the dresser, where all this sailor's stuff was spread. Coins. One dollar and fifty-three cents in nickels, dimes, and pennies. A paper with a phone number written on it. Two cigarette packs. Camels. One opened. One not opened. And then, what do I see? I see little books. Paper books that say "Tourist Information." Then, in big red letters, HAITI.

Out loud, to this whole room, I say, "Oh my, Soleil Marie."

I picked them up. On the front of one was a pretty Haitian woman, smiling so big, giant red flowers in her hand.

By the sea. That is where she stood.

I sat down on the bed. I looked at these pretty, slick pages. Pictures of the land my mama came from. I began to read: Haiti's official language is French. Deforestation—a word I don't understand—is a major problem. Sugar cane is the island's biggest cash crop.

Sugar cane. I looked to the picture. A picture of workers in the field. Smiling for the camera man. In their hands were the machetes, and the cane, yes, was standing so tall and pretty. Ready for the harvest.

A second picture had some boy with the cane in his mouth, sucking its sweet, sweet juice.

Oh, how I wanted the taste of fresh cane in my mouth. Then it was that I knew coming to the city was like cutting off my arms, yes. I looked at the faces, those in the picture. They could have been the faces of my David, my Lorgina, all my good friends who still made a life in those fields. Still free to practice our Voodoo right out under all the stars. Not to be hidden behind an old door and four roach-crawling walls. A sacrifice I had not done in a long, long time. What was there for me to do? With my baby? With my life? I could see this. I could see me maybe losing my religion. And Charlité never growing up in the ways. Big-city people with no souls. Yes. Oh, my. What had I done, me, by coming to this city? But did I want my Charlité so poor and working for the man who lived in the Big House? Then I thought in a way I hated to think.

239

To myself I wondered, If I'd told Uncle's Boy that he was to be a papa, would he have come back to my fields? Would he have loved me, and maybe make like a family? All this loneliness over my Charlité, all these scared nights when I said maybe we get kicked from this terrible apartment room, or maybe we run out of food and Mr. Gibson quits me, or maybe somebody, yes, they break in where we live because to rob—even though we own nothing. What if Uncle's Boy to find me tried but could not?

I looked at these little paper books in my lap. To take them I must. The sailor, he would not care, because—now he didn't know it, no, but he left them for me. This I knew. But stealing, that is not a thing that I do.

See now, in my pocket I keep a few shells. Shells I pick up on the beach. And I go into the Catholic church that is six buildings from where we live. I take Charlité's little plastic cup. I dip it in the holy water. To home I go and there I rest the shells, into the holy water. I say my prayers to Damballah-wedo and Erzulie and to maybe my parents and to whoever other *loa* I believe will make the shells do good luck.

So this sailor, I thought, maybe he could use some good luck. Maybe they were going to send him to that war this country was fighting so far away. I put the little Haiti books in the pocket of mine. And out I brought one good-luck shell. Blessed in good holy water, that shell had been. To his suitcase I went. Everything said *U.S. Navy* on it. Even the underwear. I thought, Where to put it, where to put it? Folded so neatly, in the top corner, was a pair of socks. I thought, Now yes, that is the place. So into his Navy sock I put his gift, his good-luck shell.

I said, "Damballah-wedo, bless this man."

And as I walked out the door, pulling my cart, I could hear my Haiti books whispering to me, brushing against the cloth of my skirt.

Emory Looney

The Atlantic, because of the setting of the sun, shimmered in aquas and golds. I'd driven to the beach to unwind a little after work. I had a Jax with me and a bag of barbecued potato chips. I'd parked by the Space Coast Arcade. Everything in Cocoa Beach, just about, had to do with space. That's because NASA was here, at Cape Kennedy, which used to be Cape Canaveral. But because the president got shot the state went crazy and renamed everything they could Kennedy this or Kennedy that.

I sat on the beach, but behind me, up at the arcade, the pinball machines rang and buzzed. Kids yelled at the machines like their voices might somehow guide those little steel balls to first base, or Mars, or the wizard's dungeon.

Sea gulls circled overhead, squawking. I tossed a chip to the littlest bird I saw, the one that looked like it needed it the most. But just like life, a big-bully gull swooped down and stole it away.

Lovers of all ages—sixteen, thirty, eighty—strolled past. Some acted like they were shell hunting. Most of the younger ones were hippies. Probably antiwar protesters and civil rights marchers. I should be like that, I thought. But no, I knew that was impossible. Something kept me paralyzed, even the smallest action was beyond my capability.

I watched pelicans skim the water's surface. They were so precise. So perfect. It amazed me that animals that, when you got right down to it, were goofy-looking could be so damned graceful. Ballerinas right out there on the water.

And then, along the horizon, the shrimp boats, their nets up. Floating like bathtub toys so far, far away.

Mama always used to take me to the beach when I was a kid. We'd sit in the sand and watch those boats for hours. She'd make up stories about where they'd been and who the sailors were.

And when we eventually got tired of that, we'd turn to the clouds. She'd point at one and say, "Look, Emory, there's Old Father Time. Looks like he's smoking a pipe."

And I'd find Old Father Time, and I'd always say, "Look at how long his beard is, Mama."

But I'd spot other things in the sky, each more fantastic than the last. Often I saw dragons and castles. Lots of times I saw pretty ladies. Princesses, I told Mama. I'd always point out their long, long hair.

And sometimes we'd get silly. Like Mama would say, "Look at the cloud over there. Why, it's skinny enough to be Aunt Eudora. Well, it is Aunt Eudora."

And I'd say, "Mama, that big fat one next to it. It looks like Daddy when he wakes up in the morning. I hear him burping. It is Daddy!"

And then we'd collapse into giggles, and her arms would be around me, so comfortable and sure.

And so as I sat, reminiscing to myself, my Jax almost gone, the urge to try my childhood game came on real strong. To play Name That Cloud, right there, all by myself.

I looked up without even having to squint, because the sun was behind me. The thick white clouds rolled past. Puffs breaking up the sky's aqua blue. I expected immediately to see a shape, to give it a name. A dog, a cat, the wizard. But the more I looked, the more frustrated I got, because the shapes weren't there. There was no Old Father Time. No wizards and princesses. No sleepy-eyed, grumpy Daddy. There were just big clouds, and try as I might, they didn't remind me of anything.

It was an awful feeling. Like something was gone from me. An ability to see, stolen. When had I lost it? What was it that had happened to me? I looked at the scene around me. The few people, the birds, the pinball players up at the arcade. I felt like every single thing was moving on, doing something, achieving things. Even the old sea gulls—"flying rats" is what my daddy had called them— they seemed completely caught up in flying and feeding. They had a sense of community about them, even in their fighting. When one flew, they all flew. When one lit down on the wet sand and strolled, they 'most all did the same. Where in the world had I gone wrong?

I looked back up at the sky. The clouds skimmed by, but still nothing, as if a part of my memory or my brain power had shut down. I wondered, If I'd come here yesterday and looked up, would all the old familiar shapes in the sky be floating by? Or what about tomorrow? Maybe all this was just a momentary loss.

Then I looked down at the sand and told myself, Emory Looney, you are being stupid. It was just a kid's game. You're older now. Not being able to play a game designed for four-year-olds is nothing to get all bothered about.

The gulls were flying over, crying. They wanted food. More barbecued chips. I felt trapped, suffocated, as if there were no possibilities. I closed my eyes but I did not see blackness. What I saw was Soleil Marie gazing at me as if she really did love me. I knew what I had to do. Some way, somehow, I had to force myself to get back in that car and head down to the fields. I had to see if Soleil Marie would forgive me.

Rose Looney

 "*You* just don't know how to live life," Eudora snaps. "*You* are turning into a nasty old woman afraid to love anything but that dead husband of yours."

We are cutting red feathers out of posterboard. We are creating a beautiful, and hopefully unforgettable, costume for Luella. She has been chosen to play the Little Red Hen in the school play. She is the star. The main attraction. The little girl who will command all the attention onstage. This I have explained to her thickheaded mother repeatedly. Her thickheaded mother claims they jerked her out of the chorus and made her play a chicken because of the stutter.

I know better.

But Eudora has managed to get me off the track of Luella and onto myself. She's doing this because I've been hounding her about that damn Harry Switzer. I look up from my posterboard. My hands are getting tired, and I know that I'm developing arthritis. Eudora

243

has taken to curling her hair like Tammy Wynette's. The only problem is, she isn't Tammy Wynette—she is about twenty years older than Miss Wynette. She wears pink rouge and has switched from her usual blue eye shadow to gold. And she looks ridiculous. So I tell her so.

"Eudora, say what you want about me, but you look ridiculous. You're dressing like a fool." I refine the point at the tail end of my feather.

"You know, Rose, I may be wrong here, but you sound like you're jealous of me. Yes. That's exactly it. Jealousy."

Now this is what it has come to between Eudora and me. We bicker. She thinks it's because age has given me a hard head. She says I never used to disagree with her so. I tell her she never used to behave so.

I put down my scissors to rest my hand. I look at the work Eudora has done. Her feathers are awful. Crooked and pathetic. I think to myself, I'll redo hers later. I look at that snappy little face of hers.

"Eudora," I say, "I have not been jealous of you, ever. Not one day in my life. But you and I both know I call them as I see them. Harry Switzer is a married man, for Christ's sakes. You are a forty-some-year-old woman. Why wear your hair like you're fifteen?"

She slams her scissors down on my supper table. The coffee in my cup shakes. "What in the world does my hairstyle have to do with Mr. Harry Switzer?"

I lean a little bit closer to her. It's a gut reaction. I keep my finger planted on the table. Otherwise I'll end up shaking it in her face. "Unfortunately, Eudora, you have always been a woman who could not live without a man. But that's okay, I don't discredit you for that. But Harry Switzer, with all his mumbo jumbo, has Luella scared out of her wits, you acting like you're a teenage medium, and me having to play mother to your daughter because you don't seem capable of doing it anymore."

There. I've said it. It's been on my mind for months, gnawing at me.

I feel better already.

But I have made her angry. I can tell by the tight, tiny line of her lips. Perhaps I said too much. Maybe I should have waited and

presented my case more gently. No, no. I don't think subtlety works
on Eudora these days. I watch as her fingers furiously mangle a
posterboard feather. Eudora does not know it, but I've been saving
chicken feathers at work. I plan to glue them all over these paper
tail-feathers, as a surprise for Luella the night of the play.

"Listen. Listen," Eudora is snapping. She tosses the mangled
feather to the floor. "I don't know the problem between you and
your son. And I'm so sorry you lost that baby, but that was seven
years ago and you have no right to make claims on my daughter or
to insult the way I'm bringing up my little girl. And as for Mr.
Switzer, he's helping me instill spiritual values in my little girl.
Don't tell me you don't believe in spirits, the way you go around
clutching that penny bracelet of yours."

"You are right. You are exactly right, Eudora," I say sarcastically.
But as usual the sarcasm flies past her. I hold out the last posterboard
feather at arm's length and admire it. I say, "In fact, I think we
should all get together and have one big old damn séance. Call back
Charlie and Junior and let them have a go-round with your Mr.
Harry Switzer."

I glance at Eudora, past my perfectly trimmed feather. I've confused her into silence. I've planted an ounce of guilt.

That's enough helping her for one day.

I'm carrying in my box of chicken feathers when I see him. My
God, from the distance, maybe fifty yards, with that black car behind
him, I think I'm having a hallucination. I think Charlie is walking
right at me.

"Hello, Mama," he calls.

"Oh, my," I murmur. I didn't know what to say. Out of nowhere,
after so many months I've lost track, my son walks up to me on a
sunny late afternoon. As he approaches, I see his face increasingly
clearer. The firm jaw. The high cheekbones. His beautiful blond
hair that, of course, he got from his daddy. But I am frozen. What
am I to think? But then I know.

"What's wrong? You're in trouble." It's a question, but I state
it as fact.

He grins. His father all over again. I feel my heart break.

245

"Nothing's wrong, Mama. I just wanted to see you. Let me get that for you." He takes the box from me.

I fumble with my key. I notice Charlie's penny dangling off the bracelet, bright in the sun. I notice it because my hand is shaking. I watch the key go in the lock. What in the world is wrong with me? I'm a wreck. A complete wreck. I push open the door and my son says to me, he says, "After you."

He's blond and he smells like sweat. One quick flash lights up my brain. Charlie the day I met him. Tan and sweaty in his cop uniform. Somewhere, back in my sinuses, I get that awful rush that signals tears coming on. But I tell myself, Girlie, batten down the hatches.

I go set my purse on the couch. I hear Emory say, "What in the world . . . ?"

He's looking into my box of feathers.

"They're for Luella. A costume for school," I say. "But don't tell anybody."

My son nods and sets it in the hallway. I watch him. Why didn't he warn me?

"If I'd known you were coming, I would've fixed us a roast or something. A cobbler."

"That's why I didn't tell you. I didn't want you going to any trouble," he says, and he walks into the kitchen.

I wonder if he's being sarcastic. *I didn't want you going to any trouble.* But I don't say what's on my mind. Instead I say, "How about some iced tea?"

"That'd be good." He's sitting at the supper table in the chair he always sat in as a boy. Old habits, you know. He looks around the kitchen. I think he's uneasy. "Jesus, Mama, this place is falling apart."

"Oh, really?" I say. This time it's me being sarcastic. "And I suppose you're going to stick around and fix it all up." I hand him the tea.

"Well, I might. I just might do that."

I sit down. The shock of him showing up out of the blue is mingling with a desire to make the best of it and to figure out why he's really here.

"How's your job going?" he asks.

So that's it, I think. Money. I feel like saying, How much do you want? But instead I say, "It's okay. They gave me a promotion a few months back." And I realize I don't look like somebody's mother—soft and fresh and young. No. I look more like a butcher. Chicken blood splattered on my smock. I wish he hadn't caught me like this.

He begins to mumble, but I make out, "I'm sorry you have to work."

I let that go by. I hit him with, "So what are you doing? How's the job market?"

He shoots me a look. The same look Charlie would give me when I'd hit a soft spot. "I'd been working at a restaurant on Cocoa Beach. But I quit a while back."

"You got any plans?" I see the dirt under my nails and I wish he had called. I look awful.

My son doesn't answer. He looks past me and out the window.

"Have you talked to your Uncle J.W.?" I ask. I can't help myself. I am playing the interrogator, I can't stop.

He still doesn't look at me, but he says, "Yeah, I went down. Spent a few weeks. Stayed long enough to know there's nothing there for me anymore."

I'm getting frustrated. "Well, how long do you plan to stay around here?"

This time he turns away from the window. This time he does look at me. And what I see surprises me. It's my son who has not grown up at all. My son who looks horribly afraid of something. But of course, Emory turned secretive long ago, so what that something is I have no idea.

"I can leave now, if you want," he says.

Now why would he say that? Why does he think I don't want him in my house? I have an impulse to touch him, to hug him. But I don't. I'm all sweat, and chicken scent, and farm grime. Instead I say, "Emory, you can't leave yet. We haven't even had a meal together."

He kind of half grins at me, and I realize I still have on the hairnet they make me wear at work. Without wanting to, but unable to

247

stop myself, I reach up and feel my hair. With every pore in my body I wish that net wasn't on my head.

Inez Temple

 My life was a fountain of change, yes indeed. But that's not because I was anything special. It was due to the times we were witnessing. The wind of change was blowing, and it was saying two words to me: voter registration.

Yes, ma'am. I'd decided that was the key. I'd heard the Good Doctor's speeches—all that I could put my hands on, anyway. And I said in response to his words, Yes, yes.

So I found myself marching in Jacksonville. I found myself sitting at the Woolworth's diner in St. Augustine, the same Woolworth's that I'd bought Mr. Pecker at. And I spoke in my church, for we were a mixed congregation. And to those folks, both Negro and white, I said to them, "You are either with us, or you are against us. It is time for equality among all God's children."

And I looked at my fellow churchgoers. And with my one good eye I saw agreement, fear, distrust, love, hate.

And then I told the truth again. I said, "If equality does not come, my friends, the walls of this country may just come tumbling down."

I think it was that little speech that caused the mayor to fire me.

But the good Lord's plans are always perfect. I still worked for Patrick Lackly and two other people besides. All the firing did was free me up to do more community work.

So this fine summer's morning I woke to the sound of Tigerlily purring in my ear. Mornings past, I would lay there, letting myself slowly wake up. But not this day. I had people to register. One person, one vote—that was the rule. My goal was to get every Negro of age in the area registered by summer's end.

I washed and dressed and then I fed the animals. I put on my black patch. I wore a patch now, over my bad eye. Except the days it cried.

It hadn't cried much lately. In fact, I can name the times. Back in 1963 it cried for weeks, right during the period that Charlie Looney and President Kennedy died. Eudora Jewel swore for weeks that my crying had been a sign. And in 'sixty-five I was at Hurton's Nursery, looking for some gladiolas. Right then and there the eye started. Three days later a bad fire wiped out the entire nursery.

Now Old Mr. Hurton tells everybody, "Inez Temple, that eye of hers knows things. Watch. And if it cries when you're around, know that trouble is coming."

And when I saw that new baby of Sara and Louis Peters—that was, I believe, last year—the eye started in. And folks whisper that the child isn't right. Slow, they call him.

Now of course, not a word of this do I believe. Certainly if this maiming of my eye was for a purpose, it was for me to learn a lesson such as humility or patience. But not for a minute do I believe it's some kind of hoodoo. If there's one thing under the sun that I am not, it's a crying Madonna.

But—rumor has its advantages. The eyepatch draws folks' attention straight to that eye. Immediately people look at it. And they've heard the whispers and stories. The mayor, when he fired me, he was swamped in phone calls warning him that Inez Temple was a witch. People saying to him, "Now you've gone and made her mad. Watch out, man. Something bad's going to happen to you."

And I say, "Nonsense." But the rumor, and I say this gently and with a humble understanding, it causes people to take notice. Tired old folk who don't want to have to sign their names to registration forms, well—they look at the patch, they look at the ground, and then they sign up.

And see, this rumor, I've made sure it got all around to the white people in town too. Lots of nice folks in Tiama, yes ma'am. But some mean ones too. Some might not like it that a Negro lady is parading 'round town getting every person of color she sees to sign up to vote.

So what do I do?

I go see Eudora Jewel. I say to her I'm visiting the diamond of my life, little Luella. Which I was, but the visit served other purposes. I told Eudora about the times my eye wept. About what folks in my part of town was saying. I sprinkled the information like it was salt falling on the tip of her tongue. And you know, I hadn't even made it out to my car before she got on the phone and started telling the world. This is all true, yes ma'am, because the first person she phoned was my friend, the good woman Rose.

I collected my papers, all the forms I had to drag with me from house to house. I was to meet Violet Gilder at the Elbow Room restaurant. She was a young Negro woman of severe promise, yes she was. She was going to be a lawyer one day. I saw it in everything about her. When she wasn't working, saving money for college, she was helping me register people. We were to have coffee at the Elbow Room and discuss the day's strategy—which blocks to work, what grocery stores and laundromats to hit. If we kept up at our current pace, by August we'd be done with Tiama, and half of St. Augustine too.

Now that was a blossom of a thought to start out with. I petted Tigerlily and said good-bye to Mr. Pecker. My hand was on the door when the telephone rang.

"This is Miss Inez Temple speaking," I answered.

That little, hesitant voice coming over the line was dear to me. God had given Luella Jewel an awful stutter. I just didn't figure it. You know that other children taunted her over it. It had to be a torture for the little girl.

"Aunt I-n-n-nez?" she says to me.

"Yes, little missy. It's so good to hear your voice."

"I'm in the end-of-the-year p-p-play. At school."

In the background I could hear her mother. "Luella, who in the world are you talking to?"

I knew, children being children, that if I left it up to Luella's own time and devices to give me the specifics, I could be standing there the livelong day. Children don't know about time, except when we tell them there's not enough of it.

So I asked her the questions: where, what time, what was her part.

"You will make a beautiful Little Red Hen," I said. "I wouldn't miss seeing you for anything in the world."

When I got off the phone I made a note of the day and time on my calendar. I wrote: *Luella's big day.*

I said my good-byes to the animals again. Mr. Pecker said in his parrot drawl, *"Adiós. Adiós."*

And feeling so good about my work, before I stepped outside I did a little twirl—me a huge woman—my yellow skirt blooming as I spun.

Rose Looney

So I'm riding home with Janelle Glisson, one of the girls from the plant. I accept her offer of a car ride because tonight is Luella's play. No need for me to squash my time together by walking home. Janelle is complaining about Lou Ellen Campbell. "She doesn't get, I'd say, even eighty percent of the feathers off," she keeps repeating. But I don't respond. I mean, I hear her, but my brain is off thinking about family matters. I keep wondering if Emory is going to be home when I get there, or if he's already flown the coop. I keep thinking about how pretty my little Luella is going to look in her Little Red Hen outfit made with real, hand-picked feathers. In my mind, I see Luella's look of delight as I hand her the costume. I see Emory smile, proud his mama is so talented. I see Eudora shocked. It's a satisfying little snapshot.

But I come out of my daydream due to Janelle whistling low and long. The woman can sound like a man when she feels like it. She's looking at my house. She says, "Well, my God, Rose, who've you got for a sugar daddy?"

I am completely puzzled. I follow her gaze to my house. My hand flies to my mouth. The front of the house gleams with a coat of fresh white paint. The shutters are painted yellow—the color they were when Emory was a boy. The place looks almost like it did when Charlie was alive. I feel this strange mixture of annoyance

251

and appreciation. I mean, it was awfully nice of Emory. But a kept house means one thing: memories.

"That sugar daddy is my son." I get out of the car. "Thanks. See you tomorrow."

For a few seconds I stand in my yard, just looking at my house. I wonder where he came up with the money. I hope that he'd saved it from all his odd jobs. "Please, God, don't let the boy be a drug dealer," I say under my breath.

I go on in. The shower is running. Oh, God. Another memory. Stop it, I tell myself sternly. But it doesn't help. I see an image of Charlie soaping up, crooning in the shower. I flop down in the chair. I am exhausted, but I'm also overwhelmed. Too much Emory. Too much Charlie. Why couldn't I keep them separated? The tears I'd been beating back since Emory walked up that sidewalk would be held back no longer. So I start in. I cry like a baby. Angrier than hell at Charlie for dying. Guilty as hell because maybe I could have done something that night to save him. Confused over Emory. How could he be so cold, just leaving me like he did after Charlie died? But then blowing back in out of nowhere, acting like he'd never left. I try to calm myself down. I say, Rose, you're just tired. That's what all this is about. I look down at my big old hands. Once they were beautiful hands. I had a saleslady tell me, years ago, that I had the hands of a model. Not anymore. Callused. The knuckles starting to get big due to my arthritis. I hold my arm up. I model my penny bracelet. Would Charlie have made something like that for some other woman? But if it had been meant for me, why hadn't he given it to me before he died?

Then I realize that my logic is hellacious. How would I ever know? I was either going to have to figure it out or take the bracelet off and throw it away. Forget about it, like I'd never found it among my dead husband's underwear.

Emory turns off the water. The pipes are so old they squeak. I say to the room, "Well, Rose, it's time to get off your butt and stop feeling sorry for yourself."

I'm fixing dinner when Emory walks into the kitchen, all fresh-showered and smelling of Ivory soap. I'm flouring chicken drums. I look up from my work. He's standing there looking as if I'm going to give him some reaction. So I say to him, "Now why'd you go and do all that work on the house?"

So my son talks back to me. He says, "Well, excuse me for living."

I look back at my drums. I know chickens so well now—each phase of their transformation from limp feathered carcasses to pink, goose-fleshed, shrink-wrapped body parts—that I wonder what in the world I'm doing having them for supper. My son goes to the refrigerator and opens the door. He stands peering into it like it might speak. Then he reaches for the milk. He opens the carton and pours it right down. I know he's doing this to irritate me. When he was a boy I always slapped his wrists for drinking out of the carton. But I force myself to act like I don't notice. I say, about the house again, "Emory, I just meant it looks like you did an awful lot of work. You did a good job." Then, because I know he'd never understand the complicated reasons why I'd rather the house fall down around me than to do anything that might trigger memories, I add, "Thank you."

"No problem," he says. Flip. Casual.

For dinner, in addition to the fried chicken, we're having creamed corn, beets, corn bread, and some fresh sliced tomatoes. I fix enough that tomorrow night we'll have leftovers. It's odd for me to think in terms of meal-planning. As I set the table and fix his plate, I coach myself. Just have a nice, quiet supper. Don't snap at the boy. Try to understand him.

He's in the living room watching TV. I go stand by the kitchen door and have a smoke to cool off before I call him to the table. I hear bells ringing and people cheering. He must be watching a game show. I take one last drag and flick the butt out the screen door. In a nice, steady voice I call, "Time to eat."

And actually, believe it or not, everything about the dinner goes just fine. He has two helpings of corn. He eats four chicken drums. He tells me about the work he did at J.W.'s farm. He describes the machete he used to cut the cane. He says the girl he wrote me about, the one he liked so much, wasn't there anymore.

"I never thought you might be working with such dangerous tools. Did you get hurt?" I ask.

"Oh, no. In fact, learning to handle the machete so well helped me at the oyster bar. Now, a shucking blade, that's a knife," he says, and then into his mouth he pops a forkful of corn and beets.

It's a nice dinner, really. I mean, we actually talk. Oh, not about anything important, but that's okay. Aimless chat is not something Emory and I do very well anymore.

And since dinner is such a success, I decide to serve dessert. In the refrigerator is a Mrs. Smith's pumpkin pie. I brew us coffee. I cut the pie. We're going along just fine. The pie isn't homemade, but I've grown out of that. And then Emory, innocent as hell, in between bites of pie, says, "Mama, how come you don't sleep in your bed anymore?"

I cringe. I want to snap at him, "That's none of your damn business." But I hold back. I say to myself, Be nice, be nice. I set down my fork. I wipe off my mouth. I say, "Memories, son. Memories and guilt."

"Guilt. Guilt over what?"

God, he could be thick-skulled. "Emory, he died in that bed. Don't you think I lay awake at night replaying it and replaying it? What if I'd called a doctor when he was in the bathroom? What if I hadn't bitched to him about this or that? What if I'd performed the heart massage just a little bit better? Would he still be here?"

I am shaking. God damn Emory for bringing this up.

But my son does something very nice then. I mean, he shouldn't have asked the question he did, but as we sit there in our silence, he reaches over and pats my hand.

"I'm sorry, Emory," I say.

And then he says the stupidest thing. He says, "Mama, do you ever play that game anymore? That game we played when I was little. Name That Cloud?"

I pull my hand away. "Oh, for goodness' sakes, Emory. Of course not. Now you put a nice shirt on. We've got to get going."

I am standing in Eudora's living room. It smells like pee. Harry Switzer gave her a cat. Claimed it would draw spirits to the house. "That cat is ruining your furniture, Eudora. Peeing all over everything," I call out.

254

Eudora is in her bedroom. Primping, I'm sure. "What? Is some-one saying something to me? I can't hear you," she yells.

I roll my eyes at Emory, who is standing stiff and uncom-fortable. He's wearing a Daytona Beach surfer shirt. I can't believe he didn't weasel out of going with me. He's holding Luella's cos-tume because I told him to. I wrapped it in red tissue paper so it has more of an air of a gift about it. I told Emory before we even got in Eudora's yard, "Don't you dare let Eudora grab it from you."

"Where's my little Luella?" I ask.

I hear the toilet flush. Luella comes out of the bathroom. She's wearing a red leotard. From head to foot she's covered in red. I study her for a second. A scattering of freckles across her nose. Shining reddish-brown hair. She'll make a perfect hen.

"Hey, pigtails, you nervous?"

She shakes her head yes. She cracks her knuckles. She looks thoroughly miserable. "Look, Luella, this is Emory. You remember Emory, don't you?"

She eyes him up and down. She plays with her pigtail. "S-s-sort of."

"Now you listen to me, Luella." I go put my arm around her. "You're going to be the toast of the town tonight. You wait and see. There's not a thing for you to be nervous about." Then I give her a good, strong squeeze.

I am very surprised when the doorbell rings. I mean, we are all there just waiting on Eudora to get her fancy tailbone in gear. I turn around. I see the figure through the screen door. My mouth drops to the floor. Luella groans. The poor little girl runs to the bedroom. And Eudora floats out, in a velveteen dress (no mind that it is six-thirty P.M. and not a degree under ninety), chirping, "Harry, I'm so happy you made it."

I look at Emory like I cannot believe what this woman has done. And on her daughter's special night. But he doesn't know the back-ground. I can't get any reaction from him.

Eudora is preening. In her long, curled hair she wears a bow. The velveteen skirt is full and long. A few years ago it would have required a crinoline. Today it should be in a trash heap. She is wearing black patent-leather pumps. "You look beautiful, as always," he says to her.

And I snort.

"Well, are we ready?" she asks.

"You ought to ask your daughter," I say. I am steamed. I think I ought to call the child abuse authorities. I think I ought to just take Luella to my house for good.

"Luella, dear, come on. We're going to be late," Eudora calls.

The familiar pounding starts up. She's throwing her ball against her bedroom wall. For some damn fool reason I say, with a business tone, "Emory."

He looks at me like I'm crazy, like, Oh no, what now?

I march past Harry Switzer, who seems oblivious to the trouble he has caused. I throw open Luella's door. "Sweetheart," I say. "Come on. We've got to get along. You can ride with Uncle Emory and me."

"But we were all going together," I hear Eudora protest.

I grab Luella's hand. She looks to be the epitome of miserableness. I drag her out the door.

"You got the keys to your car?" I ask Emory.

He jiggles them in his jeans pocket.

"Then let's go. We'll see you there," I say, looking only at Eudora.

"But why all this?" she argues. "Harry's car is big enough for everyone."

"Oh, good God, Eudora, where's your brain?" I snap. And with Luella in tow, I stalk out of that house. The sound of the slamming door is music to my ears. It's an exclamation point at the end of my anger. I am congratulating myself on solving the problem. We'll all get there safe and sound, and maybe Luella won't be a total screaming meany. Then I stop. I watch Emory unlock the doors. The Black Beauty. I don't want to have to ride in Charlie's car. Emory opens the passenger door and Luella scrambles in. But not me. I just stand there, filled with a ridiculous fear.

"Come on, Mama, get in the car," my son orders, like he's my boss. I look at him. He is Charlie Looney made over, pore for pore. Eudora's high-pitched giggle rises somewhere behind me. I look

256

my son straight in the eyes. I stiffen my resolve. "All right, Emory," I say, "I will. I will get in this car."

I slide in, but I refuse to look around. Instead I keep my eyes drilled to the windshield. I watch Tiama pass and I keep my mouth running. One long pep talk is what I deliver. And I don't know if it's so much for Luella's good as my own.

But we get there in one piece. My nerves are hanging by a thread, but I've got a handle on the situation. I'm out of the car. Luella and I will be okay. The play is to be in the school cafeteria. Children are running skitter-scatter everywhere. Parents are yelling, "Tommy, don't run" and "Melissa, behave." And the children are beaming. Giving each other those knowing looks that tonight is the biggest night in their young lives.

We don't wait for Eudora and Switzer. I say, "Let's go on into the cafeteria. They'll catch up."

I make Luella hold my hand. I want her to know I love her.

The cafeteria is hot. Even the big fans whirring overhead don't do a lot to cut into the heat. I see a flash of bright yellow and turquoise. But a big man in a gray suit has stepped in my way. I peer around him, and yes, yes, it is. It's Inez Temple.

"Look, Luella, it's Aunt Inez over there."

Luella pulls out of my grip and runs. She throws her arms around Inez. Now, it is a nice sight and all—there is nothing awful about it. But I'm not as good as I should be. Jealousy thickens my blood. But I hide it. Nobody will know. Eudora has accused me of jealousy a thousand times and has always been wrong. But not this time. I grit my teeth. This is damn poor behavior. I know it is. But no one will know. Not a soul.

So I go up and greet Inez. My heart is a cast-iron fist, barely pumping, but I'm smiling. "You here to see our girl?"

"Oh, sweetie, I wouldn't miss it for anything in the world," she says. And I know, even though Luella is still clinging to her, that my jealousy has everything to do with me and nothing to do with Inez.

"Inez, you remember my son, don't you? Emory."

"Oh my goodness, yes. How are you doing? We've missed having you around," she says. And she offers him her hand, and it's the funniest thing, but she just doesn't let go. I look at their hands, and then at her face, and then back at their hands. Emory looks uncomfortable and pulls away. I mean, he is polite but nevertheless I'm sure he pulls away. And Inez, I believe, for a real swift moment, her face turns utterly sad.

Luella is keeping a hand on Inez's turquoise skirt. A little fair-headed boy walks by and giggles at Luella. She sticks her tongue out at him.

I'm growing impatient for Eudora to arrive. I want to get Luella in her costume and see her eyes light up when we remove it from its red paper wrap. I scan faces, heads, backs. Then I feel a finger, a very persistent and definite finger, tapping like a woodpecker on my shoulder.

"We're here," Eudora announces.

I want to slug her. Now don't get me wrong. Eudora and I are still friends. I care for her. But the damn man has rattled her brain to all proportions. It is hard to take.

I turn around and eye her. One of my goals of the evening is not to look at Harry Switzer at all. Not even once. I say, "Well, I guess it's time to get Luella in her pretty outfit."

Eudora is squealing. "You're going to love this, honey. Aunt Rose and I made this with our own two hands."

I take the bundle from Emory. Beaming, I unwrap my master-piece. I've created it so that the entire apparatus can fold in on itself. I have glued all the tail feathers to a Velcro belt that we'll put around her middle. I snap open my creation. A beautiful real-chicken-feather-covered tailpiece unfolds.

"Here you go," I say.

Eudora gasps. It is a moment of triumph. I watch Luella's face. This tailpiece will give her more confidence, I just know it. She points at it. Her face goes from terror to disgust. She says, "B-b-but it's all white. I'm the Little *Red* Hen."

Harry Switzer laughs. I'm sure Eudora is smirking. I see Inez's hand flying up and down, up and down, patting Luella's back. An attempt to keep her calm.

I think fast. I know I must save the moment. My mind goes through every hen I've ever seen. I'm stuck on farmyard hens. All white, all red, never red with blazing white tail feathers. What in the world had I been thinking of? I switch over to fake hens. Ceramic chickens. No. Rubber chickens. No. I search my memory. Somewhere it has to be there. And then I get it. A Saturday-morning hen. I saw her years ago. A cartoon hen named Ruby. She had a beautiful red chest and flaming white feathers. She was the jewel of the henhouse.

So I say, "Don't you all remember Ruby, the Henhouse Queen? She's a legend. The most beautiful of all little red hens. That's because she had great white tail feathers."

And Inez joins in. "Sure, Ruby. She was a fine hen. Luella, Ruby was the greatest red hen that ever lived. Now come on, let's get you strapped into this thing."

As I fit the Velcro belt around Luella's middle, I think, Great, now I can't look at Eudora the rest of the evening either. Eudora is at her worst when smug.

But my embarrassment begins to ease once the tail feathers are on, because they are really beautiful.

Over the PA system a young female voice asks all the children to report backstage. I am a nervous wreck. Luella's little eyes flash so hopeful. She looks at her mother, who bends over and kisses her cheek.

I plant a bit wet one on her forehead and say, "Go get 'em, tiger."

Inez's and Luella's eyes meet. Luella crosses her arms so that they form an X. Inez does the same. Crossways like that, they shake each other's hands, and Inez whispers to her, "Day is dawning in America . . ."

And Luella answers her back, "And the Little Red Hen crows cockadoodledoo."

We watch Luella march off. I want to remember this moment. Her little head held high. Her beautiful tail feathers. I am all nerves and mush inside.

Emory says to me, "Great tail feathers, Mama."

I look at him sharply, but then I soften. I can see he means it.

And Luella is wonderful onstage. I know the balance between Eudora and me has shifted back to me. Her with her objections over Luella being taken out of the chorus! Luella is the whole play.

It's as if the feathers have transformed her—suddenly she is a confident, talented child. A little star. The feathers gleam under the stage lights. Her movements are completely believable, and her stutter is no problem because the acting is all pantomime. Her teacher, Mrs. Griffith, reads the story. And occasionally the chorus comes in with a song. But each action, every step onstage, is Luella's. She is carrying a huge brown basket. She is doing a chicken walk. Her feathers are outstanding. She's tossing out imaginary grains, while her lazy counterparts—a duck, a cat, and a pig—just watch. She's darling as she tilts her head questioningly, and Mrs. Griffith warbles, "Who will help me bake some bread?"

I am enthralled. Luella up there acting her little heart out. I just want to beam each time her face turns so sad as she looks at the three animals for help. And the teacher is really effective with that "Who will help me?" bit. Everything is going perfect. The audience is paying attention, Luella is shining like a star in the making. The only sounds in the cafeteria are the whirring fans and the teacher's voice.

That is, until my Emory makes a show of himself. The cat has just meowed that no, he won't help her bake bread. He yawns a huge cat yawn, strokes his pasted-on whiskers, and then curls up like a tabby-striped ball underneath a cardboard tree. All the parents are glued to the action. Some are smiling knowingly at the poor Little Red Hen's dilemma. And my son stands up and pushes his chair back so loud every eye in the house glares at him. He walks on out.

The play doesn't last long. I guess they figured little kids couldn't remember a full-length play. I am angry at Emory for leaving. I'm wondering if he's standing outside or if he's taken off. Maybe he has taken off for good again. Another thing to face.

The lights come up and all the parents are cheering their babies onstage. Eudora is blowing kisses. But Inez, she pats my arm. I glance at her. I notice her eye has started its crying. I see the path leading from her patch down her face. Probably from the lights being turned back on or something. It caused a reaction. She puts her arm around me and says in my ear, "Listen to me, Rose Looney, that boy needs you. Even if he goes off again, remember that he needs you."

Luella Jewel

The school that I go to, it's made of these real big yellow stones, like the kind of houses almost on *The Flintstones*. Tiama Elementary School. When I was four was the first time I ever came here. Mama and Aunt Rose brought me to the cafeteria for a polio shot. Red medicine on a sugar cube. There were stacks of red sugar cubes. Enough for all the children. Mama said they looked like rubies. They took me to Dairy Queen after 'cause I'd been so good about taking the medicine and all. Yeah, that was the first time at my school. I thought it was neat then.

But now I hate it.

I hate it because of the stupid girls. Just because they have store-bought clothes and pretty parents, they think they can make fun of me. I mean, last year I was in a play and I was real good and everything. But it didn't make them any nicer to me.

Mrs. Wilson is my second-grade teacher. I don't like her. I'll be glad when I go up to third. Mrs. Johnson will probably be my teacher then, and she's pretty. Mrs. Wilson has the biggest arms in the world. She threw Tommy Gitters out of our class one day, and she used just one of her arms. Because in the other she had the eraser. And her eyes, the way she looks at you, especially during math—she's just mean.

But this one day that I hated more than any other happened because stupid Mrs. Wilson asked us kids these things. She said, "The county wants me to ask the following questions. It's for their records."

I was happy at first about this. Meant less time during math period. I'm a bad adder. And then she yells, her mean eyes looking

261

at every one of us, "I want the only sound in this room to be the sound of my voice. If I hear anybody's mouth rattling it means five minutes off your recess—that is five minutes less per each rattle. Just raise your hands when I ask the questions. Mary Eversole, you will help me count hands, please."

Mary Eversole. Queen of the world. Teacher's pet. Perfect clothes every day. Shoes to match each outfit. And she was real skinny. She prisses up to the front of the class.

Mrs. Wilson says, "How many of your parents own more than one car?"

A bunch of hands went up. All of us are looking, seeing how we compare. Of course, my hand doesn't go up. All the kids who have the cars get this look on their faces—like they'd just been handed a billion dollars so they're better than anybody else in the world.

"How many of you have more than three brothers or sisters?" Jason Brown, his family is huge. I think there are like ten kids.

And then Mrs. Wilson asks, "How many of you have a parent who is deceased?"

All of us, we looked at Mrs. Wilson and then at one another. What in the world did she mean?

"Deceased," she said. She wrote it on the board in pink chalk. Then in blue chalk she wrote D E A D. " 'Deceased' means 'dead.' Do any of you have a dead parent?"

The whole room is like one kid. Everybody lets out a big breath. Everybody but me. And those kids, they all know I don't have a dad. But so what? Whose business is it, anyway? Maybe I *never* had a dad. Maybe Mama had just borrowed that picture from somebody. Maybe she knew that I didn't have a dad but decided to make up a story. She probably thought it would make me feel better. Kids with the gift probably don't have dads. They're just born. That had to be it. Because nobody had shown me proof of a real dad.

So I decided I'd just sit there—like the other kids—without putting my hand up. Who knows, if I put my hand up I could be messing up those county records.

But then that stupid Mary Eversole, she says like she's real sweet, "Mrs. Wilson, Luella's daddy is dead."

And Mrs. Wilson looks over her glasses at me. And all the kids start making goof noises like it's a big deal. Like I'm the purple people-eater or something. They're all making big eyes at one another, and Queen Mary Eversole is making her hyena face behind old Mrs. Wilson. I put my head down on my desk, hiding my face with my arms, because I can tell my face is getting splotchy. And even though I'm a second-grader, I kind of cry a lot. But nobody will know it this time. I feel my face getting really hot. It's on fire.

Mrs. Wilson says, "Luella?"

But I didn't answer. I just kept my head down on the desk. I didn't raise my hand to no more questions. Forget it. I didn't care if the old county had straight records. Wasn't their business anyhow.

And then recess happened. And I was still upset. And still thinking over not being actually born at all. If everybody had left me alone I wouldn't of gotten in big trouble.

Mrs. Wilson had said, "Line up for recess. Single file."

But not me. I stayed put. I waited with my head on the desk until I heard all their feet shuffle out. And Mrs. Wilson's voice. She goes, "Luella Jewel, what's wrong with you? Do you have lead in your behind today? Get on out there with the others."

So even though *I* got in trouble, it was Mrs. Wilson's fault. She's the old lady who made me go play. Here's how it happened: The girls arc playing dodge ball—not on the court but underneath the trees. And the boys are playing on the jungle gym. The girls keep whispering. Nobody wants to talk to me. Priscilla Hindrin whispers, but not so quiet—I can hear her—she whispers to Mary Eversole, "God, her dad's dead and her mom's got lots of boyfriends. I heard my parents talking about it. They said Luella's mama is white trash."

"Yeah, so Luella must live in a garbage can," says Queen Mary. And she starts laughing and making her monkey face.

I'm so mad now. I'm not going to let them get away with it. So I yell, at the top of my lungs, "I am not white t-t-trash! And my daddy's not d-dead. He lives in"—and my mind moved fast, back to geography class—"P-P-Paris, France," I lied.

Mary Eversole taps her tiny patent-leather shoe. She says, "Luella, my mother says that when a person stutters it is a sign that they are lying."

So I yell at her, "I am not l-l-lying."

But all the kids are singing, "Liar, liar, Luella's a liar."

I can't say a word. Because I'm so mad I know I'll stutter. And if I stutter, they'll say I'm lying. Even if I'm not.

So there was nothing left for me to do. My anger was inside me like a tiger. Taking over everything I did. It caused me to slap Mary Eversole. Right on her face.

But that made everything worse. She scratched me and screamed and hollered. What was I supposed to do? I had to scratch back.

And then out of nowhere Mrs. Wilson was there, and she was dragging me away with just one of her big old arms. I felt the tips of her red fingernails dig into my skin. Claws. It really hurt. I wanted to bite her so she'd let go of me, but I managed not to.

As we headed down the corridor toward the principal's office, I heard Mary Eversole crying behind me, screaming, "She tore my mole! Oh God, I want my mother. She tore my mole!"

Inez Temple

It all started on a good March morning. The end of March. April just days away. My garden was absolutely busting with little buds. And I'd taken the day off. Because I was pooped. I'd been cleaning houses, watching people's children, working for the Negro Community Action sunup to sundown, with not a break at all for near to a year. So I do believe taking a day of rest was in order.

I was anticipating the first taste of tea with just a little honey and lemon in it when I opened my front door, to go get the newspaper, you see. But there on my doorstep somebody had left another basket of flowers and also a loaf of raisin bread. This had been going on for about four months now. People had gotten wind of that story about me, that tale about how my eye knew things. The people in this town, some had gotten in their minds that if they left me offerings—apples, oranges, flowers, bread, even once a freshly killed chicken packed in an iced cooler—that they would somehow gain protection. Protection from what, Lord, I do not know. They ought to be putting that effort into the church, or into their neighborhood, or even into their own households.

This was such a mystery to me when it all began. A neighbor clued me in. She said, "Miss Temple, it's because of that eye. People are protecting, taking care, 'cause they know about you. Think they're going to get blessed."

Just imagine people having such foolish notions.

My full, good intention, of course, was to give everything back. But most don't leave their names. They think somehow I'm just going to know it was them. So what I do is give it all away. I give it to a variety of folks who, because of bad luck and bad times, really need it.

Like last week a fruit basket was left. I took that over to Pearl Waverly's. That good woman with seven mouths to feed. Now you know she can use that fruit. And the chicken—well, that went to a soup kitchen in Jacksonville. I got one of the young neighborhood men to drive it in for me.

I walked down my cobblestone steps and picked up my newspaper. The whole earth that I saw at that very instant was dew-shined. Very pretty. Very pretty, indeed. On my way back inside I retrieved the flowers and bread. The flowers, I decided, would go to the county hospital. There must be somebody stuck in that place whose flowers stopped a long time ago. The raisin bread would go to the children's home. That is, after I enjoyed a piece with my tea. Tea and raisin bread—you know that tastes good.

Yes, I fed my animals, giving Tigerlily an extra helping of milk because we were on vacation. Mr. Pecker, I gave him a brand-spanking-new cuttlefish.

And finally, at my tiny kitchen table on which sat a beautiful red geranium, I settled down to my tea, my one piece of raisin bread—my gift—and the morning paper.

Straightaway I went looking for news of the Good Doctor. You could not pick up a newspaper in any city in this country and not read about him. And I mean on any day of the week. He was three pages back with a nice picture. A snapshot taken of him when he spoke to a group of college students in Manhattan, Kansas. That's what the newspaper said. And it said he was traveling to Memphis, Tennessee, to lead a march and talk to the good folks and to city officials.

I was reading the article, which was just a news article with nothing special in it, but reading its every word just the same because, see, I loved that man. He was hope in a bleak, bleak sea. But I'd boarded his boat, and I was discovering it to be a beautiful ride. A direct and steady and determined ride, despite the rough seas.

Yes, my thoughts were fine and flowering. Being positive about the future, that's how I'd come to be. But just as if somebody had taken a power cord and pulled it out of the socket, the light snapped shut on my good thoughts. Goodness gracious, what had happened? I felt like a knife was being ripped through my chest. I was all fear and shakes. I placed my hand over the picture of that good man. And said to myself, This man is in trouble and I know it. I wiped my hand over my face. Yes ma'am, the good Lord knows this is the truth: The eye was weeping. Some might say I was being crazy. But as sure as the sun rises and sets, I knew something was wrong in Memphis.

I went to my whatnot drawer and got my notepad out. From by the telephone I got my little black phone book. I flipped it open to *I* for important. I ran my finger down the numbers I kept there. The church. Community Action. Rose Looney. Patrick Lackly. There it was: the Southern Christian Leadership Conference. I said to myself, right out loud, "Inez Temple, they are never going to believe you."

But I had to try. You can't ever let somebody not believing you prevent you from trying. I wrote in man-sized handwriting:

Dear Sirs,
    I know this letter may sound crazy, but with all the goodness you dear folks possess in your hearts, please take my words seriously. The good Dr. King is in trouble. Something bad is lingering in Memphis. I can offer you no proof. I have not one scrap of a detail or date. It's all my intuition, and it's telling me

something awful is waiting in Memphis. Please, believe me. Please, please, don't let our good doctor suffer.

> May the Lord guide you,
> Miss Inez Temple

I addressed the envelope, slid the letter in, and prayed, "Dear Lord, guide this letter to the proper hands."

At the post office I put two stamps on it. Now I knew that two stamps weren't going to get my message there any faster than one stamp, but I sometimes did this. If the letter was important right down to my soul, I gave it an extra stamp for good measure.

As I drove home, I saw the spring stormclouds building off over the Atlantic. I knew that by afternoon the rains would come. Normally this would make me just as happy as a bee soaked in pollen. But not that day, no ma'am. I still had not managed to shake the fear. The awful fear.

At home I pulled all my blinds. I said to my grandmama and mama this and that. I said to them, You all believed in signs. I remember that well. I remembered how my mama could read the steam rising off a soup kettle. Especially if it had good, fresh marrow in it. And if I didn't feel good, Grandmama would go out and bring in fistfuls of wild herbs. She'd throw them in broths and teas, depending on my ailment. She was half doctor, half priest. I said to her once when I had the croup and she was making me drink something that had grass in it, I said, "Grandmama, are you making me drink magic?"

"No, baby, this is just good old-fashioned hoodoo."

And let me say, it worked. By the next day's light I felt fine. Just fine. How foolish I'd been as a young woman, ignoring their knowledge—in fact, not even wanting it.

I put on a pan of water. It'd be store-bought tea for me today. I didn't know what herb or combination those two women used to beat back the bad, ominous blues. I said, "Thank you two for giving me croup-fixing tea. But I sure wish I had a memory of your other cures."

Yes, the blues had settled in as firm and stony as my childhood croup. But I had no medicine for it. Me, Miss Blue-Skies Positive Thinker, knew things were going to go from bad to worse. I sat down in my rocker and opened the Bible on my lap. But it just didn't seem to do no good no ways. Not a single comfort in there could I find. I fell asleep while reading Luke.

When I woke up, rain was pouring in my window.

Luella Jewel

I was watching the funeral on TV at Aunt Rose's house. This was the second funeral I'd seen in just a couple of months. The first one was for the nice colored man. All week long—when I wasn't at school or being yelled at to do home-work—I stayed glued to my TV or to Aunt Rose's. That's all they talked about, him getting shot in some city north of here. "The big cities are going to burn down," my Aunt Rose kept saying.

And there was pictures of it in all the newspapers. I know, because my Aunt Inez—I went over there with Aunt Rose—she had those newspapers stacked all over her house. And both of them eyes of her were crying. And she didn't talk much. Not to me at all.

But this one I was watching this time, it was a different funeral. Summer vacation had just started. The man killed was the man who was going to be our president. He was so young and handsome. I'd seen him on TV before he died. My mama had said, "What a fine-looking man he is."

And my Aunt Rose had said, "Luella, that's the brother of President Kennedy. You remember John-John and Caroline at the funeral for President Kennedy, don't you? Well, this man on TV is the president's brother. He's going to continue all the good work the president started but didn't get a chance to finish."

And every time after that when he came on TV, I'd run into the living room and watch him. Because, see, at night, when I looked out my window at this big star that was almost always there, I'd say, "Please, God, let that Bobby Kennedy be my daddy."

So don't you think it was kind of weird that I wanted him for my daddy, and then he ends up dead? Especially in light of me having the gift and being without a dad and all.

On the TV this reporter was outside some place asking people who walked by what they thought about Bobby Kennedy getting killed. Everybody was sad. Even one man who was old enough to be a granddaddy looked like he might start crying. And I looked at my mama and at Aunt Rose. Both of them were crying. My Aunt Rose kept shaking her head and wiping her eyes with those big hands of hers.

I'd been thinking so much about it. So I decided to ask them. "That man you say was my d-daddy—was he as good of a man as K-Kennedy?"

My mama looked away. Aunt Rose seemed surprised. But she answered me. She said, "Oh yes, Luella, your daddy was a fine, fine man."

So I looked at my mama. "Then if h-he was so good and really my d-d-daddy, why didn't you take me to his funeral? And how c-come we n-never visit his grave?" I looked back at the TV. They were talking about all the cards sent by people. I think he said something like eight hundred million zillion sorry cards had been sent to Kennedy's wife. How many had my mama gotten? All I knew about was Mama's boyfriends. I knew that Switzer-kitzer didn't have a brain and that he was born in Illinois. I knew that Bobby Reynolds had three dogs, none of them was the same kind either. But about the man they all say was my real daddy? The only thing I knew was his name. Burl. There weren't any pictures but one, and I wasn't in it. Nobody talked to me of him. If he was really real, why hadn't they ever taken me to the grave? Switzer-kitzer wanted me to talk mumbo jumbo to my dead daddy, who might have been just my mama's lie. I didn't want to talk to no ghosts. I just wanted to know things about him. I mean, if he was really my dad I wanted to know if he was like Kennedy. I looked at the sad TV faces. I looked back at my mama, who was lighting up a cigarette. "I want to see my d-daddy's grave," I shouted.

Aunt Rose jumped up and flipped off the TV. "The child has

just seen too many people killed in too short a time. That's all. Poor child growing up in a time when all the good ones get gunned down."

Nobody was answering me. My Etch A Sketch was in my lap. I threw it on the floor. I shouted again: "I want to go see my daddy's g-g-grave!"

Mama looked at my Aunt Rose. Mama's mascara was snakes down her face because of crying for Kennedy. "What are we going to do?" she asked.

My Aunt Rose said, like she was real mad, like she'd just stubbed her toe, "Child, you're too young to see his grave. Get that straight right now. When you're older, things will be different. Until then, just get used to it and quit hounding us."

I hated them both right then. I wanted to go see my Aunt Inez. She never talked to me mean. "I'm leaving and I'm never coming back," I said.

And I walked out, but I didn't have no shoes on, so I couldn't go very far. I couldn't get to Aunt Inez's. And she wouldn't come get me without my mama's say-so. I'd tried that before. I couldn't wait until I was growed up. I would marry somebody as handsome as Kennedy and have ten million jillion trillion children. And we'd be rich too.

I went in my mama's closet. I tried on her black high heels. I walked into the kitchen with them on. Clop, clop, clop. One day they would fit. I got out two Cokes and carried them into the garden in the backyard. Aunt Inez had given us a concrete bench to put in the garden. It made us look rich.

Carrying the Cokes real careful because I could trip in Mama's shoes, I walked over to the bench. I was playing like I was sixteen years old. And Bobby Kennedy was alive. He was my boyfriend. My very first. I sat, like I was a lady, on the bench. I smiled the same way I'd seen Mama do at Switzer-kitzer.

"Would you like a cold drink?" I offered Kennedy. My voice was real flowery, just like the lace curtains I'd seen in store windows downtown.

And of course, since this was my game and nobody was here to mess it up, he said, "I'd love a cold drink."

And so I drank my Coke and thought about how when I got older I'd have to drink it out of a glass so that I'd come off ladylike.

Then Kennedy was back and saying, "Luella, don't drink your soft drink so fast. It might make you sick."

He was not my boyfriend anymore. He was Daddy. He was happy I was his daughter. I saw his face. He was smiling at me. Proud of me. I put my hand in his. My hand was real tiny compared to his man's hand. And I said, "I'm sorry, Father. I won't drink so fast again."

He put his arm around me. Kennedy, my daddy. He whispered in my ear, "That's my good little girl."

Soleil Marie Beauvoir

Damballah-wedo is good and angry at me, yes indeed. This I say to myself as I rocked my sick baby. This child was hot like a flame, and I had no money. Not a dime. Not a single penny. Sweating so bad. I pushed some of my hair back that had fallen to my eyes. I hold my Charlité so close. But because we have no money for food, she doesn't weigh much no more, and neither do I.

I looked to this room that I didn't have the dollars to pay for anymore. Mr. Gibson at the Jupiter Motel took from me my job. It was after they killed that Negro man we called king. Murdered him, oh yes they did. And to go to work? No, I could not. I stayed in my room for two days to mourn. To light candles and pray. To try to see him safe to the other side. Mr. Gibson didn't believe this, no.

So for three weeks I walked the city concrete. Where to find a job, where to find a job? And all I heard was this: "Your English is not good enough." They'd say it loud like I had no ears. Or to me they would say, "A bad time to be job hunting. Off season, you know."

And all those three weeks I'd say to myself, What did I do to Damballah-wedo to make him so angry at me? But once Charlité fell sick, once Damballah-wedo started punishing this baby—making her be so fussy and irritable—I quit asking.

I looked at the face of hers. That sweet, pretty face showing the fever. Big red splotches caused by her crying burned deep in her skin that had no more color. I touched my baby's burning face and a picture happened in my mind. The big wheel Uncle's Boy and me was riding when I realized a life was with me. It had big colored light bulbs all over it. "Baby of mine, you've got a carnival on your face," I whispered to her. "And it's so, so pretty. We're going to travel past the trouble, yes."

But my baby didn't smile back. She didn't act like I'd said words to her at all. What to do, I had no idea. How sick was my child? Was this fever just a passing shadow? In the cities I was without *connaissance*, so no answers did I have. My friend Judy Gabinski, she was not at home. Many nights she'd show up with milk and bits of food from that restaurant. Stealing for a cause, she called it. Maybe tonight I'd hear her knock at my door, and maybe I'd open up and she'd be standing there with what she calls pastrami sandwiches. And maybe milk. Or orange juice. Yes, some orange juice might make better my baby.

The sound of stuff, plaster and all, crumbling inside my walls starts up again. Rats. They was inside these walls, and to hear them walking made me so scared. Made me hold Charlité closer. I'd seen one once inside my room, by the toilet. Judy Gabinski brought to me a trap. But to use this I could not, because how do I keep my child out of a rat trap? How do I tell her not to stumble over it or play with it, and know for sure she would listen?

But so early in the day it was. And already there was the sound of the rats in my walls, and my baby's wailing had not stopped all night. I wished I still had the milk in my breasts. My ladies in the fields had milk for their children until maybe the babies was six or seven years, sometimes more. But not me—to eat good enough I had not. So no more rich goodness for my baby.

Still holding onto Charlité, I reached over to my coffee table and pulled the holy candle closer to me. With one hand I struck the match and lit the candle. And to my baby I said, "Charlité, every-body loves you. God loves you. The Virgin Mary loves you. Your grandparents love you. Yes, Damballah-wedo loves you. Soon this sickness is going to leave this baby. Soon my baby smiling again she will be."

I tapped the tip of her nose. This always makes Charlité giggle. Charlité's green eyes didn't answer me back, though. She just rubbed them with her tiny fist. Then she whimpered and coughed, whimpered and coughed. I thought about my dog that I'd left back in the fields. My good black dog, who always protected me from the things I could not see. Who did I have anymore to protect me from such things? Where was my child's papa? Where were my *loa*?

And now here, look at my ugly room. No breeze in this place. The air hanging still and thick with no good smell.

I looked at that candle flame doing its dance in my awful room. I said to it, "Please, Damballah-wedo, do me some good."

But his answer came fast and quick, and no good tidings did it bring. The rats in the wall. The falling, falling, falling of plaster. The sound that was like an evil *loa* giggling low and wicked in my ears.

Up I stood. I pulled Charlité to her legs, but she flopped on the floor and kicked and screamed. Now where did she get that energy? This fever fed her in mean ways. I didn't think I could take no more—a screaming sick baby, rats in the walls, heat that made your skin want to leave your bones and walk away, smells that made breathing a bad thing. Suddenly I felt like a bobcat dying in a hunter's trap. What does the bobcat do? I wondered. He escapes. Even if he has to chew off his own paw, he escapes. It was then I knew that, if we stayed in this airless room in this city where the *loa* aren't welcome and the earth can't sing 'cause it's buried under concrete, we would die.

I summoned every prayer in my body and lifted that heavy child into my arms. We ran from my room. Charlité, she was hanging onto me, screaming her sickness and unhappiness to anybody who had ears to hear. We hurried down the hall. It smelled like dead garbage. I pushed open the lobby door with my bare foot. Charlité's legs were dangling down 'round mine. This would never do. I let go of her. I knelt down so to look straight in her fevered eyes. "Charlité, baby, listen to Mama. You're going to have to do some of this walking yourself. You may feel bad, but you are old enough to walk on your own. You have to, so we can go get well." And my baby, so scared she looked—but she nodded that pretty face yes. From the winds blowing in my voice, she must have knowed that this crying, fussing stuff had to stop. So we half walked, half ran, me and Charlité moving as fast as we could. And in my soul I pushed us, because, see, this is true. I had one thought, and it screamed, yes it did, through every bone in the body of mine. It screamed, "Go to the sea. Go dip yourself and that baby in the sea."

Emory Looney

My mama was standing there in her work outfit, her hairnet in her hands, looking like she was fighting back the tears. My main thing was to get in the Black Beauty and be miles down the road before she started her bawling. I just couldn't take that. I'd been back for two days, and I had only intended to stop by for an afternoon, tell her the news, and be on my way. But she just begged me to stay the weekend. So I did.

Things had eased up a little bit between us. I mean, we could actually have a conversation without one of us jumping down the other's throat.

"Are you sure you don't want me to give you a ride to work?" I asked.

"No, I think I could use the walk," she said as she fiddled with my shirt collar. Then she said, "I do not understand why you insist on doing this. You are as hardheaded as your father."

I knew I wasn't going to get away easy. I knew I should have just snuck off in the middle of the night. "Mama, if I hadn't enlisted they would have drafted me. You know that. There was no way I was going to get out of this."

That's exactly what I said to my mama, and maybe it was true in a nonemotional sense. But what really happened is, I went down to J.W.'s to see Soleil Marie so I could try to get my life straight, and she was gone, vanished. Just as if I'd never mattered. And nobody would tell me a thing. Not a one of those field fleas was talking. And I didn't dare ask J.W., but he wouldn't have known anyway. So I said to myself, "Fuck it. She probably never loved you anyhow." I thought and thought about it, I studied on it for months. I had to convince myself Soleil Marie was really out of my life. Once I did that, I figured the only option I had left was to sign up.

"But son, there's a war on."

How come my dear sweet mama could be such a thorn? "Mama, that's the point. Would you be any happier if I'd gone to Canada?"

She didn't answer me, which was probably best for both of us.

I looked down at her. I do believe she'd shrunk a little with age. I put my hands on her shoulders, and immediately I knew that gesture was the wrong thing to do, because big old tears started coming down like rain. So I said all those things I knew a dutiful son was supposed to say. "I'll write. And I'll tell you every place they send me. And if I can I'll come home on leave."

But it didn't help. She just stood there like I'd taken the world away from her. I did not understand what difference my enlisting made. I hardly ever visited her anyway. I gave her a bear hug. "It's going to be okay," I told her. I kissed her forehead and started toward the Black Beauty. She ran into the house. I thought that was pretty weird, but I went ahead and got in the car. I turned the engine over and there she came, the screen door that I had diligently repaired a few months ago slamming behind her. She was carrying a grocery bag.

"Wait for your care package," she yelled. "Eudora and I made you some cookies—oatmeal-raisin and sugar cookies. And there's some fruit in there, plus a couple of ham sandwiches."

"Mama, I'm only going to Jacksonville."

"I know, I know, but you might get hungry." She pushed the

bag at me. Immediately the car filled with a sugary smell, and I got hungry when I hadn't been hungry at all.

"Thanks," I said.

"Now you be careful, son." She was wringing that hairnet in her hands.

"I'm always careful, Mama. You take care of yourself. Don't work too hard," I said, and slid the Black Beauty in reverse.

As I pulled away and cruised past the prison, I saw her in my rearview mirror, a lone little woman getting tinier and tinier until she just wasn't there anymore. My good mama, who, despite herself, loved me. At least I'd finally figured that much out.

I drove out of town without even the radio being on. I didn't want it. Didn't want any noise of any kind. I had a little bit of that old mother-guilt. It kicked up every time I saw her or talked to her. Sometimes it was there if I just thought about her. But this time, I rationalized, I had no choice but to leave her. None at all. I was going to be an Army man. I was going to serve my country, home of the brave and the free.

That made me laugh out loud. If we'd been free, I wouldn't have been signing on to some monkey-assed war. Now, I'm not a guy who's particularly well informed about world politics et cetera. But for the life of me—and I'd tried to find out, I really had—I could not understand what we were doing in Vietnam. Well, maybe whoever is my big boss once I'm in will explain it to me, I thought.

I reached in Mama's care package and pulled out a baggie full of sugar cookies. I chowed down on them and thought about my plan. I was going to spend a night in Jacksonville. Maybe go to a few bars. I mean, I'm not a big drinker or anything, but it was my last night of freedom before the following morning, when I had to jump on a bus and go to Georgia for boot camp. I might as well go out in some sort of style.

My one quandary in all this was what to do with the Black Beauty. I couldn't leave it with Mama. She wanted nothing to do with the car. "Memories, son. You know what that car does to me," she'd said over and over and over.

Figured I'd just leave it at the bus station. Somebody would steal it, or maybe they'd have it hauled off. It didn't really matter to me.

I just knew I didn't want to sell it. If I sold it, I'd be forced to think in terms of value. And I didn't want to do that. I didn't want to think anything of my daddy's was valuable. Of course, the car wasn't worth much anyway, not since I'd driven it into the ground.

But then I got to wondering. If I left it at the bus station, because that's a place of business, they'd probably eventually call the police. And the police would trace it to me. And then they'd try to find me by contacting my mama. And then she'd get all hysterical. No, that wouldn't work. I'd have to leave it someplace other than a business.

So I drove along A1A. And I thought about my impending meeting with Uncle Sam. And I thought that once I was in boot camp I'd write J.W. down at his cane farm and tell him what I was up to. Maybe tell him that if Soleil Marie ever returned, to tell her that I looked for her. I mean, hell, what did I care what he thought of me anymore? Didn't seem like it mattered if he knew I was on terms with one of his workers.

A car passed me on a double yellow line and I honked at him. Damn fool. I wondered where Soleil Marie could have gone. Why did she leave? I told her I'd be back for her. I kept my word.

And then I said to myself, Emory, boy, you are an idiot. You've kept her waiting for years. All wrapped up in Daddy-hate. The girl is probably married to some big-muscled colored man and has a screaming houseful of dark-skinned babies. Yes, that's probably the truth. And the thought of it didn't make me too happy.

In fact, it kind of deepened my funk. Mother-guilt and now Soleil Marie–guilt. Hell. Hello, Uncle Sam. Don't you make me feel guilty too.

I could feel guilty faster than any person I knew. If I was visiting someone, my Mama for instance, I'd feel guilty because I hadn't seen them in so long. And when I'd leave them I'd feel guilty for not staying long enough or for staying too long. And if I saw a person on the street who looked like they didn't have any money, I'd feel guilty because of the dollar bill stuck in my pocket. Hell. Maybe the thing for me to do was never hang around anybody. Or get in debt to anybody in any way. My own man, owing nothing to nobody.

And then I thought, Emory Looney, you are a hypocrite. Look at yourself in your daddy's car. You talking about him like you hate the ground he walked on, but you sure have driven this car of his to hell and back. If you hated him so much, you shouldn't be driving this heap. Even if you did tear it up. Even if you planned to have it for only maybe another eighteen hours.

Well, I said to myself, to hell with it. Dump it now. Thumb a ride to Jacksonville.

That idea caught my fancy. It was an early solution to my car problem, kind of a funny, good thing to do before I married Uncle Sam. So I started looking to the roadside for the perfect spot. A rest area wouldn't work, and I couldn't drive in the dunes; I'd get stuck before I was in very far.

Then about a hundred yards ahead of me I saw the dilapidated sign: COQUINA MOTEL. That sign used to be done up like a neon firecracker, but no more. The old place was as abandoned as hell. The sign still stood, but no neon filled its veins. Kids had taken potshots at it. Bullet holes riddled it from top to bottom. I slowed the Black Beauty. I pulled into the drive. It was a shame, really. The old motel looked haunted. Its windows were mostly all busted out. Weeds grew tall, not giving a thing else a chance to live. Broken glass littered the parking lot. Kids must have come out here and vandalized the place on a regular basis.

I pulled the Black Beauty up so that it faced the Atlantic. The water was so beautiful, the waves crashing in on the shore in white furls, and the ocean beyond a deep, perfect green. I had this crazy impulse, but it was my day for indulging in such things, so I did it. I ran down the dunes to the shore. I stripped down to my skivvies and took a cold, deep plunge. It felt absolutely wonderful. The waves were perfect for bodysurfing. They had lots of volume and power. I bodysurfed for probably close to a half-hour. A few people walked the beach. I decided I didn't care if they saw me in my underwear. I walked out of the water with my drawers bagging, but nobody even looked.

As I laid on the beach, the sun warmed and dried me. But it didn't dry my underwear. I couldn't put dry jeans on over wet underwear. I looked around. No shelter in sight except for the crumbling motel. Oh, well. It was my only shot. I grabbed my clothes and ran back up the dunes. I tried the office door. It swung open with a creak. I looked in. The place was trashed and smelled like mildew. Spider webs hung from the ceiling. Jesus, it was creepy. The office phone was torn from the wall. The venetian blinds were coated with dust and webs. A WELCOME TO THE COQUINA MOTEL sign was on the wall facing the front door. Perfectly centered. Just a little dust, as if the place was still in business.

It was pretty dark, and hard to tell what might be a dustball or a rat, so I stood just inside the door and tried looking out for anything that might crawl, as I pulled off my soaked underwear. As fast as I could possibly manage it, I stepped into my jeans and then, without shutting the door, got the hell out of there.

I opened the Black Beauty's trunk and got out my duffel bag. I took Mama's care package out of the car and wolfed down both sandwiches and ate another cookie. I couldn't finish them all, so I made room between my undershirts and shaving kit for what was left of the care package, and then set the duffel bag on the hood.

I checked the interior for any personal belongings. Nothing— clean as a whistle except for the glove box, which had one of Mama's rose-colored scarves in it. We used to always give her something rose-colored for her birthday. Jesus, that was a long time ago. The scarf must have been in there since before Daddy died. For a second I considered leaving it, but then thought, No, maybe it belongs with me. It was dusty and soft, and there was something so sweet about it I almost wanted to cry, which was stupid, since that scarf had been in there all the while I owned the car and I had never given it a thought until now. But shit, the Army was soon going to own my ass—why not take a little bit of my mama with me. I put it in the duffel bag.

Then I rolled up the Black Beauty's windows, locked the doors, and slammed them shut. But there was still one thing left to do: the license plate. I managed to unbolt it. I stuffed that in my duffel bag too.

Despite the sea breeze it was hot. I wiped the sweat from my eyes and then took account of the Black Beauty. She had been a jewel when he owned her. And she was a damned hardy car. She just kept going, no matter what I did to her. Even though I'd torn her up, she looked kind of good like that. Parked, big and silent. Those headlights like unblinking, unswerving eyes staring out at the Atlantic. Hell, I almost felt sad. I patted her side. "Good-bye, Black Beauty," I said. "You're a good old gal."

And then I walked off. Right out of the Coquina Motel, past its beat-up sign, and down the road. And I didn't look back, even though the impulse was there.

Instead I stuck out my thumb and looked at the asphalt road glittering in the sunlight. I looked into the distance—away from Mama and Daddy and the Black Beauty. But mostly away from Soleil Marie. I saw the highway far ahead melt into a muddy mirage. To ease the awful quiet I said out loud, "Well, Uncle Sam, here I come."

Soleil Marie Beauvoir

It was not the sight of my swamp buzzing in the moonlight, no. It was not the cool, cool earth under my feet. It wasn't even the sight of all the herbs and flowers growing free and wild—ingredients that would bring all the strength back into my baby's body, no it wasn't. It was the scent of the fields that told me I was back where I belonged. That sweet sugar scent filling me with its magic. And filling Charlité too. "Smell that, baby?" I said to my child. "That is the smell of home. That is the smell that is going to make us well."

The moon, it was just a slice in the sky. But still it shined so pretty to give us the light we needed.

We'd been doing the walk for days, but how many I do not know. I said to myself, "Soleil Marie, just start walking. It's the only chance you and your baby have."

So we did. I left my friend Judy Gabinski a note. Where I was going I told her, I did. If she ever needs me, she'll find me. And then we started off, following the sea as far as we could, because its coolness helped save my baby. Kept that awful fever from eating her alive. We'd walk by night (sometimes, though, Charlité, she was too sick to walk for long. So I'd carry her a ways until no more could I go either), and by day my baby and I, we'd sleep in parks or on the beach near some kind of shade, and always food I'd find for us. 'Cause people, see, they waste so much of the good food. Just throw it out like it was bad water. It's a good thing Charlité and I would walk by when we did. That I had not so much pride that I couldn't dig through a garbage can or two. Stopped all that food from just not serving anybody, that's what we did.

But now, thank all my *loa*, we were close. Just so close. The night sound of my fields came on like a huge band. Bullfrogs, crickets, cicadas, night birds whooping. I knew these fields oh so well, like every point of them was familiar, like the way the calluses on the hands are known.

As I walked I felt the knife under my skirt hit my thigh. The knife reminded me of my pace, when I'd slowed too much or when so fast I was going that I would tire too soon.

Past all the favorite resting places of my *loa* we went. And to them each I gave my greetings. "Hello, Damballah-wedo," I said as I passed his palm tree. "How do you do, Cousin Zaka," I whispered as I passed his oak.

"Hello, Papa. Hello, Mama." This I whispered over and again. For them I felt were with me from the moment I took in the good sugar smell.

I would, too, give my greetings to Erzulie, yes I would, but first I had to make it back to my old house. There, waiting for me, I was sure, would be my old dog. My Charlité would love having that old dog back, this I knew. Somebody to play with, wrestle with. So to see that dog we must.

Then to Erzulie we'd go, and then to some good, deep rest. And what was running in the back of my mind all along was a hope so light you could see through it: Maybe Uncle's Boy was back. Maybe he was sound asleep in the Big House dreaming of me.

The moon was high in the sky when finally I made it through the field and into the clearing. We stood there, Charlité holding my hand, and already I knew the child was glad to be home. "It smells good here," she said.

I squeezed her little hand. "Yes, yes, it does."

And then I thought about my good friend Lorgina's words, the ones she spoke to me the day I left these fields. "You will come back, Soleil Marie. And when you do, your house will be here to meet you, just like you left it. Because this house is like part of your body. Nobody else, not a soul we know, can live in it. Just you."

And she had been so right to me. There was my old house on its stick legs. Broken down but pretty in this moonlight. To believe this was too much. We was home, really home.

I throwed back my head and to the sky I whistled. This is the call my dog knows. By this call she'd know I was home. I waited for some time, circling the house, and then again I throwed back my head. Again I whistled. Charlité said, "Mama, my dog is gone." I thought she might start crying. She started fidgeting. We were both so tired we needed to lay down. It was the rest we had to have. But to believe our dog was gone I could not. Surely somebody out here had taken care of her. Surely that dog never left. I tried maybe six more times. Nothing. No dog. She did not come. This was not good. This could be like a bad thing.

But me and my child, so tired we were and still sick that I just couldn't keep crying for the dog. I had to give my greetings to Erzulie and then to sleep we had to go. In the morning I'd ask my questions. I'd know about Uncle's Boy. I'd know if my child had a papa or no.

We walked past my good house. Back into the fields we went, just on a little farther. The good, sweet air was healing my baby and me already, this I knew. The frog music, so loud it became. Louder and louder, I just followed it and soon I was at my pond.

And pretty it was, I tell you. Gleaming like a gentle, deep eye under the moon. Charlité looked around her, she did, and then became all quiet, peaceful. Almost a smile. She remembered these fields. As I lifted my skirt and took my blade from the string I had it tied to, I said, "Charlité, we're going to find your papa, I promise you." The stand of wild cane moved in the wind, whispering its

282

song to me, telling me it was good that me, Mambo Beauvoir, was back.

I put my hand to one tall stalk and to it I said, "Thank you for giving yourself to me. Thank you for your good sweetness that's going to make whole and strong my blood and Charlité's blood."

This blade I had, no machete it was. I had to work hard at cutting that stalk. But cut it I finally did. And then because to offer some to Erzulie and make enough for Charlité and me, I had to cut it to more pieces. My hands, they were shaking. I kept saying, Just a little more, just a little more. No strength did I have, but the cane so important it was to me that I had to finish the cutting. Had to make the offering.

I was bent over the cane, like that, cutting for our good life, when I heard the sound in the fields. Coming straight at me it was. Now this was a sign that I'd been gone from the fields too long. Because if this had been the old me, I would not have been afraid. The old me knew not a thing, nothing, would hurt me in these fields. But the city had stolen *connaissance* from me. Weak and scared I was. I'd have to sit in the swamp for many a day and listen. And learn again.

But not time for that yet. So scared I was. The sound nearing, nearing. I made this motion to Charlité for her to stay quiet, for her to lay down. Her eyes turned scared, but down she went. I laid my self flat over my baby. I waited. Hearing the animal move closer. Trying to judge its distance. Grass snapping. Leaves rustling. Wild pigs in the field. I wanted to run, but too afraid I was.

Then the sound stirred clear, no more rustling in the reeds. The animal was at us. Silent. Smelling of swamp. Something pushed at my face. I jumped. Its cold snout butted into me. Up I jerked my head and out I went with a long, long cry because all over my face, up and on it, our dog was licking me with that slobbery, thick tongue. But I hugged that dog, so hard had I missed her. And so stupid I felt for the fearing.

There we were, the dog, Charlité, and me, by the pond, ready to take and give the offering. Charlité was petting the dog's behind. She looked up at me and said, "I'm naming this dog Judy." I heard myself laugh so pure I thought that I was already a different person than the one who'd been miserable in the city.

I reached for the offerings, all the time listening as the fields swelled with animal sounds. One piece of cane to my mouth I put. I felt myself glow as its sweetness filled me. I throwed one section into the pond. For Erzulie. I said, "Thank you, my good friend, for helping us home." I knew, when I was all okay and could manage myself in the fields the way I should, I would give to my Erzulie a chicken. For soon it would be time to start with my life again and put things in the patterns they belonged. To try to do something about my Uncle's Boy. I gave a bit of cane to my dog, and I told Charlité to rest up against me. I gave her the cane. This child, she knew exactly how to take the goodness from it. She downed all it could give. Then she says, "Mama, do you think I'll see my papa tomorrow?"

"Child," I whispered, "I hope so." And I stroked her pretty hair and then them eyes of hers grew so heavy—but not so much with sickness, just with sleep.

I watched her sleeping face in the moonlight. And big old Judy laid down beside us, but she did not close her brown eyes. No, to watch our every thought, that is what she did. I relaxed so deep. I felt the sugar breeze blow over us, comfort us. In the morning I'd find out about Uncle's Boy. Maybe in the morning he'd see his daughter. And the last thing I heard, because no more could I keep my eyes open, was them herons flying overhead. Looking for a place to land, them.

Rose Looney

The news from my son is not good. I am sitting at my supper table, trying to recover from the double shift I worked Friday, reading and reading his letter and chain-smoking until I'm green.

Dear Mama,

I thought I ought to write while I have the chance. The scuttlebutt is that something "big" is up. That's what my buddy Langford keeps saying. The guy thinks he's a beatnik. He says stuff like, "I hear it's big, man, really big. Can you say, man, Cambodia?" He's black but he's okay—my best friend. And his scoops are almost always on the money. Hate to say it, but I almost hope he's right about this. I mean, sitting around camp just waiting to get your ass shot off by Charlie isn't fun. Too much time to think and make things up. (Don't worry, Mama. Charlie is what we call the enemy here—it's nothing personal.) I know I sound like things are shit here, but I don't want you to worry. We're all pretty much keeping our cool. I'm in with some good guys. We're all homesick as hell. And real tired of the rain. Monsoon season. Mud up to our asses. Sorry for my language, Mama. It's just being here and all. By the way, thanks for the brownies. Sgt. Lawrence, you know, the buddy I share a tent with, he said to tell you they were the best he's ever eaten. He's a hell of a good person. Married, with a little baby. I don't have it tough at all compared to him. Listen, Mama, I got to get out of here. You keep writing to me, though. It's always a good feeling not to go away empty-handed at mail call.

Your son,
Emory

I'm trying to read between the lines, trying to get a hint if he's been shot at. If he has seen anybody killed. If he's been sick at all. Now I know that I'm being unreasonable to think that my son, out of all the sons over there, would happen to be lucky enough to not see any action at all. But I can't stop hoping. And one of the ways I keep my hope buoyed is by trying to understand what's not written down. If I keep rereading until I'm convinced that what's on the paper is exactly what's going on, then I'm okay for another day or another hour. And where in the hell is Cambodia? And what in the world is my son doing there?

For the umpteenth time I reread the letter. I can't deny it. There are holes in that letter as big as China. He might as well have just signed his name to a blank piece of paper. It would have been just as scary, just as uncertain.

I light another cigarette. I'm sick to my stomach with worry. Just give it up, girlie, I tell myself, give it up. I decide that I ought to try to rest. Maybe my shakes are due partially to just being worn out. I go in and lay down on the couch. For a minute I let myself consider my bed. A big, soft mattress would feel mighty good, I tell myself. But think about it is all I do. Hell will freeze over before I try laying in that bed again. Maybe I'll sell it. Get rid of the monstrosity for good.

Sleep starts creeping in on me. I cover my eyes with my arms. Images flicker behind my lids. It's my own private, incomprehensible movie. Me at work bumping into slaughtered chickens that hang ready for inspection like worn-out breasts. But my movie is jumbled, unreal, and scary, because the chickens are all mixed up with pictures of Emory and Charlie. I see Emory on Charlie's police motorcycle and Emory singing at the Bonfire. It's Emory who's dancing with me as all the customers watch. But where is Charlie? I don't know. I don't see his face anymore. But he's there. I feel it. My mind flips through images like wind whipping through a photo album. I see a jungle. What I think Vietnam looks like. And I don't see my Charlie or my Emory, but dead chickens are everywhere. Riddling the ground like blisters.

I don't wake up until the following morning, and even then it's not of my own accord. I wake up because somebody is pounding on my front door like all hell has broken loose. "Just a damn minute," I call. Now who in the hell could be bothering me this early in the morning?

I get off the couch and look out the window. Harry Switzer, big as Judas Priest, is standing at my front door. He has made a mistake. I am in no mood. I check to make sure my housecoat is all buttoned, and then I open the door.

"What is the big idea?" I ask.

"I'm so sorry, Rose. I know I should have called you first, but Eudora said there was no time. She said I should just run over here and tell you immediately."

"And you always do what Eudora says. How interesting." He is in his usual weekend outfit—khaki shorts and an embroidered

African-looking shirt. Like he's some kind of witch doctor. What a fool.

"Eudora and I, we made, well, we made a *contact* this morning."

"A contact. Aren't you two at it a little early this morning?" Right then I should have slammed the door in his face.

"Rose, can I come in?" He was using his real polite salesman voice.

"You got five minutes," I tell him. I push open the screen door. He sort of half bows as he walks by me. What a quack.

"Into the kitchen," I order. "Sit at the table. I'm going to fix myself some coffee." I was actually enjoying being rude. "How's Mrs. Switzer?" I ask.

"Fine and dandy. She's at her Garden Club meeting this morning. In fact"—he looks at his wristwatch—"she ought to be arriving home just about now." He smiles at me. Smooth as a snake. Eudora could really pick them.

I watch the coffee percolate. I'm not even going to sit down. I want him to understand how much I detest him.

"Well, Rose, I know you're not a believer—in the supernatural, that is—but something happened this morning that Eudora and I feel you must know about."

Great. He woke me up to tell me some hocus-pocus mumbo-jumbo story. I pour myself some coffee. I don't offer any to him.

"We were working on the Ouija board. The Ouija is an instrument we mediums use to—"

I snap. Already, so early, I'm close to boiling. I don't need this. My mind wanders back, in a flash, to the images of last night. Emory, chickens, a husband that I can't stop thinking about. "Cut the crap. I know what a Ouija board is. Get to the point, because your five minutes are running fast." I look at my rooster clock above the stove. I do this by force of habit. I unplugged it weeks ago because I finally couldn't take any more of its terrible racket.

"Rose, I don't know how to tell you this, but we contacted Charlie today."

Charlie, my dear husband. The man who haunts me by day and night. The man who is like a sacred thorn in my side. I feel something well up inside me. It is a rolling, uncontainable anger. I mean, I am reeling mad. Harry Switzer should have never said my husband's name. Never should he have involved my family in his baloney.

"And something is terribly wrong. Rose, Charlie told us he's locked on this earth."

I eye the mop that is propped between my sink and the refrigerator. It is a good mop, old and heavy. Not like the kind they use today. Its handle is sturdy, hard oak.

"He says you won't allow him to pass to the other side. He asked me to tell you to please let him go."

I fill with the kind of blind anger that makes everything crystal clear. I grab my mop. I say to him, "Harry Switzer, don't you ever, ever use my husband's good name to try to manipulate me into one of you and Eudora's games." And each time I say the word "ever" I strike him across the face with my mop handle.

He is shocked. Frozen. I've simply had enough of him and Eudora. I hit him again. He covers his face with his hands, so I hit his ribs. I say, "If you ever, ever step foot in Eudora's house again, I will find you, and I will beat you again. I will beat you so hard you will wish you never lived."

He kind of crouches and moves out of his chair. He's shielding his face, but I see the damage I've done. The swelling eye. He moves past me, but I'm right behind him. I follow on his heels toward the door. I say, "Don't you ever, ever step a foot in my house again."

And I just can't stop myself. He's so close to the door. Almost gone. I swing my mop hard. I connect right across the shoulders. He yelps and pushes open the door.

I follow right behind him. I watch as he runs out of my yard. I yell at him, "To your car, Mr. Switzer. Or do you want more of my mop?"

And I see his hand fumbling in his khaki shorts pocket. He pulls out his car keys. "When you least expect it, right on that boneless skull of yours," I yell.

I notice that as he drives away he doesn't even dare look back.

I walk into my house. Rose Looney, you are crazy, I tell myself.

But I tell it without much guilt. It's what the damn quack had coming to him. From way back. But despite this bit of smugness, I know my job is not finished. You can't just physically beat a man and expect him not to retaliate. Insults, slaps, threats go just so far. You've got to go for the jugular. You've got to finish the job in a clean sweep. What do the French call it? *Coup de grâce,* I believe. I did learn a few things from living with Charlie.

I set my mop back by the refrigerator. I pick up the phone and dial directory assistance. "Jacksonville," I tell the operator. "Yes, do you have a listing for a Harry Switzer? S-W-I-T-Z-E-R."

In less than a minute the operator is reciting the number. This is so easy. Why hadn't I done this sooner? The Garden Club. Well, that's nice, just getting home from her meeting. I dial the number. After just one ring I hear a pleasant middle-aged female voice.

"The Switzers' residence."

"Hello, Mrs. Switzer?" I ask.

"Speaking."

She sounds awfully nice.

"You don't know me, but my name is Rose Looney. I just beat the hell out of your husband. But I can explain."

Luella Jewel

 The scariest part was coming up. It was when I had to hug the tree just to keep from falling hundreds of feet down to the bottom of the ravine.

I come out here all the time. By myself mostly. Just because I want to. It's like my secret place that Mama and Aunt Rose don't know about. I mean, I don't think they know about it. They don't ever come out here, and they never mention it. It's in the woods behind our house, out about one mile. I used to think it was a trillion miles, but it's not. I come out here to stay away from them. And to crab.

See, Mama and Aunt Rose aren't speaking anymore. Not since Aunt Rose got rid of that old Switzer-kitzer. Mama said Aunt Rose tried to kill Switzer-kitzer. I sure hope so.

But Mama won't let me play over at Aunt Rose's anymore. She says I'm to never go over there as long as I live.

And being home with Mama isn't any fun. She nags me all the time. "Clean your room." "Wash the dishes." "Why don't you act more girlish, more feminine?"

And also, she plays solitaire. Like all the time. That's all she does. Except when she's nagging me. And she cheats at it too. I saw her peeking at the pile you're supposed to keep turned down. And also, I saw her rearranging the shuffling cards, to get the ace to come up. But at least she's not playing tarot anymore. She hasn't tried to read my fortune, or get me to talk to dead people, since Aunt Rose beat Switzer-kitzer.

This oak grove is really pretty. Sometimes I think I just want to live out here. Stay away from the kids at school forever. Not have to take orders from Mama. I hate having just a two-person family. People think I'm weird because of it. Maybe I'll move out here to the grove and have eight million kids.

To get past the oak without falling, I have to grab ahold of it. I mean, I could go around the side that's opposite the ravine. But it's so thick with roots and palmettos I'm scared of getting into a nest of rattlers. I'd rather take my chances on the ravine side—where there's nothing but oak roots falling like rope to the bottom. I make sure my bamboo crabbing pole is stuck far into my back pocket. In my shirt is the paper bag with bread in it. Bread balls are my crabbing bait, see. I hug the tree. This part scares me so bad. I can't do anything wrong here. No mistakes. I hug it. And real slow, I move my feet all along its base until I've made it across to where the path starts again on the other side. I have to be so careful not to let anything suddenly scare me. Like a big breeze gusting.

How many people, I wonder, know about my bayou? Sometimes nobody is there except me. But not so this time. Down at the far end was some Negroes fishing, but too close to my spot was this little boy. I'd say maybe two years littler than me. And his daddy.

I thought, Wow, they are really lucky they weren't in my spot. Because I have this special crabbing hole. I just found it on pure luck. But I mean it, it's full of crabs. I just throw in my line, and it's like within seconds I've got a bite. Mama don't even ask me where I get all the crabs. She probably thinks I'm going down to the pier.

I pull out my paper bag and begin rolling up bread balls. Best bait in the world for crabs. I've seen Negroes use chicken neck. I think I'll try it sometime. But I doubt that can be any better than bread balls. I squat down at my crab hole. I see their air bubbles floating to the top. They give themselves away. I couldn't help but hear that little boy and his daddy.

The daddy was saying, "Now Jeff, you cast this way. With a smooth swing." This was a dumb place to be casting.

I baited my pole and dropped my line into the dark green water. I watched the boy out of the corner of my eye. Him and his daddy seemed to be having a fun time. He tried to cast like his daddy had done. But he caught the line on a tree branch. His daddy didn't yell or nothing. Just went over and unhooked it for him. He said, "Let's try that again."

I decided to try to mind my own business. But I just couldn't. I counted how many times it took before the boy landed the line in the water. Six whole times. But after that, once he and his daddy both had their lines slung out there, they sat down by each other and just talked. But real quiet so as I couldn't hear them anymore.

"Bite, you little bastards," I said, as I looked down at my crab line. I'd been learning dirty words from this guy David Harris at my school. I learned last week how to point my middle finger in this special way. The kids call it shooting a bird. But I didn't think that was dirty. This new boy, he's Puerto Rican, he showed it to us at lunch. He said it meant "hello" in Spanish. So when I got home I shot a bird at Mama, and she slapped my face and said if I wasn't careful she'd wash my mouth out with soap.

The little boy and his daddy started laughing. I wondered if they were laughing at me. But then I felt that tension in my hands, the sign that I had a nibble. My crab string was pulled tight. "Gotcha!" I said.

Real carefully, I pulled the crab from the water. Oh, he was pretty too. A Blue Boy. The very best kind. Big sky-colored pinchers.

I stood up and rested the pole on my shoulder. I strolled over to the boy. I walked up right behind him.

And when he turned around, I jerked that pinching crab over my shoulder. I waved it right in front of his face. I was trying to manage it so the crab would grab the boy's nose. It would have hurt. Probably he would have bled. But the pole and the crab were swinging too wild.

It didn't matter, though. He was scareder than scared. Screamed like he thought the crab was going to eat his face.

He jumped up and ran, yelling at the top of his lungs.

God, it was *so* funny.

Flying Home

Inez Temple

 I woke from my good dreams to the smell of smoke. And I thought, "Oh, dear Jesus, somebody has finally decided to burn me down."

It would have been a meaningless action on someone's part if they had. I mean, since the Good Doctor was killed, since nobody heeded my warning, I'd just given up. No more Community Action. No more helping people I didn't even know. Every day I just went and cleaned a few houses and came back home. Stayed out of the mainstream, far away from people.

Now, a burning house would just cap this off real well. Don't you know it.

I got out of my bed and checked the house. My old bird, Mr. Pecker, was sleeping. Everything was in its place. I slid on my slippers and walked outside. A nice cool night. There was nothing wrong with my house. I walked down my cobblestones and looked left and right. Not a thing.

I turned to go inside but walked almost right smack-dab into a spider web. I stepped back. I paused. To not admire it was impossible. The moonlight showed off the web's pattern. A work of beauty it surely was. Those frail lines of light spinning first long and round and then tighter and tighter to the web's center. Spokes connecting it all, holding it all together. And every spoke and every line eventually led to the lady in the middle, that plump little spider sitting there like a black jewel. A diamond in the center of her intricate setting. My impulse, yes, was to surely touch it. To put my hand to the spoke on the outside, farthest from the center. What could be the harm? Lady spider might feel a pluck, one or two vibrations, and that's it. But no, I held myself back. Because stronger than my urge to pluck the web was my desire to see its pattern preserved. A world far larger than herself this lady spider

295

had spun. It was a marvel. A breeze blew, and the entire web shimmered. But not a spoke, not one line, gave under the pressure of the wind. And it looked like lady spider just held on, enduring the ride, like this violent and momentary disruption was just part of life.

"Sleep tight, lady spider," I said. And I went on back in my house, and shuffled to my bed, and got back under my covers, hoping that no more strange smells would interlope on my sleep.

And oh my goodness, the dreams I had that night. Grandmama, Mama, and me all alive together again. Reliving our entire lives in the span of just one night's dreaming. Grandmama and Mama were teaching me things—all that knowledge I'd ignored when I was a girl. Lemongrass is good to calm the nerves. Hibiscus root cures constipation. And oh my, to protect oneself from enemies leave a sachet of ground magnolia leaves, sandspurs, and garlic on their doorstep. And through the whole night I was not Inez Temple, grown woman with a patch on my eye. I was a little-bitty barefoot girl, no bigger than nine or ten, struggling to remember everything they said. They whispered about cures and herbs and spells, and even about spirits that my grandmama insisted had powers over us. She talked about some spirit named Damballah-wedo, about how he had powers both good and evil. And she sang this little rhyme. And I knew that rhyme in my waking hours. But here in the dream it was different. My grandmama said, "Day is dawning in Africa and the cock crowing cocoriko. Damballah-wedo landing in America, praying for freedom cocoriko."

Why it got all changed in my dream I have no idea. But you know now, sometimes you can be dreaming and thinking too. That's how it was for me. I was dreaming these great, clear dreams but also thinking to myself, "Remember this. Remember that. Don't forget any of this."

And through it all, seeming to last the whole night, hovering just under the dream words, came my grandmama's voice chanting her riddle to me. Over and over, a whisper in my ear. She chanted to me, "Truth will come easily because, child, shiny buttons will never blind you. Wolf cries, crocodile laughs, snake words shining like pearls will never blind you. But my grandbaby, even though you may never be blind, you may not always know what you see."

By morning time, I was exhausted. It was like my body and soul had been working all night long. But even though my body was tired, my spirit was just a little happy. And happiness, you see, is not something that had seen much of me lately. No. The world's sweet fruit had all been plucked—there was only sourness, it seemed. But as I got out of bed and stretched my arms over my head in an attempt to get the sleep kinks out, my attitude wasn't so gray. It was like I saw just a glimmer of my old energy hovering somewhere in my room.

I went into the living room and took the towel off Mr. Pecker's cage. "Good morning, pretty boy," I said. And then, just on a pure whim, I unlatched his cage door. Tigerlily was meowing outside. I'd just slide her breakfast out the back door and let Mr. Pecker enjoy some exercise.

At first my little bird didn't know what to do. I stuck my finger in and offered it to him as a perch. I brought that little bird out, and I said, "Fly, Mr. Pecker. Go on."

His wings were a beautiful sight. Flapping sure and colorful. Up to my curtain rods he flew. The vet had told me Mr. Pecker might live a total of fifteen years. So I figured the time he had left ought to be fun. His bright eyes spied the room. And then he began to flit from drape to drape, from china cabinet to couch to table. He chirped clear, clean notes. "Have yourself a good time," I told him.

Into my kitchen I went for my morning ritual. Out the door with the cat food. Then to my hot tea and bread and jam. I sat myself down and considered my dreams. They were as real as that little bird flying in the next room. I thought about that cocoriko rhyme. I had remembered it only as a little childhood saying. I'd even taught Luella: "And the Little Red Hen crows cockadoodledoo." But the way it was in my dream—it had power behind it like it was a prayer, like it might empower a person who chanted it. Then I thought about all those little cures Mama and Grandmama sprinkled through my sleep. I realized how much knowledge I had squandered through the years. How I'd never really given any deep thought or homage to learning the good things they knew. Oh yes, now I respected them and loved them. And I knew to stay honest and hardworking. Those things they taught me. But there was so much more. My mama and grandmama never called themselves Baptist or Catholic or Seventh-day Adventist. Their religion went beyond all that. Their worship dealt with the earth and all good things growing from it. It dealt with believing everything in this world was alive and had a purpose. That every little thing mattered. Could affect you. Oh my, I had certainly done some slipping from them. How in the world would I get back?

And then to myself I thought, Well, the first thing you can do is let some light back in this house. The day they murdered the Good Doctor I shut my curtains, and I had not reopened them—as if that silly act might shut out the violence. Seemed like the dream was going to help do something about that. I needed my whole house lit up. I needed to behave with a renewed sense of energy.

So me, a woman who'd acted glazed for months, began zooming from room to room. Up with the blinds. Wide open with the curtains. The look of my house was awful. It needed a cleaning. In my head the checklist started. Wash the windows, wax the floors, polish the furniture. Don't wallow in yourself anymore, Inez Temple, I said to myself. Goodness, it had gotten so bad the last few months that if somebody walked up to my house and went to knocking on my front door, do you think I would have answered it? No, ma'am. Seemed as though I'd spent a good portion of the last few months refusing to respond to the outside world.

And it is entirely possible that if I had not had my wild whim that morning to open up my house again, I might never have known that Eudora Jewel was standing, like a scared little dog, on my front doorstep. Yes, she was. I was going about setting my house straight when I looked up from my dusting and saw her. It was a puzzling sight.

I set down my polishing chamois and swung open my door. "Eudora Jewel? My, missy, what are you doing here? You been standing here long?" Her long streaked gray hair was pulled off her face and up in a ponytail. Her cheeks glowed. That woman loved rouge, she did.

"Can I come in, please?" she asked. She was so tiny that I wondered how in the world she ever gave birth. Seemed like that kind of pain would have caused her to crack.

"Well, sure. Don't mind my mess. I'm cleaning."

She grunted and waved my words away with her hand. Then she walked in my house but didn't sit down. She just got right to the point. "Inez, I need your help. It's Luella. I don't know what to do with the child. First, the other day she comes home screaming and crying, saying something about some dumb boy and his father. I couldn't make out the problem. Something about a crab. But it had her in a tizzy. And then she switched off the boy and started in on me. Started screaming she hated me. Now she won't speak to me. She won't eat. All she'll say is she wants Aunt Inez."

Well, my, my. Things coming home to roost. Yes, they were. "Has Rose tried talking with her?" I asked.

This woman's face screwed up like I'd thrown salt in it. "Rose Looney and I aren't on speaking terms," she snapped.

That was disturbing news. Quite a shame. I stood there and looked at her. At wits' end due to trouble of her own making. Never settling things with her daughter about her daddy. Behaving like he never existed, to cover up her good-hearted crime. And here it was, the first day I open up my windows in a long time, and already somebody was here asking for help. "Truth will come easily to you," my grandmama had said. Well, it looked like it was time for some of that truth.

"I'll talk to Luella for you. But it's just her and me. No interruptions. No ground rules. Okay?"

Eudora nodded at me, looking sober as a judge. Then she said, "Don't get us in trouble, Inez."

"Looks to me like you're already in trouble."

And then I shooed her out of my house. I told her I'd be over in an hour or so. I watched her as she walked out to her car. She looked scared. Probably thought one of these nice Negroes in my neighborhood might attack her or something. "Stay calm, Eudora. Nothing bad is going to happen," I called to her. She nodded my way and climbed in the car, but not a smile did she throw me.

Mr. Pecker was perched on top of his cage chirping. I opened the little wire door, offered him my finger, and put him back in his house. Enough free-flying for one day.

I walked into my bedroom. I decided to dress in my favorite colors, purple and gold. I took that old paisley cloth off my head and watched as my one gray braid came tumbling down. I thought, Now maybe I have not paid attention like I should have to my mama's and grandmama's ways, but I'll fix that. I studied my hair. Below my hips my hair fell. Yes indeed, even at my worst, I never considered cutting that hair. Oh no, not even once. Hair is a link to the generations. No good deed could come from cutting it. Mama told me, from the time I was a baby, "Nobody in our family—from way back—cuts their hair. It connects each of us to one another, both living and dead. Don't you ever harm a single hair on your precious scalp."

I coiled the braid back on top of my head. It was a grand stack of hair, it surely was. And I hid it under my scarves of gold and purple.

I was out my front door and heading to the car, keys in hand, going to see Miss Luella, when my neighbor called to me from across the fence. Mrs. James was watering her tomatoes. They were good, thick-stalked tomatoes too.

"Good day, Miss Temple. Did you hear the news?"

No, I had not heard any news. I had my phone disconnected the week the Good Doctor was killed. And the same day I canceled my newspaper subscription. "No, honey, what news?"

"The mayor's mansion. Last night. It burned to the ground."

Now that really gave me pause. "Well, isn't that something," I said. "They know how it happened?"

"Nope. Not a clue. At least ways, that's what the morning paper reports."

"My, my. Well, I'll see you later, Mrs. James. Have a nice day."

She nodded at me and went on with her watering. But I just shook my head to myself. It was a strange sensation to feel like a conspirator when you had absolutely nothing to do with what happened. But that's it, that's exactly what I felt like.

I knew I was going to drive straight to that mansion and have a look. I had to. This I had to see for myself. Goodness, how could I have smelled the smoke? But then I said to myself, Oh, who cares, Inez. Just go with it.

I pulled up behind the fire inspector's car. The yard was roped off with bright yellow plastic ribbon. And I just gasped. I mean, to the ground that house was. And still smoldering like it was the entrance to hell.

I got out of my car and ran up the still neat, tended green lawn. The inspector, a big, sweating man with glasses and a clipboard, yelled, "Whoa there. What do you think you're doing?"

"I'm sorry. I just wanted to look," I said.

"We don't need any lookers. We've got work to do here," he grumbled, and then started walking around to where the rear veranda used to be.

"Yes, sir," I said. But I looked anyway. I looked to where the staircase had once been. My heart felt like breaking. Gone, burned. Not a trace. I searched that charred rubble. Certainly something must be left of it. I looked at a scorched beam. Black with steam rising off of it. I knelt down and got a better look. "Goodness gracious," I whispered. And in my mind I thought, Damballah-wedo landing in America, praying for freedom cocoriko. Because under that scorched, still steaming beam was the staircase newel. That carved Mama and Papa and Baby burned on the edges, but still intact. I felt like shouting for joy.

I called to the inspector, "You have a good day, now." And as I walked back to my car, I knew what I would do. Tonight, under cover of darkness, I would retrieve that newel. And to my house I would cradle it.

I was claiming it for my own.

As I walked up to Eudora Jewel's house, I heard glass breaking. Somebody must be throwing quite a fit, I thought.

I knocked on the door, and Eudora opened it looking absolutely whipped. Now it was her who was giving up. "She's breaking her Flintstones glasses. She says I lied, that I never went to your house, and that you're really not showing up."

"Well, maybe she needs more than a talking to," I said, and I walked on in.

"Luella," I called. And around the corner, out of the kitchen like a shot, ran Luella. Her face was swollen from crying. Her hair was just a mess. Tangles like she'd been pulling on it, ratting with it. But those big eyes of hers lit up when she saw me. She ran to me, a pint-sized storm that was all noise and no rain. She didn't say a word to me. She just hugged me and sobbed like it was the end of day.

I patted her back. She was a good little girl, really. She just needed to know some things. That was all. "There, there now," I said. "What's all this screaming and fussing at your mama? Things need some clear light on them, little missy."

I took her hand. "Come with me," I said. "Let's go outside to our garden." She couldn't talk because those tears had been so severe she couldn't catch her breath. I just returned to patting her back. I rubbed and patted. Rubbed and patted. It was a good way to soothe a body down.

We went out and sat on the old concrete bench I'd given them. The site of my blinding. But maybe that was okay. Perhaps there was nothing so wrong with losing an eye when a person had plenty of other ways to see the world. And it had grown into such a fine garden. All variety of things sprung up. Fern and blossoming plant alike. And that good oak sprinkled soft, healing shade.

I pushed some knotted, wild hair out of Luella's eyes. I put my arm back 'round her. "Luella, little girl, it's time for me to tell this story. Time for me to tell you some truth."

Eudora Jewel

My little girl, who says she hates me, is sitting in our backyard being told all about her father by a colored woman. My best friend, Mrs. Rose Looney, is right next door at home doing who knows what. Probably trying to figure out a way to kill my next beau. She tried to kill my last one, Mr. Harry Switzer—a gentleman from Jacksonville who makes his living as a door-to-door salesman. And what am I doing? I am sitting in my dead husband's favorite chair—a royal-blue recliner—and staring at his picture, which I hold in my hands.

I am not a bad woman. My morals are as airtight as should be expected. They don't live up to Mrs. Rose Looney's standards. I'd have to practice total abstinence to make her happy. But I am not a floozy. I care deeply for my men friends. And also, my dear husband died so long ago. I was still young. My hair didn't have one streak of gray in it, not a single strand. And my figure—it's still lithe and trim, but back then I could barely walk down the street without attracting a few wolf whistles. So what would Mrs. Rose Looney have me do? Curl up like a ball of dust and die? Like she did?

I talk a lot to Junior. Not when my daughter's around, of course. When I'm alone. I know he understands my life-style. Sometimes I walk right out there to the grave-garden, where Luella is now, and discuss things with him. Other times I try to contact him by looking at his picture. These are the things he tells me: he doesn't want me to grow old alone; he doesn't want Luella not having a male figure in her life. There have been moments when I've asked right out loud, "Junior, ain't I doing the right thing? Ain't I?"

And until recently I always thought he answered me. I thought his approval was something I woke up with in the morning and took to bed with me at night.

But maybe not. This is how messy my life has become. Just maybe he never heard me.

He is twenty-three years old in this photograph. I snapped it on

New Year's Eve, 1948. He's standing by our front door waving a bottle of champagne, holding it aloft like a trophy. We'd only been in the house a month or so—we called it our love nest. Even back then his smile is so sweet and sad. That's one of the most beautiful things about my Junior: he possessed the most bittersweet and gentle smile of any man I'd ever met.

After he died, I decided that without Junior there was no Eudora. I did not exist. But as I said, I was still young. I need companionship. In fact, several years back I had this beau who told me, "Eudora, you are a vibrant woman."

And I was until lately. But because of my recent troubles, I can barely summon the strength to put makeup on each morning. These are the names of the clouds shadowing my life: Mrs. Rose Looney. Mr. Burl Junior Jewel. Miss Luella Mae Jewel.

I am no longer on speaking terms with Mrs. Looney. She has always been a tough woman. But after her husband, Charlie, died of a heart attack right at home, she grew—well, there's no other word for it—harsh. And jealous. She is jealous of my men friends. I just know it. And actually, I think she never forgave me for delivering a fat, healthy baby girl after she miscarried. She wants Luella to be her child. And everyone knows that things between her and her son, Emory, are not what a mother would wish. I'm not college-educated or anything, but I've got intuition, and I know she wishes Luella was hers.

My poor little girl, I know the child needs a father. But haven't I done my best to find her one? My relationships just haven't worked out, that's all. And as far as her real daddy goes—what good is a dead father? Memories don't hand out discipline or good-night kisses.

So what do I get for trying to be a lady, a good citizen, and a devoted mother? A child who won't speak to me. A best friend who tries to kill my men friends. And a situation whereby at this very moment a colored woman is the only person my child wishes to speak to—and believe me, I know that Miss Inez Temple is a good colored woman, but nevertheless she is telling *my* daughter about *my* husband.

I think over my actions and for the life of me I can't see where

I've been a bad mother or an uncaring wife. In fact, every beau who's ever stepped inside this house has been introduced to Junior. I point to his picture on the living room wall and I say, "This is my husband Junior, and I'm sure that if he was alive he'd be pleased to meet your acquaintance." Of course, I don't tell them that he's in the yard beneath the azaleas.

Then again, if I've been so wonderful, why do I feel so awful? And why am I not on speaking terms with anybody but the dead? I gaze down at Junior's picture and see that same old unchanging, tragic smile. I say, "Junior, baby, what am I supposed to do?"

But this time I have no words to put in his mouth. I don't know why I've run out of things for him to say, but I have. And I know that all the messages from the grave were just a game—my way of not facing my life's sorry circumstances.

I have no idea how late it is, but I know Luella and Miss Inez have been outside for an awfully long time. And this is a chilling thought. It makes me consider the horror of what happens next, of what is unleashed when Luella walks back in this house armed with a new knowledge. It means I'm going to have to share Junior with my little girl—he's no longer my private property, my fantasy husband who approves of my every move. I know that Luella's demands on her dead daddy will grow, and then he'll no longer be a spirit guide on the Ouija board that I can manipulate. He'll be a real force to reckon with.

Here I sit, in this old tomb of a house, knowing that outside my daughter is holding Miss Inez Temple's hand and growing very powerful. And I also know this: Even though Rose Looney and I are different, even though she will never understand my need to have a man around, we share a problem.

The recliner creaks as I get up. I hang my husband's picture back on the wall and then run my hands over my hair to make sure my ponytail is still in place. Everything seems strange. If I let myself go, I mean really go, I could imagine that the recliner and my old couch and the TV and the pictures on the walls and all these gorgeous knickknacks aren't really mine. That everything between now and the moment my daughter walks back in this house is pure imagination.

I stand very still, waiting for that back door to open. But inside my head I'm thinking, Eudora, you and Mrs. Rose Looney both might need to regain some friends among the living.

Rose Looney

Every photo of Charlie I can find I have set out on the bed. These photos I haven't looked at since before he died. No. I just couldn't bear it. Kept saying to myself, Don't look at them, the memories will be too much to handle. But now I can't bear not getting on. I've decided I've got to get over him, or go crazy.

Our life is all there, in shades of black and white. Me bringing Emory home from the hospital. Us at the beach, proudly showing off a sand castle that looked more like an igloo than a palace. Charlie playing at the band shell one Fourth of July. There's even some pictures of Eudora and me. The person I saved from Harry Switzer who won't even so much as speak to me anymore because of it.

I peek out my bedroom window expecting to see her on her porch, running those ice cubes down her throat for the benefit of the prison guard across the street. She'd taken to doing that again since I got rid of Switzer for her. But no. I am surprised. Eudora's nowhere in sight, but Inez Temple's car is parked out front. Something must be up over there. Is it Luella? She's my cost in all this. She's how Eudora repays me for helping her. Won't allow the little girl to come see me anymore. But I watch her a lot. I watch her from my house. And I know Eudora can't keep her from me forever.

Frustrating—that's my life in a nutshell. I look back down at the photos strewn across the bed. Then I look at my penny bracelet. It has not been off my arm once since the day I found it. Not once. I hold up my arm and watch the copper dangle in the muted sunlight. "Penny, penny, did Charlie mean for you to be for me?" I ask. But of course, like always, there is no answer.

Flying Home

I'm fed up. The pictures aren't helping me get over anything. Memories or no memories, it doesn't matter. I start in on my bent again. What if I'd called an ambulance just as soon as Charlie's attack had started? What if I'd never gone in that bedroom and started a dumb crossword puzzle? What if—during our entire life together—I'd nagged at him less? What if? What if? Oh God, it's just no good. At some point I say to myself, This wondering, this second-guessing, has got to stop.

Maybe some tea would taste good. I leave my bedroom and touch Emory's boot-camp graduation picture as I walk past it. It's in my living room in a frame I bought at the Woolworth's. Handsome boy. I haven't heard from him since that letter where he told me his friend enjoyed my brownies. I think, Come home, Emory, in one piece. Just come home.

Into my kitchen I go. I pull an ice tray from the freezer and drop a few cubes in a glass. I look out my kitchen window. It's from there that I can see Eudora's backyard.

What I see gives me kind of a half-chill. Inez Temple sitting on that bench, talking to Luella. And Luella is sitting with her hand in Inez's. In the midafternoon sun, the garden shimmers. I can see everything. Luella's quiet, she's watching Inez's face. This is serious stuff. This isn't just a casual baby-sitting session. After all, Eudora hasn't even left the house.

And then I think to myself, Jesus Christ, is Inez telling her about her daddy? Is she spilling the beans on us? My God, we could end up in jail.

I am about to go into one of my furies. Throw an absolute tantrum. But you know, I must be just too damned tired. I think, Oh hell, who cares if Luella tells everybody her daddy's buried in the backyard. Nobody is going to believe her anyway.

Scenes of Junior's death swell up in my mind. In retrospect, they are almost funny. We sure were frantic over that. Stealing the body and digging up almost the whole damn backyard. Charlie really went out for Junior on that one. Yes, he did.

But what had I done? What about me? I stayed trapped, I say to myself, just trapped. I mean, here I stand in my old kitchen, all by myself. Charlie, Charlie, Charlie—he's almost all I think about.

I remember Harry Switzer's words. I mean, Switzer was wrong to do what he did. But maybe, in a way he didn't realize, he was right too. I don't mean about Charlie being trapped on earth, unable to pass to the other side. That was just so much of his supernatural crap.

But there was a grain or two of something honest in his words. It was twisted, but it was there. It's not Charlie who can't go on. It's me. I have to give Charlie up. I have to go face him, go forgive him and myself, and then maybe get on with it.

Of course he made that penny bracelet for me, just believe it. I put my hand over the bracelet. "Just believe it," I repeat the words out loud.

I look around my kitchen. The kitchen where Charlie and me had so many meals. The kitchen where he'd come up to me in the mornings and put his arms around me while I stood barefoot at the stove, fixing him scrambled eggs. I think about that grave of his I've never visited. I think about that bed I've never again slept in. I look out the window. I see Inez, who is most likely, right at that moment, telling Luella all about her daddy. Helping her come to terms with him. Charlie's grave is but ten minutes from my house. I don't know if I can do it. But maybe it's worth a shot, I say to myself. It's better than me just standing in here in my yellow prison wringing my hands, rehashing my life, replaying the tape. So do it. Don't even think about it. Simply do it.

I pick up the receiver. I dial the number. She answers the phone. I check. Inez is still in the garden with Luella. "Hello, Eudora," I say, fighting to keep my voice steady. "I'm calling to ask a favor."

There is a big pause. I hear nothing but her breathing. I consider hanging up. But no. I've gone this far. My kitchen—I believe its walls will just cave in on me if I stop now. I decide there's nothing for me to do but barrel on. "Eudora," I say, "I need your help." Another pause. Still no response. I feel salty, betraying tears mounting behind my eyes. I continue, if for nothing else, to stop the tears. I say, "I need for you to go with me to the grave." And I know my eyes aren't strong enough. I know they can't contain the flood that's about to break out. And it starts. They blind me. The tears obliterate the whole damn world. But I decide I won't let them stop me. I decide I have to go on. Between sobs, I blubber to my old friend, "I think it's high time I bury the hatchet between him and me."

Emory Looney

I crouched belly-low in this tall grass, hoping like hell that all the things that could go wrong didn't. Charlie had been shooting at us on and off for three days. I was past sleep. It all started when they shot the hell out of our loudspeakers. We used them to broadcast the wildcat radio stations we picked up out here. You know, a few guys with a transmitter playing all the tunes Uncle Sam wouldn't let us hear. Like Hendrix and Cream. But Charlie came at us invisible in broad daylight. It was noon. Most of us were inside, out of the sun, eating Army-issue crap out of tin cans. And Charlie starts banging away at the speakers. Nothing else. And we didn't hear from them again until we moved out twenty-four hours later.

Fucking Charlie knew how to get on our nerves.

So I'm belly-low, like I said. I've not seen any real action. I mean it's true, the speaker thing was the closest I'd gotten to a gook fight. But I knew my time would come. And also, I knew the litany. By heart. It went like this: Charlie could wipe out my ass any second. Or just maim me, maybe blow my legs off. But forget Charlie. Let's talk about the snakes. Back home we had water moccasins, rattlers. Here they're called cobras. Let's talk about the rats the size of baboons. The only thing we didn't have to worry about, or so said my buddy Langford, was booby traps. "No booby traps in Cambodia, man. Just a bunch of NVA over there, shooting down our throats like we're chicken feed. You'll see, man. You'll see."

I tried to be so still, so motionless. I tried to concentrate on the sounds. Occasionally I'd hear a bird. Or I'd hear wind rustling through the reedy grass and the trees ahead. But then I'd hear mortar fire. Crackling, crackling like it was inside my brain. And I knew, I knew maybe the way my friend Langford knew—by a feeling that ate away at my stomach lining—that all shit was about to break loose.

The point man started up again. He must not have had confidence in Langford's prediction of no booby traps, because the boy was spooked. Every few feet he'd stop and we'd go down. And I'd think that every step he did take brought us closer to hell.

But as we moved on, the village came clearer into view. And this thing happened to me. It was like déjà vu. Because this place didn't feel like I was on the other side of the world fighting gooks. No, it was all familiar. I'd done this before. I'd walked through a field scared out of my mind before. I'd approached a clearing with palm trees and a wood house before. Back home, approaching my man-hood. Falling in love with Soleil Marie. A field filled with animals I feared. A clearing ahead holding for me the unexpected. I removed my sunglasses—they were rose-colored, and the lenses were heart-shaped. The only way to see the war, said Langford—who was as black as the ace of spades. I wiped the sweat from my eyes and looked again, without everything being tinted a rose shade. The colors, the deep greens, the thick vegetation, the trees. Hell, just like my backyard when I lived at J.W.'s.

And because of this, because of this feeling of familiarity, the stakes suddenly grew. There couldn't be slant-eyed people in this village ready to kill me. It would be all wrong. Ever since I got over here, that's what's been haunting me: the eyes. Almond-shaped. Like Soleil Marie's. Like Langford's. So for a few minutes I just couldn't believe it. I was in a place that looked like home. And these were just people. Minding their own business. Not out to shoot my ass.

But then the mortar rounds started their familiar popping. No, this wasn't Florida. Florida was what was unreal. I looked through the beautiful green reeds. I half expected to hear the heron and their lonely cries, but instead from the east I heard thunder: F-4s rolling in. Death birds shooting through the sky.

This was going to be a bag of shit.

And then the whistling sounds and the explosions so loud your teeth rattle. We're bombing and I didn't know why. All I wanted at that very moment was to sink into the earth. To be covered in dirt, to drown in dirt. If only my legs would give. If only the shaking earth would suck me in. I'd be safe. Safe.

A smell blew in from the west. It was a gut reaction. I thought it would be sweet, like my cane field. But God no, I looked at that smell. It was a smell you could see. Napalm. Like the strongest gasoline you can imagine. I think, Man, we're killing this land.

I look to the sheet of napalm. The sky is raining fire. I looked at my buddy Langford. He was ahead of me. He turned around, whistling. He smiled real big, as if he'd seen a woman he wanted, instead of the end of the world, which is what this was like. "Emory, my man, this is it. This is something else."

And I was about to say, "Langford, you're full of shit." But I never got those words out of my mouth. Because right then that village lit up like a Roman candle. And mortar fire was everywhere. And NVA were coming at us like rats. And I knew I was going to die. But I kept firing anyway.

Soleil Marie Beauvoir

Oh, yes. The powers, they were back. Just like I'd never left these fields. I mean, they weren't back in a sudden, no. I had to sit down—for long hours, yes—and listen to the swamp. In my house, in the dark but with every candle burning, me and Charlité, who'd grown so fat and healthy like a little bee, listened to what the birds had to say. We listened to the sound of grass snapping as the panther or the bobcat traveled the night toward their good food. So much there was to relearn. So much to hear.

But by that day, the one when I'd bundled so many stands of cane so much bigger than me—when Uncle walked up to me and stared over my head and blurts, "Got a letter today. He's in 'Nam. Says if you're here to tell you hello. So hello"—well, by that day the powers they were back. Rolling through my veins like rain.

To thank Uncle for telling me I could not. The big man didn't give a chance. But I run over to where Charlité was playing with some other children, she. By the old cane truck. And I hugged her, and I says to her, "Baby Sweet, he's been thinking about us. You're going to have a papa, after all."

And so happy I was, this is true. He had come back for me, everybody told me so. And now he was sending me messages. A tiny hope is much better than sand where nothing grows.

So that night, me and my people, we decide to hold church. To thank every *loa* I could speak to. This was my plan.

And up in my house my baby and I dressed all in white, and I said to her, "Maybe one day you'll be a *mambo* too.

And down the steps we walk. We are like two queens, yes we are. I looked to the sky to where the sun was going down and said, "Bless this earth, Damballah-wedo. Bless this earth, Erzulie. Keep Uncle's Boy safe, him."

I studied the place for our worship. I thought, What to do? Who to draw? But really, I knew all along. I just asked the questions, yes, to maybe please any *loa* who were hanging near.

I went to work fast with my flour and sugar. Ogu-badagri, I wanted to speak to him. The Little General, my people call him. He is a *loa*, yes, who knows all everything about war. When he lived like you and me, in the flesh, a great warrior he was back in Africa. So I drew him big. And in his hands I sprinkled out a machete. For strength, no? But all around I sprinkled sugar flowers. And down by those big feet of his, I drew a bird. Pictures of peace, I said to myself. I wanted Ogu-badagri not to make more war. To help my Uncle's Boy. This was the meaning.

And soon it was that my church people started coming in. And the boy bringing the drum shows. And I check all my rum jugs. I light the candles all my people had brought to Ogu-badagri. To the chickens in the pens under my house I look. Already I had bathed these chickens. In milk and cinnamon. I poured it over their bodies. This is, no, a consecration.

I snapped my fingers. The drums began.

I kissed this earth in front of Ogu-badagri. I raised myself back

up. I saw Lorgina was holding my Charlité's hand. Smiling my
child was. *"Ave Maria,"* I cry.

"Ave Maria," they return.

"Ave Pater," I cry.

"Ave Pater," they return.

The drums, they were getting so furious. I lifted a rum jug to
my lips. Drank it full, I did. And then I passed it on. To each of
my people they drank from the jug. And it became time, because
the Catholic stuff was over and my people, restless they were. I
snapped my fingers. Three people ran and brought to me the chickens.

And each one of them I gave to Ogu-badagri. Feast for the battle,
yes. Five chickens I gave to him. And this song my people was
singing as I gave the chickens to him:

> *Oh, Badagri, a ferocious general you are!*
> *Oh, Badagri, you know the sounds of battle*
> *because it is you, our Little General,*
> *who throws the thunder grumbles*
> *and heaves the lightning blasts.*
> *Oh, Badagri, a ferocious general you are!*

It was just as this machete, mine, was making the last offering,
that Ogu-badagri came on. In my friend, a *houngan* now, David.
With those eyes closed he was. But jumping from woman to child
to man, flicking his imaginary machete. Being ferocious. But then
he began this twirling. Twirling, twirling, twirling. I knew this to
be a bad sign, yes. Because Ogu-badagri doesn't twirl unless danger
is happening. Not like Erzulie, who twirls for fun, to show herself
off. But no, twirling he was, tighter and tighter. And then Ogu-
badagri does this really bad thing. While he's spinning, off he goes
with David's shirt. And into a candle he throws it. Out again he
pulls it. But the shirt is aflame now. And he's waving through the
air, making that flame flash in the night, causing my people fear.
And I know what this means. I feel it sudden and wild. I say to
myself, My Uncle's Boy is in danger bad.

I run to my Charlité. "Go upstairs, now, Charlité. Hurry." And
she knew the look in my eye. It was the look she never tests.

313

Up the house steps we run, because to save my Uncle's Boy I must.

I am nonstop motion inside my house. I am lighting candles. My child, she is looking at me like crazy I am. "This is for your papa," I say, and then I tell her to sit on the floor by the window. Which she does, but I know she's scared. Then I run over to the trunk by my bed that I keep plants on. I push them all onto the floor. Some of the pots break. I don't care. I take a deep breath before I open this trunk. It belonged to Papa. It holds his magic. It's filled with powers I hoped never to use. I lift the lid, and there, inside, lying on Papa's old blanket, is an osprey's foot and its thin, white skull. A stone arrow so sharp it can break the sky. My papa's bow. A wild boar's hoof. Three bells made from bone and steel. And the jar. Full of heron feathers it is. Special, powerful feathers. I take the jar from the trunk and bring it to Charlité. When she asks me what for, I don't answer. I go to my porch and bring in my white candle. This is not a candle I burn so often. White is the color of pure space, and it is through space I must fly.

I light the white candle. The flames from inside and out reflect on my window. The drums beat like anger. I sit on the floor and say to my confused Charlité, "Lay between the V of my legs. Let me hold onto you. Now don't you be scared." And she does just like I say to her. She leans into me, and with one arm I hold on, and with my free hand I take a feather from its jar, a big dark-blue heron feather, and I offer it to the flame. Sparks fly, and I think, Good, good.

When this feather is but ash, I close them eyes of mine. And I rock my child back and forth. And to a special place I go. Deep, deep inside myself. To that place where my soul does the seeing. I put all my energies to my Uncle's Boy. He is in so much fear. This I know. I see flames that are trying to eat him. And bullets that are flying on evil wings so close to his sweet flesh.

I begin my humming. Outside this house, mine, the drums still beating they are. I know Ogu-badagri is still there, spinning and fighting. I pull a second heron feather from my jar. To the flame it goes. Deep in myself I say, Fly us, wings, fly us to my Uncle's

314

Boy. And I sink deep, deeper, still rocking with my child, still seeing my Uncle's Boy in so much danger.

But the wings are taking shape now. Slowly they grow. From my body they grow. Springing out from my soul. Deeper and deeper. Shaped like leaves and oh so pretty, they are lifting me up, up, up.

I know if I can stay in this place, keep my energy pure, I will soon be flying. The sound of the drums begins to fade. Now I hear only the wind. Blowing through my beautiful feathers.

My Charlité and I, we feel our feet are off the ground. These great heron wings are filling our souls. I hug her so close to my body and look below me. The fields are shimmering, singing, below us. The wind is fresh and sweet, it is. Deeper, deeper I go.

The fields edge so slowly into sand. And then no land is there. But beautiful water stretching so far. And stars on our shoulders. My Charlité is holding on fast and tight. But I keep our bodies going, because I know this journey, it is so far. And I am growing so tired, but I say inside myself, Beat, wings, beat. And they do. Like two huge muscles, they keep us going.

And then deep within me I see fields again. A new smell fills me. It is a death smell. And I know not my fields are these. I fly over, searching the earth below. And then in my whole body I see fire. It is a devil's place, there. But I see it is where I've got to go. Where my Charlité and I must fly.

"Holy Mother Mary, full of grace," I whisper in my child's ear. And then we swoop down. Into the awful heat and fire. Fear fills me everywhere. But this I know, I must be so close to my Uncle's Boy. He is near, he is near, he is near. These words, they are my chant.

I am hovering above the destroyed earth now. I see the deep scars cut into her by this devil war. I see the destroyed trees, the ruined farms. I see places where people and *loa* once lived, in ashes or flame.

I cannot breathe. I must find him soon. Beat, wings, beat, faster must we fly. I see the sky in front explode into fire. Manmade death birds fly over me. Shadowing me. I shield my child's face from the sight. I hear the death birds' hum, but it is not the hum of life, like mine.

I look again to the earth. I know it is the eye of the bird I must use. I turn my face sideways. The eye sees each blade of grass that still lives. And then, through the choking air, the eye sees a yellow patch. Closer and closer I fly. Toward the yellow. Toward the yellow. I feel like a bird flying through hell to see the sun. I know that hair. It is my Uncle's Boy's hair. It's the hair that grows on my Charlité's head.

With my great heron wings I swoop to the earth. There is confusion and fear, and blood flows over my wings. But I have got him. I have got him. I have got my Uncle's Boy.

Inez Temple

After I left little Luella, after I had calmed down her soul by telling her straight out and simple who her daddy was and why it was so important to always feel connected to him, I decided to do a little soul-calming for myself. I'd say it was a bold action that put me back at the mayor's mansion. And don't you know my heart was beating like a wild turkey's as I crossed that yellow plastic ribbon that screamed KEEP OUT—CRIME SCENE.

But yes ma'am, I did it. And now that sweet ebony newel—only slightly charred around the edges—was sitting in my living room right between my couch and my rattan chair. And don't you know I felt good about it. As if my action had helped that dear family whose likeness was carved into that wood rest a little easier. Fancy thoughts, I know. But as I ran my hands over their faces, letting my fingertips be my eyes, I knew I had done something good.

I also knew that my evening escapade had left me pooped. In fact, I had no sooner gotten the newel into my house as when my eye started weeping full force. I knew it was because I was exhausted. So I pulled shut my drapes and thought about just going straight to bed. But I was even hungrier than I was sleepy. Just a sandwich—that was my thought. Mr. Pecker was squawking at me, so I opened his little cage door and offered my finger. He hopped right on it. I brought him close to my good eye and said, "Mr. Pecker, how do you do tonight?" Then he startled me by flying up to my shoulder and perching. It's amazing how much breeze a little bird's wings can produce.

Mr. Pecker and I headed into my kitchen. "Little bird, how about you and me having a ham sandwich?" I said. I pulled out my package of cold cuts and some bread and mayonnaise and a nice piece of lettuce and sat down at my kitchen table to enjoy it. I gave Mr. Pecker a few nibbles of the lettuce. Seemed the closer I came to finishing that sandwich, though, the hungrier I got.

So I went over and stared into the refrigerator, and as I was standing there pondering what to eat next, I consumed five pickles. I wiped the tears off with the back of my hand and thought, Inez Temple, real food won't do. You are craving some sugar. So I started in on some tangerines somebody had left at my door last week. I sunk my thumbnail into the fruit's soft, orange flesh and breathed in its fresh smell. I ate three of them.

But it wasn't enough. I said, "My, my, what is wrong with you?" And then I went and got into my cookie jar. It was brimming with oatmeal-raisin I'd baked myself. I stood there leaning on my counter, eating away. I lost track after my sixth cookie. I knew I was going to make myself sick, but there wasn't a thing in the world to do about it. I was starving for sugar, as if I needed energy.

I clucked to the little bird on my shoulder, "Your mama has gone nuts," and then I went straight for the dates that I hid behind my canisters of flour and sugar. That way, I tell myself, they are hard to get to so I won't gobble them up as soon as I buy them. But no ma'am, gobbling didn't mean a thing to me that night. I tore open that package and like my life depended on it ate down an entire package of sweet dates. I checked the wrapper: eight ounces of dates—yes ma'am, and they were all in my belly.

I stood there, amazing myself at my appetite, Mr. Pecker nipping at my head scarf, when the biggest urge of all hit me. I keep my flour and sugar in blue plastic canisters. I looked at the one with *Sugar* on the lid. I looked at my faucet. And back at the sugar canister. I knew what I had to have. No question about it. I took

317

a glass from my sink dish drainer and filled it with cold tap water. I got a teaspoon out of my silverware drawer. I knew perfectly clear when the last time was I fixed a concoction like this. It was twenty-some-odd years ago. In a rickety motel room for a pregnant Rose Looney. And just look what happened to her. Don't do it, Inez Temple, don't do it. That's what I was thinking as I removed the lid from my blue canister. I stared down at the beautiful, crystal-like white powder. In my mind's eye I saw the cage that floated at the bottom of Rose's glass that day. I knew how seducing its sweet bars could be. I thought about my guilt. How I'd felt responsible for what was going to happen to the Looneys and Jewels—especially their children. And then I reasoned, But Inez, you did a good deed for Luella today. You helped her ease up just a little. What can you do for Rose's boy? And I told myself, Nothing. He was a world away, fighting in some far-off war. How in the good-gracious sakes could I do anything for that boy? I just shook my head and wiped off some more tears and plunged my teaspoon into the sugar. Not a thing I could do for that boy. Nothing for Rose either. So I might as well drink what my body is craving. Just drink it and stop this awful urge and go straight to bed.

So, like I was a possessed woman, I threw three heaping spoonfuls into my glass of water. Then I stirred it, and stirred it, and stirred it. Dissolve, little bars, dissolve, I said. And when my hand was tired from stirring, when I thought I couldn't hold that spoon another minute, I brought that blessed or cursed mixture to my lips and began to drink. All of it. One long, luxurious swallow.

And as I drank, my kitchen disappeared. My head blossomed with the sights, sounds, and sweet smells of a sugar-cane field. I mean, my body—I think that was still in my kitchen, but everything else about me was in the exact field I'd seen a long time back, when I thought those pills prescribed for my eye were causing me to see things. I felt the hot, strong winds and smelled the sweet cane and I saw one of those heron birds circling in the sky above me. I kept drinking the sugar water, but there was no end to it. I felt the wet ground underneath my bare feet. The fields were rich, overflowing with life. I wasn't at all afraid. But I was thirsty—so thirsty.

I looked ahead of me, where there was a clearing, and I saw the back of a young man, a soldier, walking, walking. One time he paused, and he felt one of the big old leaves of a cane plant growing wild at the clearing's edge. The bird seemed to slow, and I decided it was following him. Up ahead was this old stilt house with a big, windy porch. That soldier, he walked with a purpose, like he knew exactly where he was going. And indeed he did. He went straight to that house and climbed its wooden stairs. I could never get a good look-see at his face, though. As I drank I tried, I even squinted—he was too far away. But I know this. When he reached the top of the stairs, he threw open that screen door and called out a woman's name. It was a strange name, sounding like music. As the water gurgled down my throat, I hoped with all my strength that the soldier was Emory Looney. I kept drinking, and then everything in those fields calmed down. The animal noises stilled and the wind grew gentle and that heron flying overhead, she glided down down down. She cried a joyful sound when she landed on that good, cool earth.

And then the glass that seemed like it took ages to drink was empty. And the picture show in my head evaporated. But I knew that the soldier boy was safe and sound inside that house. And I was no longer hungry, no longer thirsty. I thought, Inez Temple, you are a strange woman. You got more of your mama and grandmama in you than you know. As I took the glass from my lips, I felt like the burden of a thousand years had been lifted off my shoulders. Mr. Pecker squawked and flew onto my kitchen counter. I set the water glass down beside him. I walked out of the kitchen, humming, feeling joyful, because I had absolutely no compulsion to hold that glass to my good eye, to gaze down into it for a sign.

See, this time I knew—in my bones and in my soul—that once and for all there were no glistening grains of sugar haunting anybody.

Sugar Cage

Connie May Fowler

ABOUT THIS GUIDE

The suggested questions are intended to help your reading group find new and interesting angles and topics for discussion for Connie May Fowler's *Sugar Cage*. We hope that these ideas will enrich your conversation and increase your enjoyment of the book.

Many fine books from Washington Square Press feature Readers Club Guides. For a complete listing, or to read the Guides on-line, visit
http://www.simonsays.com/reading/guides

READING GROUP QUESTIONS AND TOPICS FOR DISCUSSION

1. Referring to her own husband, Rose tells us early in the novel, "I've never trusted him." How exactly does the issue of trust play out in Rose's life?

2. What happened in Rose's childhood to make her so "afraid of night and day and everything in between"? And what caused the "sunshine walls" of her marriage to Charlie to turn so abruptly into a stifling prison?

3. It is in the context of this ambivalent marriage that Connie May Fowler first introduces the paradox of her "sweet poison" metaphor, or the sugar cage. How does the idea of the sugar cage work, and how does it come to represent the arc of the novel as a whole?

4. Describe the different "cages" with which each of the novel's characters must contend, and explore the individual journeys each character takes.

5. By the end of *Sugar Cage*, do you believe any of the characters have found/will find personal freedom? Who will remain imprisoned (whether by sorrow, fear, or bigotry)? Explain.

6. By the time Inez Temple dissolves the "haunting" grains of sugar at the bottom of her glass in the novel's closing paragraphs, Fowler has treated us to a remarkably expansive journey through recent American history. Many of the signature events of the last half-century stand as powerful backdrops to the events in the novel, from the bombing of Hiroshima in 1945, to the assassination of Dr. King in 1968, to the grisly conflict in Vietnam. Discuss the effects of Fowler's decision to punctuate and color her fictional characters' experiences with shades of a much larger and more familiar story—the modern American experience.

7. What does Rose mean when she says she has let Charlie's "hot wind burn me to a crisp"? Standing in her cramped kitchen with Emory's letter tucked in her apron pocket, Rose invests the ordinary aroma of an apple pie with out size significance. The smell, with its all-American suggestions of "domestic peace, happy homemaking, perfect children, and all that other malarkey," starkly belies the reality of Rose's situation. What is Fowler doing here? Why does Rose feel that if she burns her pie, her life will be finished?

8. Why do you think Fowler tells the story through the eyes of nine different characters? How would the novel be different if it were told only from the perspective of Rose? Emory? Inez?

9. Which character would you say is the most "reliable" narrator? Why?

10. What is the significance of the recurring image of the heron in *Sugar Cage*? What is happening in each of the heron's appearances?

11. What other symbols and images emerge and tellingly recur throughout Fowler's novel? Consider, for instance, the ebony jewel, Black Beauty, the 'cane fields, goldfish, and the Coquina Motel. What does each represent?

12. What similarities and differences exist between the willfully enchanting magic of Soleil Marie, the mambo, and the involuntary magical visions of Inez, the self-professed descendant of a long line of "good, old-fashioned witches"? Is their Voodoo all of a piece? Do you suppose Inez will continue to recover, in her dreams, the lessons and traditions of her ancestors?

13. "It was the smell of sugar, and it was so sweet and strong it caused a picture to crawl up in my mind. It was the picture of a woman...pregnant with a rising belly." Why does it make perfect sense that Emory automatically associates sugar with conception? What is going on here? Discuss the significance of sugar in Emory's life.

14. In referring to the vast Indian burial grounds of Florida, Fowler subtly evokes the dark legacy of the Native American genocide. Along with the loss of countless lives, the ancient traditions of spiritual magic and intimate communion with nature have all but disappeared in North America. The mass graves commemorate the inestimable tragedy of a heritage forever lost. Discuss how this theme dramatizes and informs the following: Soleil Marie's frightening isolation in Miami; Luella's oddly comforting dreamscapes in Junior's garden; and Inez's powerful sense of affinity to the engraved ebony staircase in the mayor's mansion.

15. What kind of a man is Burl Junior Jones? What do we learn about him in his brief, haunting narrative? "It is my awful luck that I did not come home to my true self until too late." Beyond his name, what do you suppose Junior's true self might be? What might Fowler be leaving unsaid here? To what degree does Charlie, in the end, "come home" to himself? What about Rose and Eudora?

16. What specific techniques does Fowler use to distinguish the voices of her narrators? How is it that each is almost instantly recognizable?

17. Who was Charlie's mother? What sort of childhood did he have? How are his experiences reflected in the dynamics of his adult life? Discuss his impromptu homecoming. Is Charlie changed by this experience? Explain.

18. "Truth will come easily because, child, shiny buttons will never blind you. Wolf cries, crocodile laughs, snake words shining like pearls will never blind you. But my grandbaby, even though you may never be blind, you may not always know what you see." At the close of the novel, Inez recalls these words spoken by her grandmother for the second time. How is Grandmama's prophecy both challenged and confirmed over the course of the book? Although Inez is literally blinded by the rake at Junior's gravesite, in what ways does her uncommon ability to "see" come to shape the entire course of *Sugar Cage*?

Q: *Sugar Cage* began as a short story written to fulfill a writing assignment for a graduate fiction workshop. Who or what inspired you to develop it into your debut novel? And at what point in the process did you begin to sense the enormity of your project, with its sprawling historic scope and rich evocation of love's magical healing powers?

A: *Sugar Cage* started life as a short story titled "The Auction," and was written to fulfill a class assignment. My professor at University of Kansas, Carolyn Doty, encouraged me to try to transform those tentative twenty pages into a novel. I was petrified and had no idea of where to begin. The story was set in Kansas—which is a place I didn't understand deep down in the recesses where writers truly do their work. So I changed the setting to Florida, which was the place I was deeply homesick for, and the novel immediately began to take shape. I simply took it one day at a time, immersing myself in stories that were as familiar to me as my own skin. In this way *Sugar Cage* is a memory book—as many first novels are—
torn from the pages of my own childhood experiences and family legends.

Q: In interviews, you've said that you "write what you know," often drawing directly from your own experiences to develop the subjects and themes in your fiction. How does *Sugar Cage*, in particular, reflect your childhood in Florida?

A: I had a most unconventional childhood. Poverty and violence were ever present but mitigated by truly magical moments—usually moments when a connection was established with a person outside the family (for instance, the women Inez Temple is based on) or with nature. In terms of the details of the book, much of it is factual. Charlie Looney is based on memories of my own father. I was a child when Reverend Martin Luther King, Jr. brought the civil rights movement to town. The Jewels were styled after my parents' best friends. When the women became widows, they, like the women in the book, became fascinated with crystal balls, tarot cards, and parapsychology. Because during part of my childhood, we lived in a tenement motel, I was exposed to many kinds of people—all races, ages, religions. All of this is drawn upon, in *Sugar Cage* and, I might add, subsequent novels.

Q: How did you address the challenge of creating nine distinct and instantly recognizable voices?

A: When I was small I had a speech impediment and because it was difficult for me to verbalize, I listened—a lot—so I became the proverbial fly on the wall, listening to the stories around me, soaking in people's stories and speech patterns. I think it was back then that I fell in love with the rich tapestry of the English language. So writing in nine different narrative voices was not a problem. Keeping their lives on track, however, was an entirely different matter. I had file folders overflowing with information on each character and a giant chart with their life lines mapped out. If I changed, for instance, the date of one character's birth, it upset my entire fictional universe and everyone's life would be affected.

Q: Emory is the only figure to narrate his story both as a child and as an adult. As a result, we are able to witness firsthand how his boyhood experiences and relationships directly influence his impulses and actions as a man. Tell us about how you created Emory.

A: I relied on my knowledge of men I knew, men I'd grown up with, mainly my brothers Jimmy and Bubba and my childhood friend, Scott Morse.

Q: Which other characters' voices presented particular challenges to you as a writer?

A: The main challenge was to keep the voices consistent. So, for instance, if I was going to work on Rose Looney's narrative, I would reread her previous passages so that I would be immersed in her voice and world.

Q: Did you know where the novel would end when you began writing?

A: Yes. The end of the novel was always there for me and I wrote toward it. The images of Soleil Maria flying and of the soldier returning home acted as visual lighthouses for me— guiding me through the narrative and these people's lives.

Q: Inez Temple is an unforgettable character. Did anyone in your own life serve as her model?

A: Yes—the love she showed Luella and the life-saving role she played in the little girl's life were taken from my own experience with a woman named Vivian (Inez is very much related to the Miss Zora character in *Before Women Had Wings*). Physically, I patterned her after a woman I knew in Kansas.

Q: How did you come to be familiar with Voodooism? Were you influenced by any other artists who have also drawn on African and Haitian religious traditions (i.e.: Zora Neale Hurston, Ishmael Reed, Chinua Achebe)?

A: As a child I knew people who believed in grassroots forms of Voodoo and was, of course, fascinated by it and virtually all other forms of religion that I happened to encounter. But I also did a sizeable amount of research in which I relied primarily on anthropological, religious, and sociological texts. As for Zora Neale Hurston, her work continues to have a tremendous influence on my writing.

Q: One of the most striking aspects of the novel is the way Soleil Marie's Voodoo rituals are so thoroughly intertwined with her Catholicism. Is this religious hybrid one of the legacies of European colonialism in Haiti? What exactly is the history behind this?

A: Yes. As the catholic priests spread Christianity and Catholicism throughout Haiti, Voodoo didn't go away, it simply cross-dressed. So while the priest thinks the parishioners actually know that the Virgin Mary is Erzulie, the Voodoo Goddess of Love, in disguise. But this phenomenon isn't restricted to Haiti. Theologians call it the localization of religion.

Q: *Sugar Cage* vividly relates the uneasy tensions and violent undercurrents of the Civil Rights movement in the 1960s. What role did the adults and teachers in your own life play in the struggle? How do they inform your ideology and politics today?

A: My mother was one of the most Leftist individuals I have ever known. My father, to put it succinctly, was not. Fortunately, it was my mother's politics and sense of justice that rubbed off on me. I'm proud to be a liberal—and to me that means a person who believes that all folks have an inalienable right to be treated with dignity and fairness and kindness—for their humanity to never be denied them—and that's our duty to not give this idea simply lip service but to actively work in our communities to try to effect positive change.

Q: What themes do you find yourself consistently addressing in your work?

A: The changing face of religion in an increasingly technological society. How do we transform the burdens and sorrows of the past into a viable and hopeful future? How does the individual live a balanced and decent life if he is divorced from nature? Humankind's duality—good versus evil, tolerance versus intolerance—and its effect on families and individuals.

Q: How does the writing process work for you? In the eight years since the publication of Sugar Cage, how has your writing evolved?

A: I think I am just beginning. Writing is an amazingly intricate activity—the process is as mysterious to me today as it was the first time I ever put a pen to paper. And I'd like for it to stay that way. But I'd also like to get better at it. Maybe that's what I love most about writing—every time I sit down I am presented with the opportunity to clarify a problem, to test my intellect and creativity, to hone my perceptions and insights, to write with a greater measure of honesty.

Q: What other books would you recommend that reading groups add to their lists?

A. *The Poisonwood Bible* by Barbara Kingsolver. The Stone Diaries by Carol Shields. *Fair and Tender Ladies* by Lee Smith.

Q: What would you most like readers to get out of this novel?

A: Insight into the lives of the characters which in turn sheds light into their own lives.

Q: What is next for you? Are you working on a new project?

A: My latest book, *Remembering Blue*, will be published in January 2000. And I've started work on my next project, a murder mystery titled *The Problem with Murmur Lee*.

Connie May Fowler is an essayist and screenwriter, as well as the author of three other novels, including *Remembering Blue* and *River of Hidden Dreams*. In 1996 she published *Before Women Had Wings*, later a successful "Oprah Winfrey Presents" movie, winner of the 1996 Southern Book Critics Circle Award, and paperback bestseller. She and her husband, Mika, founded the Women With Wings Foundation, an organization aiding women and children in need. They reside in Florida.

If you liked SUGAR CAGE, you will also enjoy these other highly acclaimed Washington Square Press titles:

Jewel
Brett Lott
0-671-03818-4
$14.00/$21.00 Can.

The View from Here
Brian Keith Jackson
0-671-56896-5
$14.00/$20.00 Can.

Walking Through Mirrors
Brian Keith Jackson
0-671-56894-9
$14.00/$21.00 Can.

The Color Purple
Alice Walker
0-671-01907-4
$14.00/$20.00 Can.

Some of these titles feature a readers club guide.
All WSP readers club guides are available on-line at
www.SimonSays.com/reading/guides